GW01080852

*Mothers & Other Loves*

*Also by Wendy Oberman*

Family of Strangers

# Mothers & Other Loves

Wendy Oberman

HEINEMANN:LONDON

William Heinemann Ltd
Michelin House, 81 Fulham Road, London SW3 6RB

LONDON   MELBOURNE   AUCKLAND

First published 1989
Copyright © by Wendy Oberman 1989

British Library Cataloguing in Publication Data

Oberman, Wendy
Mothers and other loves.
I. Title
823′.914 [F]

ISBN 0 434 53164 2

Photoset by Deltatype, Ellesmere Port
Printed and bound in Great Britain by Mackays of Chatham

FOR MY SON BENJAMIN WITH MY LOVE

for Tracy and Debra

for Robert, Ruth, Daniel and Karen

for an old friend

and for Barney and Lily Oberman and Bella Sherman

# *Acknowledgements*

*Mothers & Other Loves* would never have seen the light of day without my agent, Gill Coleridge; my editor, Laura Longrigg; Juliet Morrison whose patience and dedicated research was invaluable; and Edith Sampson whose special care of me during this time of my life has kept me sane.

'Of all human struggles there is none so treacherous and remorseless as that between artist man and mother woman.'

George Bernard Shaw

# Chapter One
## 1938

On September 2nd 1938, Cassie Fleming arrived at the port of Le Havre in France. A big-boned voluptuous 22-year-old, she was apple-pie fresh with tawny eyes and thick golden hair. Home for her had always been New York's smart Upper East Side, but now it was time for Cassie to travel. What she didn't know, for she had never travelled before, was that the pleasures of travel were reserved for those who came from lands that were not threatened by the thumping jackboot of Adolf Hitler's rapacious armies. Cassie knew nothing of the refugees who were looking for sanctuary. She had sailed the Atlantic from her native America in perfect luxury.

Excited, and nervous, she had left a much-loved father and a strong mother to come to France to paint. Painting was as necessary to her life as her requirement for food. There was nothing particularly dramatic about it. Even as a small child she had used crayons and paper to communicate. It wasn't that she couldn't use words, she just didn't like them as much. As she grew her work had been indulged, but that was all. Her mother, Jane Fleming, an unusual woman who was a full partner in a New York legal practice, had done nothing to decry Cassie's aspiration – she was too intelligent for that. She had merely insisted that Cassie major in History of Art, hoping that the possibility of working in a museum or even as a critic would be enough for her daughter. But Cassie had still longed for the smell of turps and oil.

So Jane told her husband, Clinton, 'The girl had better go to Paris. If she has it in her to be a good painter she'll find out there, and if she doesn't, she'll find that out too.'

Her father, who always deferred to his wife in matters relating to Cassie's upbringing, put aside his deep need for his daughter and told her briskly it was time for her to begin her life.

*

Cassie hung over the rails watching the ungainly bulk which only hours before had been a great ship ploughing the deep waters of the Atlantic as it submitted to the self-important little tugs that pulled and pushed it into its berth; she felt the sudden sharp edge of unwanted homesickness. Those around her might see a fashionable young woman in a tailored black suit and a hat with a little brim and a slender feather, but she certainly didn't *feel* very grown up.

It had been arranged that she would study at the celebrated Ecole des Beaux Arts. In America it had all seemed wonderful, but now that she was actually about to set foot in France she was terrified that she might not be a good artist. She wanted to turn around and see her parents standing by the cabin door. She needed them to tell her to go on down the gangplank. Everything would be all right – they were just behind her, she told herself, just as they had been on all those other first days, at school and at college. But they weren't with her any more, they were a long way away, on the other side of the vast ocean. She tensed her shoulders, feeling the sharp wind as it whipped over the silver-grey, land-bound waters of the harbour – it hadn't seemed quite so cold in New York. She breathed in a different smell, one she had never encountered before – a rich, sweet odour of tobacco mixed in with the stench of fish and sea. It made her feel much better.

Cassie was not travelling alone. She had come with her friend Beth Sinclair whose own father was a well-connected merchant who played golf with Cassie's banker father. Beth had no desire to study anything in Paris. A sensual but sensible girl with straight brown hair and breasts she was proud of, she just wanted to have a good time. She hoped Cassie would grow bored sooner rather than later; then perhaps they could go to the South of France and Italy, and maybe even Germany, before returning home. Beth was not unaware that six months in Europe would give her a certain social cachet.

The two young women, one as blonde as the other was dark, found their way into the Customs shed for the formalities of landing; a bare, anonymous place where uniformed men and mounds of baggage ruled over the confused and displaced. Finally, after all the anxiety of the journey, the thrill of her arrival in a foreign place touched Cassie. She turned to Beth and grabbed her arm, wanting to share everything with her.

'Look around you, it's so different from home. Can you see the men, they're smaller, wirier somehow. They move quickly, have you noticed that? Everything is French here, Beth, even the grime.'

2

As soon as she said the sentence she laughed at herself. She knew she was being stupid, but she didn't care. She was in another world, in a wonderful dream.

Not so Beth, who stumbled, and complained – a lot.

'How are we going to cope, Cassie? No one seems to speak English.'

Cassie ignored her. She had taken the trouble to learn French – well, not that much, but enough to get by. She tried her new skills on a porter.

'S'il vous plaît, Monsieur, ce train est pour Paris?'

She was slightly put out when he answered in English, 'Yes, this is the Paris train.'

The journey to Paris enhanced Cassie's sense that she was in fairyland. She looked out at chateaux like enchanted castles. There were villages with ponds set in velvet green fields. It was all so prettily laid out – almost too prettily; but the perfect neatness was invaded by the aroma of delicious garlicky food coming from the restaurant car. When a bell rang summoning them to table, Cassie almost ran the length of the corridor in her eagerness to eat.

'I think this is truly the beginning of my life,' she told Beth as she tucked into warm French bread that she had smothered with rich yellow butter.

Beth ignored her. The smell of the food and the movement of the train was making her feel sick.

They reached Paris in the evening. It was raining, the gloriously regal grey stone of the city seemed to dissolve in the soft, inky dusk. Cassie had never seen such beauty. She thought briefly of her New York with its sharp, jutting skyline that soared protectively – and threateningly – over its inhabitants. Here she saw grace.

Rooms had been arranged in an apartment owned by a Madame Pétier in Rue Vavin, off Montparnasse – not far from the art school that Cassie and Beth were to attend in Rue Bonaparte. Madame Pétier was a secretary and, she informed the girls on that first night, scrupulous about her work. She showed them around the apartment which was located on the fifth floor of a rather pleasant building which was like nothing either of the girls had ever seen. The large brown door on the street opened onto an enclosed cobbled courtyard. This in turn led to a glass door, behind which was the actual entrance to the building. More like a corridor, the hallway was dominated by an ornate but rather rickety lift which couldn't inspire a great deal of confidence. Madame Grés, the concierge, who Madame Pétier informed them was not to be trusted, was located behind another glass door at the front of the building. Apparently, Madame Grés was too interested in affairs that were none of her concern, in particular Madame Pétier's affairs, or rather lack of them. It was, of course, to be Madame Grés who would inform Beth, the one who had time to listen to such matters, that Madame Pétier had once been the mistress of an important man. It was he who had rented the apartment for her. He was, Madame Grés assured Beth, a very generous man – even though he had acquired a younger mistress now.

How different from the impressive buildings their families occupied on the Upper East Side where there were no concierges who gossiped with the tenants, just attentive superintendents who served and never fraternised. The apartment itself was very comfortable; there was a small hall, and off to one side a corridor which led to the bedroom that the girls were to share. It had two neat brass beds, and plenty of hanging space behind a blue cotton curtain. There were drawers in a wooden tallboy that Beth quickly discovered was balanced somewhat precariously on three ball-shaped feet and a small book. This was revealed to be Flaubert when the tallboy overbalanced under the strain of an enormous number of clothes.

'I think I'll have a shower,' said Beth.

'I, er, didn't notice a shower in the bathroom,' Cassie said quietly. She couldn't think of any way to warn Beth that the primitive little iron bath and the huge rusty taps were very distant relatives indeed to the steady, steaming comfort of New York's plumbing.

Beth took a thick white towel from one of her cases. Cassie had to say something.

'It's not quite like we are used to,' she managed.

'I know. Whoever heard of not having a bathroom attached to your bedroom? I mean, we have to share it with Madame Pétier. I can't understand how she can bear it, let alone how *we* feel.'

It took Beth no more than a moment to go to the bathroom, and return to the bedroom.

'No bath?' Cassie asked.

Beth lay down on the bed, her back turned away from Cassie. It was obvious that she couldn't speak.

Madame Pétier's own room was located at the other end of the corridor. She made it clear that she had things to do in the evening, and did not like to be disturbed. She also explained that she liked to dine alone, always on *bifteck* and *haricots verts* which she purchased from

4

the *traiteur* who sold cooked food just a few yards from the entrance to the apartment building.

'It would be best if you took your aperitif at the hour I wish to dine,' she said in slow but excellent English, 'and then the kitchen will be free for your use when you return.'

So that is how, on her first night in Paris, Cassie found herself on the Boulevard Montparnasse. Lured by what she had heard about its special atmosphere, she could not wait to sit on the terraces of the Left Bank cafés. She'd heard of the Deux Magots and the Café Flore in St Germain. She wanted to go and sit in the Closerie des Lilas. She was excited by the idea of the Dôme, the Select, and La Coupole. She was sure that was where the real artists went.

Beth refused to go with her, she was tired. 'I can't understand why you want to rush out. Tomorrow we can dress properly and sally forth.'

Cassie laughed. 'I'm not waiting till I'm properly dressed. If you think I could possibly spend my first night in Paris in my bed, you're crazy. I want to see it all, and feel it, and listen to the people talking French. . .'

'You are the one who's crazy. Definitely,' said Beth as she rolled onto her side away from Cassie.

On her way out Cassie thought it would be correct if she bade her landlady a good evening. She had seen her lounging on the chaise longue in her salon.

Madame Pétier had removed her grey suit and put on a pale pink peignoir. She still had on her black silk stockings and her suede shoes. Cassie was very impressed with the silk stockings and the shoes, but she was not so taken with the white bandages that Madame Pétier wore under her chin, nor with the bandage across her forehead. She immediately assumed that Madame had had a terrible accident, but her landlady explained that it was all part of her beauty treatments.

'The one for the chin is to eliminate the jowls, and the one here,' she said, pointing to her forehead, 'is to smooth out the creases of age.'

Cassie had nodded, muttering 'of course' as she backed out of the room. Her hand touched something soft and furry. She jumped.

'My red fox,' Madame Pétier said, trying not to laugh.

Cassie looked around wildly and saw a foxskin lying on the back of the chair. The head was pointing in her direction; she could have sworn one of the eyes winked at her.

Shutting the front door rather shakily behind her, she resolved not to

5

bid her landlady good night, or indeed good evening, again unless they actually met each other in the corridors. She wasn't quite sure what other beauty treatments Madame Pétier might have in her repertoire.

Cassie followed the crowds that thronged the huge boulevard of Montparnasse, she stared into the brightly lit cafés, at their crowded terraces with table after table crammed into a row, with another row behind, and another and another. Each little table, whether it had just one occupant or three or four, was no bigger than the next. Waiters carrying small trays laden with drinks and coffee cups threaded their way through the maze of tables and chairs, served or cleared, took their money, offered the change and began again.

Cassie crossed the wide cobbled boulevard, carefully avoiding the trams and the tram lines, and found herself outside La Coupole, but she did not go in, she couldn't. She watched the women who, she recognised in her naive way, conveyed an offer of a particular kind of hospitality with their chic clothes and rich red mouths. Suddenly she was aware of her American self, and felt very provincial in her suit and hat. Impulsively she took off her hat, ran her fingers through her hair, and stuffed the smart trilby with its elegant feather (bought with such care in Saks's exclusive millinery department) into her handbag, not caring that such treatment might well render it unfit for future wear.

Down one of the small side-streets, Cassie noticed a little café that somehow didn't seem as daunting as the more fashionable places. There was no glass terrace, just a doorway. Inside there was a bar crammed with gossiping women and hard-drinking men and others who stared into each other's eyes. There were tables at the side of the room, and more at the back. She pushed her way through, absorbing the atmosphere, and recognising once again that same rich smell of tobacco. She sat at a small table to the side and asked the waiter in her best French for a Pernod – everyone had told her it was a very French drink. It tasted horrible, just like medicine, but she kept sipping it and told herself that it was an acquired taste and she would grow to like it.

'You drink it like this, Mam'selle,' the waiter said in English – was her French that bad? – and he poured some of the carafe of water that he had put on her table when he had served her drink, into the glass. He stirred it, and she saw that the liquid had become cloudy. She felt such a fool; obviously it was supposed to be diluted. What a hick she was. She managed to smile her thanks, and took another drink – she still didn't like it, but she would have to finish it now, all of it, the waiter was watching her. She longed for a frosty Coca-Cola.

Cassie looked away from the waiter and noticed a slender, dark-haired young man appraising her. Happy to be a part of all the bustle around her, she lifted her glass to him. He understood the invitation even if Cassie did not and he joined her.

It was the movement of his body that captivated her. Despite the crush he stalked rather than walked – like a panther, she thought, lithe and slender. He was well dressed, in a suit with a white shirt and a red and grey and black striped tie. He would have been very respectable if it weren't for the hat which he wore on the back of his head, and the raincoat slung over his shoulders as if it were a cloak. It seemed to her, an American abroad, that he encapsulated the particular quality of Paris – elegant, insolent and worldly. As he sat opposite her she saw that his cheekbones were high, the skin white, the eyes brown – not soft, but shiny bright under thick, black lashes. She noticed his hands immediately, they were long with slim fingers that curled around his glass. His mouth was full, a perfect Cupid's bow, but there was a hardness there too. Cassie felt a shiver of sexual excitement that was all the more shocking because she had not even spoken to the man yet. She played nervously with the carafe of water, swishing some more into the Pernod, hoping it would weaken the aniseed taste. She knew she was embarrassed almost to the point of fear.

'Where do you come from?' he asked in almost perfect English.

'New York.'

'It's a long way from Europe.' He had nice teeth, they were very white and even. 'Why have you come? It isn't comfortable to be in Europe now.'

'I've come to study painting.'

'You would be safer in New York.'

'What do you mean?' Cassie asked. 'Oh,' she continued, suddenly realising her stupidity, 'you mean what is happening in Nazi Germany. But it isn't going to affect you in Paris, is it?'

The man laughed.

'You don't understand, do you?' he said.

'Pardon?'

'Europe is a continent shying away from the inevitability of war. Whilst Paris prepares itself for the cold, its inhabitants cling to the peace laurels of the Munich Agreement between the English Prime Minister and the Führer and tell themselves not to think of Czecho-

7

slovakia and Austria. Paris is a city of the dispossessed – the ones who have run away from the possibility of a perfect life under the protection of the glorious Third Reich. We foreigners have to carry identity cards with a special profile photograph showing our right ear.' He smiled at her. 'That would not be a problem for you, you are young and you are quite lovely. There are some women who are not happy to expose their neck to view.'

Cassie blushed. No man had spoken to her like that before. She had to think of something to say – quickly.

'You said "we foreigners". Where's home for you?'

'Vienna.'

'The city of Strauss waltzes and Sachertorte.'

'And Adolf Hitler.'

Cassie nodded. 'Is that why you left?' she asked.

'Yes.'

'You don't like Nazis, I gather.'

'Oh, it's more than that. Personal, if you like. You could call it a blood feud.'

'You are Jewish?'

It was his turn to smile.

'We understand Jews in New York,' said Cassie said with perfect ease. She held out a hand. 'I am Cassie Fleming.'

He took her hand, and she was aware of the dry, almost flaky, texture of his skin.

'And I am Joshua Gottlieb.'

'I've told you I am studying painting. What do you do?'

'In Vienna I was a gynaecologist. Here I write poetry and hope for a visa to somewhere.'

Joshua ordered a bottle of *vin du patron* and began to explain how the French idealism of the mid Thirties had given way as the threat of war increased.

'Spain is about supporting a cause in someone else's land, but the French in particular don't want sirens howling on their territory, or even their own evacuees from the Maginot Line pouring into this already stretched capital with automobiles piled with beds and bicycles and perambulators, with their gasoline stored in kettles and champagne bottles – they are French after all. When the Munich Accord was signed they saluted Neville Chamberlain. The British have never been so popular in France. The idealism of the International Brigade has been buried along with Czechoslovakia, Austria

8

and Sudetenland. "Peace in our time" by all means, but at what cost?'

Cassie rocked on her chair, she was tired, bemused too, but stimulated and excited. She was part of the real world, she was listening to the stuff of front-page news. Girls in snow-white dresses at senior proms flaunting college seniors were a long way from Joshua Gottlieb's experiences.

'You are ready for sleep?'

'Yes.' She got up from the table. 'And you are right, it is a long way from New York.'

'Do you know where you are going? Would you like me to walk you home?'

'I would like that very much,' she said, ignoring the little voice that said, 'You are mad, Cassie Fleming. Who is this man? You know nothing about him, you have only ever spent time with young men whose backgrounds are the same as yours.' She was light-headed and the romantic quality of the broad boulevards lit by flickering white lights served to heighten the unreality. She wondered if he would kiss her; she hoped she would see him again.

At the door to her apartment building he asked, 'Will you meet me tomorrow night, at nine o'clock, in the café?'

'Yes.'

She let herself into the apartment, it was quiet and dark, and she crept into her bed. Her feet felt cold so she wriggled her toes and curled up on her side. She wished Beth were not asleep, she had so much to tell her. . .

Joshua was quite surprised at himself. Cassie was so different from the women he normally cared for. She was a blonde girl, almost gauche in her manner; he liked luscious semitic women with knowing eyes. When he had first seen her across the café she had amused him with the business of the Pernod, he had thought her pretty, and her smile charmed him – that was all. When he had sat down with her, her innocence had excited him, but it was her warmth that drew him to her. It was ridiculous. She was a girl on her first visit to Europe. He was an exile, suffering the loneliness and bitterness of displacement. He would not allow it to get out of hand. A young American, however warm and attractive, was not the kind he should dally with. His life as a Communist activist couldn't allow such luxuries. He glanced at his watch, it was eleven o'clock. There were still things to be done and he hurried to his discreet rendezvous with the man from Moscow.

A few days later Cassie made her way to the Rue Bonaparte. It was registration day at the Ecole des Beaux Arts. She was very nervous, scarcely able to drink the huge cup of hot coffee and the delicious croissant that Madame Pétier had offered her. She had dressed very carefully in a skirt and jumper. She wore a row of pearls around her neck and her hair had been brushed until it shone. Beth had gone with her to register, but she had put on a pale blue dress with her pearls as she was going to meet Sarah Parker, a friend of her mother's, whose husband was attached to the Embassy. She intended to fulfil her obligation to her father by registering, but that was as far as she would go with her art studies. She had discovered that Paris had much more to offer the discerning and attractive young American – shops and parties and gossipy lunches, and that was the world that Beth wanted.

Cassie's needs were different. Having registered at l'Ecole she learnt that she should also find an *atelier*. She had no idea what such a thing might be, but an Englishman standing nearby helped her and explained that it was an art studio where an organiser would provide models, and a professor would come once a week to comment and to judge. There was a fee of course, could Cassie manage it?

'Yes, but where do I find such a place?'

'I'll find out if there is room at mine.'

'Thank you. I didn't know, you see.'

'Don't worry about it.' He told her that his name was Charles Bray.

In a huge room dominated by a vast window Cassie began the task of learning her craft. There were students all around her in rows. Each one was concentrating on the business of assembling their canvases and laying out their paints. No one was talking, no one was fidgeting and no one paid any attention whatsoever to the young woman seated on a chair on a raised platform who, having disrobed behind a small screen, was completely naked.

'What made you come here?' Cassie asked Charles, mindful that the same question had been asked of her the night before. He was rather handsome in the classic English manner with clear, wide-set eyes and a good straight nose above a generous but firm mouth. He was as blond as Cassie – but his eyes were blue, and he seemed to have a very slight tan. He was wearing a grey shirt, open at the neck – no necktie – and grey trousers. He'd taken off a rather battered-looking tweed jacket. Cassie had brought a painting-smock with her. As she took it out she was aware that it looked rather too smart and clean.

She hoped by the end of the first session it might not look quite so new. She stuffed her pearls inside her sweater.

'I am an architect and fine art is a part of architecture. I feel I should learn more, and what better place to work than Paris?' he told her. 'And you?'

'I have to find out if I am any good at this,' she replied, indicating the empty canvas in front of her.

He looked at the blank space on the easel, and then back at her.

'Difficult to judge at the moment,' he said.

Cassie ignored him and concentrated on her preparations for her work, taking a pale green watercolour and spreading it over the entire surface of the canvas. She stepped back and looked at it, touching it gingerly. Of course it was wet now, it wouldn't hold any more paint until it dried. How could she have been so stupid not to have prepared her canvas! She glanced over to Charles, his canvas was ready, with the lightest covering of burnt sienna. Without seeming to acknowledge that anything might be amiss, Charles swiftly removed her canvas from the easel and replaced it with his own. She wanted to remonstrate with him, to explain that she couldn't accept the switch, but the professor had arrived. She was concerned as to how Charles would deal with the wet canvas, but it was not on his easel, it was propped up at the side, he had another prepared canvas with him. Cassie pursed her lips, she knew she hadn't organised herself properly, it didn't feel very good. She resolved not to be so disorganised again.

The episode had left her feeling nervous. She had to make a deliberate effort to quieten herself, to concentrate on the professor, on his guidance. He spoke in rapid French. Oh God, Cassie thought, I don't understand him. She was almost in tears.

'He is explaining the relationship between body and movement. Try to watch with the eye, the words will come after . . . you are an artist, let that guide you, not the mechanics.' The speaker was a small French-woman, a fellow student, standing just behind Cassie. Cassie noticed how wiry she was, just like the porters at the harbour in Le Havre, with brown button eyes and a stretched light brown skin. She would have been unremarkable, except for the low husky quality of her voice.

'Whatever you miss I will explain later.' The woman's voice was insistent, almost as if she sensed that Cassie was ready to flee the class. She handed Cassie a pastel; Cassie would have preferred a charcoal.

At first Cassie was completely confused but then she noticed that the professor's hand was lingering over the curve of the model's thigh. She watched critically and listened carefully. She managed to pick out the occasional word and she understood that he was discussing proportion, but she was fascinated by the way the light from the window fell on the skin giving it an almost luminous glow. She picked up the pastel and sketched rapidly with soft strokes, one on top of the other. The professor moved over to her, and stood watching her. Then he said in an English that was hard and gutteral, 'Your eye is in tune with yourself. You are fortunate. When I want to tell you something I will speak to you directly. What you must do is paint and paint and paint. There are no substitutes for the work itself.'

Later, after the class, Cassie and Charles and the Frenchwoman, who introduced herself as Yvonne Dubreve, drank *café crème* at a stuffy little *boîte*. Cassie loved the aroma of the rich coffee; France, she decided, was a country of smells. She relaxed into her seat: the professor had accepted her, she had made friends and that night she would see Joshua; she was very happy.

He took her to a small restaurant in Rue Jacob. The *patron*, Pierre, was a short fat man in black trousers and a white shirt with a black tie and a huge moustache. She wanted to laugh, he looked just like the 'French-style' waiters in New York.

They shared the same *couvert*. 'Do you mind?' Joshua asked. 'We do that. You see, it saves on what you call the cover charge. If two of us share one place there is only one charge.'

'Of course. I am a student too, I need to think about things like that.'

'You don't have to play those games, Cassie. You are American, you are rich. I don't mind that. You shouldn't either.'

Pierre obviously knew Joshua's habits. 'Numéro douze!' he shouted, and numéro douze, a serviette curled into a sausage shape and stuck into a serviette ring, materialised at the table and was spread out in front of them. The cutlery was laid, and two glasses with a small carafe of excellent house wine appeared. Mireille, Pierre's wife, prepared a delicious omelette, the rich, yellow kind delicately speckled with dark green herbs. As she ate, Cassie wondered with a quick stab of jealousy whether Joshua brought many girls to the restaurant.

'Are your parents in Paris too?' asked Cassie in what she hoped was a conversational tone.

'No. On the day Hitler marched into Vienna, I kissed both of them, and my sister, goodbye. I begged them to come with me to Paris. But my parents are old Austrians, like me they merely acknowledge their

Judaism.' He smiled. 'But unlike me they think nothing will happen to them. They have told me that they will leave when they are ready. They have things to do, arrangements to make. I turned away from them and took a taxi to the railway station, got on my train. I didn't look back.'

By the time Joshua had finished talking, Cassie Fleming had fallen in love with him.

She told him about Madame Pétier, and the bandages, and the red fox. It made him laugh a lot, his eyes crinkled, it changed him from a serious, almost sombre, young man into a glorious sunny one.

'I have a *chambre de bonne*, what you would call a maid's room, at the very top of an apartment house. It's a very basic room but enough for my needs. The French, like their English neighbours, did not believe that domestic staff needed any of life's niceties. They installed just one cold water tap in the corridor, but I am lucky, I have the deluxe apartment, the tap is opposite my door.' He laughed and Cassie squeezed his hand.

She wanted him to understand that she realised life had been very different for him in Austria, but she didn't know how to say such things, it would be too personal.

Later they walked, she and Joshua, along Montparnasse, down St Michel, into the Jardins du Luxembourg and down towards the Seine. He asked her how her classes had been, she bubbled with the pleasure of it all. She could see that he was enjoying her acknowledgement of her little success. He kissed her in the moonlight just near the Pont Neuf, pressing his body against hers, exciting her by the little liberties he took. His hands stroked her back, straying under her arms to the sides of her breasts, cupping them gently, letting his palms stray over her nipples for just a brief moment. It felt wonderful. She touched his face, running her fingers around her eyes, into the sockets, over the nose, lingering on his mouth.

Joshua held Cassie and he wanted to sink into her. In all his times with women he had never experienced such incredible warmth. It was as if Cassie knew his deepest hurts and wanted to comfort him. He wanted her comfort, he wanted her. He wondered if he would be able to stop himself from loving her.

When Cassie got home she discovered that Beth had been out too. She had met Marvin, the second son of a naval attaché at the American Embassy. They had eaten dinner at Maxim's, his lifestyle as a monied expatriate was perfectly to her taste.

Cassie's life took on a pattern. During the day she studied her art and

13

enjoyed the company of her two friends, Charles and Yvonne. At night they separated. Charles to a model who, in wonderful keeping with tradition, actually lived in Montmartre and Yvonne to her home in Neuilly. She told Charles and Cassie that she hated living at home, but she didn't tell them why she would not move. It had fallen to her to protect a tearful mother and two frightened sisters from an angry father who drank too much and earned too little; a man who had taken his pleasures where he could – be it from Yvonne, or from her eight-year-old or fifteen-year-old sisters, or his battered wife, until Yvonne hit him with a bottle, splitting his eyelid, almost blinding him.

'Tell the police,' she had screamed, 'and I will give them a graphic description of your prick.'

Since then he had stopped molesting the family. And Yvonne had turned her energies to her future. She had worked by day as a typist, by night as a waitress, her only aim to save enough money to buy her place at an *atelier*. She lived for her art. She had worked so hard to gather the money; every moment was precious to her. Yvonne knew it was different for her friends. Of course they were dedicated too, but it wasn't quite the same for them – they could afford to relax a little, and to laugh a lot. She had to work.

Cassie spent every evening with Joshua. Sometimes they met at a café called Le Vin des Amis off the Boulevard St Michel, which was where Joshua's intimates went. They were mostly expatriates like himself, but there were a few French. It didn't take her long to learn they were all Communists.

There was one older couple, Kurt and Frieda Greenfeldt, who, it appeared, were very close to Joshua, treating him with impassioned affection and a comfortable rudeness. They were friends from the old days in Vienna, friends who had taken Joshua's hand and guided him down the difficult, and sometimes impenetrable, path towards the dream of the perfect Socialist world.

Cassie tried to be particularly friendly to the Greenfeldts but they were not very sympathetic. The man, Kurt, was polite enough, and always greeted her, but the woman, Frieda, studiously ignored her.

She tried to mention it to Joshua, but he merely said, 'You are imagining it. Frieda is a busy woman, she knows a lot of people. It isn't deliberate.'

So the following night Cassie came into the bar and made a point of going over to Frieda who was sitting at another table with two men and a woman. They seemed to be involved in an intense conversation, but she had no intention of disturbing them, she just wanted to be polite.

'Good evening, Frau Greenfeldt,' she said.

Frieda did not answer her – her face was averted from Cassie, she seemed to be comforting the woman who Cassie could see was clearly distressed.

'Are you all right?' Cassie asked her in English. 'Is there something I can do?'

The woman looked up; she was quite young, dressed in a black coat and a pretty hat. 'Please go away,' Frieda snapped. 'This is nothing to do with you.'

Stung, Cassie walked away and went to sit next to Joshua.

'Frieda was very rude to me,' she said quietly, after Joshua had kissed her.

'Cassie, she is helping some people. I've told you, don't take it personally.' He squeezed her fingers and she felt better.

It seemed to Cassie that Joshua was touched by magic. Everyone loved him, he was their leader. Cassie had noticed such an air of kindness about him. If someone was without a drink in a bar, he would provide them with one; if there was a beggar in the street he would be the one to hand him a coin; if anyone needed a place to stay Joshua would find it. He had a network of helpers, he said. He would never tell her much about it, she never asked. There was no need – he told her what he wanted her to know. She was a part of him, he told her that. She loved that, being with him, being part of him. Often he would read his poems aloud to his group of friends, but Cassie liked it best when he read his poems to her alone. She was surprised for it seemed he wanted her approbation and she gladly gave it – his work was very good. He had a power with words, he used them, she supposed, as he had once used his scalpel, without embellishment, cleanly and neatly.

'You lift the skin off,' she told him after he had read her a poem about loneliness which had made her cry. 'I envy you.'

'Don't envy me,' he said, obviously pleased. 'Do it yourself. You can, you know. It's up to you whether you are a chocolate-box artist, or someone with something to say.'

'The difference between you and me is that you do have something to say.'

'It's just that you have not found your voice, Cassie, that is all. You will, and I shall be very proud of you. When I am an old idealist I will see your paintings in important galleries and I will say I knew her before. . .'

Cassie laughed. 'But you might still know me then.' She knew her voice sounded uneasy. She was not sure if she could bear the thought of a time when they might not be together.

On the following evening, November 6th, Joshua and Cassie went to the cinema and laughed at Charlie Chaplin, the first time that Joshua had ever missed a gathering organised by the local party. It wasn't a particularly important gathering, merely a social event – some wine and talk in a benefactor's apartment off Rue des Batignolles, just beneath the snow-white spheres of Sacré Coeur. His absence was noticed. It was decided by some of those present that the matter should be raised with Joshua. The candidate had to be Kurt Greenfeldt, the fat little man who worked staunchly and loyally out of belief and not expediency.

Kurt did not waste his time. He had agreed with his wife Frieda that the sooner Joshua forgot his American Princess the better. He met with him the following morning.

'It's ridiculous for you to get involved with that girl, Joshua,' Kurt told him without preamble.

'I am not "involved", as you call it.'

'You were not with us last night.'

'Last night?'

'We all met at Sophie's.'

'And I went to the cinema. What of it?' Joshua's voice was belligerent. Kurt decided to let the matter be – for the moment.

In another part of Paris a seventeen-year-old Polish Jew, Hershel Grynsbau, shot a German consular official named Von Rath. Two days later Von Rath died and German revenge was swift. Jews were stoned to death, their property destroyed, their synagogues burnt, they and their wives and children were hauled from their beds and transported to concentration camps. Joshua excused himself from seeing Cassie. He gave no explanation, but Cassie had overheard urgent exchanges in the café and she knew that it must be to do with the Jewish boy – his aunt and uncle who had given him illegal refuge in France had been arrested and Joshua and his friends were enraged – and very worried. Cassie spent the days working at her paintings. She realised she was changing. She no longer wore her pearls. She had taken to putting on slacks and sweaters and a small chiffon scarf tied around her neck.

Beth, meanwhile, never forgot she was an American abroad. She had made a lot of friends in the expatriate community. She spent her mornings at the shops or perhaps in a beauty parlour. She took in the

16

major exhibitions. Her lunches were always booked and in the afternoons she paid visits or rested so that she would be at her best for the evening's entertainment: dinner and dancing, or the theatre, even the opera, best of all would be a party at someone's sumptuous house. As always, she was escorted by Marvin.

'Life,' she told Cassie, 'is just one whirl of fun. Why don't you join us one evening?' Beth was sitting in front of the dressing table. She wore one of the newest angora jackets, very fashionable in America, and simply not available in Europe.

'It's not for me, thanks,' Cassie said, catching sight of herself in the mirror.

It seemed to her that next to Beth in her white angora, she had a real look of Paris about her and she was very pleased.

About four days later, Joshua waited for Cassie outside l'Ecole des Beaux Arts. As soon as she caught sight of him she pushed past Charles and Yvonne and anyone else who was in her way in her eagerness to get to him. They kissed a lot, Cassie curled into him, up against him, loving the feel of him. After feverish caresses, wet kisses, and tantalising glimpses of flesh, Joshua had to say, 'It's too public, let's go to my room.'

She let him guide her there, let him undo the buttons of her coat and take it off her shoulders. He could see the hunger in her eyes. It excited him deeply. He pushed her sweater up and undid her brassière. He gazed at her breasts, touched her skin. She felt so good, he wanted to bury his face in her gorgeous flesh, and lie in her for ever. Joshua understood that Cassie was different from him, but he didn't care about that. He never discussed ideology with her, there was no need for that, others filled that role. Cassie made him feel loved. It was a strange emotion, not one he had ever experienced before, and it banished the pain of partings.

Cassie watched the man on top of her as he touched her breasts, rubbed his face into her. No boy had ever made her feel so achingly soft. She felt as if she were melting, there, just between her legs. She trembled, suddenly nervous as he hooked his fingers under her light cotton knickers and slipped them off her body, kissing the little red ridges the elastic had made on her skin.

She lay very still and watched as he removed his own clothes. She had never seen a naked man before. She'd looked at statues, and at paintings, but Joshua wasn't a statue – his flesh would not be cold and ungiving to the touch. She glanced over at him, he had turned away to put his clothes on a chair. She saw the ripples of his back, his smooth arms, the curve of his tight white buttocks – she averted her eyes, she was shy.

'Cassie, Cassie, I won't do anything you don't want me to do.' His voice was soft and so loving.

She opened her arms to him and he lay down beside her. She could not help but let her hands linger over the muscles of his back, over his chest, down over his stomach. His skin felt like velvet. She wanted to hold him. She knew what to do, her girlfriends at home had talked about it enough . . . and Beth had done it. She took him in her hands, he was so beautiful, so hard, so smooth, she ran her nails over him, she felt his shiver as if it were her own. Afterwards he held her. 'Thank you,' he whispered. 'Now it's your turn.' His hands travelled over her, between her legs, and he slipped his long fingers inside her. She wanted to like it, but she didn't. It didn't feel soft and melting any more. He seemed to sense her dislike and he withdrew his hand. He kissed her deeply on the mouth.

'Oh Cassie,' he whispered. 'What kind of spell are you weaving over me?'

'No spell,' she whispered back.

'Come,' he said, pulling her up from the bed. 'What shall we do? Shall we walk by the Seine, or shall we go to a café and eat *tarte tatin?*'

'What's *tarte tatin?*'

'Upside-down apple cake and it's wonderful.'

They chose the Dôme. As Cassie sat next to Joshua, holding his hand, feeling him holding hers, she remembered how nervous she had been on her first night in Paris. She wanted to tell him about the little hick of a girl who had stayed outside rather than brave the Dôme's daunting reputation, when a shout made her turn around. Charles and Yvonne were sitting at another table.

'Join us,' Cassie called over to them.

With much hustling their chairs were vacated, their coffees were carried over and they sat down.

'Charles, Yvonne, meet Joshua,' Cassie said.

'Hello,' said Charles, offering a hand. Joshua shook it and turned to greet Yvonne.

'So you're studying with Cassie,' Joshua said.

'We have to study in order to perfect our art,' Yvonne answered sharply.

'Of course, life is about trying to attain perfection, isn't it?' said Charles.

'When one is young,' Joshua said, smiling, and suddenly Cassie saw the lines around his eyes. She realised she had never asked Joshua how old he was.

'So are you enjoying yourselves?' he continued, and Cassie knew he was patronising them.

'I think we are all aware, Joshua, that this is not a time to enjoy Paris.'

'Really?' said Joshua, casting a hand around the café which was jammed with people talking, laughing, drinking and eating.

'I think Cassie is referring to the political situation in Europe.'

'Do you know about the political situation?' Joshua asked. He was stirring sugar into his coffee.

'I have a rudimentary knowledge,' Charles said.

'Gleaned from the few newspapers that can be bothered to put in some reports on the Nazis in between the cricket results and Mrs Chamberlain's latest outing to a charity ball.'

'You know as little about England as I do about Germany,' Charles said slowly.

'At least we are agreed on that.'

He turned towards Yvonne; the Englishman bored him. At 31 years of age he had other things to do than spend his time with people without ideals. He was more taken with Yvonne. They talked of art, and life, and the hard work of survival. Cassie and Charles found themselves excluded from the conversation. Cassie was very uncomfortable, she sensed Joshua's condescension towards Charles and assumed that he felt the same way about her.

'Rubbish,' he said later. 'I don't feel judgmental. Just don't pretend an involvement with this fight, this is a matter for Europeans.'

'Charles *is* a European,' Cassie said hotly.

'He's an Englishman.'

'Is that different?'

'Yes, it is.' Joshua's voice was sharp. 'They are not part of the continent of Europe. The Empire, the King, the old school, that's all that matters to them and too many of them have a liking for the New Order. I am not fooled by your Mr Bray's pretty words.

Cassie didn't like the way Joshua condemned her friend, it was the first time she found cause for criticism – here was a bigotry she had not heard before. She didn't want to think about it. She tried to lighten the conversation.

19

'But he does look like a Greek God, don't you think? It's those beautiful patrician features and that wonderful golden hair.' They were sitting in the gloom of Notre Dame, not because they wanted or indeed needed to go to a place of worship, but because they both liked the sanctity of the huge cathedral with its dark opulence and the slender flickering candles of the supplicants who came to offer penance and pleas to a forgiving Saint.

'You find him attractive?' Joshua asked. He was laughing at her, she was looking so serious.

'No, no, of course not,' she replied quickly.

'Why not?'

'Because of you, that's why.'

'There are other men in the world for you, Cassandra Fleming,' he said very softly, his voice whispering in the lofty silence of the great cathedral.

Cassie was frightened. Was he falling out of love with her? She dismissed the thought – he was looking at her so gently she wanted to cry with the pleasure of it.

She was surprised when Yvonne told her that she didn't like Joshua.

'But you got on so well at the café.'

'He's facile, that man. He makes glib statements. He sees himself as a victim of the nasty world, and we are stupid because we have not experienced real hardship. He doesn't know what any of us feel or do. He judges us because we don't wear badges that say "I have suffered".' Yvonne snorted with anger. 'I think it is very bad behaviour and I am telling you, Cassie, you should protect yourself from a man like that. He will hurt you.'

'I don't think he means to be like that,' said Cassie, dismissing Yvonne's comments.

She wouldn't heed warnings, she had no need of them. Her art was flourishing. In the cold of the Paris winter she learnt that when she twisted and twirled her brush she could make suggestive shapes and designs that excited her. She began to use a knife in her work. She learnt about the use of shadow, and of highlight. She learnt to understand composition and design. She went to galleries and studied the masters, sometimes she copied them so that she could understand their technique in order to master her own fledgling style. Picasso had an exhibition at the Paul Rosenberg Gallery. Cassie went with Charles, but was disappointed. There had been twenty or so paintings depicting flowers in a vase. There was one of a frying pan, and two that explored his window casement theme. She had stood in front of them, her pad in her hand, but then she put it back in her bag in disgust.

She almost stormed out of the gallery. Charles was puzzled at her fury.

'Why are you so angry?'

'The man has it within him to make people think with his work. I mean, I know it's a silly example, but it's like Joshua and his poems. He uses his poems to say something, he doesn't just paint nice scenes with his words. He challenges and he hurts sometimes. He's taught me to expect more.'

'I hope you don't ever expect too much,' Charles said thoughtfully. They were walking through the Rue de Rivoli towards the Louvre. Charles needed to look at a Rodin. Usually Cassie loved the Rue de Rivoli, she thought the arches opposite the Jardins des Tuileries were so romantic. She and Joshua had kissed there one night. But her mind was not on kissing.

'What do you mean?' she asked, although she knew exactly what Charles was saying. Neither of her friends liked Joshua and it distressed her – it showed on her taut face. Cassie was incapable of hiding emotion.

Paris was a city for shoppers, and watchers, for intriguers, and lovers. Joshua was one of those who did the kissing and the whispering but on a Sunday morning it was different, he and his friend Kurt Greenfeldt became shoppers. They liked to go to the second-hand book market, near Notre Dame. Here they could forget their habit of intrigue and use the hour they allowed themselves to forage for the likes of Dashiell Hammett, or Virgil, or Racine. They shared a love of literature; that was how they had met. Greenfeldt had been a publisher of fine books in Vienna, Joshua had been one of his subscribers. As the son of a rich merchant Joshua had, despite being a medical student, been able to indulge his taste for beautiful irrelevances, and leather-bound books were a particular pleasure. However, even as an indolent student, for that is what he had been at the time, Joshua had admitted to a sense of discomfort in his world of privilege whilst too many laboured in the dark world of deprivation. Greenfeldt had taken him to a meeting of those who thought as he did; after that matters became clearer – he had to change things. The imbalance within society must be evened out – by revolution. There was no other way. In the meantime Joshua concentrated on his studies and became a gynaecologist – and a good

21

Communist. He took his pleasures with women, and shared his friendship with the Greenfeldts. It had stayed that way, even after they came to Paris – until Cassie.

'You are going to have to stop seeing her,' Kurt told him as he browsed through a yellow, crinkled, but as yet untorn edition of Fitzgerald's *Tender is the Night*.

'We have already discussed this once and there is no reason for me to stop yet. I will when I am ready.'

'Joshua, don't make complications for yourself.'

'I don't think she is a complication.'

'Don't be naive. You have a special job to do here, an American girlfriend is not going to help you.'

'I cannot see how Cassie can interfere with my work as a courier for Moscow. If I am lucky I will manage to help a few people escape from the Fascist nightmare. I will try to spread the word here in France and explain the proper alternative to Fascism. But I can't do too much of that otherwise I'll get kicked out to God knows where. So I talk to the French and try to get them to talk to their compatriots.'

'You know very well that you are highly thought of. Up to now you have been very successful.' Joshua stopped browsing and looked into his small plump friend's round pink face.

'Kurt, if you think that my relationship with an art student whom I find attractive is affecting my activities then you should inform those who make the decisions.'

'I just want you to keep things under control, that's all.'

The pink face had turned a little pinker. Joshua didn't want to hurt his friendship with the Greenfeldts whom he cared for deeply. They had offered him affection where his parents had only offered formal loyalty.

'I am, I can assure you,' he told Kurt. 'Now let's stop this talk of the women in my life.' He emphasised the word 'women', trusting that it would have the desired impact.

After leaving Kurt, Joshua went and sat in a café near the Seine. Absently he ordered a whisky. He knew that Kurt was right, his involvement with Cassie was getting out of hand. He needed her love, but it was not compatible with his principles. As he drank the ice-cold liquid he wondered what he was going to do.

When Rebecca Rothenstein, a genuine refugee from Hitler's brutality, came to Paris just before Christmas, Kurt decided to send her directly to Joshua. To be more precise, it was actually his wife's idea, for her zeal far exceeded his.

Just seventeen with a smooth cap of black hair and huge sad eyes, Rebecca had come from Berlin. Her father and mother had both been teachers, and determined Communists. Rebecca's father came from a very poor background. The son of a Rabbi, he had long ago swapped his religious convictions for what he considered to be the more realistic goals of an equal world. At a Party meeting he had met a fragile beauty from Berlin. They had fallen in love and married. His prosperous jeweller father-in-law was sympathetic to his views and life was comfortable for the Rothensteins – their union had been blessed by a much-wanted daughter. On that terrible night of November 10th Rebecca's parents had been dragged from their beds and . . . who could know for certain, hopefully deported, and not shot. Her grandfather had been forced to scrub the paving stones of the Unter den Linden, and her grandmother had killed herself rather than face the mob.

Rebecca rapped on the door of Joshua's small room as Cassie's long golden hair slithered over Joshua's chest, as one of his hands grasped her head, kneading it with his fingertips. He pulled on his clothes hastily as Cassie rearranged hers, and then he opened the door.

Rebecca was neatly dressed in a black jumper and skirt, beneath a black and white coat. She carried a black handbag and a small brown case. Her pretty face was etched with exhaustion and grief. As she told her story, Joshua prepared some tea. It was always cold in Joshua's room, there was a fire, but ill-fitting windows sucked away its heat. Cassie drew a chair nearer to the fire and offered it to Rebecca.

'Let me help you,' said Cassie, 'I can rent a room for you.'

'No, I would prefer just to stay with someone. It would be quite adequate, thank you.' She spoke a difficult English.

'Listen, I have money, use it. That's what it's for.' Cassie quickly reached for her own handbag, took out twenty dollars and handed it to Rebecca. The girl took it, folding it into the palm of her hand. She did not put it in the pocket of her neat black and white coat, nor did she put it in the black handbag which she had left by her case near the door.

Joshua spoke to Rebecca softly in German. Cassie could see he was being gentle with the girl. She left shortly afterwards, feeling awkward in their presence. They certainly did not need her – they had an exclusivity of suffering which shut her out. Joshua was fussing over the little German waif. She couldn't understand what they were saying and when they spoke in English it was merely out of politeness. She shut the door of Joshua's room behind her, and the click re-emphasised her sense of dislocation. Before Rebecca had arrived, she and Joshua had been kissing each other, touching each other – as they normally did in the afternoons. Paris was two worlds for Cassie, her *atelier* and Joshua. When she was painting she was not with Joshua, when she was not painting she was with Joshua. She had no idea what to do. She went back to the apartment in Rue Vavin – perhaps Beth would be there, but then she remembered that Beth was going with Marvin's mother to take tea with Mrs William Bullet, the wife of the American Ambassador. If that were not enough, a famous Hollywood film star whose on-screen speciality was the role of the hero, was also expected to grace the proceedings.

The remnants of Beth's preparations littered the room, discarded afternoon dresses, hats and shoes, an open perfume bottle, lipsticks – some with, but mostly without their tops – a block of mascara, its brush sticking to the little mirror, spilled powder; she had even left the light on. Cassie didn't like the chaos. She looked at herself in the mirror, her lips were red from Joshua's kisses, she rubbed her hands over her nipples, she ached for him. She turned and walked out of the room, pausing only to turn off the light. She went to the Beaux Arts and worked on a still life, some fruit. She mixed her paints – vermilion and purple – taking licence with the apples and pears, and tried not to think about Joshua alone with the girl. It was silly, after all Rebecca was just a young refugee.

Joshua allowed Rebecca to sleep on his bed that night, he told her that he would use the little couch under the window. She did not want to go out; she was, she confessed, exhausted. He went down to the *charcuterie* on the corner of the street and purchased a chicken and some tomato salad. She ate a little and then excused herself. 'May I sleep now?' she asked. She did not bother to take off her clothes, just slipped under the covers and fell asleep.

Joshua thought about Cassie as he lay on his little couch. He wished she had not offered the money, it was crude somehow, and Rebecca had been so embarrassed. He wondered why Cassie hadn't seen that, she should have, she was an artist, she should be sensitive to the situation of others. But he could not help but feel uncomfortable that he was with Rebecca whilst Cassie was alone. He remembered that he and Cassie had been kissing when Rebecca arrived. He thought about her lips against his chest, he shifted in his bed and touched himself. Cassie had such a wonderful ripe body . . . so different from the thin little girl in his bed.

Rebecca started to cry in the early hours of the morning. The attic room was lit with the Paris night as Joshua got off the couch and went to her, put his arms around her and tried to calm her.

In her own bed, in her room, Cassie was restless and buried her head in her pillow. She could not sleep, nor could she put on the light for she did not want to disturb Beth. Besides, she had had enough of Beth and her gossip about the film star who had said they simply must see Berlin.

'He told us it is absolutely gorgeous,' Beth had told Cassie. 'The German soldiers are apparently so handsome and charming. He could arrange. . .'

'Actually, I don't think they are my kind of people. They kill anyone who does not agree with them, and in particular Jews and Communists.'

'Well, the Jews and the Communists aren't our problem. I mean, they aren't really anything to do with us, are they?' Beth had had her back to Cassie, otherwise she might have seen the real anger in Cassie's face, and then she might have stopped, or have chosen her words more carefully.

'They have a great deal to do with me. They are human beings, as I am a human being, whether or not I agree with their politics or their religion. As a matter of fact, I met a young Jewish girl today. Her parents have disappeared, dragged out of their house by your handsome and charming soldiers. Her grandfather was made to scrub the paving stones of one of Berlin's smarter streets and her grandmother has killed herself.' Cassie's voice was very quiet.

'Cassie, get off your high horse. . .' It was then that Beth turned around.

'Oh, and there is one other thing. I am in love with one of them, a Jew that is, and probably a Communist.' If Cassie had any pleasure that day it was from the expression on Beth's face.

A peace of sorts was made in the morning.

'It's no good you just lecturing me, Cassie. I don't know any of your refugees.'

It was only later when Cassie was telling Charles and Yvonne of the previous night's happenings that she became really aware of her own situation for the first time. She was no longer part of Beth's world, Joshua had changed that. But nor was she a part of his, she had seen him with Rebecca and she knew they had a natural kinship that excluded her.

'I know how you feel, Cassie,' Charles said quietly. 'I, too, am a voyeur in the theatre of events.'

25

'Is that what we are, Charles, you and I?'

'For the moment,' Yvonne said, 'we all are, and I pray God that we stay that way.'

'There *will* be a war, Yvonne.' Charles spoke very quietly.

'There has to be,' added Cassie.

'Perhaps. I don't want to face it just yet. I cannot help but wonder if we will all survive. I, for one, don't want to live with M. Hitler's New Order.'

'Fortunately, Yvonne,' said Charles, 'there are quite a lot of us who would agree with you.'

'And America, what does America feel? Will she come in on our side, Cassie?' asked Yvonne.

'Don't make me ashamed,' Cassie replied, thinking of the all-American film star's infatuation with the Third Reich.

Joshua was waiting for her in their café. He greeted her with a kiss.

'I let Rebecca stay last night.'

Cassie looked at him.

'She slept in the bed, and I stayed on the couch until she cried in the night, and then I tried to comfort her.'

'And did you?' Cassie tried hard to keep the tartness out of her voice.

'I don't know. My heart was not in it, I'm afraid. I wanted you.'

'Oh Joshua.' Cassie linked her arm in his. They were walking now, their hips touched, their strides matched, they fitted each other perfectly. 'I realised yesterday that I am not part of your world, and neither am I part of mine any more.'

'What do you mean?'

'My experiences here have made me different. I see differently, I feel differently.' She gave a little laugh. 'I am in strange territory. And I don't feel as if I have any fellow voyagers.' She laughed. 'Well certainly not Beth at any rate.'

Joshua smiled, the kind of smile that made the skin around his eyes crinkle. It was as if her heart actually contracted, as if it were being squeezed by her love.

'Will you meet her? At least you can learn a little of my old world.'

'If it would please you, but it may not be a good idea, it may heighten your sense of separation from us all.'

A formal rendezvous never took place, not because the participants were unwilling, but because Joshua and Beth came upon each other by chance in the hallway of the Pétier apartment. Madame Pétier herself was a witness to the exchange. She wouldn't have listened because she was not a curious woman, and she didn't much like either of the combatants, but she did like Cassie a great deal. She found the young American to be a thoughtful person who never intruded but was always courteous, unlike her friend.

Beth was in the hall, dressed in going-out clothes – a suit, hat and gloves – when the doorbell rang. Madame Pétier was about to open the door, but Beth, expecting the faithful Marvin (whom Cassie had yet to meet), pushed Madame Pétier out of the way in her rush. The Frenchwoman was about to speak her mind when she realised that Beth was disconcerted. Instead of the slight, diligent but extremely flat-featured American, they were confronted by a young lion. Madame Pétier was instantly aware of his sexuality. Had she been a younger woman, she might have revealed her own. The thought momentarily brought back feelings that had long gone. He introduced himself.

'I am Joshua Gottlieb.'

'Oh,' Beth simpered, 'Cassie's Joshua.'

'You bitch,' Madame Pétier muttered under her breath, knowing instinctively, as Beth did, that Joshua would not have liked that description.

Joshua ignored the comment. 'Is Cassie here?' he asked Madame Pétier.

'No, she is at her painting class.'

'She stayed late, then. I was delayed and she was not at our café. I assumed she had come here.'

'She's finishing something, I suppose she got lost in it. That's the way she is,' said Beth, her voice indicating that she was the one who was privy to Cassie's arrangements and not Madame Pétier. 'Are you going to interrupt her?' Beth asked.

'No, I will go to the café and wait for her.'

'Well, when she gets there perhaps you and Cassie might like to join Marvin and I for the evening. We are visiting some American friends for a little civilised behaviour. I find the, er, French who don't travel, if you will forgive me, Madame Pétier, are different from us.' She smiled at Joshua and ignored her landlady. 'Cassie tells me you are an Austrian doctor.'

'I was,' Joshua answered sharply. 'Now I am a Jewish poet.'

'Without a country to live in.'

'Oh, I will have one.'

'It must be so difficult for you. After all, most of us feel we have enough Jews of our own.'

Madame Pétier took a sharp intake of breath.

Joshua smiled to himself; he loved a barb or two, except of course that, in this case, the opponent was hardly worth the effort.

'And where did your family come from, before they were American?' he asked Beth.

'I beg your pardon?'

'Your pedigree – mine is Jewish, although we lived in Austria for at least seven hundred years. Where do you come from? You look quite semitic to me, are you Jewish too?'

'Absolutely not.'

'But you are not an old American family. That's obvious.'

Beth tensed her shoulders. What an awful young man, she couldn't see what Cassie could possibly see in him. His manners were appalling. Even more disgusting was his assertion that she looked even a little Jewish. Why, that was ridiculous. Her maternal grandmother hadn't looked Jewish at all, otherwise her Irish grandfather would never have married her, she was sure of that.

Noting her discomfort, Joshua was satisfied. He nodded her a farewell, and then turned to Madame Pétier and, with great charm, kissed her hand.

'I don't like him,' Beth said, after he had shut the front door.

'Oh I do,' said Madame Pétier. And she did, but not for Cassie Fleming. Joshua Gottlieb, she surmised, was an ambitious man, and despite his sexuality, a cold one too. Cassie was still a virgin, Madame Pétier could see that, and she recognised that the handsome Austrian was used to worldly women like herself. All it would need was a shrewd little hussy to excite Joshua Gottlieb's appetites, and her young American friend would be swept away by a tide of passion in which she would have no part.

When she finally reached the café Cassie was aghast, she was over two hours late.

'I didn't realise the time,' she said, kissing Joshua on the mouth. She was tired. She had been working on a nude, it was difficult for her; although she was mastering the techniques of tone and line, she was still painting pictorial images. She knew that constant work was important, the artist could only emerge with unremitting practice. Her anguish, for indeed it was anguish, was that she could not find the artist within her, only the technician.

'I was late too,' Joshua told her. 'I had to go to a meeting myself. I was anxious that I had missed you so I went to your apartment. I met Beth.' Cassie didn't miss the stress he laid on the words 'I met Beth'.

'Dinner is off, then,' she said with a straight face.

'Dinner is off, but we could always entertain Madame Pétier.'

'She's a fine lady.'

Joshua nodded, he would have liked to have known Madame Pétier in her youth.

Cassie was drinking her Pernod. She had grown to tolerate it.

'Joshua,' she said quietly, 'I don't want you to think that Beth is anything like my own family. I mean. . .' She coloured up. She was being disloyal but she had to explain that her parents were different from Beth's. They had not talked about their families before, it was as if both of them had tried to separate themselves from their backgrounds so that they could come together without encumbrances. Now that Joshua had met Beth there was a shift in emphasis for Cassie. He had come through her door and she had to make him understand that it could be a comfortable place for him.

'My mother is a lawyer, my father a banker. They are liberals, democrats in the real sense. Some of their friends are Communists.'

Joshua smiled, he could not help it. She was so intense, this girl of his, so proud, but he was also uneasy. He was not used to exclusive relationships. He was a man who normally enjoyed many women. At first he had loved it, especially her trapped sexuality, imagining how it would be when he released the power in her. But recently he had begun to realise that he and Cassie had different needs. The exchange with Cassie's friend, Beth, had identified the reality of those differences. Cassie epitomised the capitalist way of life. He was almost ten years older than her and his Communism was deeply engrained in him. He believed there were no alternatives and Cassie represented the very system that he wanted to destroy. Despite an affluent beginning, Joshua enjoyed his life of survival, it sharpened him, gave him a sense of place. Cassie needed the reassurance of a more certain existence. It was different with Rebecca. She came from the same culture as him – lapsed Judaism and a Teutonic sense of what was proper. He had begun to spend time with her, they discussed their shared beliefs.

Christmas was coming and after a blissful three months Cassie experienced a horrifying bout of homesickness – all the more terrifying because it was unexpected. She longed to hear her parents' voices, to feel their physical presence, and she missed Cleo, the generous, kind black woman who had come to work for the family before Cassie had even been born. She was as much a part of Cassie's life as America itself. The thought of a Christmas without Cleo's roast turkey and cranberries was unbearable. Cleo, who cooked and cleaned and cared for the Flemings, was no maid, she was Jane Fleming's friend who had nurtured her and raised her child. When Cassie had left, it was Cleo who wept to see her go.

'I'll be coming back,' Cassie had told her.

'Not the girl who is leaving now. She won't be back.'

And in Madame Pétier's ornate little salon, Cassie realised how right she had been. She was different now, she wanted to go home so much, but what would there be for her in America? She wished she were still that little girl who sat at her father's knee, but the stuff of her childhood was all gone and, suddenly feeling frightened, she longed to have it back. She found unsatisfying consolation in the knowledge that she need not face the implications of this for the moment – at least not until she had found the artist in her.

She was surprised that Beth was staying in Paris for Christmas. She would have expected her to return, but Beth had no intention of returning from Europe alone; it would look as if she had turned tail and fled whilst Cassie stayed to enjoy the riches on offer. And in any event there was Marvin. Beth liked him a lot.

Cassie confided her homesickness to Beth.

'Don't you long to see your parents and even just to see America?'

'No, I am fine here,' said Beth, and Cassie could see her surprise. She supposed it was to be expected; in a sense Beth had never left America.

Charles was going to England for the holidays. He was flying, he had told Cassie, from Paris to Croydon, an airfield just outside London. 'Why don't you come with me?' he asked.

'I can't leave Beth at Christmas. And Beth won't leave Marvin.'

'And there's Joshua!'

'Oh, of course there's Joshua. But as he is Jewish Christmas isn't as important to him as it is to me,' Cassie said quickly, not knowing whether that was true or not.

Joshua told Cassie that on Christmas Eve he and some friends would be gathering at Frieda and Kurt Greenfeldt's apartment. The older couple, who seemed to think they had proprietorial rights over Joshua, always made Cassie feel frivolous. Of course, she was invited too. But when she told Joshua she thought she should be with Beth – they had been invited to drinks at the American Embassy – he had agreed willingly enough.

'Join us later, if you want,' was all he said.

Joshua told her, when she asked, that his parents celebrated Christmas in a formal manner: a huge dinner the night before, as was the custom in Austria, with all his relations present.

'Despite our Judaism, we would light the four traditional candles at each side of a wooden crown. As a child I loved it.'

Cassie realised it was the first time since they had met that he had talked of his life in Austria. She would have liked him to have said more, she needed to know of his roots. But he offered nothing else. It bothered her that she knew so little about him. She was sure he must be missing his home, especially at this time. However it did not stop her wondering how Christmas could be celebrated without honouring the birth of the Son of God.

She gave careful consideration to what she might give Joshua for the festivities. She wanted it to be special and she explored the Faubourg St Honoré for an indulgent luxury. No, she didn't like the soft silks, the handspun shirts, the monogrammed leathers. She had noticed recently that Joshua's shirts were beginning to fray, just a little. Joshua was always impeccably dressed, his tie just so . . . his hat perhaps a little rakish, but nothing that might be considered improper. He wore a raincoat – she wondered if it was going to be warm enough for the winter. It was then that she decided – a cashmere scarf . . . and perhaps a beautiful shirt. No, only one present – he would consider two excessive.

After she had completed her purchase, Cassie went back to her canvas. She was still working on the nude. Could she give it to Joshua? If she gave it to Joshua would she change it? She stood back from the easel, examining the lines, the textures. Her colours were interpretative, harsh. If it were to be an offering to Joshua she would want to reveal not just the body, but the essence too. She stared at the canvas and understood that it was too bland; there were no shades, no mystery. Quickly she squeezed grey onto her palate, mixing it with white and just a touch of pink. She worked at softening the lines, at creating the mystery it lacked. She took a red pastel and defined the outline, and then, because she thought it too hard, she rubbed at the lines with a soft cloth. It was coming, she could see that. She worked for many hours. When she had finished she stepped back. She had painted herself. She was the gift for Joshua.

31

She showed it to Yvonne the next day. Charles had already returned to England, and she was quite relieved. She knew that he would understand the personal statement and she felt unable to deal with that intimacy.

Yvonne told Cassie she was very brave, and she hoped she wouldn't get hurt.

'Why do you keep saying that?'

'I just want you to be aware that Joshua Gottlieb is a man who will put his own needs before yours.'

'Well, I know that. But he needs me.'

'For the time being.'

'I know that too,' Cassie said, too quickly.

They were going to have lunch. Cassie had a present for Yvonne. She had chosen Yvonne's gift almost as carefully as she had chosen Joshua's. She had noticed that Yvonne had very little money, but she had to be careful – she did not want to insult her friend by buying a gift that was too expensive, nor one that might be considered a necessity. That would be equally insulting. She had chosen gloves, beautiful, soft leather gloves. She had wrapped them carefully and slipped them into her handbag.

Yvonne was embarrassed, she had no gift for Cassie.

'You don't give in order to receive,' Cassie said quickly. In truth, she had been surprised that Yvonne had made no mention of an invitation over the holiday period, but she supposed that was the way in France. She would have liked to have spent some time with Yvonne. It would have helped to be with a family.

'Do you have a big family?' she asked Yvonne. She knew so little about her friend.

'Two sisters.' Yvonne was looking at her very directly. 'It isn't very easy for us, especially as I am not earning now.'

Cassie immediately understood that Yvonne had exposed herself, made herself vulnerable. She was shaken by the confidence, she realised that it placed their relationship on a different level – the bounds of politeness had been removed.

'Will you understand,' Yvonne continued, 'if I don't take your gift?'

'Oh, but I want you to have it.'

'Please, Cassie, I don't want to take the present. There will come a time when I shall demand them, now it is enough that I have your friendship.'

Cassie stared at her, she thought of Rebecca and the dollars she had forced on her. She felt very stupid.

'But I tell you what,' Yvonne said, 'I will allow you to pay for lunch. I'm starving and I was only going to have an omelette, but the *coq au vin* is wonderful here.'

Cassie smiled, she knew that Yvonne was mollifying her.

'Where did you learn your English?' she asked, glad to change the subject.

'At school, and then I did lessons. I thought I would get a better job.' She paused. 'And I did, but I couldn't get excited about a typewriter.'

'What *do* you get excited about?'

'Art . . . and people.'

'Today I am interested in the people. Are you in love, Yvonne?'

'No,' Yvonne said sharply, 'I am not.'

'Oh, Yvonne, you sound so – well, final. Have you been hurt?'

Yvonne saw Cassie's anxious face; she was really becoming very fond of this American Miss, but what could she know of hurt, real hurt? Briefly Yvonne recalled the first time her father had entered her, the horror, the humiliation, the pain, and the terror. No, there would be no love in her, not for a man.

Joshua had chaired a meeting of his executive on the day before Christmas Eve. It was late when the comrades left. His back ached. The situation was bleak, it had not been a good meeting. They had met because Moscow had indicated that another group of travellers would be allowed haven. And this time he was expected to go. Of course such an opportunity could not be wasted; a chance to end his exile. But Cassie, his beloved Cassie, what was he going to do about her? He ran his hands over his face. Oh God – unconsciously, he had called on the old deity – what had that woman done to him? He must control his need for her.

He didn't realise that Rebecca was still there until she gave him a whisky.

'Where did you get the bottle?' he asked.

'Kurt. He thought you might need it.'

'I do.'

She moved quietly, even before he was aware of it. Her movements were sure, demanding, unlike Cassie who was always looking for reassurance. He always had to be in control with Cassie, careful not to let himself give in to his needs. Cassie was not ready to give up her

33

virginity. Rebecca was thin but her fragility was an illusion: her breasts were hard, her stomach flat, her legs wrapped around him like strands of wire biting into him. Uncompromised sex. He gave it everything he had.

On Christmas Eve itself, in a glittering room filled with power-seekers (for the really powerful had other places to go on such a night), Cassie listened to the burr of conversation and wished there was one person she could actually talk to, unaware that there were certainly those who looked at the young woman in the soft blue silk dress and pearls. Hearing the American voices was almost painful.

The air of Paris which had seemed so attractive now smelt stale. The light had no quality, she wanted homespun America. She had received her parents' presents the day before, a beautiful black leather handbag from Jane, a book of Walt Whitman's poems from her father – they used to read Whitman together. She couldn't bear to stay in this room with so many reminders of her home country so far away, strangers were better roommates on this particular night.

Cassie joined Joshua at the Greenfeldts'. She took presents, of course, crystallised fruits and a good cognac from Fauchon. She thought that was the right thing to do since she had no idea who would be there and in this way everyone could share the delights. She had loved going into that shop. The array of food and the glorious presentation had thrilled her. Joshua's present was to be reserved for a private moment.

Joshua had drunk a lot by the time she arrived. He needed to – he would see Cassie. He felt very bad that he had betrayed her. Cassie mattered to him, but Rebecca was his own kind. And Rebecca was going to Moscow with him – she had pointed out that it made sense. He had to tell Cassie, he would tell her after the Christmas celebrations. He had told Rebecca that there was no question of him explaining anything until after the New Year.

He greeted her with a shout of joy and a kiss. His cheek felt hot against her cold cheek. She wrapped her arms around his neck and kissed him on the lips. She knew her mouth was soft and full. As she drew away from him she saw that his eyes were open – she always closed her eyes at a kiss. She ran her fingers over his mouth to clean it of lipstick. He giggled and she realised he was a little drunk.

Cassie noticed that Rebecca was looking at them. She was surprised to see her, she had had no idea that the young German girl would be there. She hadn't seen her since that day of her arrival in Paris.

There was drink, and laughter and sadness. Joshua and Cassie sat together, stood together, drank together, ate food together. Joshua read his poems. There were about eight of them in the room, Cassie only knew the host and hostess and Rebecca. Another man, rather quiet and nervous with glasses, was not introduced, nor were a rather jolly couple who, it appeared, were related to Frieda Greenfeldt. But Cassie didn't care, Cassie was happy.

Later that night they went to his room and she gave Joshua his presents. He thanked her for the scarf and put it on, admiring himself in his little cracked mirror. 'Quite the dandy,' he said.

He opened the painting carefully, cutting the string with a little knife, undoing the paper rather than tearing it. He lifted the canvas out and placed it on the bed. Cassie could hear her heart beat, it was the first time she had ever shown Joshua her work. He stood and looked at it, he walked back and then forwards again.

'Well, do you like it?'

'Very much,' he said. 'Very much indeed.'

'It will have to be varnished later, in about six months.'

'Will it?' he said carefully.

He made a ritual of hanging it, finding the nail, banging it into the wall, positioning the picture where he wanted it. But somehow it was not enough, she wanted him to say more about her work, she wanted to discuss it. Instead he said, 'Now I can look at you from my bed whenever I want. Come here, Cassandra Fleming, come here and let me love you.'

She went to him on the bed, but it took some moments before she could kiss him. With the touching, however, the white-hot shaft of pleasure burst through her and she leaned her head back, relishing him. He removed the pillow, placing it under the small of her back, lifting her legs up. His tongue slithered over her, in her hidden places, he was taking care, she could feel that, and her body answered him. It was going to be good, she knew it was, the tips of his thumbs tantalised the skin of her face, she tried to trap them, at least one of them, in her mouth.

'I love you,' she whispered.

'No, you mustn't.' The words were like ice-cold water thrown on a warm-wanting skin. He had moved away from her, he wasn't touching her, what was happening?

'Cassie, listen to me,' he said, and he pulled her back to him, holding her, trying not to respond to the need in her.

35

'Don't love me so much. I can't give you a future, so there is no point.'

'But. . .'

'I can't, that's all there is to it. I don't want to talk about it.'

He got up off the bed, wouldn't look at her, and lit a cigarette. She'd never seen him smoke before.

'Why are you doing that?'

'I have tried to tell you before. I don't want to be harsh with you.'

'I mean the smoking.'

'I smoked in Vienna. When I came here I stopped. Now I have gone back to my old ways.'

She knew he was trying to tell her something, she didn't want to hear it, she wouldn't hear it.

'Don't you want me any more?' She was crying now. . .

'Of course I do, it's just not right. Not now.'

She took heart from that – maybe later, maybe that's what he meant.

He saw the pain in her and wanted to hold her.

'We are travelling on separate paths, you and I, Cassie. Those paths have crossed and it has been wonderful.' Why was he sitting down on the bed? Why was he holding her, he shouldn't be doing that, but she looked so wretched, so small and so wanton.

'It wouldn't work. Don't you see, it won't work.' He was touching her; he mustn't touch her, he knew that, but she was reaching for him and the agony of denial was sweet pleasure too.

She knew it was different, he was holding himself back. He caressed her, but there was no kissing. He was not going to make love to her. She did not know what to do, she wanted him so much. She could feel he wanted her, she could feel his penis against her. That restored her, she would give him pleasure. She turned him onto his back.

'No, Cassie,' he whispered, but he did not move away.

She ran her lips over his stomach, she had done that before. She kissed the inside of his thighs, she had done that before. But now she took him in her mouth, she had never done that. She felt him shake as she opened her mouth and took him in and then she slid her mouth back up and then down again, and up and down, and up and down. He felt enormous, could she manage – he seemed so big – but yes she could because she wanted to. She flicked her tongue and used her teeth on him.

'Cassie. . .'

She heard him, she could feel him holding her head, a hand reached for her breast, cupping it, squeezing it. Rasping breath, he was shuddering, he was coming, she pulled him further into her – she could feel him at the back of her throat – she sucked him faster and faster, used her fingers over his shaft. She could taste him. He spilled into her mouth, she swallowed him, loving him.

'Oh, Cassie, Cassie. . .' She looked up at him and saw he was in tears.

Cassie was incapable of accepting that Joshua no longer wanted to see her. At first it was the flimsy excuses for missed appointments, and then it was the awkwardness when they did meet. Loving him so desperately, she told herself she would have what she could, when she could. She made excuses for him to herself, clinging to those excuses to justify his cavalier behaviour. Madrid's surrender, the German outrages against the Jews, Czechoslovakia, Hitler moving on Poland – Cassie turned it all to her own end, telling herself that Joshua was needed by those with no hope, but even so, in the grey mist of justification a dart of black asked, but why is there no place for you? She would not answer that blackness. Instead she would sit in Pierre's café night after night and she would panic as she nursed her Pernod. What time would he come? What would be his mood? Would he come at all? Mostly he did, sometimes he didn't, but still she waited.

Charles told her that she should play hard to get. But Cassie couldn't. . .

'You are becoming obsessed,' said Yvonne, and for a moment Cassie wondered if it were true.

She felt as if the sun had gone in, there was no light anywhere, just the blackness of Joshua's absences. She was in turmoil at all times, there was nowhere her mind could find peace.

But then Joshua asked her to go on a trip to the Swiss Alps with him and the sun came out again.

Charles and Yvonne protested that she would be missing the event of the year, the Arts Ball when the students took over St Germain, even invading the terraces of those holy places, Deux Magots, Café Flore and Brasserie Lipp. Even Beth was attending the ball, she was going as a slave girl. Cassie would have liked to have seen that but Joshua wanted her to be with him and that was enough.

'Why do you have to ask her?' Rebecca asked. She was brushing her hair.

'Because you don't just throw someone out like yesterday's dishwater. You tell them properly, with care.'

'There is no way to do it with care. Every day that you don't tell her makes the situation worse.' She looked at Joshua in the mirror. He was putting his cashmere scarf on.

'Why are you wearing that scarf? The weather is warm now.'

'I like it, that's why. And I like the painting, so don't touch that either.'

He walked out of the room slamming the door behind him. He knew he was wrong to ask Cassie to go with him to the mountains, but he missed her and he told himself that he would not touch her. They would spend time together and in the peace of the country he would explain that he would never see her again.

There were about twenty of them on the trip, and there were large huts to sleep in, perhaps seven to a room. Cassie felt shy and a little awkward when she realised it was assumed that she and Joshua would be sleeping together.

But that was nothing compared to the toilet arrangements. When Joshua told her it was a hole in the ground, she laughed, but all humour evaporated when she entered the little hut and realised that she had to squat. She felt quite sick and she could feel her feet sinking into what she hoped was damp mud.

The campsite was beautiful. Set low in the mountains, it was in a clearing which seemed to have been made for it, and just a hundred yards away, easily visible through the trees, was a lake. Such natural perfection calmed Cassie and she ran down the slope until she reached the gently lapping water. She pulled off her shoes and waded in, feeling the clean water wash over her legs. It wasn't that the primitive facilities no longer mattered, it was just that their importance was diminished. She enjoyed the quiet and the emptiness.

Hans, a Swiss, who offended the French at lunch by consuming his food directly from a tin instead of undertaking the important preparations and rituals that were necessary before they could enjoy a meal, suggested a trek through the surrounding woods. 'To get to know our place,' he told Cassie enthusiastically.

It was all right then, Joshua held her hand, half pulled or pushed her, stayed close to her, she could breathe his breath. The others, she knew quite a few of them, were indulgent of young lovers.

That night, around a camp fire, Joshua gave a reading of his poems, and Cassie sketched him – the young lion silhouetted against a black sky, his admirers ranged around him. She loved it.

But when he lay next to her and she wanted to turn to him, to hold him, to enjoy him, he pushed her away, albeit with a gentle gesture.

'Some of them aren't asleep,' he said.

He was quiet the next day; she wanted to speak to him about their situation, but could not. It was as if a web had been spun around her vocal chords, preventing her from even finding the words she needed. So she said nothing and simply touched him in the sunlight. He allowed that and walked with her into the woods away from the others, held her, kissed her, put his hand between her legs. She sank to her knees and reached for him.

'Cassie, don't, listen to me.' He tried to raise her from the ground but her fingers were already touching him. 'I am going to go to Moscow. I am trying to tell you that I won't be seeing you any more.'

'I know,' she said but still she didn't stop.

And Joshua berated himself as he gave into Cassie's mouth.

On the way back to Paris he repeated that he was going to Moscow and that he would not be able to see her, he would try of course, but he had things to do. Cassie said nothing.

She asked if she might have the poems he had read at the campsite.

'Of course.' His voice was kind, it was unbearable.

'I'd like to see if I can place some of them for you.'

'I doubt that anyone will take them, but I would be happy for you to try.'

Cassie was grateful to have a link to him, but she did not tarry. She took the pages he was holding out to her and said, 'Come to the café when you can. I am always there.'

'I will. Good luck with the poems. Let me know what happens with them. And work hard at your paintings.'

She couldn't speak, the tears were choking her. He was patronising her, she hated that. She walked away from him quickly, wondering if he was looking at her.

Cassie took Joshua's poems to the Editor of *Pariser Haint*, a publication whose bias would be too Zionist for Joshua's taste, but whose literary quality was renowned. At first the Editor took just two of his poems, and then he asked for more. Cassie put Joshua directly into contact with him.

Her efforts on his behalf brought them together again briefly and he bought her dinner at Pierre's. It wasn't an easy evening, particularly as he made it clear that they would not be going to his room.

'Why?'

'I have told you. We have no future, Cassie, it has to be over.'

She shook her head.

He looked down at his plate and concentrated on cutting his *bifteck* into neat little squares, but he didn't put any of the pieces into his mouth.

'You really are going to Moscow?' Cassie asked hesitantly.

He nodded.

'At least I can understand your reasons for wanting to go there. But you don't have to go. I can talk to someone, my father has connections in important places. I mean, if I can help you wouldn't have to see me – once you got to America. I mean, I'll probably be here painting away and you'll. . .'

'No, Cassie.'

'Don't stop seeing me, not before you go. Please. Just come to the café. I know you have arrangements to make. But at least we can meet for a drink.'

He didn't answer her, but the following night he was there. He wanted to tell her that his poems were to appear every week. He admitted to being very excited. He was going to delay his departure, but he was still going, he didn't want her to nurture hope. She touched his leg with her hand, and lied when she said, 'I understand.'

Rebecca was not pleased, but Joshua gave her no choice. Within a short time he became a sort of celebrity, to be fêted, invited and even copied.

Cassie continued to work, it was all she had now, and through her hurt came her voice. Her sketches were short and furious. She did a watercolour of eyes, round eyes, horizontal eyes, drooping eyes – but all sad. She developed her use of shadow, using black in its starkest form to convey a sense of impending tragedy. Walking in the street one day she saw a travelling circus. She took out her pad and sketched as much as she could, noting the colours, the gaiety, the crowds who watched. She painted the scene in rich gaudy colours, the clowns in their brilliant reds, vermilion, crimson madder, crimson lake, and yellows – cadmium, citron, and yellow ultramarine. For the trapeze artists in glittery blue, she mixed cobalt blue with white to give them a luminous quality. The faces were white masks with red lips, the crowd, a mixture of old and young and children, were unformed, only their eyes blocked in; she didn't work on the mouths or noses at all. The effect was grotesque, and then she took her black shadow and used it to disfigure the work.

Her fellow students commented and debated, her professors argued with her.

'But this is what we are about now, isn't it?' she told them all. 'The mad laughter before the black storm.' If Cassie had bothered to look she would have seen incredulity on the faces of those around her, not because of the force of her statement – there were many who felt as she did – but because it was not a sentiment they would have expected from Cassie Fleming.

She spent her hours with Charles and Yvonne (apparently it was all over with the model in Montmartre) but saw little of Beth and her beau Marvin. She did join them once for dinner. They brought a date for her, Alfred Fitzgibbons, a New Yorker too. She had sat with them in one of those antiseptic restaurants in the Champs Elysées that offered foreigners a taste of 'La Vie Parisienne' which Cassie found to be a watery version of the real thing. She listened to the two men give her an evaluation of the European situation from behind the barricades of isolationism. In a moment of total clarity Cassie realised she couldn't go home any more. She felt intolerably lonely – she was no longer an American. Nor, she knew now, was she a European.

She explained her feelings to Charles.

'I understand more than you think. I have a girlfriend at home, her mother is my mother's best friend, you know the sort of thing.'

Cassie smiled. They were sitting in a little café in Place du Tertre. It was a balmy evening, Cassie's hair was lifting in the breeze. Charles would have liked to have sketched her.

'I could hardly believe what I was hearing when my girlfriend said that after visiting Germany she had to admit that the country was being run very efficiently.'

'That's not so extraordinary. Beth said she wants to go there because she's heard the officers look divine in their uniforms.'

They giggled together. It was a nice moment.

'You told me you want to be an architect.'

'I am an architect. I qualified in England.'

'Is your father one too?'

'No, my father is a barrister, the kind of lawyer that stands up in court.'

'I know about them. I've seen the photographs. They wear dresses and wigs,' said Cassie, but she was laughing. 'Seriously though, what made you become an architect?'

'Actually, I want people to live in better conditions. I think architects can change the status of people in a more real way than any politician or mere dreamer. It all starts with the home: if people live in

41

amenable surroundings they feel better; if you send them to a better designed school they will study more; if their place of work is pleasing they work harder. It makes sense.'

'You make it sound very simple.'

'Underneath all the talk, I think it is.'

Cassie didn't notice that Charles couldn't look at her, but then Cassie wouldn't have noticed. She was conscious only that Joshua wasn't there for her any more. The only time she saw him was when she waited for him at Les Amis du Vin, but he seemed to have stopped going there as much, so she would wait for him outside the newspaper offices or on the corner near the Greenfeldts' apartment. Once she went to his apartment house, but she saw Rebecca. Obviously the German girl had acquired a room there too. She didn't want Rebecca to see her, somehow she looked an ungenerous person.

She was sitting near the Greenfeldts' when Joshua found her and told her that he didn't want her to wait for him, anywhere, ever again.

'Please, Joshua, it's the only time I see you now, you're always so busy.'

She slipped her hand under his jacket, running her fingers over his shirt. She waited for his hand to reach for her. He always used to do that, and more, in a dark alley where few walked. She loved the feel of his hands.

'I've told you, don't do that.'

She knew he was irritated but she couldn't help herself. She put her hand on him, slid her nails over him in the way she knew he loved.

'I've told you, Cassie.' His voice was so cold.

'Please can I at least see you at Pierre's, tomorrow, to talk?'

'I'll try, but don't expect me.'

On the following night Cassie sat at a table and waited. She was totally indifferent to the fact that she had actually sold a picture to an Italian tourist that day. She had taken one of her nudes to be framed, the man had stared at it and at her, and then he'd offered her one thousand francs. She hadn't even smiled her thanks. Cassie had learnt to understand the female form. She liked her own body; sometimes she would look at herself. At those moments she knew she was pretty, but she only looked at herself when Joshua fed her with his presence. In the time of his absence she had become another person, unsure of herself – her appearance had changed. No longer the apple- pie-fresh girl, she was almost haggard, an observer might say old for her years, and sad. The yearning for him swamped her. Ordinary tasks could not be faced, they accused her – the crime was failure, of not being good enough to hold the man she loved, and that sense of failure so communicated itself that the simple, the mundane, became Herculean obstacles that reminded her of life. And life was over there, somewhere in another room, whilst she sat trapped in her own longings, unable to take the simplest pleasures.

She was aware that she had a letter from her parents in her bag; she hadn't answered it, not because she didn't want to, but because the effort required in composing joyful prose was something that could not be contemplated. There was also a banker's draft in the envelope, to be put into her account at her American bank, but that was another task too burdensome to be faced. She knew she was in overdraft, but she knew equally that the Bank would simply charge interest: they knew her father's cheques came every month. And, anyway, now she had that money from the man who had bought her painting. Suddenly she couldn't wait to tell Joshua; she glanced at her watch, it was seven o'clock, he was never normally that late. He must have been delayed, he had said he would try and come. Perhaps he was still at the newspaper. Yes, that was it, there must have been a problem there. She should go and meet him there, that was the best thing to do. There was a moment's hesitation, but she pushed it away; this was no time for doubts.

Hurriedly she paid for her drink, pulling out a large note, scattering smaller notes in all directions. Quickly she gathered them together, stuffing them into a zipped section of her handbag, anxious to be on her way. She didn't even check her change. She was aware that Pierre was looking at her curiously. It bothered her – she wanted to be anonymous, he might talk about her, worse he might laugh. Ridiculously, she wanted to say, 'He's still at the newspaper, that's why he isn't here. I'm going to meet him – that's all there is to it, stupid really.'

But she said nothing for, through the window, in the Paris rain, she saw him, walking across the road quickly, an anxious, but joyful expression on his face. He was carrying his poems under one arm. She watched as he greeted a small, slight wisp of a girl whose dark hair clung to her head like a cap. He kissed her, just lightly, but a kiss on the lips.

Cassie felt herself go red, she wanted to bleed, but there was no wound. She walked quickly from the restaurant, they were still together, their heads together as they talked. Cassie could hardly bear to look, but equally she could not turn away.

'Joshua?' she called, wanting him, loving him, hating him.

The wisp-like girl – Cassie could see now it was Rebecca – saw her first. Blind, silly Cassie, immersed in her own wanting, not reading the exit signs, not even seeing them.

Joshua walked over to Cassie, after Rebecca had pointed to her. Cassie could scarcely speak for the pounding and rushing inside her head.

'Yes?' he said.

'Did you forget you were meeting me?'

'I don't recall having an arrangement for this evening.' His voice was even, polite almost.

'But we were supposed to meet.' She knew she was crying.

'No, that is not correct.' The voice was so patient, it was too patient. 'I explained I might not be able to meet you.' And he was gone.

Had he explained that? Had he said that? She was sure he hadn't, but perhaps he was right. But he'd kissed that girl, he'd looked into her eyes, she'd seen that, she'd seen the way Rebecca had looked at him. Oh God, it hurt, like a dagger in the ribs – no, lower, in the stomach. The pain would not stop, it would be all right if she could die of it.

Later, in her bed, she'd asked God to let her do just that, she'd wept and begged, all she could see was the kiss, the touch on the lips, the shape of his head as he bent down to find Rebecca's mouth, the light in his eyes. It stayed with her, every gesture, haunting her, eating away at her, smothering the rest of life.

Cassie had stayed in her room for days, unable to face the necessities of life. Beth had been unsympathetic.

'You became obsessional, Cassie, the guy was trying to get out of the relationship and you wouldn't let him. Don't you see, it had to end like that. You didn't give him a chance to behave like a gentleman.'

Yvonne cared. Yvonne held her. Yvonne fed her. Yvonne stroked her.

'I can't stop thinking about him, I can't stop caring.'

'You will – you'll get better. I promise you, now that it really is over – it's the hoping that is bad, when you still pray for happy-ever-after.'

She prayed that Joshua would come to her, but Joshua didn't come – Charles did. He cared for her too – but not as if she were an invalid, like Yvonne. He eased her hurt. He forced her out of her room, criticised her work, shouted – yes, shouted – at her artistic inadequacies, bullying her unkindly, making her turn to her work as her solace and her friend, praising her small successes. She grew to rely on him, she found a haven in him. They were alike, she and Charles.

44

After a little while he made her laugh, and she agreed to go to a restaurant with him, and then he courted her. It was easy for Cassie to love Charles. She had nowhere else to go. Joshua no longer wanted her, she had no place in America. A good, caring man reached out to her and she turned to him to bury her hurts.

They were standing on the little gallery, high at the top of the Sacré Coeur, looking across Paris towards the Seine, when he asked her to marry him. He had decided to go back to England.

'I am sure there is going to be a war, Cassie. I don't think it will be an easy time, but I love you and I think we can survive it, together.'

Cassie could feel the wind pulling at her hair, was it making her eyes water too?

'I will never leave you, Charles. I will be a good wife to you.'

'I don't need a good wife – I need you to love me.'

'I do,' she whispered, realising that she meant it.

Charles didn't wait for the ceremonies. On a hot summer's night in the darkness of his small room he loved her, seeking the curves of her body with gentle hands and a soft mouth. She felt the ache flood in, and then the shudder started and washed over her – releasing her from herself for just a moment.

'Oh God, oh God,' she whispered.

And Charles held her, wishing she had said his name.

She and Charles booked a telephone call to her parents: Cassie was insistent. The line was distorted but she could hear her parents and that was pleasure enough – she even demanded to speak to Cleo. When her father took the receiver back she put an embarrassed Charles onto the line. He formally asked for her hand in marriage. Amidst the crackles a speedy trip across the Atlantic was promised – by both sides.

Jane said little on the telephone. Her letter asking Cassie to come home with her fiancé before the nuptials was despatched the same day. It had been impossible to talk properly on the poor connection and it worried Jane. Cassie had written letters brimming over with her Austrian boy and now, just a few months later, she was telling them that she was going to marry an Englishman. Jane was sure he was charming, Cassie wouldn't care for someone who wasn't, but she knew her daughter. Cassie was a proud, sensitive young woman and if she had been hurt and was offered solace by someone she would take it without thinking of the consequences. The English were not an easy nation, they had their rituals and Cassie was a spoilt American. Jane wondered how it could possibly work.

Beth had already returned to America. She was going to marry Marvin, a most suitable match.

Cassie wrote to Joshua, care of the newspaper. It was a careful note, telling him that she was engaged to Charles and that she was going to live in England. She gave him her address, in case he ever needed anything. She sealed the envelope, and then ripped it open again. She couldn't help herself, she had to add something else.

'I love Charles, I want to be a good wife to him, I want children. But I will never forget you, you are part of me and still I long for you.'

He came to her room to say goodbye. He spoke little, just walked around and opened the curtains to look at her clothes hanging in an ordered line, pulled out the drawers and studied the contents as if to seal the memory of their time together. He kissed her on the forehead and wished her well. She wanted to cling to him, but he was gone, shutting the door behind him. She wanted to run after him, to bring him back, for just a few minutes more. She would have done it, but she heard Charles' voice at the door, greeting Madame Pétier, and she knew it was too late.

# Chapter Two
## 1939–1941

Jane's letter advising caution had failed to persuade Cassie that she should take a more leisurely approach to her marriage, and she and Charles married in a small, gloomy church off Montmartre on August 4th 1939. Yvonne and Madame Pétier were their witnesses.

Immediately after Charles and Cassie arrived in England, Charles joined the Air Force. Conscription had started in the previous April – even women were being encouraged to enlist. The propaganda machines churned out inspiring messages and stories and the country prepared itself for war.

Charles' parents, Edwin and Deirdre Bray, a well-mannered couple, had coped with their son's marriage as best they could. They had been shocked by the speed with which he had made his choice and indeed by the very choice of his life-partner – they had always assumed he would marry his childhood sweetheart, Florence Aspel. They had been so close until Charles went to live in France. But Edwin and Deirdre loved their son as best they could and so they had no choice but to welcome the young couple.

Of course, when they had first received Charles' telegram informing them that he had married, Deirdre had been quite upset. She had wanted a proper wedding for her son, and had always secretly looked forward to that event; nevertheless she pulled herself together. The girl was obviously quite suitable, the daughter of an American lawyer, so it seemed – however, it was surprising that it was the mother who was the lawyer, the father, apparently, was a banker. Deirdre secretly wondered about the suitability of sending one's single daughter to live in Paris; a boy was different, they needed to know a bit about life.

She had steeled herself, for not only had she spent time with Florence who was so obviously sad – 'It was quite awful,' she had told her husband – but Florence's mother too had claimed many hours. She had not confined herself to the niceties to which her daughter restricted herself. For she was the mother who had held the sobbing girl and Deirdre Bray was her best friend, they had been at school together; such a long intimate relationship allowed for honesty.

'Your son is an uncaring beast,' she had stormed at Deirdre.

And the awful part was that Deirdre had to agree with her.

A statuesque young woman, so obviously well-bred, nicely dressed, with just a slight tremor in a firm handshake to betray what were obviously nerves, was a pleasant surprise. So was Charles' obvious happiness. The only difficulty was the girl's almost pig-headed determination to work as an artist. Deirdre Bray came from a line of women who believed that the role of wife was an honourable enough profession.

England was a shock to Cassie. She had grown used to Paris and her easy life. There had been no rules of behaviour, no one else to consider but herself – rich soil for the seed of first love. But the wife of a young Englishman of proper breeding would be expected to live in a very different way. She would not only have to abide by the rules of marriage, which would mean a sort of intimacy with total strangers, but she would also have to learn how to live in England.

In 1939 London was the centre of the largest empire the world had ever known, an empire built on discipline and the good character of the motherland itself. For an American it was another world, a world of tea-drinkers divided by class as well as money where it seemed to Cassie that the essential ingredient for success was to know one's place. It was going to be difficult for Cassie Bray since she did not understand such divisions.

She found her mother-in-law polite, but nothing more than that. On the other hand, she liked her father-in-law, he made her think of her own father. On their first night Edwin Bray had opened champagne and made a little speech.

'To Cassie. I did not expect such a beautiful daughter-in-law. I bid you welcome to our family, to our home and to our country.'

Cassie would have liked to have kissed him, but she could see that one did not do that in England. She felt awkward and drank too quickly, her head felt quite dizzy.

Charles had a sister, Evelyn, a tall, rather fine Englishwoman. With her white-blond hair, high cheekbones and her skin of peaches and cream, she resembled Charles, and their mother. But Evelyn had different eyes, and brows. Her forehead was wide and flat, the brows thick and straight, her eyes were brown and direct – that part of her, and her character, came from Edwin's side of the family. She had two daughters, Victoria aged eight and Louise aged six, from her marriage to a sensible, sturdy man named Harry – he was a solicitor.

'Solicitor?' asked Cassie, her voice carrying just the slightest inflection.

'A lawyer,' Charles intervened, trying not to laugh. He turned to his sister. 'I would imagine the word "solicitor" has a slightly different meaning in America,' he told her as he moved away to fulfil family niceties.

Evelyn smiled. 'We think we speak the same language, but I expect you will find that we don't at all.'

Cassie glanced around her parents-in-law's drawing room. It was a formal room painted in cream with green velvet drapes, highly polished antiques and paintings in the style of Stubbs – even in the August heat it was chilly in that room. She thought of the smells of Paris, but she spoke of New York.

'There are a lot of differences. I suppose I have to expect that the transition won't be that easy.'

Her sister-in-law squeezed her hand. Already Cassie knew this was an uncharacteristic gesture. 'I am sorry we don't live in London. Our home is near Bath, in the country. I would have liked to have been within visiting distance of you but I am sure it won't take that long for you to find your way, and to settle down. Charles loves you very much.' She laughed – a dry, nice sound. 'You'll find somewhere to live, and learn how to cope with our appalling plumbing.' It was Cassie's turn to smile, the rudimentary bathroom with its brown linoleum floor hadn't even the charm of Madame Pétier's stylishly outmoded facilities.

'I wish you were nearby too. I think we can be friends, can't we, Evelyn?'

It wasn't a question. She liked this woman.

'Will you paint here?' Evelyn asked.

Cassie nodded. 'Of course, but I think your mother is rather shocked. She hopes I'll grow out of it.'

'I don't think there is anything for you to grow out of, as you put it. I expect an artist has to grow *into* her work.'

'Oh Evelyn, I hope all English women are like you.'

49

'Are all American women like you?'

'There are a few good ones.'

Their shared mirth could be heard all around the room. Faces turned enquiringly. Cassie watched them and realised that she might not have a lot in common with the rest of the Bray family. She needed to see Evelyn, and Evelyn was not going to be there.

As if hearing her thoughts, Evelyn said, 'When you find your own home, and meet Charles' friends, and make your own, life will assume a familiarity and the transition will be over.'

Cassie smiled her thanks; of course Evelyn was right, what were language difficulties anyway? She hadn't even been able to speak French properly when she had first arrived in France and yet Paris had become a home of sorts that had radically altered her perceptions of the world.

They rented an apartment in Kensington not far from Charles' parents. It had three good rooms, one of them faced north and Cassie immediately commandeered it for her studio.

'Will you go to art school?' Charles asked her. 'It might be a good idea, it would put you in touch with what is actually happening here.'

Cassie agreed with him, but did nothing about it. She wanted to enjoy being married. Sadly it didn't work out that way. Weekend leave was a treasured moment in a difficult time. She would long for Charles' arrival home. The sheer pleasure of being alone together was wonderful. She loved the sex. She told Charles, 'I think the sexiest thing in the world is a naked body with just its wedding ring on.'

He'd laughed at her and tumbled onto the bed with her and as he slid into her Cassie changed her mind. 'I'm wrong, the sexiest thing in the world is you inside my body.'

Cassie learnt quickly that all that pleasure had to be preserved and brought out and examined and remembered when Charles was not there. She steeped herself in the business of setting up a home in a strange country where a request for something different from the normal pattern was met by incredulity. Central heating was not to be contemplated, refrigerators were still an exception, drapes were called 'curtains', and washing-up meant doing the dishes. She had still not grown into the manner of things – let alone had a chance to form her own relationships – when the Phoney War was over and the real fighting began.

The false sense of security and the humour of the barrage balloons vanished. London became a city under siege and Cassie learnt of the real stuff of England. She fell in love with a city that relinquished the luxuries of peace with a courage that at first confused her, before she too became enmeshed in its struggle: she too was at risk, and she too learnt the language of the Blitz.

She lost count of the nights spent huddled in the tube station, sharing rations and kindnesses with strangers who might be dead the next day. But the bombing raids somehow spared Kensington. It was quite extraordinary – whilst most of London swallowed its dust and rubble, little enclaves escaped the devastations. The quiet squares where Cassie lived and walked seemed to belong to another time, except that there were no railings any more: the iron had been taken away and melted down for armaments.

Cassie missed Charles desperately – for despite the street camaraderie London was a lonely city when you were a foreigner, and a foreigner who did not conform. She missed her friends, even Beth. And she worried about Yvonne, and Madame Pétier too – she was frightened for them, constantly wondering how they were coping with the Occupation. As for Joshua, he filled her private thoughts. She told herself she would stop thinking about him once she knew he was safe.

She no longer missed her parents as much as she had done when she was in Paris. Of course she wanted to see them, but they were no part of her life now. They were safe in an America that was still a spectator in the war. They constantly wrote and asked her to come back to them. She did her best to explain that her place was in England now; she didn't know whether they understood or not.

Deirdre and Edwin were kind to her, frequently inviting her to their home, introducing her to young women of their acquaintance who shared her anxieties. She made passing contacts, in particular with Claire Brooke-Everett, the youngest daughter of a baronet. Claire was a writer, agonising over an American poet who had spent the summer loving her. Now he was enjoying a Frenchwoman in New York. Cassie liked Claire, in the shared intimacy of Claire's distress she was almost tempted to talk of Joshua, but she didn't, it would have devalued Charles.

She committed some of her time to a local hospital, doing whatever was asked of her as best she could, whether it was visiting the injured, comforting their children, reading to those who could not read, operating a small trolley that sold tea and buns, even scrubbing floors and toilets when there was no one else to do it. But despite her investment in the life around her, she was happiest when she could spend her hours with her oils and her charcoal. She sketched the faces of the Londoners, trying to capture the stoicism, the grief and the humour. One night she watched as a young woman was prised out of a fresh crater that had been her house. An off-duty nurse, a small woman – they needed someone small, there wasn't much room in the hole – had crawled in and literally pushed the badly injured girl up to her rescuers. They had joked and sung, and Cassie had joined in, they asked her to.

'Keep her spirits up,' they said.

Just as they lifted her out the girl died, her heart simply stopped beating. She had been just eighteen – even her youth couldn't prevent her death.

When she got back to her flat Cassie tried to write to her father about it, but she never posted the letter. In the morning there seemed little point.

Charles came back when he could. But Cassie knew that he was finding it difficult to adapt to her domestic needs. She never discussed it with him but she tried to comfort him physically. She thought that he might gain a brief respite in the oblivion of sex so she tried to make their time together special.

On one particular night's grace when it had been so cold that her throat hurt and her fingers curled up inside her gloves, her toes were pinched and numb, and her breath hung on the still air, she had refused to go to the tube station – the nightly shelter from the raging sky. Cassie spun on her heels and turned to face him, she was a little smaller than he was, and she liked the fact that she had to look up to him.

'Charles, listen to me.' Her fingers touched his mouth. 'Let's go back to the flat. A whole night with my husband is not to be spent in the company of others, irrespective of Adolf Hitler.'

In the eerie blackness Cassie had guided him back – she knew the way.

He did not mind, he hoped there would be a raid, he needed the danger. It was necessary for him now. Charles found his times with Cassie disorientating. He was more comfortable with the business of war. His daily bread was the reality of death; illusions, for that is what they were to him, of the order that Cassie offered him were unacceptable. He was nervous away from his squadron. He preferred the company of his fellow flyers, but mindful that he had a wife he forced himself to be congenial and caring.

Cassie held her husband's quivering body, she stroked him as she had never stroked him before, she felt him high inside her body – there

52

was a softness in her flesh, an openness about her, and she had clung to him, almost sucking his essence out of him, feeding on him, needing him.

And Charles had let her, content for her to do the foraging. He was tired. He loved Cassie although fear and excitement had almost extinguished his sexual appetite. But not totally, Cassie's wanting finally reached him, and he drove in on that softness, drowning out the whirr of the aircraft engines and the put-put of the guns, and the whamms of the bombs, gorging himself on his wife's sex, smelling her, licking her, biting her, wanting to devour and be devoured.

Just ten weeks later Cassie knew she was pregnant. It was wonderful for her. She blossomed with her maturing child. She never felt ungainly, she never minded the full breasts or the protruding stomach, they were proof of the miracle that grew within her. When she first felt the little butterfly touch of her child's movement inside her she experienced metamorphosis. No longer was she a girl waiting in the wings of experience. She was now a woman – sexual, powerful, giving – born to bear a child, there was nothing finer to await her in her life.

Deirdre was thrilled when she learnt that Charles and Cassie were to have a child. She immediately arranged that Cassie would come to the house after her stay in the hospital. She would need someone to take care of her and that someone would be Deirdre since she had the help and the facilities. Deirdre might have admitted, if anyone close enough had dared to ask, that she was a little anxious too. She believed that motherhood was an extension of the role of wife. Even though Cassie was pregnant it was obvious that she didn't consider motherhood an extension of that honourable state, motherhood to her was a nourishment in itself. Deirdre wondered what would happen to Charles and Cassie's marriage after the baby.

She found the opportunity to voice her fear when Cassie allowed her to see a finished painting, depicting the pregnant mother caressing her rounded tummy. Deirdre found it a little vulgar, but she withheld her feelings, concentrating only on how important it was to make the husband feel that he was not displaced. She tried very hard to be a friend to Cassie, as she was to her own daughter; they really had rather a modern relationship, but Cassie was uneasy with her.

'What do you expect, Mother?' said Evelyn. 'She doesn't know you or Father very well, she is in a strange country, her husband is fighting a war that isn't her war and he could be killed at any time. She has no friends here, she is totally alone. It must be quite dreadful for her.'

Deirdre agreed, of course. She resolved to try and improve her relationship with Cassie but it was Evelyn's world that was destroyed first. Evelyn's husband Harry, who like Charles had joined up immediately, was killed on October 21st 1941, the night Cassie's son was born. Deirdre, surprising even herself, had cried a lot, and even damned the Germans and the war in the most uncharacteristic manner. She had been quite uncommonly fond of Harry. Unable to sleep, she had spent the night clearing out her cellar, in case Cassie and the baby needed shelter. It was quite dry, and there was ventilation from an unsealed coal hole. She herself would go to her daughter and her grandchildren. She had telephoned Charles' squadron and left a message for him and then she had contacted their old family nanny, Nanny Bristow – Deirdre knew her first name was Mary, but no one ever used Mary, it was always Nanny – asking her to come and take care of Cassie. It was not an ideal situation, there had been some problems with Nanny, but she could not deal with that now. She had to go to Evelyn.

Armed with what petrol she and Edwin could muster, she set off in the early hours of the morning. She had looked up at the sky and dared the Germans to bomb her. The journey had been frightful. To confuse an invading army, simple precautions had rendered England almost unnavigable. Names of towns were blanked out, signposts pointed the wrong way and locals were mindful of giving even a distraught Englishwoman directions. But eventually memory and doggedness guided her to her daughter's home. Deirdre tidied herself up in the car, combing her flat cap of grey hair and applying a fresh outline of lipstick before swinging her tired legs out of the dusty 1932 Alvis that had once been Edwin's pride and striding purposefully to the front door.

Evelyn was peeling vegetables, her grief all too obvious. She didn't greet her mother, she couldn't move from the sink. The mundane task was necessary, otherwise she felt she would simply fold up and give in. She just carried on scraping the carrots, her tears mingling with the peelings. Deirdre embraced her daughter, then stood with her arm around her shoulder and they stayed like that, the two of them – together in front of the sink, drawing comfort from each other. After some time, maybe ten minutes, maybe just two, neither of them knew, Deirdre put the kettle on for a cup of tea.

Quite soon, after they had drunk two cups each, Evelyn asked, 'What about Cassie? Who will take care of her?'

'Oh, I telephoned Nanny Bristow.'

'Mother, I considered her too old when I had Victoria and Louise.'

'It is a time of war, my dear,' Deirdre replied, 'and I had to do what I could.'

'She should go back to America.' Her face caught the early winter light, allowing Deirdre to see the ravages in her daughter's face.

Cassie didn't have an easy labour. The child was facing the wrong way, unwilling – so it seemed – to leave the safety of the mother's womb. Cassie was brave and bore it stoically, only twisting the top of the damp sheets of her bed into ropes that she could bite when the pains were very bad.

'She's amazing, that American woman,' the midwife told one of the younger nurses.

Charles was not with her, he was somewhere in the inhospitable sky, fighting a duel with a stranger who, in another time, might have been a friend. Cassie Bray lay on her back and sweated to bring their child into the world, whispering her words of love, and need.

'Fight, damn you, little thing, come on out, so I can see you, so I can hold you. It's just us, you and me. Come on, get out here, it's time to start the living.'

But the little thing stayed where he was, inside his mother. Cassie had no sense of time, or place, she just toiled and whispered.

Later, a lot later, a nurse came and examined her. She was vaguely aware of activity, someone else came to her bed. There seemed to be a lot of talk and then a nurse called out loudly, 'Mrs Bray?'

Cassie wondered why nurses always shouted so clearly as if their patients were not only deaf, but also insensible.

'You are doing well, but we are going to have to give you some help.'

'No, I'll do it myself.'

'You can't,' another voice said. A man, who was it?

'I am Dr David Sinclair,' came the answer to her unspoken question, 'and I am going to give you a little injection. When you wake up you'll have your baby.'

'No, I've told you, it's up to us. Go away.'

'There's a good girl, hold still now.'

She could feel someone take her arm, she fought them with all the strength she had left in her, but there wasn't much. She tried to stop the roaring in her ears – it was no use, the sensation was sweeping over her, swamping her.

'Count,' someone told her.

'Little thing,' she shouted defiantly, 'Little. . .'

If Cassie could have stepped outside her own body she would have seen a competent man and his team of women working quickly, the bulbous cord that had kept her infant alive inside his mother was now wrapped around his throat, a little longer and the cord that had sustained him would have killed him.

There were those to take care of the baby, others fought for Cassie. After two long, gruelling hours they won their battle for her life, but they had taken her womb away.

The baby was named Thomas after Charles' grandfather; Cassie resolved to call him Tom.

Charles learnt he was a father when he landed. They didn't tell him how he had almost lost his wife until he got to the hospital.

'It was touch and go,' the doctor informed him. 'I had no choice but to perform a hysterectomy. How do you think she will cope?'

'I honestly don't know,' Charles replied, 'but I'll tell her myself.'

He did not concern himself with the implications of the operation; it was enough that Cassie was alive, and that their child was well. Charles had learned enough to cherish the living.

As Cassie pushed for consciousness she knew her husband was there, with her, she felt his hand and she was glad. But the baby, where was the baby? She was asking and no one was telling her, where was her baby?

On the morning of the second day after her ordeal she was able to ask, 'Little thing?'

'Absolutely wonderful,' said Charles.

'I want him.'

'Darling, you are very weak. You've had a big operation.'

'Operation? I had a baby.'

And then she realised she was hurting.

'You had an operation as well.'

Charles was leaning over her bed, she found him so beautiful with his soft white-blond hair, his fine, almost female face, his deep blue eyes. She wanted to hold him, but the movement would require a physical effort that could not be contemplated. She was suddenly aware of disability, but she was not anxious, because Charles was not anxious – she could see that. He was smiling, so she merely asked, 'What operation?'

'It doesn't matter now. I'll tell you when you are more awake. We have a beautiful son, Cassie. Thank you.'

She tried to lift her hand and touch his face. She managed that. He was so dear to her. She looked up at him. 'I want to hug you,' she whispered huskily.

Their tenderness had become almost painful and they found it hard to even look at each other. A nurse coughed carefully behind them, her presence was almost a relief. She was holding the baby. Charles immediately shifted a little on the bed, allowing the nurse to put the boy into Cassie's arms.

'Little thing,' she whispered, 'little thing, you are my son, Tom.'

Charles had to return to his unit immediately. He would be given two days' leave to take his family home when Cassie was able to leave the hospital. He was absolutely delighted by Tom's birth. His babyhood, though, would belong to Cassie. When he grew into his boyhood, that would be the time when they would share things. But then Charles pushed the thought away. He had to deal with the business of living day by day – dreams of a future were a luxury of peacetime.

When Cassie discovered that Harry had been killed she was desperately sad for Evelyn. She tried to write a letter; it was oddly formal, Cassie couldn't work with words. She would have liked to have torn it up and sent her a sketch. It would have been easier to convey the sense of loss that way than through a few dry sentences.

Claire came to see her. She had joined the Army. Cassie was sad, she would miss her.

'Don't be ridiculous, you've got your baby and I shall have all those men.'

Cassie was not very happy about going to Charles' parents' house in Kensington, but she knew that there was no question of her coping with a baby and the aftermath of a hysterectomy alone – even without the fear of an unwelcome intrusion by Mr Hitler's mechanical emissaries of death.

She felt quite sick about the operation. Charles had told her as carefully as he could. She had been able to cope with the fact that she couldn't have any more children, but she had felt sickened by the loss of her femininity, for that is how she saw it. She'd tried to talk to the sister about it, just a day or so before she had left the hospital.

'What happens, when you have a hysterectomy?' she had asked.

'Oh, they take away your womb and all the other bits.'

'What does that mean exactly?'

'Oh, you won't have any more of those wretched monthlies, you lucky girl.'

'What do you mean by the other bits?'

'Ovaries too.'

'You mean I have no female organs left? Nothing that makes me a woman?'

'Nonsense, of course you are a woman.'

'I don't think you understand what I mean,' Cassie had said quietly and wretchedly, feeling a despair that she did not know how to control except when she held her son.

She left all the arrangements for the move to Charles, she wasn't interested – all she cared about was her baby.

She would lie for hours just watching 'little thing', as she still called Tom, asleep in his cot. She marvelled at the perfection of his head, at his tiny hands and feet, at his perfect little face. How extraordinary that all of this had come from a coupling that had been complete in itself.

Nanny was a small wizened old lady who had been partial to a cigar and was a stickler for nursery routine. She admitted she was set in her ways, but talked proudly of her babies, and it seemed to Cassie that despite an autocratic bearing, which she knew was going to irritate her, Nanny did seem fond of her charges, and uncommonly fond of Charles. He had hugged her and warned her, somewhat seriously, Cassie felt, to take special care of his family.

'They are your loved ones, how could I do otherwise?' Nanny told him.

Charles brought Cassie home just ten days after her hysterectomy. Nanny had ushered her into Charles' old bedroom with a cup of hot tea, and swept the baby off to the nursery. Cassie had tried to protest, she wanted Tom with her, but she was just too tired. She knew she must concentrate on getting well, and try to ignore her disquiet at having to surrender her child to a woman who had been designated by others to care for them both. Above all, she didn't want to cause Charles any concern, she knew it was hard for him to leave them. He was fussing around her, putting her clothes into his old wardrobe.

'It's extraordinary to think of you here in my room, the guardian of my secrets.' He pulled a wry face and Cassie smiled back, her tenderness for him almost choking her.

'I wish I had known you then, what were you like?'

'A grubby little boy who dreamed of a fair princess – and what he might do to her. Imagine, now she is in his bed.' He tried to pull her into his arms.

58

She winced. 'I hurt,' she said quickly.

'I know, and that was thoughtless of me.' He ruffled her hair. 'I have to go.' He was sad, she could see that.

'Go on, your sister will need you.'

'War is not a nice thing,' said Charles, as he walked out of his bedroom door.

Naturally the entire family, with the exception of Cassie, were going to the funeral. Her father-in-law, such a courteous man, had apologised for having to leave her. However, everything seemed to be satisfactory. Cassie could scarcely stand up, but she was glad to be away from the stench of hospitals. She glanced around Charles' bedroom. She imagined it was just as it had been when he was a boy. The walls were painted cream, the neat brown shelves were littered with the memorabilia of childhood. She noticed his school photographs, one for each year. She saw how his face had changed from the small, smiling, open-faced little boy sitting cross-legged on the ground to the serious young man with a neat haircut and pens that stuck out from the top pocket of his jacket who sat next to the masters in the middle row. Underneath the photograph it said, 'Head of School – Charles Bray'. There was a rowing cup together with some crossed oars and a photograph of the rowing eight; Charles rowed in the middle of the boat. There were a lot of books: the classics – Greek and Latin – as well as Shakespeare and the great poets, and his architectural and art books. It was all as Cassie had expected, except for the Bible and a very old, rather worn teddy bear.

She would have liked to have lingered over Charles' possessions, to have touched them and got to know them, but she was exhausted, she had to get into bed. She tried to tell her body to stop, to let go so she could sleep; she was so aware that she and Tom were alone, except for the old nanny, in the cold Kensington house that she was expected to call home for the foreseeable future.

Life with Nanny assumed a pattern. Charles returned to active service and Cassie lived with her ache of fear that a cross in the cold ground and not their bed would bring him his peace. Deirdre stayed with her grieving daughter and grand-daughters. Edwin returned to London.

Every morning he would breakfast on a slice of wartime bread and spread it with a little butter from his ration and a great deal of his daughter's apple jam. He had always had sausages for his breakfast; he admitted to himself that he missed his sausages most of all – when you could get them now, they were made of breadcrumbs with just a touch of meat. So he spoiled himself with his jam, reasoning that at his age he was entitled to indulge himself in any way he could. He insisted that he carry out his breakfast ritual alone. In any event Cassie was in bed and Nanny was not to be tolerated at such an hour.

Edwin worried about Nanny being entrusted with young Thomas – he'd questioned Deirdre's choice, but she had silenced him with a sharp response, assuring him that she had spoken quite firmly with Nanny and that there was nothing to worry about.

Cassie noticed that Nanny, along with the rest of the English nation, drank a great deal of tea, and that after several cups she would become quite flushed. Cassie wished she knew her better, then she would tell her not to drink so many cups: it obviously wasn't good for her. She could never complain about the way Nanny treated Tom. She was a bit brusque – but kind in her way.

Cassie didn't really want Nanny around her, she wanted Cleo – she needed her, she would always need her. Cleo made her feel safe, she didn't feel safe with Nanny. Nostalgia for her own childhood swamped her: crisp clear days in New York when the cold bit her lips and made her nose sore; ice skating on crisp, white ice; thick malt chocolate to drink with Cleo's hot muffins running with butter and syrup. And her father, her beloved father. There were always hours of story telling. She liked it best when they went to the Hamptons. They would sit in front of their huge fireplace – in Charles' bleak English bedroom she could smell the scent of American wood as it burnt in the American grate – and he would tell her stories and stroke her hair. Sometimes he would read to her, a favourite was *Little Women*. Cassie couldn't wait to take Tom to America, for him to sit by that fire, or to walk in the cold in Central Park, or skate in the Rockefeller Center. She thought about her mother – she missed her too, very much. They had never been that close, she and Jane, but somehow she had always known that the family centred around Jane. She might not do the story telling or even the cooking, but Cassie knew, even as a child, that Jane was the one who made everything happen just the way it should. Cassie was surprised at how much she ached for her sensible mother.

During the day Cassie would sleep when she wanted and get up when she wanted. She always went into the nursery and gazed at her son, sinking down beside his cot, just staring at him. Sometimes she would lift his covers and run her fingers over his skin, letting him feel her touch, sometimes she would sketch him. She was aware that Nanny felt

60

that her passion for her child was quite improper. Her displeasure made Cassie laugh.

Cassie wrote to Jane about her feelings for Tom; it came as no surprise that her mother had ignored her outpourings in her return letter. She had concentrated on advice and another plea to Cassie to return to America. 'How can you cope with a child in that situation? You must realise that you have responsibilities, my dear. You must think of your son – the boy has a right to grow up away from a war.'

Her father, on the other hand, had confided his own feelings for her when she was a baby.

'I know exactly what you mean,' he had written, 'I marvelled over you – you were such a miracle, Cassie, and now you are a grown woman with your own extraordinary triumph. I long to meet my grandson, come home please.'

When she had read their letters Cassie had cried a little. She did feel alone, and frightened, she wished Charles was with her. Her father-in-law was a kind man, but a very private person and she had no wish to intrude. It was hard enough that they had to live together. She envied Deirdre and Evelyn, at least they had each other. Cassie longed to hear Jane's slightly nasal voice with its dry American vowels. She missed America, there were times when she needed to touch its soil. But as the days went on she began to feel a little better. Eventually she resolved to take Tom for a walk. She knew she wasn't quite strong enough, but she couldn't bear the house any more. She had to get out. She called out to Nanny whom she assumed to be in the nursery, 'Can you get Tom ready, please, I think we could both do with some air.'

She dressed, taking great care over the swollen scar on her abdomen. She hated it and wondered if it would ever fade. She combed her hair hastily, applied some lipstick and went into the nursery.

Tom was not in his cot. She went down the corridor and knocked on Nanny's door – there was no reply. She pushed the door open and then she saw the whisky bottles and the overflowing ashtrays. She actually managed to run down the stairs and saw that the pram was gone. She tried to reason with herself: of course a nanny should take a child out. Maybe she had gone to the corner shop and would be back soon. The siren shrieked out its warning. There was a raid. Cassie could not possibly go and sit in the cellar, she sat on the stairs listening to the thud of the bombs and prayed that Nanny had taken Tom into the safety of an underground station and that they would be back when the German planes had gone. After the all-clear she made some tea, but they did not return.

61

She felt sick, she could not sit down, she just walked up and down, the length of the hall, the width of the sitting room, through the dining room, into the small library, out to the kitchen and beyond to the pantry, and back again, over and over again.

Edwin came home at five o'clock. Cassie was scarcely coherent. He gave her a brandy, and used the telephone.

'They have found a pram in Church Street,' he told her quietly, when he had put the receiver down.

'Oh Edwin, please, it's my baby, it's my baby.'

'I know, my dear,' the old man said stiffly. 'It's my grandson.'

'Where is he?' she wept.

At nine o'clock the warden knocked.

'Blackout,' he said roughly, 'the windows.'

'I'm sorry,' Edwin told him. 'We are a little preoccupied.'

'The bloody corporal isn't going to concern himself with that, is he?' the warden snapped.

'No,' Edwin said and went about the task of blacking out the night.

There was another knock. Cassie staggered to the door. A woman stood there, she was holding a baby – Tom.

'Oh God, oh God,' Cassie whispered and grabbed her child.

She went up the stairs with him, holding him tight, kissing him, crying out her hurt and anguish and relief – and love. She could feel his little mouth again on her cheek. He was dirty, and hungry, his cries mixed with hers, but he was whole, he was safe. She took off his clothes and cleaned him. She dressed him quickly, and cuddling him very close she went down to the kitchen to prepare his bottle.

Edwin was thanking the woman, whose name was Mrs Bradley, and, of course, making a cup of tea. If Cassie hadn't been so upset she might have laughed at the predictability of it.

'I found him,' the woman told Cassie, and then she cleared her throat.

'Where?' Cassie asked.

'In his pram, outside the Anchor pub in Kensington Church Street. Just before the siren went off. I didn't know whose baby it was till I went to the police station and they told me you'd reported your child missing.'

'I will never be able to thank you enough,' Cassie whispered carefully. 'I thought I'd lost my baby. I can't tell you the. . .'

'Please,' the woman said softly, 'don't. You see, I wanted to keep your baby.' The woman's knuckles were white, her voice was choking with uncried tears. 'I wanted a baby, see. My own kiddie was killed two months ago. I miss him, I miss the feel of his little body, of his fingers. Their fingers are something special, aren't they?' The woman looked up at Cassie, her eyes were bright with her unshed tears.

'How terrible for you,' Edwin said compassionately.

'Shrapnel. He was in his pram, thought he'd be safe there, in the house, but the glass in the window was shattered.'

'I probably would have actually kept him, if I had been you,' Cassie told her.

'I am sorry.' She looked utterly desolate. What a life they all lived.

'But you didn't keep him,' Cassie told her. 'You brought him back to me.'

'Well, I just remembered how bad I'd felt when I knew my littl'un had gone, and I couldn't do it. But I wanted to.'

Cassie hugged the woman. Edwin fed his grandson and put him to bed. He left the women alone in the kitchen and wondered briefly at the extraordinary nature of love.

There was no such wondering when Nanny returned insensible from the Anchor and her hours in the tube station during the bombing raid. Edwin told her never to contact the family again. The old woman muttered that she loved Charles, she began to babble almost incoherently.

'You should have thought about Charles before you went on your drinking binge,' Edwin informed her. 'Now pack your bags and go.'

But Nanny was incapable of such an act just then, so they left her in her bedroom. In the morning she left quietly and in great distress, but neither the mother nor the grandfather had the inclination to listen, although Cassie admitted that the old woman looked devastated.

'What kind of life must she have,' she mused, 'caring for other people's children, with nothing of her own? I am not surprised she drinks.'

Cassie longed to see Charles, but it was not possible. She held her baby and told him, 'We'll just have to cope, you and I, till your Daddy comes home. In the meantime I have to start painting again, that will help us both.'

The following day Edwin brought her charcoal and sketch pad to her bed, together with a neat tray set for breakfast. Two cups and saucers, two slices of wartime bread, two tiny neat pats of butter, and two large mounds of apple jam. He placed the tray on Cassie's bed, drew a chair up and began to butter his toast and spread his jam in silence. Cassie understood that Edwin did not like to talk at breakfast, but she was grateful for his presence. Before he left he brought her the post. There was a letter for her from Portugal. The letter was short.

> *Dear Cassie,*
> *I write to tell you that my husband Joshua was killed – shot – as he was helping Jewish refugees to cross the border from France to Spain.*
> *I know he would have wanted me to advise you of his death.*
>
> *Yours sincerely,*
> *Rebecca Gottlieb*

Joshua dead, her beautiful Joshua gone forever. She couldn't, no, she didn't want to believe it. No, no, not Joshua. She started to cry but the worst part was that there were no tears, the pain was horrible. She couldn't bear it. The tray slid from the bed, the cups didn't break but the dregs of tea spilled out of them to form an ugly puddle. The butter was smeared over the plates, the remains of the bread and jam stuck to the carpet. But Cassie didn't see any of that. She just saw brown eyes, long slender fingers and a Cupid's mouth and heard a soft voice. She felt as if her heart was breaking.

A child's cry called her, a child needed her, her child. She got out of bed and went into the nursery. She picked Tom up, smelling his baby freshness, and she held him so tight. This child of hers, this love of hers, would help her to cope with the terrible, terrible hurt inside. He had to help her, for if he didn't she would quite simply die of anguish.

# Chapter Three
## 1942–1946

Cassie Bray was a mother now and an artist; where, she might have asked, if she had cared to, was the wife? She tried hard to be a proper companion to Charles, but she knew she had no part in his daily living. He shared that with the men he fought with. Cassie was the one at home, the one to whom he would return – when it was all over. Until then she had to make do with what he allowed her.

She could no longer welcome him into her body. She had dried up – intercourse hurt – she derived no pleasure from touching. The first time she and Charles had made love, after Tom's birth, after the operation, the pain had whipped her. She was empty, there was nothing there. Charles was on top of her, trying to reach her, trying to excite her, but it was gone – whatever it was – taken from her, she felt, by the knife that had cut away her womb, the part of her that she had learnt, during her pregnancy, really mattered.

Because she was a thinking woman, because she was an articulate woman, she tried to talk about it.

'I am sorry,' she had told Charles, afterwards.

He lay there, away from her, but still next to her.

'Why, Cassie? I love you.'

'I love you – but it hurts me.'

He stroked her hair, she was comforted by that.

'I will go and see the doctor, perhaps there is something wrong,' she said.

But that was 1941 and doctors had other priorities.

After a brief examination, and after allowing her time to rearrange herself behind his closed curtains, the doctor invited her to sit at his desk and informed her, 'There is nothing wrong internally, Mrs Bray. The surgeon has done an excellent job.'

'But I don't feel female any more.'

Dr Fox misunderstood. 'Perhaps you might think of adoption. There are, God help us, so many orphans now. I have a case that I can think of immediately. The mother was twenty-two, she was killed by falling bricks, the baby, he's a bonny little thing, just two months. . .'

'It's not that,' Cassie interrupted – she was irritated that he could not understand her needs – 'I don't enjoy making love.'

'I beg your pardon?'

Cassie could see he was shocked. She followed his eyes as she looked around his sparse surgery with its bleak green walls, its thin cheerless green-on-green patterned curtaining. Suddenly she thought of her doctor in America, Dr Garton, he was fat and he laughed a lot. He had toys in his surgery and a cookie jar, and he always held her hand, even when she grew up. She looked at the chipped paintwork and she hated it.

'Well, I am sure with time that will sort itself out.'

The doctor was a thin, weasel-like man, with a thin black moustache. He stood up and held out his hand, indicating that the interview was over. It amused Cassie to realise quite how anxious he was to end the conversation.

But Cassie was not prepared to end matters there; she rearranged her black gloves carefully in her lap, lining them up next to her black handbag. She cleared her throat. 'You see I don't feel anything!'

Dr Fox began to tidy his papers. 'My dear, you have to come to terms with the changes inside you. Things will settle down. And now I really must see my next patient.'

But 'things' did not settle down. Cassie tried to talk to Charles, he did his best, but it was hard for him. Men he loved were dying. He himself could die.

And so Cassie and Charles became friends instead of lovers. They shared their son and the difficulties of living in Charles' parents' house. But their intimacy was gone.

When Charles was away Cassie spent her time caring for Tom, loving him with a passion that worried her mother-in-law now that she had returned from her daughter's. She bathed with him, she slept with him, she fondled him. He gave her such joy, she would look into his eyes and hold his little hands and make him promises for his future.

The most shocking event, in Deirdre's eyes, was Cassie's excitement when, on changing his nappy, she discovered his erection.

'It's distasteful,' she informed Evelyn, when the widow came to stay.

Cassie was stifled in her parents-in-law's house, she felt like a guest. Deirdre and the precious Mrs Carlisle, known as Mrs C, who had worked with Deirdre for 30 years (a crisp lady in a flowered dress and a cardigan, with long wavy hair pinned up in a bun) were always careful to be nice to her, but often when she would walk into the cream kitchen with its heavily stacked dresser and wooden table, they would stop talking. And there was nowhere for her to paint.

She would go out, wheeling the pram for hours – even when it was very cold. On one particular Friday, Cassie went to the park. It was November and rather cold, but the light was good that day – the sky was the deep English-winter blue, the leaves had gone from the trees – the branches made odd, distorted shapes. Cassie liked them, the gnarled, knotted wood attracted her. She wanted to touch them. Instead, she drew them, making them seem like an old army, petrified and distorted, warning of the ill-disguised future, under all that pleasant greenery.

'That's good, that's very good,' said a voice.

Cassie's heart stopped. She turned around and there, shivering in a thin coat, stood Yvonne. Cassie could not believe what she was seeing, she reached out and touched her friend, trying to absorb the fact that she was not in Paris, that she was in London, sitting next to her on a park bench.

'How?' was all she managed to say.

Yvonne seemed to sway slightly. Cassie could see she looked tired, her eyes had deep rings under them, her face was white, her fingernails were grimy. Cassie remembered she always used to have beautiful fingernails.

'My father, may the good God forgive him, he likes the Germans. I was so ashamed, I could not stay.'

'Oh, Yvonne.'

'I walked, as far as I could. And then I got some help.'

'Help?'

'Help, Cassie.' The voice invited no more questioning.

Cassie did not care, it was enough that her friend was there with her.

'The boy?' Yvonne asked, looking towards the pram. 'You have a son?'

Cassie smiled with all her heart. Yvonne pulled the covers back slightly and gently touched Tom's face.

'Charles? How is he?' she asked.

'I live with fear, every day, like the rest of the women. Oh, Yvonne, I think this is a women's war. It is the women who fear for their men, it's harder to do the waiting than to do the fighting. It's the women who battle for the food, it's the women who work the land, it's the women who work in the factories.'

'Paint it, the women's war. That's what you should do.'

'Look,' said Cassie, pointing to a woman pushing a child on a swing. 'That is what it's about, it's about doing it all on your own, raising your child, loving him, caring for him – all by yourself.'

'But you are not alone in that way. You have Charles' family, and you could go back to America if you wanted,' Yvonne interjected gently.

'My place is here, waiting for my husband, like her,' and she pointed at the mother and child again.

There was something about that woman that disturbed Cassie; she turned away from her, back to Yvonne. Despite the Frenchwoman's fragility, she had the extraordinary ability to make Cassie feel safe, and she realised that she hadn't felt safe for a very long time, perhaps not since she had been a child in New York. New York made her think of her father – he had made her feel safe too. She suddenly wanted to see him very badly, but at least she had Yvonne now – she had to help her, but she remembered Yvonne's pride, and she knew she would have to be very careful about the way she offered assistance.

The woman at the swings had seen that she was being watched. She averted her face without studying her voyeurs, she didn't like being the object of interest. She continued to push the swing methodically, backwards and forwards, backwards and forwards. The child, her hair neatly parted in the centre and plaited at the back, was shrieking with pleasure. The ropes of hair sailed out as the swing rocked her backwards and forwards.

'Mama!' she shrieked with pleasure, 'Mama!'

The mother smiled at her daughter. She loved to see her laugh. When the other two women and the pram were out of sight she stopped pushing her.

'Come, liebchen,' she said. 'We are going to Frau Heindt for tea.'

Rebecca Gottlieb felt she should use English in England, but her endearments and titles were always German.

She had arrived in England just three months previously. Fascist Spain had been difficult for a penniless Jewish Communist. But there were sympathisers everywhere. She would have liked to have gone to Russia, but the war precluded that possibility and so an old compatriot of Joshua's, Fritz Blum, had arranged for her to come to England on a Portuguese freighter. The captain had been entranced by the idea of rescuing a waif and her baby from Hitler and Rebecca had been very grateful to him. She had expressed her gratitude nightly. He was a kind man, not handsome, but comfortable to lie with. A big man with a huge face, he had made her forget that she was a widow and she helped him deal with the nights at sea. He showed her photographs of his family and she let him play with Elizabeth.

The child had been born just seven months after Cassie had left Paris, during the time of the Phoney War which Joshua had known could not last. He had married Rebecca and taken her and the new baby to Jaca, a small Spanish village not far from the French border and there he set up his headquarters. His job was to smuggle as many Jews into Spain as he could. The job of the Spanish border guards was to stop him. One day he stopped cheating death. He had kissed her and the child goodbye. He was very relaxed that morning, it was not thought to be a difficult mission. He'd stopped and waved when he reached the corner of the small street where they had lived. Rebecca had waved to him from the door, the sun had played games with her and she had seen him disappear into its blinding white light. If Rebecca had been that kind of person, she would have paled with premonition, but Rebecca had no such feelings. Shortly after Joshua's death she heard that the Greenfeldts had been taken – a friend discovered that Kurt had been hanged before he had even had the chance to leave Paris. Frieda survived interrogation for three weeks, the 'friend' was told she had died of a heart attack.

The captain of the freighter had wanted to help Rebecca when she got to England, but there were people expecting her, not friends exactly, but like-minded people who had been alerted of her arrival.

The *Freier Deutscher Kulturbund*, established in Hampstead, was an organisation of German Communists exiled from their homeland: writers, artists and thinkers. They helped each other and Rebecca was one of them. She was not an artist, but an administrator. She worked in their offices and lived in a small flat off the Finchley Road. She never normally went to Kensington, but Frau Heindt lived there, and an invitation to tea from the lady was not to be ignored. Frau Heindt was a tall, good-looking woman whose husband resided in Moscow at the Hotel Lux while he waited for the war to end. She liked Rebecca, and the child was particularly charming. She had told Rebecca that Elizabeth should dance. 'She has a dancer's feet. . .' Frau Heindt told

69

her. She should know: once, after the First World War, she had had her moment of glory, she had been a prima ballerina at the Berlin State Opera.

As Rebecca walked to her appointment with Frau Heindt, Cassie and Yvonne rediscovered each other. Cassie looked at Yvonne carefully, she could not help but contrast her own neat black coat, which, despite the utility requirement, still managed padded shoulders, a fitted waist and flared skirt, with Yvonne's thin brown one, tied at the waist with a belt, and which had so obviously belonged to someone else.

'Are you all right for things? I mean, do you need anything?'

'No, Cassie, I don't need "things". I need you, and little Tom and Charles.'

'And I need you,' Cassie said, impulsively putting her arms around her friend's shoulders. 'I've actually been quite alone.'

Yvonne smiled at Cassie. 'Well, you're not alone now.'

'And neither are you.'

They went to a Lyons tea shop. Cassie hated those places, so bleak with their linoleum floors, small tables, and lukewarm tea. Iced Coke, big sandwiches, and luscious icecreams, were as alien as thick rich coffee there. That day it didn't matter.

'Joshua?' Yvonne asked.

'He's dead. I had a letter.' Cassie's voice was flat. She raised her head and Yvonne saw pain.

They ate dinner that night at the Brays' house. There was sherry, from the store laid in before the war. Deirdre and Edwin had welcomed Yvonne unreservedly. A friend of Charles, a friend who had suffered, was to be treated with the utmost courtesy.

'There're no nuts, of course,' Deirdre said, as she poured golden liquid into cut glass on the silver salver. Deirdre wore a dress of dark blue with a double row of pearls. The fare was a Lord Woolton's special, corned-beef stew, potatoes and carrots. There was a tiny piece of cheese and some of the grey-looking bread. Yvonne declined the bread, but took a small piece when forced.

She admitted to Cassie that she was staying in an unpleasant room in Notting Hill Gate. She worked for the Free French. 'For refugees, you know, helping to house them.'

When the siren shrieked its nightly call, Edwin suggested they use the cellar rather than move to the tube station. Tom was put into his Moses basket; Deirdre carried the sherry. They sat huddled in one corner, listening to the thuds of the bombs and the terrible spraying hail of the anti-aircraft guns. Cassie glanced up and noticed that Deirdre was shaking. She reached over and took the woman's hand in her own. She was quite shocked when Deirdre clung to her. She hadn't realised her mother-in-law was so frightened.

When Charles telephoned – a weekly occurrence – Cassie was bubbling with excitement. Her voice almost shook with pleasure as she told him how she and Yvonne had met in the park.

'Oh Charles, it is wonderful, it's going to be just like Paris again.'

Charles, knowing it could never be like Paris again, wondered how Cassie could be so naive. Had the war touched her at all? He didn't tell Cassie that he already knew that Yvonne was in England. In fact it was he who had told Yvonne how to reach Cassie. They had come across each other at one of those anonymous country houses where men in uniforms coaxed and coached those who were to parachute into occupied lands. Sometimes Charles flew them in. He was instructed to attend a special briefing – a young Frenchwoman recently rescued from France had important things to say. The young Frenchwoman was Yvonne.

Charles did not rush over to her. He stood at the back of the room and waited until she had finished. She had noticed him immediately, he had seen her little face lift slightly in his direction. They smiled with the smile of friendship, different to the one used by acquaintances, or even the one used by lovers. At the end of the briefing she walked over to him and held out her hand.

'Hello Charles,' she said, much as she might have done if they had run into each other in Rue Vavin in a time before the fighting.

'Hello Yvonne.' And if the handshake was warmer than it might have been, neither of them would comment.

He had found a bottle of whisky – he had his contacts – and they went to Yvonne's room. She told him that she had hidden allied servicemen and some Jews until a collaborator had betrayed her.

'I know who it was, a man who wanted me out of the way. I knew about him, he raped his daughters.' She didn't look at Charles when she said the sentence, she kept her eyes down as if she were studying the rich brown wood of the carpetless floor.

Yvonne cleared her throat, she was sitting on her bed, her feet drawn up under her skirt. Her hands were clasping her knees, she was as taut as a piece of wire strung between two electric currents, just waiting for the switch to be pulled so it could explode and burn itself out.

'I was warned by someone, I don't know who it was. I just took the warning and left. Eventually I got to Chantilly. I was absolutely terrified. I didn't know where to go, the local priest found me in the church. He didn't ask any questions but he arranged everything, ferrying me to another town, organising a safe-house, keeping me hidden until the pick-up. You know, Charles,' she looked at him for the first time, 'I hugged that priest before I left, and I think it is as close as I have ever come to loving a man.'

Charles understood, he knew how hard it was to love. Mostly, though, he knew about the terror. It hit him every time he went up into the sky – as he left the ground he would feel the racing heart, the dry mouth – and he would pray. It was bad, but it wasn't as bad as the nights when he curled up into a little ball and tried not to cry, holding his old teddy bear secretly under the sheets: it was exactly how he used to be when he was a small boy, away from home, at prep school.

He didn't tell Yvonne any of that, in fact they didn't talk much at all. They couldn't, either of them, after Yvonne had said so much. They did drink though, solidly. Charles fell asleep first, there in the chair. Yvonne didn't try to wake him, she watched him for a while and then she got up and clambered into her bed. He woke with a dry mouth and an aching back in the early dawn. He studied her as she lay curled on her side – she had shown her vulnerability and her vulnerability was his own; quietly he let himself out of the room so as not to wake her.

It was shortly after Yvonne's arrival in London that Cassie found a way to help herself – and her friend, for she had not stopped worrying about Yvonne's impoverished state or her dismal room. But first she had to talk to her mother-in-law. She explained to Deirdre that it was time for her and Charles to live in their own home again. At first Deirdre demurred: after all, Cassie had a young baby, how would she cope alone?

'The same way that everyone else manages. But I did think it might be an idea if I asked Yvonne if she would like to live with us. It would be a way for me to assist her, Deirdre. She is quite alone in the world.'

And Deirdre, who understood very well that women needed each other, had not taken offence.

Cassie invited Yvonne to Sunday lunch with Mr and Mrs Bray. Over the dessert of stewed apples she made her suggestion to Yvonne. Yvonne smiled, and Cassie knew that Yvonne knew her just a little too well. She toyed with her glass, she felt quite hot, her hair clung to her neck, she badly needed Yvonne to accept.

There was a small pause; Edwin looked enquiringly at Yvonne.

Then Yvonne spoke. 'Of course I will stay with Cassie when Charles is away, but when he is home on leave I shall go back to my little room – we shall all need that privacy.'

Cassie wanted to live in Hampstead Village, near the Heath. She often took the tube to Hampstead and wheeled the pram up to the gentle lush slopes of the Heath. Despite the anti-aircraft gun emplacements she knew great peace there.

Edwin Bray knew of a house for sale in Well Walk. It had belonged to a schoolmaster who had left London for the Cumberland countryside at the start of the war; he wanted to be rid of his London residence. The moment Cassie saw the house she knew it was the right place for her: the Heath was only a moment away. She was unaware that by moving there, she was but ten minutes' walk from Rebecca Gottlieb's flat.

The house was built of solid Victorian red brick on three floors – three small rooms in the attic, three bedrooms and a bathroom on the first floor. The bath interested Cassie, it was huge, sitting on small feet shaped like lion's paws. Above it was a small machine; apparently one inserted some pennies, and out came a few miserly drips of water. It was called an ascot heater. She realised as she stared at the monstrosity that she had been away from America long enough – she was no longer shocked by the plumbing.

There was a large kitchen with a coal-burning stove, a dining room, a drawing room, and a small room that could serve as Charles' study. That room had a single door that led into the garden where there was a large shed.

'One day,' Cassie told Yvonne, 'that will be my studio.'

She showed the house to Charles on his next leave. He liked it, but had no time to make the appropriate arrangements. That was left to Edwin. There was a trust, money left by Charles' grandmother, so it was quite simple to organise. Furniture was supplied by Charles' parents. Cassie wanted to take the mementos of Charles' past, she thought they should go into his study. She wondered about the teddy bear, she couldn't find it anywhere.

Cassie began to paint as soon as they moved into the house. Her theme was as Yvonne had counselled: 'The Women's War'. She worked hard and well, her work was sparse, interesting – but there was a barren quality about it that worried Yvonne. The characters were in place, the construction of the painting was good, but it was flat, without emotion. It was as if Cassie had cut herself off from life. Yvonne remembered how she used to paint in Paris, how she had first mastered her technique but had no voice, and then the way the pain of losing Joshua had given her work a power and a perception. There was none of that in Cassie's work any more.

'What's the matter with you, Cassie? You are hiding away from life.'

They were in the little room at the top of the house where Cassie painted. It was quite bare and extremely cold, but there was a good light from the north-facing window.

'Perhaps.'

'Why?'

'Lots of reasons.'

Cassie fidgeted with her paintbrushes.

'Try one on me.'

'Just one?'

Yvonne smiled. 'Cassie, tell me.'

And Cassie, who wanted to confide in her, admitted that she felt nothing for Charles sexually.

'I think it hurts more than I am prepared to admit.'

'Ask him to touch you in other places,' Yvonne said simply.

Cassie was curious and a little tempted. She prepared herself for Charles' first leave in their new home with care. It would be the first time they had been alone in their house.

Deirdre managed to get her a chicken, an event in itself in a time of tinned Spam and corned-beef. She prepared it as best she could, cooking it slowly in breadcrumbs, the American way, with potatoes and carrots – she longed for butter and cream. She mashed apples carefully into a puree. She set the table, used only one standard light; she liked the effect more without the centre light. The fire was kindled, she bathed herself, washed her hair and tried not to be nervous.

Charles was exhausted. He was now a Squadron Leader. That morning, over France, he had lost a plane – he loved his men, all of them, but especially Simon Harris, a young man just three years out of school. He'd been frightened, he admitted as much to Charles. Like a new boy on the first day of term sitting in the Head of School's study, he had choked back his fears and tried to behave like the man they told him to be. When he died he had flown just three missions.

Harris' parents lived in Hendon. On his way home Charles called in to pay his respects. It wasn't an easy experience. Harris' mother was a young woman, she cried a lot. 'He didn't want any part of the war.'

By the time he reached his new home in Hampstead, Charles needed a bath, a whisky and bed.

He was unprepared for the seduction that Cassie had prepared. Momentarily he was irritated, but then he looked at her soft, lovely face, his son asleep in his cot by the fire, and the table set for dinner and he was grateful. He was one of the lucky ones. He caressed her shoulders, easing his fingernails along her spine.

'Charles?' she said. 'Touch me a lot.'

And understanding, he drew her close and kissed her, gently rubbing her nipples under the thin white hostess gown with its cross-over top and slender skirt. He ran his hands down over her body.

His brain reacted – Oh God, how beautiful she was.

He pulled up her skirt.

'No, darling,' he heard her say quickly, 'not like that. Slowly. I need other ways.'

'Later we'll try other ways,' he said, his heart was throbbing – he had to have her, what a wonderful girl to realise that.

He pushed her down on the carpet by the fire. The baby began to cry. Instinctively Cassie reached up towards the cot.

'He's all right for a minute. Babies should cry,' Charles said roughly. He was undoing his buttons.

'No, that's not. . .' Cassie started to say.

But Charles had already opened her legs, kissed her, run his tongue up into her.

'No!' she said again, listening to the child, wanting to go to him.

But Charles was inside her and she hurt. She lay still and let him finish.

When it was over she stood up, feeling his sperm running down her legs, picked up the baby, cuddled him, calmed him, went into the kitchen, cleaned herself and checked the chicken. Only then did she realise that she had left the room without even looking at Charles.

She walked back into the sitting room. He had arranged his clothes and was sitting in the chair she had placed by the fire for him.

'Would you like your son?' she asked in a bright voice.

'Thank you,' he said politely.

'I'll get our food then.'

'Fine.'

In the kitchen with the door shut, Cassie cried. She felt so empty and so useless, the same black horror that she had experienced in Paris. The terrible deep hole of despair, the same sense of incompleteness, the same difficulty in facing the day-to-day business of living. She looked at the reminders of the dinner littering the work surfaces and the sink, she couldn't deal with them, she hated that sinking feeling inside her, she felt so ugly.

Charles could hear her crying, but he didn't know what to do about it.

There were just another two Christmases of the war, and then it was over. There had been so many victims. Cassie's personal toll included Claire, who had been killed by a V-Bomb. There had been no ideological struggle to discuss in 1939 – there were simply the good guys who had to fight the Nazi bad guys. Then came the mushroom-shaped cloud and those who understood knew that nothing could be that simple again. The larger world's exuberant victory swung into a harsh peace.

When Cassie first saw the photographs of Hiroshima she quite simply went into shock. She sat in her kitchen, just staring at them, unable to move.

When Charles came back from his walk with Tom, he said, 'What's the matter, Cassie?'

'The matter? This is the matter!' She flung a copy of *Picture Post* at him. 'They've destroyed his chance of a future. I hate them.'

'That's a bit irrational, isn't it? They had to use the Bomb to end the war. The Japanese would never have surrendered.'

'So they fried a few children, and now it's all right.'

'No, it isn't all right. We just have to hope we never have to use it again.'

'Hope. Is that all you can offer me?'

'Cassie, I didn't drop that bomb.'

'But you would have done, wouldn't you?'

Cassie was stunned when Charles didn't answer her.

London was a bleak place, there were queues everywhere – even for the dry cleaners. Chocolate creams were a rare delicacy, children's sandals were unavailable. The bombs had left their craters, and the pock-marked skylines served as a reminder that the financial burden for a bankrupt nation was poverty. The people tired of the old order and voted for change, a socialist foundation for a new world, so they thought.

Cassie was no longer naive. She now suffered regularly from depression. She learned to recognise it and accept it, but she hated it.

There was no pattern to it. It came unbidden and there was no cure for it. But the black moods were not with her all the time, there were the good times, Tom was the one who saved her. She and Charles slept together occasionally. She liked the feel of the man as he lay close to her, sometimes she would touch his back as he lay next to her, sometimes his shoulders, his flat stomach, marvelling at the smooth texture of his skin. She liked it when he caressed her, she submitted to his penetration. She felt nothing, but at least it didn't hurt any more.

Yvonne had moved out of the house. She had a little flat off the Finchley Road which she shared with a friend. 'I have a place of my own now, it's important for me,' she told Cassie by way of explanation. Of course Cassie understood, but she missed the companionship. She worked long and diligently, and privately. She was now much more able to reveal herself in her painting, no longer sterile and flat. She created small women against the huge machines of war, big women cradling their children, ordinary women trying to reach their men over vast empty spaces. She used greens and browns and yellows; full but delicate brushwork created the figures; the landscape was provided by a palate knife and a crumpled rag dipped in the paint. It wasn't that she was trying to create a feeling of spring: the colours were muted; she didn't want the brightness of new life, she wanted the bleak colours of a hard victory. She was, in the main, satisfied. But all that work was diminished by a new canvas, born from her mind, from her terror of the legacy of Nagasaki and Hiroshima.

Cassie was tormented with visions of arid earth and scorched flesh. Sometimes she would rush to Tom and hold him, visualising a flash of light and the flesh falling from his bones. She held him tight against her as if she could shield him from the horror. She had to paint it, it was the only way she could deal with her nightmares. She tried a huge canvas of yellow and red and orange, employing her palate knife to build up the paint. The entire composition was constructed as a massive fire ball. In the corner she sketched in two tiny figures, stick figures, using crimson lake. She wasn't sure about that, so she painted them over in black. She preferred them in black, depicting the charred remains of humanity. She called it 'The Burning'.

One night as they prepared for bed Charles had tried to explain that he shared her loathing of the atomic bomb, the only difference was that he understood why the Americans had used it. Cassie wouldn't listen to him.

'I can't accept it under any circumstances.'

'You don't know what you are talking about, Cassie. You have no idea what it is like to fight a war, to continually see dying around you. Let me tell you that anyone who really understood would do anything to stop it, even if it meant dropping the Bomb.' He had stormed out of their bedroom. He had no intention of sleeping in the same bed as Cassie that night. He was incredibly angry with her. She had no idea what he – and all the others who had been in the business of death – had gone through.

'Charles.' Cassie had followed him into the hall. 'Please – just look at my painting, maybe if you saw it you would understand how I felt.'

'No.' He didn't want to see the painting.

Charles returned to the bedroom but lay still and quiet in the bed next to Cassie. He was beginning to realise that they were very different people. She was honest to the point of discomfort – he supposed it was an American trait, but he didn't like it, he preferred a more subtle approach. Charles wouldn't admit it to Cassie, but even though the war was over he found it easier to be with the men who had fought with him – particularly David Sampson, a pilot who, like him, had survived the Battle of Britain. Sometimes he didn't even want to take his weekend leaves, preferring to stay at his camp – but he was always careful to make a plausible excuse, wanting it to sound genuine.

Cassie noticed, and sought comfort in her work and her son. She relished her child, loving him with a passion that sometimes frightened her. They were best friends. They would bathe together, sometimes sleep together, and walk together. When they walked they held hands, and Cassie talked of 'how it will be when Daddy comes home'.

Cassie and Tom had their rituals. He would wake between 6.30 and 7 o'clock in the morning. When he was a toddler Cassie would hear him giggling and chattering in his cot until, bored with his own company, he would shout for her, and she would go and pick him up and bring him into her bed. They would lie in the warmth and Tom would touch her face with his little fingers and he would curl into her and she would tell him stories until it was time to get up. As he grew he left the constraints of his cot and acquired a bed – and a voice. In the night, when he needed her to chase away the witches or dragons or tigers that came to haunt him he would cry out, 'I go my Mummy bed' and Cassie would rush to him, cuddle him and rock him, and soothe him. He had a clay rabbit in his room. It was a sad toy for its ear had been broken, but Tom loved his rabbit and they would sit together and tell rabbit about the bad think and rabbit would take the bad think away.

By the end of the war Tom had grown out of muddled words and incomplete sentences.

'Mummy,' he would call when the sun roused him, 'is it time to get up?' And she would go into his bedroom and carry him – still half asleep – into her bed.

'For the morning cuddle,' she called it. She would tickle him, and he would tickle her back. The pillow fights had started when he was about three – he loved that and would laugh and laugh.

They spent many hours in Cassie's studio at the top of the house. Tom had his own paints and a pad. When Cassie started work, he did too. He would concentrate carefully, the tip of his tongue sticking out between his teeth. His glass of milk and two biscuits were just by his side, on a bright blue table. Actually it had been Charles' table when he had been a child, but it had been dark brown wood and Cassie thought it dull. She had painted it the brightest shade she could find. Charles had been quite shocked.

'Oh come on, Charles, it was only a table.' But then she felt bad. 'Did it have a lot of memories?' she had asked.

'Just the usual,' he said quite sharply.

She wished he'd said more, shouted at her for desecrating something from his past, but he said nothing, just set his lip. Sometimes, if she were honest, she was rather relieved when he went back to his base. She wondered how things would be when Charles was home all the time.

And then Charles did come home for good. Cassie saw the teddy bear the night he got back, it was on Tom's bedside table, just by the little nightlight that was left on during the dark hours. She made no comment to Charles, she realised that the matter of the bear was private for Charles, so she merely picked it up and popped it under the eiderdown, its little face on the pillow – waiting for Tom. That night when Charles went in to kiss his son goodnight he noticed that the bear was in his arms.

'What's his name, Daddy?'

'I never gave him a name,' Charles replied, 'I suppose he was just Bear.'

'That's what I'll call him, Just Bear. You can kiss Just Bear goodnight if you like.'

Awkwardly Charles picked up the bear and pecked it, feeling the spiky hairs on his lips. He realised it was the first time he had touched his bear in front of anyone.

79

Charles had joined a firm of architects in Portland Place, just a few yards from Broadcasting House. He was grateful that he could at last activate his personal view of a just society. The bombing had achieved one thing at least: it had allowed a chance to rebuild. And in Charles' view it would be the *function* of the building that would be paramount. Lives had to be made better – simple clean buildings that served that end were the way to achieve his aims. Fantasy and pretty pictures had no place in Charles' life. He worked hard, not wanting to give himself time to think; that was his way of dealing with his difficulties. He had suffered in the war, but now it was over. He had survived and now he wanted to live. He didn't want to think of the differences between him and Cassie. He loved his boy.

Charles progressed rapidly within his organisation. It was not just his architecture, it was also his style that appealed. He was never ingratiating or personal, but he achieved a kind of balance between formality and intimacy. His directors found him an easy man to deal with, his equals admired him – he was, after all, a leader of men, and his personal staff would do anything for him.

The one happy event was that Evelyn remarried, a childless widower, much older than herself. His name was George Williams and his wife had died in the early part of the war, a victim of the Blitz; he'd been quite devastated. Evelyn's grief for her Harry awoke a strange sort of protective tenderness within him that he had never felt before. It wasn't a passion, but he recognised it was a need in him. As for Evelyn's needs, George was a country gentleman, he suited her, and he was very kind to her daughters.

'They need a father,' she had told Cassie on the morning of the wedding.

'I hope that's not why you're marrying him,' Cassie said quietly. She was pinning a rose onto the pink hat she was lending Evelyn. It was a favourite from before the war, purchased from Lord and Taylor – she thought nostalgically of the luxury that had been her right then.

'Cassie, I'm a pragmatist.'

'Oh, Evelyn, that's a dreadful thing to say.'

'Is it? I was in love with Harry. I can never have that feeling again, I am not sure if I even want it – it can be quite painful, loving someone so much that you lose part of yourself.' Cassie looked away, she knew exactly what Evelyn was saying. 'I am extremely fond of George, he will take care of me. And I am rather looking forward to it.'

'That wouldn't work for me,' Cassie said softly.

'It isn't always the hearts and flowers that work. Sometimes the sensible partnerships stand more chance.'

'Ouch!' Cassie said, sucking her finger furiously. 'I pricked myself.' She pulled the needle through one last time, cut the thread and handed Evelyn her hat.

'It was very kind of you to lend Evelyn your hat,' Deirdre told her after the ceremony.

'It isn't a kindness, Evelyn is my sister-in-law,' Cassie said sharply. She was irritated, the English were so formal, sometimes it stuck in her throat.

Deirdre noticed her daughter-in-law's sharpness, she wondered about the effect of the war; it had damaged them all. She herself coughed a lot now, she tried not to show it, but Edwin knew. He fussed a bit, but she told him to stop it, she was perfectly all right.

The young Brays, as they were called, made a life for themselves. They had a lot of acquaintances. Yvonne was their friend. David Sampson was Charles' confidant. Cassie welcomed him eagerly, realising he was a Jew; she hoped he would be like Joshua. But David intended to become a stockbroker. A lithe man with good shoulders and prematurely thinning black hair, he had a wonderful humour that comforted Charles in his black moments. David apologised to Cassie for his closeness to her husband, '. . .but we watched too many good men burn to death, we bombed too many neat towns not to have an understanding beyond the normal limits of friendship.'

Cassie didn't mind, she knew that she had not shared those years with Charles. She was not envious of that time, she had had Tom. Briefly she hoped David and Yvonne might like each other, but Charles scotched that idea. 'He'll marry a Jewish girl, and soon,' he told Cassie.

But David didn't marry a Jewish girl. He chose Marilyn, a WAC with wavy red hair and freckles whom he'd met during the war. They married in Hampstead Registry Office and Cassie and Charles were the witnesses. Cassie would have liked to have made a friend of Marilyn, but she found her rather too sensible for her taste.

'You know the kind of woman,' she told Yvonne. 'She'll run a perfect home, have the perfect children and eventually do the hospital visiting thing. We had a dreadful dinner with them. She obviously didn't approve of me at all.' Cassie's eyes sparkled. 'I think I rather shocked her, I kept talking about how beautiful it was to touch little boys.' Yvonne joined in with her laughter.

Yvonne had decided to stay in England. The stain of collaborator had marked her father, and she could not contemplate living with that shame. With Charles' help she found a flat in Marylebone. She started selling paintings from there: Cassie's work and that of another two French artists whom she had met in England. During the day she now worked as a secretary at the French Embassy. Cassie never did find out what Yvonne had actually done during the war, but she was quite forthcoming about her position in the cultural attaché's office. It allowed her to make a lot of contacts. 'And I shall need them all when I open my gallery.'

Sometimes Yvonne would meet Charles for lunch. They never discussed their meetings with Cassie, she might have misconstrued them, and they were perfectly innocent. Except for the fact that they discussed Cassie. Charles reasoned with himself that he needed someone to talk to and Yvonne was Cassie's best friend. Yvonne reasoned that she was very fond of Charles. They never discussed Cassie intimately, they talked about her art, about her being an American – and about her obsession with Tom. But despite her rationalisation Yvonne did feel uncomfortable sometimes, as if she were betraying her friend. She would tell herself that it was important that Charles had someone to talk to, someone who was loyal to Cassie, after all she and Charles were friends – it wasn't just Paris, or even Cassie that had cemented them together. It was a night in an anonymous English country house.

Yvonne had no interest in men, she took her pleasures, privately, with women. She had discovered her preferences at the hands of a kindly British Lieutenant just a few months after she arrived in England – she would have liked to have shown Cassie those delights, but despite Cassie's difficulties with Charles Yvonne knew that she would never be excited by a woman's body. Cassie Bray was a woman for a man.

By the summer of 1946 Rebecca Gottlieb had grown accustomed to her life of exile, but she was quite inured against English society: her work, her child and her friends precluded her from forming any kind of relationship with either the people of England or even the land of England. She missed Joshua, the grief was very bad sometimes, but she learned to contain herself and wait for it to ebb, knowing that it would return. England was not her adoptive land, it was just a place to stay – until she could go home to Germany. She missed her country and blamed the Fascists for taking it from her. She dreamed of a time when she could go back to a cleansed land – a utopia of equals, just as her beloved father had dreamed. Rebecca was not a woman to delude herself. She had known she was not the great love of Joshua's life, she was his friend. She was like him, they came from the same stock, they had the same ideals, but it was Cassie Fleming who had been his lover. Rebecca wished it had not been like that. She told herself he would never have been happy with Cassie, his politics would have separated them, but she knew of course that he had never forgotten the American girl. She tried not to think about it and told herself that in time it would have been different – but there had not been time, Joshua had been killed, and he had never seen his daughter grow, he had never learned to love Rebecca. The lesson Rebecca had learned in childhood that one could not change the unchangeable was a very hard one. . .

On a particularly warm Sunday, Frau Heindt, who knew of Rebecca's loneliness, suggested a visit to the seaside, to Brighton, just a train ride away. Rebecca felt nervous, she didn't want to leave London, the idea of travel made her insecure.

'We have a visitor, Dietrich Brundt, who has travelled here from Berlin. He's here from Berlin to help us return home.'

Dietrich Brundt was a good-looking man with thick sensual lips and huge brown eyes. He wore his brown hair neatly parted on the right side and swept back from the temples.

'We are building the new Germany. I know it sounds pretentious, I don't mean it to be. Life in our world won't be easy at the beginning. We have to flush out the Nazis, frankly we have to start again. Are you willing, Comrade, to be part of that? To give your child the chance to grow up in an equal society where everything is possible?'

He was talking as they sat in the second-class carriage of the train that was taking them to Brighton. As they travelled through a countryside that didn't interest her she told him, 'I have been waiting to go home, I want to go back to Berlin.'

'Excellent. I will arrange accommodation for you.'

'I will need a job,' she said absently, touching Elizabeth's hair. The child was excited. She was looking out of the window. Frau Heindt had told her they were going to see the sea.

'You will work for me,' Dietrich told her, letting her know with his eyes that he thought her pretty. If Rebecca had looked she would have seen that Frau Heindt was well satisfied. The stiff old lady in her baggy black suits and jumpers and her two rows of beautiful pearls that were never hidden, had long wanted to see a flush of pleasure in Rebecca's cheeks.

It was she who walked Elizabeth along the promenade at Brighton, past the pale-turquoise railings that prevented a fall onto the shingles below. The beach at Brighton wasn't sandy. Elizabeth was rather disappointed, but later in the day, after they had looked at the Royal Pavilion, a palace that had once been the home of a decadent prince (Elizabeth heard the grown-ups discussing its façade as if it were some disgusting eyesore; she thought it rather pretty with its three domes and gracious proportions), the tide went out and there was lots of wet sand to walk on and to crunch her toes in. Frau Heindt took off her shoes, and her stockings; she intended to paddle too. As she took Elizabeth's hand she turned back to Rebecca who sat on the pebbles with Dietrich, her feet pulled high under her, her black hair curled for the day, her lips reddened.

'The girl has to be a dancer, never forget that.'

Dietrich smiled. 'I will ensure that she goes to ballet school at home.' He squeezed Rebecca's hand. 'And you will be able to watch her,' he told Frau Heindt.

The old lady smiled kindly and shook her head. Before Rebecca could say anything she had walked off across the wet sand, encouraging Elizabeth to dabble her toes in the breaking surf.

'Her husband has gone missing,' Dietrich said quietly.

'What?'

'We expected him in Berlin, but he is not at the Hotel Lux. We don't know where he is. She will not come back until we find him.'

'You will,' Rebecca said.

She felt so peaceful; it was a long time since she had experienced such an emotion. She was going home. She only wished it could be with Joshua. She pushed the thought away. She knew she looked nice that day. She was wearing a good black skirt and a pretty blouse with a flattering collar. She'd taken her coat off, she could feel the warmth of the late sun on her face. She glanced at Dietrich, she saw that he found her attractive, but then she noticed the thin gold wedding band on his finger. She made sure she smiled at him. After all, he was going to find her accommodation, and a job, and even a ballet school for Elizabeth – then she turned her back, and lay down on the shingle, allowing herself to enjoy the gentle air of England. She watched Elizabeth as she played at the water's edge. She had collected a group of stones, piled them one on top of the other, as if they were a castle. She danced around the castle, ignoring the shingle, a prince courting a princess high in a tower. She bowed and leapt around, using her arms and her head to convey her love for the princess. It didn't take long for Rebecca to realise that quite a number of other people were watching Elizabeth too.

On the morning of September 23rd 1947 Cassie took Tom to school for the first time. She dressed him in his grey trousers, grey shirt, red tie, and grey blazer. She put his red cap on his head; the blazer was a little too big, the shirt cuffs had to be rolled back, but still she could see the pride in his eyes. She took his hand and together they walked to the school. At the gate she kissed him; he turned away from her, and then ran back and put his arms around her neck, hugging her very tightly. Then he walked into school.

'Where did you get that wonderful smile, Thomas Bray?' she heard the headmistress say and Cassie burst with pride.

She watched another boy, crying, clinging to his mother, and she thought of her boy, marching in on his sturdy little legs. She knew he was frightened, she always knew when he was frightened. It was his smile; he only smiled like that when he was scared. At five Thomas Bray started his lessons.

# Chapter Four
## 1949–1953

Tom met his American grandmother, Jane, when he was seven years of age. Cassie had stubbornly refused to go back to America before – she and Charles did not have enough money of their own to finance the tickets, and she felt she could not accept her father's offer to help. She had no idea that the reason Clinton had not come to England to visit her was not an identical stubbornness: he was a very sick man, a heart attack at the golf club had almost killed him. He no longer worked, simply nurtured himself for the day when Cassie would bring her son to see him.

It wasn't that Cassie hadn't wanted to see her parents, she missed them very much, but it was a question of pride, she was a married woman now. So she worked at her painting, storing the money she made from occasional sales much like a squirrel husbands its nuts, in a pile she could see. Cassie didn't want that money to go into a bank – she wanted to count it, to feel it and, most important of all, to see it. The crisp five-pound notes were kept amidst her underwear, just to the left of the lavender sachet that she used to keep the intimate clothing sweet.

She had collected £155 when she heard that her beloved father had died in his sleep – he'd been just 58. Tom went to the funeral with her. Charles had offered, but she had declined. She knew he was working on an office building off Threadneedle Street in the City of London, a narrow, twisting relic of the old city where old money and new conspired together – it was an opportunity for Charles to make his mark – Cassie understood that it would be very difficult for him to be away from his work at such a time.

She and Tom flew from Croydon to Idlewild. It took fifteen hours; they stopped to refuel at Shannon and Gander. Tom felt quite sick, but he was a brave little boy. The steward fussed over him and the pilot allowed him into the cockpit; he really enjoyed that, sitting at the controls. Cassie watched him from behind.

'Why don't you pretend you are a pilot, just like Daddy was in the war, swooping down over Germany, and killing all those Nazis so that the war can end?'

Tom looked up at her, he seemed to smile into her. She reached over and touched his shoulder and he turned, burying his head against her body. He was tired. She picked him up, not something she did often any more, he pushed her away sometimes now, and she carried him, as if he were still a baby, back to the seat. He fell asleep, lying contentedly against her, and Cassie felt a sense of oneness with Tom that almost frightened her.

As she tried to find a comfortable position in the awkward aircraft seat Cassie thought about her father. It seemed impossible that he wasn't going to be there at the airport to meet her. She remembered their last farewell, he had hugged her and told her to go into the world and take what was hers, but to be careful never to take what did not belong to her. The tears stung her eyelids at the memories of walking in Central Park on Sunday afternoons while Jane enjoyed her one indulgence of the week, a sleep on her bed. That was the time when Cassie and Clinton would walk to their little lake in Central Park, just up from 55th Street. Cassie loved that place. There were rich red-brown rocks right in the middle and her father used to tell her a story of the mermaid who lived there who when the moon came out used to climb onto the rock and sit in the silver glow and watch New York. One night, determined to see the mermaid, Cassie had waited until everyone was asleep and then she had slipped out of her bed, put on her thick red winter coat with the velvet collar, and her thick gloves, socks and shoes, all over her nightdress, and had tiptoed to the door. She had tried to open it, but it was locked. Her mother had discovered her in the hall. Cassie had thought she would be very angry; instead she said, 'There are no such things as mermaids, but if you like we can go and check.'

They had hailed a cab, and if the cab driver thought that it was odd to see a girl out at that hour of the night, especially a girl in a nightdress under her coat, he had said nothing. Jane had asked the cab to wait, they ran through the park, the moon was full, the rocks looked different in the quiet light, but there was no mermaid. Cassie had been heartbroken.

'I think it's important that we don't tell your father the mermaid doesn't exist,' Jane told her when Cassie had finished her tears. And Cassie never told him – not even the next Sunday when he sat down by the lake and started the story again. She was anxious to protect her father from the reality that there was no mermaid. It had taken her several years to acknowledge her anger at her mother for destroying her dreams. She looked down at Tom and realised that she had been seven years of age then, as he was now. Gently she woke her son, kissing his eyes, his nose. He was bemused at first, reaching out for her instinctively, stretching, and then, 'Ow! My ears!'

'Oh darling, it's the pressure. Here,' she said, rummaging for a handkerchief in her handbag. 'Blow hard.' He took it and tried, but he huffed instead of blowing.

'Oh Mummy. . .'

'Try one of these,' the amiable steward said – Cassie noticed he had dark blue eyes – and he offered Tom a boiled sweet.

'I feel sick,' the little boy said, shaking his head.

'Come on,' Cassie whispered. 'You can do it. It'll help. See, I'm doing it.' She opened her mouth and showed how she sucked the sweet and swallowed. Tom put a peppermint in his mouth. Gingerly he swallowed and sucked.

'That's it, keep going,' the steward said as the plane sank into a low shallow descent, lurching a little. Cassie's stomach literally churned. She realised she felt very unwell. She was sweating. Tom clutched at her. She ran her hand across his forehead.

'Mummy, you're hot,' Tom said, looking at her anxiously. 'Are you all right?'

'Not wonderful,' she replied.

'I'll take care of you,' he said, as the plane sank lower still. He grabbed the arms of his seat. 'At least I will when I feel better.' They both laughed and held each other's hands tightly.

The plane swooped low and Cassie said, 'Look down there – it's the Hudson River.'

She tried to ignore the tightness in her throat as she pointed to the Statue of Liberty, but the tightness turned to tears and Cassie Bray knew she had come home.

The noise and apparent confusion of Idlewild Airport swamped her, there was a strangeness about it all. Everything seemed different to her. She shook her head, she didn't want it to be like that. Tom wanted to go to the toilet. She stopped a porter to ask for the washrooms, he had a smiling, large face and an ebony skin, his lilting voice was a reminder that soon she would see dear Cleo – she remembered how she had needed Cleo when Tom was born.

Tom was tugging at her hand. 'Mummy, what's a washroom?'

She explained that in America the toilet was called a washroom. Tom was confused by the wording, he thought the English and Americans spoke the same language. Cassie laughed.

'When I first went to England I had to get used to "toilet",' she told him.

'But you lived in Paris?'

'In France it's called "la toilette" and I once went on a camping site where all they had was a hole in the ground.'

'Uuk,' said her fastidious son.

Despite Tom's protestations, they both used the women's room because she wanted to keep him with her. When they'd finished he held open the door for an elderly woman. She walked through, followed by a younger woman and then a child. Tom was amazed that no one said 'thank you'. Others streamed past them and Cassie realised that she and her son must have stood there for at least five minutes whilst Tom held the door open. She pulled herself together, and took his hand. 'Come on, darling,' she said, 'I'd forgotten -- no one does that here.'

Jane was waiting for them when they had cleared Customs. A thin woman, her slightly tanned face was very lined, her thin blond hair, a poor reminder of Cassie's thick mane, was swept up into a bun at the back of her head. She wore a black coat and a small black hat which seemed uncomfortable on her head. Jane was a woman made for trousers and thick sweaters, somehow when she wore those she was at her most female. In the neat clothes of her sex she looked somehow disjointed. Cassie would have liked to have rushed to her and hugged her, but her mother was not a woman to encourage such intimacies. She embraced Cassie, but let herself be touched rather than touching back, and when Cassie had kissed her, leaving a lipstick stain on a white cheek, she had rubbed it off quite deliberately. Yet her voice – so gravelly – was soft when she said, 'I am glad you are here.' Cassie knew she really meant it. She resolved to spend some time with her mother, she resolved to try to know her a little better, the way she hoped her son would know her. She watched her mother bend to greet Tom, saw the way she put both her arms out to him, formally, but with an extraordinary tenderness that the boy immediately recognised. She took his hand, and they went together. It was the first time that Tom hadn't held Cassie's hand.

Cassie let Jane get the cab – it would have been hard for her, she had forgotten that you had to push your way past others, she was used to queuing now. Jane managed to get one, but as she was opening the door a couple barged past them and pushed themselves in first. Cassie was shocked.

'Those people were so rude.'

Jane smiled at her daughter. 'You have been away too long, Cassie. This is New York.'

The homecoming was bitter-sweet. That was when it really struck her that her father was gone. The apartment seemed so empty without him, but Cleo was there, dearest Cleo, she hugged Cassie – and Tom. Beth was coming for drinks in the evening, other friends had left messages inviting calls. None of it mattered – her father was not there any more. She went into her bedroom, a pretty room still decorated in rose and white with matching chintz curtains and quilts on the two beds. It was exactly as she had left it, but the memorabilia of childhood was put away, as if Jane had acknowledged the passing years. Cassie smiled at that. She drew the drapes back – how quickly her vocabulary had reverted! She looked down at the teeming city, she could see Central Park from her window. She ran her hands through her hair, it was difficult – she wanted everything to be the same, but she knew even then that the ten years in Europe, an English husband, an English son, an English life had all eaten into her American self. Cassie wondered where she belonged. She saw herself, one foot in England, one in America, doing the splits across a huge sea. She would have liked to have sketched it, quickly. She worked like that – etching her ideas crudely and then defining and refining. She would have liked to have talked to Yvonne, wondering how she coped with her French self in Anglo-Saxon England. But Yvonne was not there whereas Beth was on her way.

She arrived at 6 o'clock. They tried with the squeaks and yahs of their teenage years to bridge the emptiness of the years apart, of their different experiences. Beth enjoyed being married to Marvin. They had a daughter, Emily – she was three. Marvin had decided upon a political career and to further that end he worked in the Justice Department in Washington while Beth sat on the right charity committees. She didn't see as much of her parents as she used to. Marvin's family were quite demanding, and of course they had all the best connections for

Marvin's career. She was sure her mother and father understood. They were very close to her younger brother who had married a really nice girl he had dated at high school. They had three children who kept her mother busy. Beth was wearing well – neat hair, outlined lips, a sweet hat, an elegant dress. Cassie envied the dress and the hat.

'Tomorrow we should shop. We could lunch at the Stork Club, be good, wouldn't it? They still do the greatest lobster salad. I doubt you'll have had as good a one in all your years in England.'

Cassie smiled. 'I haven't had a lobster salad in ten years, Beth. And I want it, and a black and white soda, and I want to shop too, but not tomorrow.' She touched her friend's arm. 'After the funeral. OK?'

'Oh Cassie, how thoughtless of me. I am sorry.' Beth swirled her martini in its glass. Cassie could see she was genuinely embarrassed. She felt great tenderness for Beth.

'Tell me about your little girl,' she said.

'She's very sweet. She's three now. I dress her at that wonderful children's shop, Bests, of course. You won't need to go there, Tom is able to get the real thing in London.'

'No he can't. We have rationing. We can't get what we want.'

'We had rationing too.' Beth was indignant. 'It wasn't all romance here. Marvin was in the navy – in the Pacific. There were times. . .'

Beth stopped, Cassie covered her hand with her own.

'I know. It was our war, we women. Yvonne and I discussed that, she made me do a series of paintings about it. They're not good enough, though, I couldn't get the passion somehow.'

'Yvonne?'

'My French girl friend from Paris. You remember her?'

'Oh yes, the funny little thing, with the frizzy black hair.'

Beth wanted Cassie to make social arrangements. She would organise a little dinner for old friends, and a lunch for the girls. But Cassie declined. This was a time for her and her mother, and for Tom. She hoped Beth understood. Of course she wanted to see Marvin and little Emily, but there was so little time. They would do it on her next trip.

The funeral was difficult, as funerals are. Momentarily Cassie wished Charles was with her, but she comforted herself that at least she had one of her men with her, her Tom, a little boy in his English school clothes, his cap straight on his head, his coat neatly buttoned, who stood amongst his American relatives holding his mother's hand and comforting her with his presence as he watched a man he hadn't known being consigned to his Maker. She wondered if he should be there, but that morning he had insisted. 'Daddy isn't with you, so I will be, it's my place,' he had told her.

She looked down into a perfectly formed English face, with its grey-green eyes and button mouth. He was quite determined, she could see that, and she felt a respect for him. At one point, when the coffin was lowered into the earth, she faltered, remembering the feel of her father, his eyes, his laugh. It was Tom who tightened his grip, it was Tom whose fingers curled into hers. She glanced over at her mother. Jane stood very still in her neat black coat, she held a bright white handkerchief in her fingers which she had twisted into a thin rope, her fingers plucking at it continually. Cassie watched her mother grieving, remembering how she had twisted the bedsheets into ropes when she was in labour. It made her feel very close to Jane. She wished she could help her, but her mother was such a private woman Cassie was sure she couldn't even let her own daughter share her loss.

The kith and kin gathered after the ceremony. Jane and Cassie were perfect hostesses. And Tom played the little man. The maiden aunts clucked and wondered over him. Jane's brother-in-law praised his stoicism.

'He's very English, Cassie, so polite.'

Robert Fleming had been born fifteen years after Cassie's father. The two sisters had been born in between. Robert Fleming the Second (named after his grandfather) had married late. He loved his wife Mary Anne very much. They had three children, he was proud of them.

Tom's great-aunt fingered the cloth of his jacket and stroked his blond curls. His three American cousins, two girls and a boy aged nine, eleven and twelve respectively, were appalled by his good manners. They found it quite difficult to talk to him, as he did to them. There were no shared experiences. Television was new to Tom. He watched it, of course, avidly, although *Howdy Doody* seemed very young to him. He had just begun to understand *Biggles*, and *Just William* was a whiz. Tom was very proud that he had just begun to play cricket. The Americans knew nothing of that. They talked of the World Series, and about Joe Di Maggio of the Yankees. Tom's American cousin Robert tried to explain the principles of baseball as he helped himself to squares of rich Hershey chocolate. Tom would have liked to do the same, but he had already taken two pieces and he didn't know how much each person was allowed. He tried not to look at it, but his mouth was watering. He concentrated on the conversation, putting his hands behind his back so that he wouldn't give in to the urge to take more.

'Baseball sounds like rounders to me,' he said.

'Rounders! Is that a good game?'

'Girls play it.'

'Then it's not the same as baseball. Was your Dad in the war?'

Robert obviously wanted to change the subject. Tom understood that very well. Rounders was not even a game worthy of discussion.

'He was a pilot in the RAF. He was a very brave man.'

'My father was with Eisenhower. He planned the battles and the invasion of Europe.'

Tom was stunned. He looked across at Robert's father, a small man with a nice face, but no match in Tom's eyes for his own hero father. He couldn't think of anything more to say. He excused himself and went to his mother. He decided to stay close to Cassie, he felt safe with her.

She held him very tight that night. They shared her bed, neither of them wishing to be apart from each other, but who was the comforter and who was the comforted was impossible to say. They did that quite often in England too, when he had his 'bad thinks', as he called his nightmares. Charles never approved. Cassie told Tom, in the darkness, that when she was little her father used to climb into bed with her, when she had her bad dreams. Her mother never used to come. Once, when her father had been away, Jane Fleming heard her daughter's cries and had come and sat on the bed, and soothed her a little, pushing her hair back from her forehead in kind, unhurried movements, but she did not get into bed with her. In the morning Tom had asked his mother, 'Why didn't Grandma let you sleep with her?'

'She said it wasn't right for children to sleep with their parents,' Cassie told him lightly.

That was the last time she and Tom shared a bed.

Tom liked Cleo, she made him something called waffles and corn muffins that he thought were very nice. There was much more food here than at home, but he didn't stuff himself with chocolate; he wanted to, but he knew one didn't do that sort of thing. Of course, when Cleo gave it to him, he took it – it was only polite. He would go into the kitchen and sit with her whilst his mother and his grandmother talked. He decided his grandmother was absolutely smashing, so much nicer than his English grandmother who treated him as if he didn't exist. His American grandmother asked him his opinion on things, such as what did he think of America, did he like it, had he felt the minister made a good job of the funeral; he particularly appreciated that question, it made him feel as if he were a part of it all. He hoped he would be able to come to America a lot.

'Next time I am sure we will bring Daddy. Then we'd show those stuck-up cousins of mine just what is what,' he told Cleo as he munched his way through a third muffin. He liked the butter and the strawberry jam, no one seemed to mind how much he took.

'What do you mean by "stuck-up"?' Cleo asked.

She was sitting opposite him at the table, her big black arms were crossed in front of her. Her head was on one side. The radio was on. Cleo, like all Americans of that time, loved the radio, especially *Amos and Andy*. Tom couldn't understand it all. He liked the adult American television. On Saturday night they had watched *Show of Shows*. He thought Sid Caesar was very funny.

'You know, stuck-up.'

'I don't know stuck-up.'

'Sniffy, then.'

'Oh, sniffy,' said Cleo.


Whilst Tom sat with Cleo in the long narrow kitchen dominated by the huge refrigerator that they called an ice box, Cassie sat in the elegant living room. Like her mother she wore black. The two women were companionable rather than intimate. Cassie talked of her life in England, and her work.

'Tell me about Charles?' her mother asked suddenly.

'Charles?' Cassie replied, startled at the question.

'How is he? How does he cope now, after the war? It can't have been easy.'

Cassie watched her mother flick ash from her cigarette into an ashtray. She noticed that Jane had wonderful legs, unconsciously she recrossed her own, aware that hers were good too. Her mother always amazed her, her directness quite shocked her: how could she answer such a direct question? It could be taken as polite interest, but politeness was not a part of Jane's character. Cassie had never discussed personal matters with her parents. She couldn't start now. Gently she deflected the question.

'The war took away our youth and our innocence, we all lost something,' Cassie replied carefully. 'I suppose, if I am honest, that is why I feel a little strange here.' The words came out before she was even aware she was saying them.

94

She knew she should have been shocked at her admission that she felt strange in America, that it was wrong to feel that way. America was her home, but then she knew that wasn't the case any more and she actually felt better for saying it. Jane looked up, encouraging her to go on.

'My experiences have separated me from you all. You remember I thought that I'd lost Tom, in the Blitz. I don't think I will ever get over the scare. It's something you cannot visualise if you haven't been through it. The worst ones,' she was aware that she was rubbing her face, 'were the doodlebugs. When the noise stopped you knew they were coming – and you just prayed they weren't coming to you. I lost a girl friend, you know, her name was Claire, and my brother-in-law too. And there was a friend in Paris, a good friend.'

Cassie suddenly stopped talking. She realised she had said more to her mother in those few moments than in all the years she had lived with her.

'I can see that it has changed you, and, yes, you have lost your youth. But then, of course, you were a little girl when we sent you to France. Now I have to cope with a young woman who is a mother and a painter. Did you bring me some of your work?'

'No, I didn't. But there was no reason other than the speed of our departure.'

'You'll come back, with Charles. Soon.'

It wasn't a request. Cassie smiled wryly.

As she and Tom were only staying a very short time, Cassie tried to deal with her loss privately. She wanted to show Tom a little of New York. Of course she would have liked to have gone to the galleries and tried to discover what was happening in the American art world, but it was Tom's time and so they went to the Empire State Building. He gazed down at the straight avenues that criss-crossed New York and the huge American cars that from the 139th floor looked like tiny models of the real thing.

'You can't see the people from up here, can you? I mean you can't see what they look like,' Tom said.

They went to Saks on Fifth Avenue and Bonwit Teller and Bloomingdales on Seventh. Cassie bought make-up and perfume and stockings. She selected shirts and sweaters for Charles. She couldn't buy him trousers: he had his own tailor in London. At Bests they purchased clothes for Tom and he had his hair cut. But Cassie had been in Europe for a long time, deprivations were what she was used to. The sheer abundance of everything, clothes and cars and stockings and furniture, even the food – its mere availability – was a shock.

She noticed that all the children looked so well. No one had that pasty look about them in America; the good air, and food, but mostly, she was sure, it was life without bombs that gave them their rude health.

After the shopping they stood outside St Patrick's – the little boy in an English boy's suit, a white shirt and a tie, his mother in utility clothing, smart, but modest – they were an obvious couple. Cassie looked around her, for a moment she was confused as to what to show Tom. But as was his way, he showed her.

'Oh Mummy, look.' He grabbed her hand and they ran towards a drugstore that Tom had spied just opposite where they had been standing. Cassie saw it was a Schrafts. At last a real black-and-white chocolate soda. Tom had pushed his nose up against the glass, gazing in wonder at all the icecreams on offer to the customers. Cassie wanted to laugh – he actually licked his lips. The land of the free had seduced a boy. They walked in and sat at the counter, Cassie had to haul Tom up, his hair had become ruffled, but his tie was still neat.

The waitress picked up his accent immediately.

'Just talk,' she said to Tom, 'I don't care what you say, honey, you just sound so cute. You know, I am Jewish,' she confided to Cassie, 'and I really salute you and your Prime Minister, Winston Churchill.'

Cassie had to explain that she was an American, and that Winston Churchill wasn't Prime Minister any more. At her obvious disappointment, Tom interjected that he was English and that his father had been a fighter pilot in the RAF. And Cassie remembered that Charles was a real hero.

After rich luscious dollops of icecream they went to meet Jane. She had insisted on going to her office. 'I have to catch up on some work,' she told Cassie.

'Don't you think you should take it a little easy?'

'I certainly don't. I am going to need to fill my hours. After all, you are going back to England, and I have to get used to that situation, because then I will be alone.'

Cassie felt the stab of guilt, she shouldn't be leaving Jane alone. It was all very difficult, for she knew her mother needed her.

'I don't suppose you would consider coming to England?' she asked gingerly.

'No, I wouldn't.' There was a sharp look and Cassie understood that a journey across the ocean without her husband was not something she could contemplate. 'And I don't want you worrying about me. It won't be easy in the beginning, in our way we had a very close companionship, your father and I, and I am going to miss him badly. But I have my work, and I have my friends. I think I am going to get involved with the theatre too.' Cassie looked at her questioningly. 'I have become quite involved in that area, through my clients. Broadway is retrenching, the new world is the silver screen. We have to fight back. I shall enjoy it.'

'You are the most extraordinary woman,' Cassie said, and despite herself she took her mother's hand. Unexpectedly, Jane squeezed her fingers back.

'It's my loss that you won't come to England, you know,' Cassie said, meaning it.

They took the subway to 42nd Street. Dusk had come to New York and the city was alive with lights. When they got out of the subway at Times Square Jane told Tom, 'They call this The Great White Way.' Tom's eyes were sparkling, at home he would have been in bed by now, but not here, for he was going to the theatre with his mother and his grandmother. However, he was not prepared for the number of people who seemed to be sweeping down on him. He clung to Cassie's hand, he wished he could have been carried, he felt as if he were going to be trampled by all those enormous figures.

'Look, Tom,' his mother was saying. 'Over there, the Camel sign.'

'Camel?'

'It's a brand of cigarettes and there are smoke rings coming from the man's mouth.' Tom was amazed by it all.

As they arrived they saw a crowd milling around, but they weren't waiting for a play – just as Jane had said, the cinema had come of age, and openings were no longer for the theatre, they were for movies. Cassie lifted Tom up so he could see what was happening.

The Hollywood Stars came out at night and glistened in sequins and furs and tuxedos. They were delivered, all shiny and beautiful, in black limousines. Barricades blocked the sidewalk and the fans flocked to watch their favourites lit up against the night sky by white glaring beams from searchlights mounted on trucks. Cassie was jolted, her memory was of searchlights probing a black sky for enemy planes, and she had to shake herself.

Jane manoeuvred them through the crowds. As they walked up Broadway Cassie saw that indeed most of the theatres had succumbed to the lure of the silver screen. But there were still the musicals and they were going to see one called *Brigadoon* written by Frederick Loewe and Alan J. Lerner. It was at the Ziegfeld Theater on the north-west corner of 6th Avenue and 54th Street, so they would have to take a cab. But Jane had wanted Tom to see Broadway first.

They made their way into the handsome auditorium with its banks of plush seats. The orchestra, in its dark pit just beneath the stage, was making twanging sounds that Cassie told Tom preceded the flood of music that would fill the theatre once the lights went down. Tom looked up at the endless curtains and wondered just what was behind them. Gradually the theatre darkened and there was hushed silence, the music swelled, the curtains opened onto fairyland, a myriad of colours whirled on the stage. The kilts and sporrans, the long dresses and neat little caps had little to do with the real Scotland and yet for Tom it was the real world of make-believe. He saw the painted moon, and the mountains and the river and he believed he could have walked onto the stage and out into the mist and heather. He sat there bound by the magic of the stage, he was so happy, he forgot there was anyone else around him, the story was unfolding just for him, he was part of it.

Cassie had little recollection of the performance herself, she had spent the time watching her son. His fine face was angled forward as if he wanted to breathe in the very spirit of it all. His mouth moved with the music, his feet twitched with the dancing, he laughed and he sighed. When it was over he still sat on his seat, as if transfixed.

'Tom,' Cassie said. 'Come on, darling, it's over, we're going home.'

He turned to her, almost shocked that she was there, for the first time in his life he had not even been aware of his mother. Later Cassie asked him whether he had enjoyed the play.

'It was wonderful.'

'Would you like to be an actor?' his grandmother asked, almost amused.

'No, Grandma. When I am older I would like to be the person who tells the actors what to do.'

When they got back to the apartment, Cassie told her mother, 'He's a determined little boy.'

Jane was very impressed by her grandson and she resolved to be his friend. She was sorry she was mourning, it prevented her from getting to know him better, but she owed that time to Clinton and herself. Jane knew she had been the dominant partner in the marriage, but that was only because his quiet strength enabled her to organise and control things. She had loved him very much, there had never been anyone else for her from that first time she had met him at a senior prom. He had been there with another girl, but Jane had looked into his warm tawny eyes – Cassie had his eyes – and she had seen a humour and a gentleness there that she knew she needed. She wondered how she was going to cope without him. She sat in her favourite high-backed wing-chair drinking a whisky with ice. Her thin hands were a marvellous foil for the heavy diamond she wore. Her fine face, so like her daughter's, was lined, her eyes were dull; her voice, though, was still clear and strong.

'I am sorry I haven't been able to spend more time with Tom. I wonder what he thinks of New York?'

'I think he is thrilled by it,' she heard Cassie say, 'but you know, Mother, I find New York almost a shock, there is so much of everything here. We have so little.'

Jane heard her use of the word 'we', she knew it was unconscious, but it placed Cassie in England.

'You should go home soon,' Jane told her daughter.

Cassie had felt very sad at leaving her mother, she wanted to cling to her and, indeed, uncharacteristically, they had done just that – but not for too long, the long embrace had been saved for Tom.

'When will we see Grandma again?' Tom had asked, trying to swallow his tears so that he could perform in the manly manner as required by his status as an English boy.

'Very soon. Very, very soon,' Cassie replied. She was lucky she didn't have to hide the tears – she didn't want to, why should she, she was grieving for her father, she was leaving her mother. Tom comforted her, putting his arms around her shoulders, kissing her cheek, patting her back, and she felt a little better. She even slept a little on the flight home.

Charles met them at the airport. He kissed Cassie and shook hands with Tom. Cassie managed to bite back a comment. She suddenly realised that she was going to miss Jane.

It was that night, when they were in their ordered bedroom performing their nightly rituals, that Charles informed her Tom would be going away to school in September.

'He'll be going to prep school. It's a very important time in a boy's life.'

'Going away?'

'Yes, he's been at his pre-prep school which prepares them, and then it's normal for an English boy to go away to his preparatory school which is, if you like, the intermediary stage, and then when he's thirteen he goes to his senior school.'

'My son is not going away from me at the age of seven and a half, Charles.' Cassie climbed into her bed, she was wearing a new pale blue, filmy nightgown from Bonwit Teller. She hoped Charles thought she looked attractive – after all, she had been away and she did like the feel of him.

Charles had been dreading this conversation. He had known that Cassie would be difficult, but there was no alternative, Tom was down for his own preparatory school, where his father had been before him. It had not been an experience he had particularly liked, but he felt it had contributed to his development. He wanted that for Tom too, and it would lessen the boy's bond with his mother, which in his view was unhealthy. He had discussed the matter with his own parents whilst Cassie had been in America. They had been totally supportive, unlike Evelyn who had said that Cassie was a superb mother, and should be given the right of choice.

'It's barbaric anyway, Charles, you know that, and I know it too. We were both horribly homesick.'

'We got over it.'

'Maybe. . .' Evelyn's tone was quarrelsome.

Evelyn discussed the question of Tom's education with her husband, George.

'I think Cassie will take him back to America rather than let him go away,' she told him over their evening sherry.

'Bit of a strong reaction on her part, I would have thought. She should stand her ground, talk to Charles, that would be the right way. There are some excellent day schools in London. Why not send him to one of those?' George replied complacently. He rather liked his American sister-in-law, but he was glad he wasn't married to her.

At that very moment, Cassie was talking to Charles.

'Let me make myself clear, so there are no misunderstandings. If there is any question of my son being sent away to a boarding school I will leave you and I will take him back to America.'

'That's outrageous,' Charles shouted.

'It may be, but that's the way it is.'

There was war in the Bray household. Deirdre came to see her, Edwin came to see her, Evelyn supported her. Yvonne sided with Charles, a betrayal that Cassie found difficult to swallow. She wrote to Jane, the reply came on a Monday morning.

'You are married to an Englishman, the English way is to send their sons away, you have to accept that.'

But Cassie would not.

Tom was aware that a battle was being fought. He felt most unhappy about it, he didn't want to go away from home, but equally he wanted above all to have a peaceful life, and he reasoned that if he went away to school there would be no more arguments.

'I'll go, Mummy,' he told Cassie over breakfast in their warm comfortable kitchen where he and Cassie shared warm bread fresh from the oven. The kitchen was home to Tom, it was the place where he came after school to share his secrets with his golden-haired mother.

'No you won't,' she told him.

And despite himself he was glad, he didn't ever want to leave that kitchen.

When Charles came home that evening he found his wife and child sitting together by the fire, their heads almost touching.

'You are too old to sit with your mother like that,' he said sharply.

'We are doing my homework,' Tom said quickly.

'At boarding school the boys all do their homework together. It's fun.'

'I've told you, Charles, Tom is not going to boarding school.' Cassie's words cut through the air like a knife. Tom watched his father's face, it remained impassive, but he said, 'I wouldn't have thought it was appropriate to make comments like that in front of Tom, Cassie, but if you wish to do so, you must.'

Charles walked from the room and went into his study. The door was shut, it remained so all night. In the morning, over breakfast, Charles asked, 'And what school *do* you intend Tom to attend?'

In his eighth year Thomas Bray entered the junior school of Linchester School for Boys, as a day boy.

The ritual of school life absorbed him. It was a school steeped in the traditions and the majesty of an institution that had been founded by Queen Elizabeth the First. It prized the pursuit of truth and of individual responsibility above all else. Tom flourished in such a place, he found studying easy, he excelled at games, he made friends amongst the popular, and the not so popular.

One of the least popular people at Linchester School was Mr Barclay, the Latin master, who entered the boys' lives when they were just eight years old. He was a tyrant of a man who strode the classroom with a

101

short sharp step and an equally short sharp stick. When they were ten years of age he expected them to have got beyond declining verbs, but still he would test them. *Amo, Amas, Amat* – those who could decline would watch in relief as the black-robed figure moved on to another small boy's desk. Like all tyrants, Mr Barclay had his particular victim – his was Westerman, a small boy with fine bones, a gentle face, and soft brown hair. Mr Barclay quite simply terrorised him, for lesson after lesson he would stand by his desk, banging his sharp stick against the palm of his hand, and when Westerman stuttered, as he always did, and muddled up his declensions Mr Barclay would shout at him, and slap his knuckles, warning of the greater threat, the cane. Westerman stumbled and wept inside, he was so frightened. The mistake would inevitably be made.

'My study after break,' Mr Barclay bellowed on one such occasion and the boy grew visibly smaller. The rest of the class sniggered, all the class but one, and that was Tom Bray. He was next. Mr Barclay smiled. Tom Bray was his favourite, Tom Bray was a true Latin scholar.

Bray stood up. 'I haven't learnt the verb, Sir. I can't do it.'

'Rubbish, of course you know it,' his teacher said.

'I don't, Sir, and so I should get punished like Westerman.'

'Well I. . .'

'The cane, you said, Sir. I'll come with Westerman. How many can we expect, Sir?'

Mr Barclay had no choice but to administer the punishment, but there was no righteous pleasure in it for him for he knew that Bray was challenging him. He wanted Westerman snivelling and then the exercise would be worthwhile, he didn't want the class hero there with Westerman, giving him courage.

'Go first,' Tom told Westerman. 'Yell if you must, but try not to cry.'

Westerman nodded, he wasn't so frightened when Tom was with him, but when he was alone with the tall master he felt his knees shake, and he crumpled. That was better. Barclay grabbed his cane. 'Bend over!' he roared as he flexed the cane and slashed at the boy's buttocks. Tom could hear Westerman's cries, he clenched his fists, he could have killed Barclay there and then with his own cane. When Westerman came out he was white and red-eyed, a beaten boy. Tom went in, Barclay almost balked at the sight of him, but he swished his cane, and, anticipating Tom's self-control, hit the buttocks lightly. Tom screamed and cried . . . Barclay was shocked – he didn't think Tom Bray was a coward, but because he liked to hit boys and liked to hear them cry even more, he hit harder. He heard the crying he wanted, even Westerman was stunned. But what Westerman didn't see was that when Tom stood up his eyes were dry, there were no tears. Barclay averted his face, he couldn't look at Bray.

Westerman comforted Tom and took him back to the class, he became the protector. The boys gathered round and the bruises were examined; Westerman's were worse, far worse. Grange, usually the class bully, took him to Miss Langton, the English mistress, and held his hand whilst she dressed the cuts, trying to hide her concern. Westerman was a hero.

Cassie was appalled, she wanted to take the matter to the headmaster but Tom stopped her.

'You don't understand, Mum. It's not done.'

'But Tom, you *know* your verbs, the treatment of Westerman is barbaric and you subjected yourself to the same medieval torture. I mean, what you did was splendid, but he hurt you, for God's sake, and I won't have that.'

'Mum, please stay out of this.'

Cassie looked at her ten-year-old son, his buttocks were lashed, but his eyes were hard, his mouth set. And Cassie knew she wasn't going to the headmaster. She wasn't sure whether her son was a hero or a fool, but he certainly had values, she was quite awed by him.

Mr Barclay strode into the classroom to take his next Latin class with his short sharp steps and carrying his short sharp cane. He turned to Westerman, glowered at the boy and demanded *amo, amas, amat.* Westerman stood up and stared at his tormentor and began his verb, his voice shook a little but there were no stumblings, and when he had finished the class cheered.

'Well, Westerman, you seem to have profited from the little lesson of the other day.'

'Oh I did, Sir,' Westerman replied, turning to gaze at Tom.

At the end of that term there was the first school play. An English master from the senior school came to direct it; his name was John Bravington. He auditioned every boy, but he had already decided to give Tom the role of Henry V in a children's version of Shakespeare's play the moment he saw him. There was no question of giving it to anyone else, the boy was a talent.

At the age of ten bordering on eleven, it was difficult to deal with motivation and character; it was more a question of drilling the actors, which is what Bravington did with all his cast, except for Tom who asked the questions himself.

'Why did Henry want to make war on France? What did Shakespeare really mean by "O for a Muse of fire that would ascend the brightest heaven of invention"? Did Henry like Pistol? Why did Shakespeare use those characters?' The questions went on and on, and they were not just confined to the text. 'Where should I stand, what should I do with my hands? Are you sure Henry should look like that?'

John Bravington was quite bemused by his leading actor.

The play was not a particular triumph but Tom received rapturous applause. He relished every moment of the acclaim, he loved being in the limelight. He knew then, with the sound of the applause ringing in his ears, that he would do whatever he had to do to ensure that he would always receive the cheers.

Cassie noticed John Bravington immediately after the performance, she found him rather attractive, he was a rangy, good-looking man with particularly nice blue eyes and tight, brown, curly hair which was improved by the grey that streaked it. He had a limp too which somehow added to his appeal. She was glad that she was wearing a new black suit, its skirt carefully shortened to show off her slender legs and the jacket well-waisted to take advantage of the curves of her body. She knew she was a good-looking woman.

'Mrs Bray?' he enquired after he had managed to reach her through the thronging parents weighed down with their own self-interest, anxious to talk about their children.

'Hello.'

'He's good, isn't he?' said Bravington.

'I think so.'

'You are an artist?' Bravington asked.

'You know my work?'

'Tom told me about you.'

'Oh I see.'

'And then I went to the Dubreve Gallery. Your work is good too.'

Cassie laughed. 'But do I match up to my son though?'

Bravington didn't know how to answer her.

And that was how she and John Bravington became friends. At first their link was Tom but then a young couple with two children, Julius and Ethel Rosenberg, were sentenced to death for passing on America's atomic secrets to the Russians. Cassie was enraged that they should have to die for such a thing. She wanted to be in America so she could make her protest as an American, but she was in England. She did her best, organising a petition for clemency, standing on cold corners, collecting names, summoning whoever she could to meetings. Charles thought it ludicrous – one couldn't change the unchangeable – but Bravington agreed that there had to be voices raised for the Rosenbergs. 'One voice can be lost, ten voices can be lost, a million voices have to be heard,' he told her.

Even after the appeal failed they still worked hard: more petitions, more meetings, more telegrams. America would listen, Cassie was sure America would listen.

'Cassie, you are deluding yourself, the climate in America is allowing a Senator from Wisconsin to scourge whoever and whatever he likes in the name of patriotism,' Charles told her, but not unkindly.

'In the end they won't do it, I know they won't.'

But just a month after the Coronation of Queen Elizabeth II with its bunting, and mugs and street parties, the executions were carried out, Julius and Ethel Rosenberg were electrocuted.

Cassie turned her anger into art. At last the image, composition and technique came together. She created bodies that seemed to float in space. At first sight it appeared that all was calm and serene, but then on a closer look you became aware of the subtle twists that allowed the ugliness Cassie saw to pervade their somnambulistic state. They were figures in agony, drifting through space and time, contorted out of their human shapes. She called it 'Death of Two Spies'. The work came easily; she sketched out the idea first on little pieces of paper and put the pieces together as if it were a jigsaw puzzle, moving the separate elements around until she had the whole. She used her favourite system of brush and rag and palate knife, layering the paints thickly.

When she had finished it Yvonne offered her a one-woman show. Together they selected her best works. At the preview Cassie's peers turned up at Yvonne's gallery and saluted her, her idols came too and nodded their accolades, and then the press – self-appointed arbiters of public taste – reported upon the work of Cassie Fleming. For just one night Cassie Fleming became a celebrity.

But on the night of her triumph, after the celebrations, Cassie sat huddled in her kitchen, hugging her knees, playing host to the black dogs of anguish, unable even to fight them. It wasn't that it hadn't been a wonderful evening – it had. She had worn a white dress with a little white cocktail hat and long gloves. It had been quite an extravagance, but why not, how often did one become a star? She had drunk too much and when a journalist had asked her why she saw the world as rotten, she had replied, 'Oh, but it is, we take perfection and we ruin it. Look at children, they are a perfect example. They begin their lives fresh and perfect and we destroy them, don't we?' Tom had been watching her, he had frowned at her, she had never seen him frown before. She'd tried to tell him that she didn't mean him, she meant the world, but he had backed away from her; she had felt horribly sick. Charles had brought her home, and then he and Tom had left her alone – she had wanted Tom, but when she'd gone up to the room he had pretended to be asleep. She'd touched him, but he hadn't moved. She was sure he was awake, she could hardly hear him breathing. When he slept his mouth would open and his breaths were deep. Tonight his mouth was shut and she couldn't hear the sounds of sleep.

Charles found her in Tom's bedroom. He led her out of the room.

'You'll wake him.'

'He isn't asleep.'

'If he isn't, he wants to be, so leave him alone. You should go to bed.'

'There is no point in going to bed, there is no comfort. Oh Charles.' She leaned against him as he led her towards their bedroom, her dress was slightly twisted, her hat had fallen off somewhere – she hoped it was in the house.

'Why don't you love me any more? You used to love me, but it's gone wrong, I know it.'

'You're drunk.'

'Yes, but it's because I'm unhappy.' She sat down on the bed and looked at her feet, the white shoes were dingy – grey round the toes. She twisted her leg to see if she could see what state the heels were in. She couldn't manage it. She wrenched them off and threw them across the bedroom. 'My father wasn't here because he is dead.'

'I am sure that hurt you. I can understand that you would have liked him to have seen your triumph. But you should be excited, not drunk.'

'I don't like the way you speak to me,' Cassie told her husband. She got up from the bed and went downstairs to her kitchen. She wanted someone to love her, and no one did, and it was her evening. Her son should have been with her, not shunning her, faking sleep. Where had it all started to go wrong for her? She knew, of course. It was in Paris, that woman, that bitch who had stolen her man, if it hadn't been for her Joshua would still be alive, and that was the worst part of all. It was a dreadful shock to realise that she still loved him, Cassie hadn't thought about him for so many years, but the reawakening of her memory of him on the night of her triumph reaffirmed his place; it was all the more terrifying because it was so unexpected.

Cassie went out into the garden, it was cold, early November and the grey night was quiet. She could hear a dog barking in the distance, but otherwise there was no sound, and no light to disturb the hour. In New York it had never been quiet at night, in Paris it had never been quiet at night. It struck her as somehow rather appropriate that only in London, the place where she had chosen to live, was there absolute quiet. She went back to the kitchen and sat on the floor again, still hugging her knees.

She had no idea what time it was when Tom came down the stairs, but it must have been about four o'clock. He made her tea, made her drink it all and then took her up to bed. Cassie hugged him tight.

'I love you, Mummy,' he said, 'but you are drunk.'

'I know,' she said, as she fell asleep.

# Chapter Five
## 1954–1958

Even after the Rosenberg affair was over John Bravington had remained a part of Cassie's life. In America Senator McCarthy was pursuing all those suspected of being members of the now-outlawed Communist party with all the fervour of the bigot. The suspects were hauled in front of his committee and asked if they were, or ever had been a member of the Communist party. Even those who were merely classified as 'sympathisers' lost their jobs and risked going to prison. Jane Fleming knew some of the victims, a lot of them were her friends, and she was appalled at how some turned their backs on those who needed help. She knew McCarthy's main prosecutor, Roy Cohen, too, but she didn't boast about that.

A concert pianist friend of hers decided she would leave America rather than face an inquisition.

'Admission by default, for invoking the Fifth Amendment is no protection these days,' Jane told Cassie on a crackling line from New York to London. 'She'll need sanctuary – will you take her in?'

The woman was an Austrian refugee, Ingrid Bloch. 'I suppose the name was Polish or German before it became Austrian,' she had told Cassie cheerfully. Ingrid was a likeable woman who stayed with the Brays for just two nights before going on to Paris. Her circumstances reminded Cassie of Joshua – what would he have said of God's Own Country?

Charles was kind to their guest, but he made it clear that he believed war forced people to take a stand for what they believed in. 'There is a horrible war going on in Korea. The Communists are the enemy and America is suffering. I don't totally condone that kind of behaviour but I understand why it has been allowed a loose leash.'

Cassie bit back a furious rejoinder. There was no point in even trying to say anything to Charles. She wondered how it was that they had ever been close. Instead she turned to John Bravington for friendship. Cassie didn't have many friends, it wasn't that she didn't need people, but it was a simple choice: her art or a social life, there simply wasn't time for both. When she wasn't working Tom filled her hours; his needs, his requirements had to come first. Charles and his world were part of her existence too, but in a peripheral way. She made an effort on occasions that required her presence, after all she was Charles' wife and she liked to give him her support, but often she felt superfluous. Dressed as the occasion dictated, she would feel out of place, and she could hear herself speaking as if from a great distance; her jaw would ache by the end of it all.

She confided in Evelyn, but Evelyn lived in the country and whilst she would willingly mutter the appropriate platitudes, she couldn't relate to Cassie's difficulties: her attitude was that one got on with the job of being married whether one liked it or not.

'I am not desperately happy. George is a nice man, but a bit of a bore. The girls have grown up, so I've made a life for myself. I am going to sit on the bench.'

'Pardon?' said Cassie. She tapped the telephone, thinking it was distorting her sister-in-law's words.

Evelyn laughed. 'I am going to be a Justice of the Peace, sorting out footpath rights and driving offences and petty thieving, that sort of thing.'

'Oh God, I am stupid, we have a similar expression. I just didn't think.'

It was only after she had put the phone down that she realised she had used the word 'we' to ally herself with America. She scratched her head and walked into her huge kitchen. Money and time had transformed it into a white and yellow paradise, with blue trimmings embellishing long work surfaces. She made herself some coffee – she always bought fresh beans at a dusty little corner shop in Soho nudged in between electrical shops and film companies and places of ill-repute just off Old Compton Street. It was an Aladdin's cave of delights that made Cassie remember Paris – but she would never go back to the French capital. Charles wanted to but Cassie always made excuses. 'The past is gone,' she would say, 'and I don't want to see how it has changed.'

She brewed her own coffee the American way, loving the pungent smell and the rich darkness, and laced it liberally with cream. The drink had become her fix. Her morning ritual was to await the arrival of her own Mrs Mop. Over coffee they would talk together of this and that and then Cassie would go to her studio and paint. After her first exhibition Charles had transformed the garden shed into the perfect place to make her art. He had taken great care with the plans, consulting her and listening carefully to her comments. He had incorporated a wall of glass into the structure so that the light would be perfect for her.

'It has to face North,' she told him.

There were shelves and drawers and cupboards – in just the right places. There was a sink and an electric point for a kettle. On the day the builders finished he had presented her with a lock and key for the door and Cassie had hugged him. She linked arms with him.

'Come on, let's go and look at it together.'

'No, it's your place now. I have finished my design.'

Cassie had gone into the unfilled space and looked up at the pointed timber ceiling that Charles had created.

'Mum,' said a voice behind her. She spun round on her heel towards the voice and held out her arms to Tom.

'You'll do great things here,' he told her.

'I hope so, oh I hope so.'

Cassie still talked with Yvonne, but not very often. Yvonne's gallery, now located, through Charles' good offices, in Cork Street, had become important. She herself had become something of an expert in Expressionist art. They were still close, but not as close as they had been. If she were honest, Cassie would admit that she was slightly awed by Yvonne's new social status.

With Tom's progression into the senior school John Bravington became his mentor and friend too. Bravington had his 'boys' who would come to his home after school. His wife Sarah, who seemed a rather retiring sort who had little to do with her husband's life, would prepare scones and cream and rich red strawberry jam. It was very comfortable in the front room where they would gather around the highly polished brown-tiled fireplace with its grey marble mantelpiece weighed down with memorabilia. The lounge suite was covered in a rough grey fabric with a light design of orange and green flowers. There were white crocheted head-rests to protect the furniture from hair-cream. But no boy ever leaned backwards on Bravington's afternoons. There were about eight of them, the stalwarts of the drama society, and Tom was their acknowledged leader, Westerman his self-appointed lieutenant. Tom acted in most of the productions; his father's fine face and his mother's rich golden hair made him the perfect idol. But Tom's aspirations lay elsewhere. He wanted to produce his own plays. At the Bravington tea parties he extolled his ideas, and Bravington allowed him his forays into Shakespeare and Sartre and even the contemporary John Osborne. The discussion of theatre led always into wider issues and it was there that Tom learnt about socialism.

Cassie didn't mind, she approved of John Bravington. Although in her late thirties now, Cassie was fresh and lovely and she was attracted to the school teacher. Nor was she unaware of John Bravington's interest in her. She liked the look of his body, but there was never more than a very brief acknowledgement of all this in a small touch, or a look. He was a married man.

Tom and Charles shared little. Tom preferred his grandfather Edwin, spending many Saturday mornings with the now-elderly widower. Edwin was something of a philatelist and he liked nothing better than to sit quietly and sort his stamps and talk to his grandson. 'Look at this one, Tom. Canadian – beautiful, isn't it?'

'Yes, and it seems to have been issued when Canada was still a Dominion.'

Then they were quiet for a few moments, rifling amongst the new packets of stamps that Edwin had purchased that week.

'And look what we have here. I do believe it is India, 1936,' Edwin announced triumphantly.

'Oh let me see,' said Tom, picking up the little piece of coloured paper with the tweezers that had to be employed when looking at the stamps. 'It's a beautiful colour.'

Edwin nodded happily – he had no idea that Tom hated stamp collecting. The boy could have cheerfully burnt the lot, but he knew how much they meant to Edwin so he pushed his boredom away and applied himself to the business of collating the stamps.

Deirdre had died in 1955, a 'lung condition', the doctors called it, but the family knew it was tuberculosis. In her last years she and Edwin had spent as much time as they could in the mountains of Switzerland, but Deirdre didn't enjoy being abroad. 'I suppose Switzerland is the best place to be, it's an ordered country,' she told Charles sadly just before their final visit. Edwin was a lonely man without his wife, but he kept to himself, and Cassie allowed him that dignity. She was immensely fond of the old man and would have liked to have talked to him of her difficulties with Charles, but good behaviour didn't allow that.

Charles mourned his lack of closeness with his son. Privately he felt that Tom was a little soft, he was sure that, had he gone to boarding school, they would have developed a more conventional male relationship, sharing their masculinity. Instead his son sought the company of his mother far too often for Charles' liking. He discussed the problem with David and Yvonne, they both told him that he should try and spend more time with Tom. David even suggested Saturday visits to Twickenham – he went with his own boys – but Charles was enmeshed in the routine of his work and he worked weekends too more often than not. He was the senior partner in his practice now, clients made demands on him at all hours, his design teams had to be cherished, without his secretary Margaret to run his life he would have been quite lost.

It was John Bravington who guided Cassie to the National Council for the Abolition of Nuclear Weapon Tests. She had been easy meat for proselytism, her own terror of the Bomb was a very real thing, which she had manifested on canvas. She had never exhibited this picture but she allowed Bravington to see it. He persuaded her to allow a showing at the Council's offices, and suddenly she found herself amongst like-minded people for the first time in many years. Tom was very proud of her.

Having been shown photographs of the victims of the Bomb by his mother, Tom too was a committed opponent of nuclear weapons.

'I want a world to live in,' he told his unimpressed father.

'No idiot wants the Bomb to be exploded,' Charles responded. They were having Sunday lunch with the Sampson family.

'It's a deterrent, you see,' the elder Sampson boy interjected over a large mouthful of Cassie's excellent roast beef. He hadn't meant to speak with his mouth stuffed with food, he was rather embarrassed by his outburst, but he was a Captain in his Military Corps at school and he knew about that sort of thing.

Tom shifted in his chair and glanced around the table, at his father whom he knew so little, at Sampson maximus, the prat who had spoken, and Sampson minimus who ran rather well. He liked Mr and Mrs Sampson, and even wished sometimes that Cassie were more like Marilyn. She was a sensible, undemanding woman, but then she wouldn't understand the nuclear disarmament debate whereas his mother was a seasoned campaigner. Cassie had her face averted from the table. He knew the look, she didn't want confrontation at that moment.

112

'I have a different view,' was all he said, bowing to his mother's wishes.

Cassie knew that Charles was not particularly impressed by her active commitment, but she ignored his stoic silences and even went to committee meetings. It didn't take her long to realise that she was not an organiser, and she retreated from the administration of the protest, happy to be simply one of the protesters.

She had gone on the Women's March against the H-Bomb Tests, responding to the request that it should be a silent and dignified protest. All the women had worn hats and neat clean shoes, like badges to allay onlookers' fears. They topped their middle-class attire with the sashes of the suffragettes.

It was natural, then, for Cassie and Tom to go together on that first march to the Atomic Weapons Research Establishment at Aldermaston.

On Good Friday of Easter 1958 they went to Trafalgar Square in the heart of London under the steely and quite possibly disapproving eye of Admiral Lord Nelson set high on his grey column above the lions of England. It was a sunny day, but cold. Nevertheless there were quite a lot of marchers, although not enough to fill the square. Very British and therefore quite orderly in their behaviour, they gathered behind the huge black flag with the inscription 'March from London to Aldermaston' embellished with the CND insignia. An observer of that first march reported that it was interesting to see so many families with children, and a disproportionate number of young people. It seemed as if they knew their time was coming and wanted a say in their future. They brought their music with them, mostly jazz, some skiffle. An ideologist might have disapproved of their wanting to have a good time as well, but they were by no means put off by that.

Not everyone on the Aldermaston march was walking all the way, just the intrepid ones, distinctive in anoraks with rucksacks slung over their backs. Cassie was going the whole way too, she wore a raincoat over her trousers. Tom had the rucksack, she carried a large bag stuffed to the brim with food and drink. Tom had teased her, had she hired herself out as caterer for the entire march?

Tom was walking with his friends, whilst Cassie had arranged to meet up with John Bravington. She and John greeted each other with a friendly kiss, but Cassie suddenly felt awkward. John Bravington had a wife and children, he should have been with them on a Bank Holiday weekend. . .

'None of the family came with you?' asked Cassie quickly.

'The girls are still only five and eight – Sarah didn't feel it was a suitable Easter outing. She's taken them to stay with her parents in Devon – my father-in-law is a policeman.'

Cassie would have liked to have drawn John's embarrassed face as he described his domestic situation.

After the speeches the march moved off and Cassie let John take the heavy bag from her. Their first stop was to be Turnham Green, chosen specifically because there was a tube station there for those who wanted to be home for supper. A night in a church hall was not to everyone's liking.

Suddenly mindful of the inconveniences of communal sleeping and even more importantly the possible lack of toilet facilities, Cassie momentarily balked at the idea of such discomforts. At her age was she not entitled to privacy? She dismissed the thought. She had promised Tom she would come.

Stealthily, so he would not see, she looked across the faces to find him. She so enjoyed him, he was tall with good straight legs and a fine patrician face – arrogant, some might have said – with a sensuality that even Cassie could see softened him.

The day was long, but friendly, the mood was good and hopeful, wellwishers on the way shouted encouragement. There was the occasional heckler, but the main difficulty was the endless walking. John was a comfort, though, he made her laugh and she was very glad that she had heeded his advice to rub her feet with methylated spirit for the two weeks prior to the march, and she had insisted that Tom do so too. The smell had been disgusting and Charles had really been rather rude about it.

She dispensed a lot of sandwiches, she was glad she had made so many. Tom kept coming over for them and she managed to refrain from reminding him of his earlier disapproval.

Tom was walking with a girl called Kate whom he'd noticed when they had first arrived in the square. He couldn't miss her with her wonderful mass of dark brown hair. He had wanted to talk to her, but he couldn't think of anything to say. She'd got over the problem.

'Are you going all the way, or just to Turnham Green?'

'All the way. And you?'

'All the way too.' She laughed totally unselfconsciously. He'd liked that. He noticed how open her face was, there was nothing contrived about Kate. She didn't even wear mascara.

114

She'd walked with him, lengthening her stride to match his.

'Why have you come on the march?' she asked him.

'My mother made me aware of the horrors of the Bomb. She went into shock when she saw those photographs of the survivors of Hiroshima. Once I knew about it there was no other way to go.' Tom pointed to Cassie without really looking at her. Kate looked across at Cassie and he could see the surprise on her face.

'That's your mother? She doesn't look old enough to be anyone's mother!'

Tom knew she was right. Cassie was a beautiful woman.

'And she's not a predictable mother either – she's an artist. What are your parents like?'

'Nice and typical.'

'You still haven't told me why *you* came on the march.'

'I saw the photographs of the survivors too.' Tom was very struck by her self-assurance.

He discovered that she was taking her A-levels a year later than him. She moaned about Chaucer, he extolled the drama of the *Canterbury Tales*.

'I'm interested in language too,' she told him. 'I want to be a journalist.'

'And I'm interested in the drama of it. I want to produce plays.'

He was worried in case she was cold. He wanted to put his anorak around her shoulders, but she claimed she was perfectly warm.

It was dusk by the time they reached the night stop. The damp had got to Cassie and she shivered. She wrapped a white scarf over her head, crossing it under her chin and tying it at the back. She was quite unaware of the way it made her eyes look so enormous.

'I hate the feel of the wet air,' she told John, by way of an explanation, 'it's the only characteristic of my adopted land that I really dislike.' She laughed and then changed her tone of voice. 'But, you know, recently I have felt great waves of homesickness. It's funny, really, when I'm in America I long for England and its civility, but when I'm here I think of cold crisp days and the sound of American voices and I miss the smell of New York. It has a special smell, every city does. New York's is excitement. I think everyone should be allowed to go to New York once every, say, five years on the National Health, just to get the senses going.'

Cassie knew she was talking too much, she felt awkward – she wasn't used to spending so many hours with a man other than Charles. She wondered where Tom was, her eyes scanned the crowd for him and she found him immediately, the leader of his little group. He looked cold, her motherly instincts came instantly to the fore – he would need a drink, she had hot milk in a flask and Ovaltine – and some of Charles' brandy. Deftly she filled the four plastic cups she had with her. Others would need warming too. She spooned out granules of the famous wartime drink, poured in the brandy, and finished the task just as Tom reached her. Suddenly selfconscious, she tried to shield him from her love. She handed him the cup and managed to say, in a level voice, 'Cold, darling?'

He nodded and took the mug without a 'thank you'. She wanted to correct his manners, but she knew better than to comment, instead she busied herself handing out the other cups. Eager hands and 'thank you's' made her smile. She noticed that before taking a sip Tom had offered his drink to a girl with brown hair and extraordinary translucent skin. Cassie made a point of talking to her.

'Are you here with your parents?' she asked her as she handed another cup to Tom.

'No.' There was a laugh. 'My parents are Tories. I am not sure what horrifies them more, a daughter who considers the Bomb to be abhorrent or a Socialist Prime Minister.'

Cassie smiled.

'You came with friends, then? Surely you aren't alone?'

'None of my contemporaries care about the Bomb. Actually, it's separated us.'

'I'm sure it has.' Cassie was instantly sympathetic. 'Are you going home tonight, or are you sleeping over?'

'Oh, I'm staying. And my parents know where I am . . . I'm not a runaway, or anything like that. I mean, I don't like their politics, but I like them.'

The girl smiled and Cassie found her self-possession extraordinary. She couldn't have been more than seventeen, almost the same age as Tom.

'You must be Tom Bray's mother. I'm Kate Sullivan, Tom and I sort of know each other.'

'I am sorry we haven't met before,' Cassie said. 'Do you know each other well?'

'No, not really, not at all actually.' The girl blushed. 'I mean, I noticed him at Trafalgar Square, and er. . .'

Cassie realised Kate was floundering. 'So you walked together,' she finished for her.

116

The church hall was littered with sleeping bags, Cassie was surprised at the passionate response the march had provoked. There were some people on the route who, disgusted by the aims of the marchers, had closed their pubs, their fields and even their churches. Others were unexpectedly supportive and had offered refreshments and hot drinks. Some of the marchers, exhausted by the walking, tried to sleep, but mostly people sat around and talked whilst the young danced. Cassie sat on her sleeping bag and watched Tom with Kate. In the half light the girl's hair cast a halo around Tom's neat golden head. Cassie wondered how they would look locked together, with their arms around each other. She was sure she wanted him to be in love, she wanted everything for him. Charles said she loved him too much. Well, maybe she did, was that a crime? Wasn't that why she had come on this march in the first place?

Cassie thought about Charles and realised that she minded the coldness between them. She wished he was more involved with her life and what was important to her, she resented his aloofness in matters of principle. Perhaps the real reason she had come on this uncomfortable march was because she wanted to shock him, make him react to her; he didn't, not any more. She was cold, she wanted to go back home to her own bed, but she knew Charles was expecting her to do just that – so she wouldn't.

Later, on the other side of the hall, a boy and a girl fumbled in the dark, a cloud of hair and a sleek head came together in a first kiss. If Cassie had seen their expressions – awe and joy – she would have been able to tell Tom and Kate that they were on their way to falling in love.

In another darkness, in another room, a man lit a cigarette and glanced at a clock on a bedside table. The hands showed it was 10.45 pm. A light was turned on and the man threw back the covers. As he started to dress a woman said, 'I thought you were staying.'

The man turned towards her. 'I would like to, but I can't believe even Cassie could cope with sleeping in a church hall. She'll find someone to bring her back.'

'You'll never leave her, will you?'

The man sat on the bed, by now in his trousers. He took the woman's hand. 'I never said I would.' His voice was very gentle.

'Go home, Charles.' The woman's voice sounded tired.

Cassie found the second day of the march very difficult. It was bitterly

117

cold, and it rained incessantly, then snowed. It seemed as if the cars sought her out and splashed her more than any of the other marchers. John stayed by her side and kept her spirits up, he laughed and talked and wouldn't let her give up. They stopped at a pub in Cranford where the landlord gave them free soup. Cassie remarked that she and John were in a minority, nearly everyone else seemed to be under 25. She really wanted to go home that night. Tom massaged her feet, and Kate rubbed her shoulders.

'You are amazing,' Kate told her.

'She most certainly is,' said Tom, cupping her cold toes in his warm hands, and she shrugged – there was no going back for her.

As she shivered in her sleeping bag she told herself, only two more days. On the third day they marched from Slough to Reading in the worst Easter weather for a hundred years.

But on the last day, on Easter Monday, the sun came out. Cassie noticed that the celebrities who had been missing during the long slog had arrived for the last moments. She felt they were fair-weather marchers, whereas *she* had earned her spurs. She walked with her head up between Tom and Kate, John Bravington was on Tom's left. They linked arms through a landscape that changed from a fertile, living thing to a heathland of gorse and pines. Cassie shivered, somehow it seemed appropriate that as they approached Aldermaston the earth should cease to flower. There was marshland and shallow, dirty-looking pools. In her mind Cassie saw horrible creatures mutated by radiation. Unless those horrible weapons were stopped, she could foresee a life where the natural order was a thing of the past. She clutched at Tom's arm. 'It's horrible, isn't it?' she said very quietly.

'It's bizarre really, they seem to have chosen the most sinister place to make their weapons,' Kate responded.

Eventually they reached the place where the bombs were made, and Cassie stared with a sense of fear at a building that might have been innocent if it were not for what took place there, and the pipes that seemed to lead to nowhere. As they marched around the perimeter fence her fear was replaced by a rage that money that should have been used for living was being spent in the pursuit of death. She noticed that they had been joined by others, it seemed to be a huge contingent and now the column of marchers stretched as far as the road was visible. Someone said that there were at least four thousand. The sheer numbers impressed Cassie, and this was only the beginning. She began to feel better.

'We're going to succeed, for sure, I know it,' Cassie told them all. And she laughed at the evil place where they made nuclear arms.

It was three weeks after the Aldermaston march that Tom received his call-up papers. He and his parents knew that he was going to do his National Service. Cassie had wanted him to apply for deferment, go to University first and avoid what she considered to be an unnecessary exercise. The whole business was due to be phased out and a three-year university course would preclude any necessity to serve Queen and country. Cassie didn't just dislike nuclear arms, she hated all forms of militarism.

Charles decided it was time for he and Tom to talk. He invited his son into his study, the small room on the corner of the house with the single glass door that led to the garden. During Tom's childhood Charles had kept that door open in the summer, he had liked to hear his wife and his son whilst he worked. These days, he had acquired the habit of resting his feet, minus their shoes, on the fender in winter, a habit which had given him chilblains.

Charles sat in his favourite wing-chair, upholstered in brown leather, its arms well worn. He reached behind him, extending his arm to pick up a ship's decanter, its flat base filled with the whisky that he so enjoyed.

'Join me?' he asked his boy for the very first time.

Tom was unnerved. Aware of the unease between himself and his father, he was unprepared for this sudden intimacy. He coughed, needing the small space that such a deliberate act gave him. He was not sure how to respond, he would have laughed at the irony if he could have – his childhood hero was a stranger to him.

'Thank you,' he said as Charles poured a small amount of the whisky into a thick, ornately cut tumbler, grateful that his father hadn't waited for a response to the invitation to drink together. Charles prepared another glass, a larger one, for himself.

'Your mother would prefer you to apply for exemption,' he said after he had drunk heavily from the tumbler, 'but of course there are no grounds.'

'I didn't say I wanted one,' Tom said quietly. He had had so many hopes, dreams almost, when his father had come home from the war. He had worshipped the man, wanting to be like him, but during his childhood his father had simply not been there. 'Daddy can't because he has to work' became the expected response to any possible outing of mutual interest. Occasionally there had been a cricket match, or rugby at Twickenham. But it was Cassie who had been his childhood.

119

'Look, Tom,' Charles was saying, and Tom forced himself to listen, 'National Service is not a pointless exercise. You are not going to enjoy basic training, no one does, but if you get on the right course and mix with the right chaps you will have a good time. Make a man of you.'

'You think I need that, do you, Dad?' Tom asked as his father averted his eyes from his.

Since the Aldermaston march Tom had spent most of his time with Kate. She was unlike any other girl he had ever met. Most girls just giggled, didn't have ideas. They layered on the mascara and presented themselves at obligatory birthday parties where the boys sat around in groups and tried cigarettes while the girls gossiped and waited to play Postman's Knock. Tom too took his turn outside the door and did the kissing, but with Kate it was different. They fitted each other.

He loved holding Kate, and touching her, and looking at her. He could hardly bear to be apart from her. On the days they had to be separated he would telephone her as soon as he got back from school. They would spend hours talking of this and that, and of important things too. Cassie would yell at him to get off the phone, even Kate's mother would voice a complaint. So they would put the telephone down and wait a little while and then one or the other would call back. They rationalised to furious parents that they couldn't see that much of each other, they had to revise, so they needed to talk.

'But whilst you are talking you are not studying,' Cassie said.

'I study, Mum,' Tom snapped. Cassie could hear the irritation in his voice, she wanted to laugh, but she knew it would not be right, and in any event she had no wish to laugh at Kate. She liked her and she wanted Tom to have a girlfriend.

Late at night, when she had finished in her studio, she would brew some tea, and take it to Tom. There were always two cups on the tray; she would sit on his bed, one foot curled under the other as he talked of her. She would always introduce Kate into the talk by asking how she was. Cassie liked sharing Tom's thoughts, it made her feel a part of the loving.

Tom joined the army in August 1958.

National Service wasn't easy for him – he was the only schoolboy in his group. The first few days, when he was kitted out and got his jabs, weren't too bad, except for the fact that the others didn't talk to him very much. They shared cigarettes and dirty jokes amongst themselves. They obviously regarded him as different. In class-ridden England

Tom should have known his place, but he didn't restrict himself, he wanted to overcome their reticence even if they resisted letting him in. He would get his food and sit with them.

'God, this is like school muck,' he said on his first day.

'Some of us are quite glad of it. We don't all sit down to banquets in our homes,' one, Peter Johnson, told him.

'I didn't say we had banquets at home, I just said that this wasn't the finest food I've tasted.'

'It's the "finest" I've tasted, it's hot and it's filling . . . some days I didn't eat at all,' another, Michael Donnelly, who had been out of work, told him, smothering his eggs in brown sauce.

Tom told them that he'd walked to Aldermaston, but no one seemed to care very much.

Tom remembered the conversation he had had with his father about being a man on the day the Drill Sergeant made him pick up a bucket that wasn't there, fill it with water that wasn't there, and walk across the shiny billet-room floor. After a few steps he was told to mop up water that wasn't there which had spilled from the bucket that wasn't there, with a mop that wasn't there, and continue to walk across the shiny billet-room floor. He was stopped and told to mop up three times. At first he wanted to laugh, but then he saw it as a drama exercise, he wouldn't think of it as stupid, he would give them a performance. When he had managed it, the Sergeant picked up a bucket that was there, filled it with dirty water that was there, and flung the contents across the shiny billet-room floor.

'Clean it, soldier,' he told him. 'I don't need acting performances from smart-arsed public-school boys who think they are going to end up as National Service Officers. I've been in this army for twenty-five years, soldier, and I have earned these stripes, no bloody accent got them for me. So you get down and start cleaning this floor, and remember, this is the army, you aren't in the fuckin' theatre now, this is the real world.'

The Drill Sergeant took the rest of the platoon out into the mud and then made them march back into the billet room, caking the floor with thick brown ooze.

'The rest of you men better bull your boots whilst your floor is being cleaned for you. Oh, and just in case Soldier Bray thinks he is getting off lightly, I'll just get his boots into the same state as yours.'

And the Drill Sergeant took Tom's boots which he had worked on for hours, carefully pushing the polish into the little holes, building up a sheen that he could see his face in, and threw them into another bucket of dirty water.

There were men who cried. Tom didn't cry. He was self-contained, and he was a survivor. He forced himself to swallow the insults, to function as one of a team, not to think as an individual and, hardest of all, not to have any expectations. He learned just to grit his teeth and long for it to end. The others noticed that.

After the incident of the billet-room floor, as it became known, they were nicer to Tom, he hadn't whinged, he had got on with it, and they singled him out for that, respectfully, but there were no intimacies. He didn't want to make his mark, however – he just wanted to be one of them.

And then came the incident in the shower. Cyril Freeman, a strong man – the Drill Sergeant never ordered him to carry an imaginary bucket of water – touched him whilst they were lathering themselves. Tom didn't react, he stayed in his place, continuing to wash himself, aware that Cyril was watching him. He finished, turned off the water, and picked up his towel, throwing it around his shoulders, wishing he could wrap it around his waist to cover himself. Instead he walked slowly, hoping the blush was not showing as his blood beat furiously through his shoulders into his face. It was only when he reached the lockers that he realised two others, small men, friends of Cyril, had been watching him. They stood in his way.

He said, ' 'Scuse me,' and they stepped to one side.

Tom dressed carefully, aware of them all the time. As he left the washroom he heard them laughing. He didn't mind that, their laughter didn't affect him. As he crossed the billet, Peter Johnson called out, 'Come on, Tom, we're playing cards. Let's see what a public-school-wallah can do.' He realised he was almost shaking, except that he was too strong ever to allow himself to shake. It was during the second hand of poker that Johnson remarked, 'So you aren't a pouf.'

'Why, are you?' Tom asked, and the laughter that greeted him was almost as good as the applause on a first night.

Tom got letters. Cassie wrote sharp accounts of life in Hampstead, and heartfelt truths about her feelings for him.

'I miss you, Tom, your room is so tidy, and I get to use the phone whenever I need it. No excuses when it doesn't ring . . . I can't say it's because no one can get through. How is it for you? Are you all right? Do you get enough to eat? I love you, my boy.'

He could sense her loneliness and it irritated him, he had always known she was emotionally dependent on him, and now, in that place away from her, he began to dislike it. He wanted to be free of her passion for him. He had a passion of his own now – Kate – and he ached for her. It was a physical pain. He would lie in his bunk imagining her with him. He thought of her as she had been the night before his enlistment . . . half undressed, wild and hot, just the way he'd always dreamed a woman would be, the feel of her, the smell of her. He had entered her for the first time that night. He had worried briefly that he might hurt her. At the moment that his penis pressed against her he had felt her shudder, he had drawn back, but she had raised her legs and using her two forefingers had opened herself for him, showing herself to him. He had slid into her, feeling the soft warmth, and he had not been able to control himself. It had been wonderful, he had felt his buttocks tense as he pushed deeper into her, loving her. Afterwards he caressed her, wanting closeness between them, wanting to roll his face in her flesh, but she had opened her legs again. 'Come inside again, please.'

She had taken him in her hand, using just two fingers on him, and he was hard again. He had taken his time, letting them both feel the movement of his penis, taking it out as far as he could, plunging it in as hard as he could, and then doing it again softly and gently, kissing her breasts, her mouth, her ears, her eyes, her nose. He saw her face beneath him, twisted into an expression that could have been pain or pleasure, and he heard breath sharp and shallow, faster and faster, and he moved in and out of her trying to keep pace with her need.

'Yes, yes,' she whispered, his tongue licked at her nipples, they were hard and tight, he wanted to bite them. It was the most exciting moment of his life. And when he relived that memory, the reality of barrack life disappeared briefly.

But at least there was a camaraderie now.

'You must admit that you didn't make a good start,' Pete, as Tom now called him, told him. 'That foppish remark about the food, some of the men in here don't have a good meal ever, and hot food only about once every three days. Life, sunshine, is not quite what you think it is.'

'And you, Pete?' Tom answered lazily, 'how often do you have a hot meal?'

The son of a clergyman in a particularly affluent 'living' punched the architect's son in the ribs, and the architect's son grinned.

Cassie was missing Tom terribly. Pretty Hampstead was empty without him. She could hear her feet crunching the grass as she went for

123

her walks alone and at night there was only one cup of tea to make. Charles always worked late. But there was a comfort for her, and it came as a surprise. Kate telephoned her quite often, it was interesting how much they had in common. Cassie discovered that she wrote, that she wanted to earn her living as a writer. Her parents wanted her to be an almoner, the thought horrified Kate.

'Can you imagine?' she told Cassie. 'I would become a cross between a headmistress and a mother.'

'Is that what your mother is like?'

'No,' Kate said quietly, 'she's a shadow, so self-effacing that I have no idea whether she is real or not. My father dominated my life as a child, he brought me up to read and think and do . . . he wanted a son, you see.'

Cassie made a sketch for her, she called it 'He Wanted A Son, You See' – it was of a mother, pale, almost ephemeral, a child, strong, clear, but outlined only, except for the hand that the man, powerful, with dark-grey pink-tinged skin, was colouring, giving it form, identifying its shape. Kate loved the sketch. She showed it to her mother and told Cassie, 'She just said "very nice, dear".'

Cassie had laughed. 'Don't worry about it, she probably couldn't understand why it wasn't finished.' When Kate didn't laugh back, Cassie had put her cup down and covered Kate's hand with hers. 'I am sorry,' she said, 'I shouldn't have said that. She is your mother, and that was cruel of me.'

Yvonne came to the studio to see the new work and Cassie told her of the conversation, and that Kate had been lovely about it. 'But of course it hurt her, it was unforgivable of me; it's terrible to realise that your own mother has let you down.'

Cassie had seen Yvonne's quizzical look. She chose to ignore it at the time, but later she felt badly. She telephoned Charles and asked if he might be able to get home for dinner. She couldn't confide in Charles, but at least there would be someone to talk to. Cassie was working on a series of paintings depicting the Aldermaston march, she knew the imagery she wanted, the feeling of youth on the march, punctured by the few older faces, but it wasn't working, it was glib somehow. There was no tension, no soul in the work. Since Tom had gone she had felt lost, empty, and the black despairs she so loathed haunted her – those horrible shadows took their hold again now that Tom was not there. She fought them as best she could, pushing them back just enough to enable her to function.

She was in the kitchen when Charles came home.

'No letter today?' she said.

'Well I hope not, the boy has far too much to do, and I hope he is starting to settle in.'

'Charles?' Cassie paused with the frying pan in her hand. 'I mean, you do think he's all right, don't you? He sounded, well, different in his letter. Perhaps we could ring the. . .'

'What?' Charles exploded.

'All right! Don't snap! I only suggested that we call to see how he is doing.'

'He's not at a holiday camp. He is doing his National Service. If he has the time to feel anything, he'll feel bloody miserable and homesick, and sick to death of the mindless grind. What the hell do you think he's doing, woman?'

As Charles slammed out of the kitchen Cassie cupped her face in her hand, stroking her lower lip. She knew she'd been stupid. She followed Charles into his study, he was standing behind his desk.

'Neurotic mothers,' she said, 'what can you do with them?'

'It's not what I do with you, Cassie, it's what you do to Tom.'

'What are you talking about?'

'You smother him. Let him go.'

'What are you talking about?'

Charles came out from behind the desk. He knew Cassie was missing Tom. He was so sorry, he wished he could help her. They had been close in the beginning, but after Tom was born she had changed, and then of course so had he – the war had changed them all.

'Drink?' he asked, going to pour them both a whisky, both of them large. 'I know how important Tom is to you, but in order to be a good parent one has to know when to draw back.'

'But of course I do. I don't interfere with him, I let him live his life. I don't interfere with him at all.'

She was angry, he could hear it in her voice. He wondered if he ought to pursue the conversation, to talk further, but he knew she wouldn't listen, and what was so sad was that it was not belligerence. She had no idea of her possessiveness, and he knew she would never believe it. He'd once discussed the situation with Jane during one of their holidays in America. She'd told him that she blamed her husband: he'd loved Cassie too much, so now she loved too much. Charles wondered if perhaps the fault might not be Jane's for not having loved enough. He glanced at his watch, it was 7.30. He wondered if he might manage to go out at around nine o'clock. . .

125

He didn't leave in the end, Cassie looked so damned sad. And she'd made a good dinner, he'd opened some wine, they'd spoken of his new project off Fleet Street, he'd even managed to talk about the concept easily, something that was difficult for him, his designs were so private. Cassie understood that.

For once she too spoke of her feelings about her work, she said she felt like a police inspector who has to find the murderer, she was slowly trapping him, stalking him. She knew she had become obsessive, it felt as if she were riding around in a circle trying to get to the centre, and then finally, magically, simplicity arrived.

'You come to a sort of truth for yourself, it is how far you can go each time, on each work, because you are reaching for your own way.'

He listened to her, he was interested, she was opening herself up in a way she had never done before. He was curious about the analogy of the murderer, this was a violence in his wife that he had never perceived before. He was curious about that. He wanted to offer the thought that perhaps Tom's physical presence had blocked her artistic development because as long as the boy had satisfied her needs she had had no need to stretch and pursue elements within herself. But he felt such a view would be too contentious. For a moment he was quite exhilarated at the possibilities offered by Tom's absence. When Cassie had rather shyly shown him some sketches, he'd offered a thought about the use of colours; she'd been interested, and then excited. They'd both gone to her studio and messed around with paints, just like they used to in Paris. Imbued with wine and affection, he'd reached for her, the first time in many months. He felt her want, she ground her legs around him, massaged her breasts into him, but as soon as he entered her, as soon as he moved, she went still and quiet beneath him. It was over quickly.

'I'm sorry,' Cassie said quietly, 'I know I disappoint you now. I don't want to . . . it's just that I am dead inside, squeezed out like a fruit without juice.'

Charles looked at her. He was stunned by her honesty.

In her flat in Lancaster Gate, Charles' secretary smoked a cigarette and waited for her lover. At 8.45 she had a bath, at nine o'clock she sprayed herself in perfume, at 9.30 she poured herself a drink and at 10.30 she went to bed in tears.

It wasn't long afterwards that Tom was due to come home on his first leave. Cassie had said she would drive up and collect him. She had a red and beige Sunbeam Rapier Convertible, which she adored, and she would drive with the roof down at the slightest opportunity. Before his basic training Tom would have welcomed the chance to speed home in comfort with Cassie by his side, but now it was different. The good opinions of the Peter Johnsons of his world were suddenly more important than Cassie. He didn't think about it particularly. He just wrote back and said he would be coming by train, along with everyone else.

Cassie was disappointed when she got his letter. She had been so anxious about him, she worried about the other men, would they like him, would they bully him? She knew he was a feminine boy, his lithe slender body and fine features would not have been out of place in a girl, she had felt all of that when he had first gone to school. And how would he cope with being away from home – in a hostile environment? She knew what happened in basic training – Charles had told her, not too much, but enough to know that the aim was to break a man's individuality. And individuality was exactly what she had tried to instil in her son.

On the first day of that first leave Cassie telephoned the railway station and discovered that Tom would be arriving at 4.30 in the afternoon. She didn't work that morning, instead she cooked like a mad thing, preparing all his favourite 'goodies': chocolate brownies, coconut cake, fried chicken, potato salad. She had decided that food was to be his panacea for discomfort. There were times when she used it as such herself.

At three o'clock she changed and by 4.15 she had parked her smart Sunbeam outside St Pancras Station, a tall red-brick tribute to Victorian bad taste. She walked quickly to the ticket barrier.

Tom saw Cassie as soon as he got off the train. He groaned. Couldn't she have waited for him at home? Why did she have to spoil everything by never giving him room for himself? He realised he was very angry with her.

'Look at that wonderful-looking woman,' he heard Pete say, 'I wouldn't mind having a piece of that.'

'You would if she was your mother,' said Tom.

'Your mother? Shit. I suppose it's different if it's your mother. Mine certainly doesn't look like that.'

Tom wanted to ask Pete about his mother. But there was Cassie, right in front of him. Cassie observed that his hair had been cut – up almost around his ears; if he weren't Tom he might have seemed ugly. He looked pale, and his uniform was baggy, she couldn't wait to get him into one of his soft sweaters and comfortable trousers. She waved energetically, oh, she just longed to hold him. She put her arms up to him, she put her arms around him and hugged him. He almost hugged her back but, aware that Pete was watching, he just offered a cheek.

'This is Pete Johnson – one of my friends.'

'Hi, Mr Johnson.' Her American charm was a shock. 'It's nice to meet you. Where are you going? Do you need a lift? Would you like to stay? You're welcome.'

'Cassie!' Tom said self-consciously.

'That's very kind of you, Mrs Bray, but I am going on to my home.'

'Can we give you a lift?'

'Well, I'm going over to Victoria Station, I was going to go by tube.'

'Don't be silly, we'll drop you off, it isn't that far.'

She linked arms with Tom, they'd often walked that way, two companions comfortable with each other, but Tom stiffened and refused to take her arm. Momentarily nonplussed, Cassie stumbled – Pete Johnson was there with his arm.

Cassie was shocked when Tom climbed into the back seat, she had been sure he would sit in the front next to her. Pete sat next to her and chatted pleasantly until they dropped him off. Cassie kept looking at Tom in the driving mirror, he wouldn't return the glance, he stared out of the window, his face set, cold almost.

'Well, tell me how it is,' she said, trying to be bright.

'How what is?'

'National Service, Tom. That's what you have been doing, isn't it?' She tried to laugh. Why wouldn't he talk to her?

'Good and awful.'

'What's good?'

'The men.'

'Oh, the rest of the boys.'

'They are men, Cassie. Listen,' his voice was sharp, she was shocked, she had never heard him speak to her like that, 'there isn't very much to tell. Do you mind if I don't talk, I'm really a bit tired.'

'Of course you are.' She was close to tears, but she had to indulge him. 'When you get in have a good long soak in a bath, that'll make you feel better.'

But Tom didn't go to the bathroom as soon as they got into the house. He went to the telephone. She could hear him, he was talking to

Kate. 'I can't wait to see you,' and then the door was pulled shut behind him. When he came off the telephone Tom told her he was going to Kate's for the evening. She felt a rage, a sense of betrayal. Why couldn't they come to her? Why did he have to go there? She looked at the food: she hated chocolate brownies. She picked them up and flung them into the dustbin.

When Charles rang to enquire about the evening's arrangements she told him quite sharply that Tom had gone to Kate's.

'Good for him.'

'I've prepared food.'

'Put it in the refrigerator. As Tom is out I think I'll take the opportunity of working late.'

It was after she had put the phone down that Cassie had a premonition that Charles might not be working.

It was Kate's habit to wait for Tom on the bench just by the bus stop near her house. She was always excited, but that day, his first leave, was scarcely bearable. She hadn't concentrated at school. Her friends knew, of course, that she had a boyfriend. They'd asked her, of course, did you go to number three? Has he put his hand inside your bra yet? What did it feel like? Once, her best friend, a girl called Lucy whose black hair was cut like Elizabeth Taylor's and who wore make-up and went to jazz clubs now, said, 'You've done it, haven't you?'

'Done what?'

'I wish you'd tell me.' Lucy laughed, her face was pale without her make-up but despite the school clothes she still managed to look wanton. 'I just want to know what it's like.' The look on her face, Kate could see, was longing. For a moment she was tempted to tell her of the feel of a man, but quickly she discarded the idea, somehow it would violate the beauty of what she did with Tom.

When she had first noticed him, in Trafalgar Square, she had known she would fall in love with him. It wasn't the way he looked, although of course she knew he was quite lovely, it was almost the smell of him that had drawn her. She had felt a flutter of excitement, and she had wanted to be by his side, to listen to him talk, to look into his eyes, to see his smile. And when he had kissed her she had felt wonderful, wanting to kiss him back, never to stop, never to be away from her. He filled her up with love – she needed nothing else.

When the bus delivered Tom to Kate there was a lot of kissing and touching. They went to the park. It was just a small square of green near

129

her home, rather flat and uninteresting, but children played there, and dogs ran free, and lovers could sit. When they began the talking Tom told Kate, 'It's been hard, you know, there have been nights in the billet when I had to fight not to cry.' His voice was very quiet.

Kate held him very tight, hoping the feel of her – of her love – would comfort him.

It was around nine o'clock that Cassie decided to ring John Bravington. She had no idea if she had the right number, she just looked it up in the book and found a J. Bravington in Swiss Cottage. She remembered that he had told her he lived nearby. It was strange she had no qualms about ringing his house, disturbing his wife. She thought about it, as she dialled the number, for Cassie was not insensitive, but she told herself that if his wife answered she would simply put the phone down.

As it was, Sarah Bravington was staying with her parents in Dorset – again.

They met for a drink in the Flask pub in Hampstead. It was a noisy, friendly place with a big wood fire. Cassie sat by its warmth whilst Bravington obtained their drinks, scotch for her, beer for him.

'Do you want to talk about why you rang me?' he asked.

'No, I don't. If you don't mind. I just need some company.'

John Bravington didn't mind. He needed some company himself.

# Chapter Six
## 1959

A long way from Hampstead, in Berlin, Rebecca Gottlieb hurried across Alexanderplatz. She was anxious, she didn't want to be late. A thin, worn woman with unnaturally bright eyes highlighting a white face and greying hair pulled into a neat bun, she huddled inside her overcoat. It was not a cold day, it was just a nervous gesture. She knew she had good reason to be nervous. Rebecca was on her way to discover whether her application for reinstatement into the Communist Party, and for readmittance to her former position as a secretary at the Defence Ministry, had been successful. When she had been a secretary she had worn red lipstick, and had short, styled hair.

She had been Dietrich Brundt's lover then – and he had said he loved her. As a young rising star in the new Germany Dietrich had been destined for great things. When Rebecca arrived back in Germany in the spring of 1948 he was working as an official in the Defence Ministry with specific responsibility for Africa. He was good to her, finding her a flat in one of the new blocks built for workers that were rising out of the rubble of the burnt-out city. There was not much furniture to be had in Berlin, but Dietrich, using his position, found beds, and even a settee of a gorgeously carved brown wood with luxurious gold satin cushions. It looked odd in the utilitarian flat, but Elizabeth loved it, stroking the soft cushions whenever she passed by the piece of furniture. Rebecca did not share her child's love of its opulence, but she was grateful to have somewhere to sit. Dietrich could have offered Rebecca many other inducements apart from his love, but she didn't need anything else, Rebecca had loved him, really loved him. She had never known anyone like him before, he made her feel safe, he did things for her, to make her life better, she felt cherished by him. For the time being she had resolved to accept his marriage, there was nothing else she could do, but she had told her little girl, Elizabeth, how much Dietrich meant to her.

'One day,' she would tell Elizabeth, as she brushed her hair and tied her ballet shoes, 'we will live with Uncle Dietrich. And we will be happy.'

'Is he my father?'

'No, your father was a man called Joshua Gottlieb. He was a doctor, but he is dead now. He would have been very proud of you.'

'Did you love my father?'

'Of course I did,' Rebecca told her child.

Rebecca was astounded by the strength of her feeling for Dietrich. He was so completely different from Joshua, he was not very cultured, he was not finely built, he was a thickset man who got things done.

'The time for ideals is over. We have got our Communist State and now we have to deal with the practicalities.'

Rebecca felt safe with him, there were no mountains to be climbed, or dreams to be cherished; if it was a question of starving or buying food, one bought food, and Rebecca, after so many years, was very grateful for a full stomach.

Elizabeth did not see very much of Uncle Dietrich, as she called him. He and Rebecca took their pleasures when they could, in the office, or in the car, and occasionally, when Elizabeth was at her dancing classes, at Rebecca's home in bed. Those were the best times, when they could be really alone, without their clothes. But there were never enough hours, Dietrich's watch would be put on the side table, and afterwards, a little while afterwards, for they always lay together and talked, he would glance at his watch and sigh and hold her close. Sometimes then she would ask him what he was thinking and he would answer, 'Everything and nothing.'

Elizabeth had started her dancing classes immediately after they had arrived in Berlin. Dietrich had organised it. He found a teacher, a tall thin woman who had once danced with Diaghilev. Along with most Berliners, she had suffered terribly after the war. When the Russians came she had existed for months on ersatz coffee, potatoes and the juice of wild dandelions that she boiled in a little tin saucepan on a paraffin stove. She had given up all hope for the future, she had just existed day by day. When conditions improved a little she was grateful, but even so she had allowed herself no expectations.

But then she met Elizabeth and in the dark-haired little girl she found a new beginning, and that was not a luxury she had anticipated.

132

A wise woman, she knew that to create a ballerina she had to instil a love of dance, and so first she told the stories, of *Coppelia* and *Swan Lake*, and *Sleeping Beauty*. She played the music on an old piano procured once again through Dietrich's good offices, and as she listened Elizabeth fell under the spell of the magic world of make-believe. Rebecca too fell under its spell, but hers was a more realistic view. If Elizabeth became a great ballerina her future would be secured. Rebecca was a practical woman, the Berlin of her past had gone, the city had shocked her when she saw it again. Once it had been the cultural heartland, now it was a mass of craters and mountains of rubble that hardly allowed for the fact that they had once been houses. Cables and water pipes protruded from the ground like mangled monsters.

There was little food, not that Rebecca or Elizabeth suffered. Dietrich insisted that they take advantage of the supplies that were available in the West, despite Rebecca's protests that she really shouldn't for the capitalists were storing those supplies and taking them away from the good Germans – Joshua would not have agreed to such an activity. Joshua had believed that capitalism was the creed of the greedy. But then Rebecca told herself that Joshua had not seen the plight of those who lived under an antagonistic victor with no sympathy for those who had supported the Third Reich – whatever their sufferings. So she quelled the thought that he would say she was betraying others who could not afford the profiteers' prices. Joshua would have pointed to the banners that were slung across the streets exhorting the workers to work and build a new Germany, and he would have told her to wait for the good times. Unfortunately for the true believer, not many Germans wanted to wait that long, and thousands fled to the Western sector of the city. Not so Rebecca. In July 1948 the blockade of Berlin began and the Russians announced that technical difficulties were preventing food from reaching the city. Rebecca believed them, for the party was her religion, and Dietrich was her god.

All that was before Dietrich defected.

He had gone on a hot Sunday in August 1953, just three months after the riots in East Berlin. She should have guessed that something was wrong because Dietrich had said the workers were right, and then, to deflect her interest in that comment, he had shown her photographs of the English Queen. She had talked of the murder of the Rosenbergs, and he had answered with the importance of the Korean armistice. He had taken his wife and children – there were three of them, two boys and a girl. The daughter was the same age as Elizabeth. Rebecca had seen her once, a small square child, her hair plaited into a rope, a pleasant face but quite unremarkable; so unlike her beloved Elizabeth who was learning to dance with excellent feet and perfect arms.

Dietrich's defection was a terrible blow for Rebecca, not least because of the personal betrayal, but there was also the question of the betrayal of principle. She remembered how they had celebrated the establishment of the Democratic Republic. Dietrich had been lying to her, he was not a true believer. He was an American agent. He had left a note, admitting his duplicity but claiming the one reality was his love for her.

Rebecca did not believe him, she felt dirty, sullied by the intimacies there had been between them. She could no longer think of them as acts of passion. On the night after his departure she had lain in the bed they had shared and made herself think back over the loving, but she found that her mind shied away from the memory of his hands on her breasts, of his mouth on her body, even from the thought of the man himself. She was not shocked at the depth of her rage. She knew it was because she had trusted him.

She lost her job, of course, and she understood that. It hurt when she left the building, especially as most of her colleagues turned their backs; only a very few managed to bring themselves to say goodbye. But that was nothing compared to the look on Elizabeth's face when they lost their home. Rebecca could not bear her disappointment.

'It isn't for long,' she told her child. 'You'll see, I will be reinstated, get my job back, and then we will have a nicer home.'

In the meantime they lived in one room, and shared a bathroom and toilet with six other families. They did their cooking in their room; in the summer it was too hot, and in the winter it was too cold. Dominating the place, far too big for its restricted surroundings, was the gold satin settee.

Elizabeth would lie on it for hours, safe in its opulence, dreaming her dreams, crossing over from reality to the imaginary secret place where good triumphed over bad, and happy-ever-after was the law. The travels of Elizabeth's babyhood had marked her. She had no love of the outside world, it had proved to be unreliable. A father had been taken from her, a life in England was gone, and now she had lost a home in Berlin. At a tender age she had learnt that her deliverance from such unhappinesses could only be found within her dance, and she turned to it, loving its escapism, enjoying its disciplines, worshipping its form. And it was the same world of dance which insulated her from the pain of her mother's exile from privilege. Elizabeth's ballet teacher had taught her well and as time went on she grew to excel. At the school word came down from on high that despite Elizabeth Gottlieb's mother's disgrace the child was to be treated well, she had talent. Elizabeth was grateful for that.

She had a history teacher, a pretty young woman with blond curls, Fräulein Glint, who had taken over the role of mentor from the now enfeebled ballet mistress (whom Elizabeth nonetheless visited diligently, for she loved the old lady).

One particular Thursday Elizabeth waited for Fräulein Glint after school had finished. She was going to lend Elizabeth a book on the Kirov. They had walked together down the huge stark corridor with its black floor, down the now empty staircase, their feet echoing in the companionable silence.

'Will you dance now, Elizabeth?' Fräulein Glint asked.

'Yes, I always do my work at the barre after school.'

'And then you do your studies?'

'Yes.'

'It is a hard life for one so young.'

Any response that Elizabeth might have thought appropriate to such a comment was immediately forgotten then when she saw a boy of her own age whose father had gone to the West being ridiculed and bullied by his contemporaries. They had tied him to a chair in the middle of the playground so he could not escape their punishment – as if it were not enough that he no longer had a father. Fräulein Glint broke up the ring of spectators. The leader of the mob, the son of a policeman, was unimpressed by her anger – his father had suggested that it might be a good idea to mete out their own punishment on the family of such a treacherous defector. The boy hadn't complained, but a week later he was shot dead by French soldiers when he failed to answer a challenge as he ran across restricted ground. He was trying to reach his father in the Western part of the city.

Elizabeth realised that as long as she brought credit to her teachers and her peers no such fate would await her. She formed no really close friendships. There were girls, and, as she grew, boys too, who wanted to be her friend, but there was little time for the camaraderie of childhood: she had to dance. Sometimes she spent time with two girls, dancers like herself, Karen Weber and Ingrid Lutz. They would drink coffee in one of the city's coffee houses. Rebecca had told Elizabeth that as a small child before the war she used to go with her mother and her grandmother to shop in the Unter den Linden under the splendid arches and elegant brown façades. Afterwards they would take a coffee and a rich cake laden with chocolate and cream and perhaps black cherries. There was no chocolate or cherries, or cream, in the People's Democratic Republic but there were still the coffee houses, denuded of their former glories. Like an unclothed tart, they still offered their wares but without the glamour of former times. Of course, in the Western part of the city there was chocolate and cherries and cream – the tart still had her make-up on there. On those occasions, the girls would giggle with the festivity of it all, but they talked of jetés and arabesques and toe shoes, as well as of boys. At least Ingrid and Karen talked of boys, Elizabeth had no time, or indeed inclination in that direction. Elizabeth simply worked and worked. Her reward at the age of seventeen was an acceptance by the Komische Oper Dance Company. She danced in the corps de ballet and still dreamed her dreams – but now they were no longer of escapism, they were of being the very best, in the spotlight, the solo artiste – stardom.

Rebecca accepted her disgrace. She got a job in a laundry and waited to serve out her sentence.

And now, in 1959, when Elizabeth was nineteen, she was attempting to effect the repeal. As she stood outside the building that housed the East German Defence Ministry she quietened her nerves with thoughts of Elizabeth. The Administration of the Dance Company had decided to present a new dancer in their next production of *Giselle*. They were auditioning shortly. Elizabeth had understudied the part so many times; she wanted to dance it very much. Just the night before she had performed the role for Rebecca, turning their shabby little room into a stage, and herself into a perfect Giselle. For a girl who had never been in love, she had an instinctive understanding of passion. Rebecca recognised it and she worried for Elizabeth – what would happen to her bright, sunny child once the spectre of love pierced her innocence? Rebecca never allowed herself to forget that it was love that had destroyed her life.

'I am sorry, Fräulein, but your application for re-employment has been refused.'

'What?' Rebecca could not believe what she was hearing. 'But it's been six years now. I mean,' she looked down at her hands, she didn't even notice how ragged and broken her nails were, 'I understood the decision of the Party to terminate my employment at the time of the defection of the former Secretary, but surely now. . .'

'I am afraid the decision is final.'

Rebecca felt the tears come, it was ridiculous. She never cried, she had not even cried when Dietrich had gone, but it was so unfair, so unjust and she was a good supporter of the State, she believed in the State. She watched the official fiddling with his files. She didn't know him, he was new, she hated him, what could he know of her struggles? What did he know of slaving in a laundry, your hands constantly wet until the flesh wrinkled like crumpled paper? She rubbed glycerine in at night, that helped a bit, but her knuckles ached from wringing out the wet heavy clothes – lately it had become more than an ache. Sometimes she cried with the pain; then Elizabeth would massage her hands and she would console her anxious child.

'Don't worry. Soon I will be back at work at the Defence Ministry.' There was no question of her working in the West, she was a Communist, an East German, but now she knew there was no future for her, there was only the laundry.

She got up. She didn't know how she managed to walk to the door.

'Fräulein. . .' She turned back to the desk, she had no idea what the official looked like, she would never know, she simply didn't see him.

'Fräulein,' she heard him say, 'I am sorry, but there is no choice, these, you see. . .'

Rebecca frowned and walked back to the desk. The official was holding some letters in his hand, maybe fifteen or twenty, they were addressed to her, they were from Dietrich. Her heart fluttered. She held out her hand.

'I am sorry,' the official said again, 'I shouldn't even have told you.'

'You mean these letters were sent to me from Dietrich and I was never allowed to receive them, even censored?'

The official looked sad for her.

'Please,' she begged, 'what's the point now in me not having them?'

'I can't, they are listed and numbered.'

'Please?' Rebecca begged again.

'One, just one,' he said, holding just one out to her.

Rebecca snatched at the envelope. She ran out of the office, down the corridor, out of the building, across Alexanderplatz into a side road that led to a small square. There were apartment buildings all around, it was very neat and orderly, a small tree had been planted at each corner of the square, and in between each tree was a bench. Rebecca sat on the nearest one. Her hand shook as she took out the letter. There were no censor marks, there was no need for them, the addressee had never been intended to see the contents. It was an intimate letter, the longing clearly identifiable. Her cheeks burned as she thought of the men who had read the private words. Dietrich had written of his love, of his despair at being apart from her: '. . . *but as I explained, I had to go, if not I would have gone to prison. I couldn't do that to my children. Will you ever forgive me, my dearest Rebecca? How I long to touch you, to lie with you, to be inside your body, to be smothered by your juices.*'

Rebecca burnt his letter, she felt defiled by its public readings.

When Elizabeth returned from ballet class she found her mother curled into the gold satin settee, her face puffy from tears, ugly with lost hope. She dropped the bottle of schnapps she was carrying, the little cake a wardrobe mistress had prepared for her. Elizabeth had been organising the celebration for weeks, for she too had been sure it would be a celebration. She had invited Karen and Ingrid, and Fräulein Glint. Rebecca had no friends of her own, save for Professor Schmidt, a friend from childhood who had once lived in Dresden. Others had fallen away when she had been expelled from the Party.

'I might have done the same,' she had told the unhappy Elizabeth at the time. 'But don't worry. It will all be put right.'

Now they both knew it wouldn't. When the guests arrived all Elizabeth could do was to tell them to go away.

In the night Rebecca walked up and down the corridor outside the little room. She felt cold, but she did not want to disturb Elizabeth. She could not sleep, she needed to think. She felt utterly alone, rejected by the system she loved, and by the man she loved. She was suddenly consumed by a terrible bitterness for it was obvious to her that it had never occurred to Dietrich that his actions would compromise her. He was an unthinking man who had put his own needs uppermost. He had wanted to put his relationship right with her so he had written letters to her. He must have known they would be intercepted. How could he have been so unthinking? Loving Dietrich had ruined her life, now she had nothing for herself, there was just Elizabeth.

She was not sure when she made the decision to go to the West. Perhaps it had been that night, or maybe the next. All she knew was that she would go, she had to. It was for Elizabeth's future, she did not stop to consider whether Elizabeth would be happy there. That was not Rebecca's way. Her argument was simple: if she – a child of

Communism – could end her days as a laundry maid then what might not happen to a dancer whose mother had become unacceptable? She could not allow anything to hurt Elizabeth, so they would go, when the time was right. She felt almost rejuvenated, she could plan again.

Tom Bray arrived in Berlin in 1959. He had been posted there – to be a telephonist because he spoke fluent German. Cassie was glad. 'At least he won't have to do any shooting,' she told a worried Kate whilst Tom himself learnt that National Service, that dreaded episode, was proving to be more of an analgesic against the responsibilities of real life than a toil.

He discovered that his new home was a city sliced into two halves. He, of course, would live in the part of the city that fell under Allied control – the Western Sector. Aware that it was bordered by an inhospitable neighbour, Tom discovered that West Berlin strutted coquettishly and offered its wares to the impoverished voyeurs of the Eastern Bloc. Those in the care of the Americans, British and French knew their twin sister reeled under an inappropriate, but determined, management, and they mocked that management: they might have kept the wonders of the Unter den Linden on their side of the wall, but the way in which it had provided a perfect backdrop to the resplendent evils of Nazism was a source of shame in the post-Hitler era. It was a time to be forgotten, banished from German memory. The history books would record nothing after the First World War. The promise of a Thousand-Year Reich was obliterated. In East Germany they could talk of the Nazi horror, for they told their people that they had rid themselves of those perpetrators of evil. The Communists, whatever their nationality, had suffered under the SS – they had nothing to hide.

For a British soldier, especially a National Service soldier, Berlin meant being in an army of occupation in a now-friendly country with the enemy just a step away through a control point. East Berliners poured in by droves; the shimmering West lured and enticed them away from the spartan bureaucracy of an order that denied choice. But despite those enticements, Tom found West Berlin claustrophobic. It seemed to him that he was in a small but comfortable prison in the midst of hostile countryside. The pleasures of the red-light district were officially off-bounds to the British servicemen. Despite being warned off potent German beer as well, Tom and his friends enjoyed both such delights. And he had found a particular friend, Helga – a comfortable bleached blonde. He liked her, she filled the emptiness of his hours –

without Kate, without the theatre, Tom was quite alone, he needed solace. Pete, who had become a Unit Education Sergeant in Munich, warned that his prize for such comfort might be an unpleasant illness. Tom said he would take his chances, the National Service pastime of masturbation in communal sleeping accommodation held no attraction for him.

He liked to go to the forests that surrounded Berlin. There was a particular route that really pleased him. It was near the Glienicke Bridge, which crossed the Havel Lake that helped to separate the two halves of the city. There was a hunting lodge nearby. Helga thought it very pretty, Tom was glad the grounds offered some sort of privacy.

Elizabeth liked that particular place too. She and Rebecca used to take the subway to the crossing point at Friedrichstrasse and then get on another subway to the nearest stop to the park and walk through the trees. Sometimes they would take coffee and a cake at one of the little cafés. Elizabeth allowed herself only the coffee, she was diligent about her body, it had to be thin and spare in order to work properly.

One Sunday as they were sitting by the lake Rebecca looked across to the other side, the discomforts of her life confronted her, they were there, waiting for her – across the water. Suddenly she said, 'Don't let's go back, let's stay here. There is nothing to stop us.'

Elizabeth turned to her mother. 'Please, I understand what you are saying, but I don't want to leave. I know it's selfish of me but my life, my friends are in my part of the city, Mutti, my dancing is there, and I may even get a chance to perform Giselle. Who knows, Mutti, one day maybe, if I am lucky, I could dance with the Kirov.' She put her hands on Rebecca's shoulders, she wanted to hug her mother, she suddenly looked so small and defenceless. Elizabeth knew her life was unrelenting and she resented her mother's fate. She hated Dietrich, blaming him – recently, since Rebecca's application had been rejected, she had thought about her father; if he had lived it would all have been different. For a moment she was torn, perhaps for Rebecca's sake they ought to stay, but no, no, Rebecca's life was not in the West either, Rebecca was a Communist. 'Try again,' she heard herself telling her mother, 'I am sure you will get your job back.'

Mother and daughter were so deep in their discussion that they didn't notice the young British soldier and his German girlfriend kissing hungrily by a tree.

Rebecca shrugged, what could she say to Elizabeth? The girl's face was set and anxious and so they turned back from the shimmering silver water and took the subway back to Friedrichstrasse and the East; Rebecca was sure that the guard was surprised to see them on their return journey.

When Tom first met Helga on Easter Monday 1959, Kate had walked to Trafalgar Square along with 10,000 others to try to stop the Bomb. She was missing Tom terribly. She would spend hours in her room, lying on her bed thinking of him. She would play 'It's All In the Game' over and over again on her little blue portable gramophone. Tom had bought it for her, after a row, 'a lovers' tiff' he had called it. She couldn't even remember what it had been about, but he'd kissed her, and then they'd laughed at the lyric together: 'You'll have words with him, and your future's looking dim.' Now she cried every time she heard that line. She knew she was stupid, but he was so far away, experiencing different things whilst she was still stuck at school, in the same world that he had left behind. Would he still want her when he came back, would she still want him?

She turned to Cassie, needing the older woman's friendship. That was a strange experience in itself: Kate had kind and good parents, but they were not her friends. The gap between parent and child was a very real one. Her father was the chief cashier in a bank, a good enough position, but one that didn't run to luxuries. Her mother was first and foremost a mother, a woman who cooked and cared for her family – it had always been that way. The welcoming smells of pungent apples full of cinnamon and cloves and the sweet scent of vanilla flavoured custards or the aroma of thick savoury pies and stews were the stuff of her childhood. It was a safe life where a fine-boned but capable woman with neatly curled fair hair who smelt of violets and wore a flowered pinny in her domain, rolled her pastry and arranged her flowers. Her father, a full-hearted but blunt man with a comfortable pink face and a thick thatch of hair that matched Kate's, ruled supreme. His meal was always ready when he came in. Sometimes, when Kate's mother was tired, her father would gently send her to her bed and he and Kate would eat together. He would tell her stories of his life in the Navy, and then they would wash up. Kate noticed that on those occasions he would lay a tray for her mother, always a pot of tea, and some thinly sliced toast, and there would always be one flower laid on the plate as an offering. Kate wondered about that, but she never dared enquire why her father did that, it was private and Kate's life had its boundaries. Her parents had their world and she had hers, there was no question of them merging. To find a woman of her mother's age who reached out to her and listened to her was extraordinary, and of course Cassie opened a door into Tom's world, she was the mother of the boy Kate loved.

As for Cassie, she simply couldn't get used to Tom being away from her. She was fond of Kate, she loved young people, she was used to them, she understood their expectations, for she too still had expectations. Cassie had not learnt the acceptance and restrictions of age, it was not her way; Jane had not raised her to deal with a life without possibility. The young found it very attractive, the more mature seemed to find it particularly irritating. So in Kate Cassie discovered that not only had she found a substitute for Tom, but also – and perhaps more importantly – a friend of her own.

Kate confided in her that she wanted to be a journalist, but that there was no question of her continuing her education beyond her A-levels. Kate's father might have felt differently had she been a boy. Her mother had suggested she might be an almoner in a hospital. Kate laughed as she sat with Cassie in a dark little restaurant that served lukewarm coffee from machines that hissed out the frothy liquid into glass cups.

'I don't see you as an almoner, Kate. You'd look good in white clip-clopping down the corridor on high heels, but having to listen to other people's problems can become very painful, it can get to you. If you are serious about becoming a journalist, you ought to go and work on the local paper as a cub reporter. See if you can do some work now. Maybe we can manufacture a drama. 'Exclusive by Kate Sullivan'. I'll see what I can do – perhaps a robbery of some kind, but with a bit of human interest too. You know, the woman has no money and twenty-eight children to feed.'

'And they live in a shoe,' Kate finished for her, laughing. She wouldn't have been surprised if Cassie had found a woman who lived in a shoe.

Cassie didn't find a woman with twenty-eight children, but she did find a well-known writer who was willing to be interviewed for the local newspaper. The well-known writer was a friend of Cassie's and the Editor of the local newspaper just happened to have bought two of her paintings.

Cassie arranged for Kate to go to the writer's house one Saturday morning.

'I don't normally write at the weekend, and the kids are at music, and my wife is usually at the hairdresser's, so we will have some peace,' he told Kate when she telephoned him.

Kate went to Cassie's house first. She liked Hampstead with its winding streets and cobblestones. It was just like a small village, perched on top of a hill, isolated from the suburbia that ringed but didn't dare encroach on it. The Heath was the best part, Kate felt she could get completely lost on it. London, particularly her own suburb of Hendon, seemed to belong to a separate continent from the rural splendours of Hampstead Heath.

The writer, a literary name who sometimes appeared on *What's My Line*, lived quite near Cassie, so a stop at Tom's mother's was absolutely in order. Kate's wild hair glowed from vigorous brushing, she wore a neat blouse and a cardigan, and a pleated skirt. She had no idea quite how lovely she looked, but it irritated her that she only had her school raincoat.

Charles opened the door to her. Kate liked Tom's father, but she was slightly in awe of him. She had never met anyone quite like him before, he was such a formal man and yet he was charming to her and she did think he was terribly attractive.

'So today is the big day,' he said, ushering her into the wide hall – it had good walls for paintings, Cassie had told him when she had found the house, but she never hung her own work, she liked to show off work by her friends and her peers.

'I am a bit nervous,' Kate found herself admitting to Charles, she was surprised, it just slipped out. He put his arm around her shoulders very nicely. He didn't embarrass her in any way, it was a gentle gesture.

'I am sure you are,' he said, 'but just relax, take notes and listen very carefully. Don't miss any nuances, or any gestures. They will tell you more about a person than anything they might say.'

Cassie was squeezing oranges in the kitchen, a singularly un-appealing job, but one that she considered necessary for her family's health. She was appalled at the British vitamin intake, she wasn't surprised they always seemed to have colds. She poured Kate a glass, and made her drink it whilst she told her she was wonderful and would write a magnificent article.

'I hope Desmond behaves himself,' Charles said quietly after Kate had gone on her way. Cassie's self-congratulatory glow paled slightly.

Kate tried to remember what Charles had told her as she settled herself on a small dining-room chair opposite Desmond Case. He was a tall man with well-dressed hair and a surprisingly ugly face beneath a trimmed black beard. He had piercing eyes of a milky blue colour. He seemed very relaxed, rather kind really.

'Your first piece, is it? Well, we must make it a good one for you. You ask the questions and I'll try to give you interesting answers.'

Kate tried, *really* tried.

'Do you think of yourself primarily as a commentator on post-war Britain, or are you a novelist who tries to reflect society?'

'I suppose, like Dickens, I am a little of both.'

'Dickens used his books to expose the evils in his society.'

'He told a story.'

'Yes, but he also used his novels in a more political way.'

'Did you study Dickens at school?'

'Yes.'

'You probably did one of his books for A-level. Read Zola and Hugo, Voltaire, Racine and the great Russians, then we will have a discussion.'

Kate realised that Desmond Case was giving her trite, off-the-cuff replies. She was suddenly very angry. He was patronising her.

'Do you always feel superior to your interviewers?' she asked, aware her tone was clipped.

He seemed surprised, and then he laughed, but it wasn't a companionable laugh. 'No, just to the earnest ones.'

He offered her a sherry which she thought she ought to accept even though she didn't like the drink, it always made her feel woozy. She found the texture and the taste cloying so she drank the sweet brown liquid too quickly. He refilled the glass.

'I really don't think I would like another one,' she said.

'Aren't you old enough to drink?'

Stung, Kate swallowed the second glass. She felt quite sick.

'Are you all right?' he asked. She could feel his hands on her shoulders.

'Come here and lie down on the sofa for a minute.'

'No, I'm fine,' she said, but allowed herself to be led across to it. Her mother always made her lie down on the couch, as she called it, whenever Kate had a headache. She would stroke her head, and arrange cushions under her. But the famous writer wasn't stroking her head, he was touching her breasts.

'No.' She spoke very sharply, pulled herself up and shoved him away. She picked up her pad and ran to the front door. She could hear him behind her, but she ignored him, opened the front door and slammed it shut behind her. Kate didn't go back to Cassie, she went straight home.

She sat at her father's old typewriter and wrote her article. It was fair, she quoted Case's words, but she also remembered what Charles had said and she told her audience what she wanted them to know using short sharp observations.

'His answers were always polite but he gave no more than what he thought a novice would expect. His brilliantined hair and over-curious eyes were not comfortable on a man of his years.'

The personal observations were subbed out of the piece, but it was published and she was offered a job.

The next time Cassie and Kate met, which was the following Thursday at the coffee bar, Cassie asked, 'Did Desmond behave?'

'Why do you ask that, Cassie?' Kate replied in a level voice, for she suddenly realised that Cassie had known exactly what might happen and she was extremely angry that Cassie had not prepared her. 'Did you feel that there might be a problem?'

'No, no, I didn't.' Kate noticed that Cassie was fiddling with her coffee cup. Cassie had nice hands with long fingers, her nails were neat, no varnish, but she wore her wide gold wedding ring.

'Well there was.'

Cassie's cheeks were red now and she did not look at Kate. 'Did he make a pass?' she asked.

'Did you think he would?'

Cassie raised her head and pursed her lips. 'I hoped he wouldn't.'

'Why didn't you warn me?'

'Perhaps I didn't want to frighten you off him. Sometimes it is better not to have a preconceived view.'

'But he shouldn't have done what he did.' Kate found herself almost crying.

'Sweetie, what happened?' Cassie asked. She tried to take Kate's hands but the younger girl pulled them away.

'He touched my breasts, that's all, but no one does that unless I want them to.'

Cassie nodded. Her coat felt uncomfortable on her shoulders, she would have liked to have taken it off, but didn't. For the first time she was disconcerted by her son's girlfriend.

'It was wrong of me, I just didn't think about it. Charles reminded me after you'd left,' she said honestly.

Kate made no comment. She stirred sugar into her coffee, watching the white granules slide into the frothy top. She could hear Cassie clearing her throat. They both knew that the balance in their relationship had shifted slightly. Cassie had slipped a little from her pedestal. They finished their coffees in silence.

On a hot summer's day Edwin came to have lunch with Cassie. The sun was high in a blue sky, the flowers were in their prime, roses and irises and spray carnations packed the square beds that ringed the smooth, green lawn of Cassie's English garden. Foxgloves vied with lupins for attention. Edwin had pottered a little, he liked to work in Cassie's garden whenever he came over, but that morning when she had collected him after breakfast he had said he was tired. She had suggested he should take advantage of the gentle heat so he had taken a book and settled in a chair facing the sun. His straw hat was perched firmly on his head. Cassie had watched him for a few moments from her studio. But seeing that he was comfortable she had turned back to her work. She was preparing a series of paintings on the subject of motherhood. Birth had been easy, infancy and childhood had not taxed her, but the concept of the young adult had bothered her. There were numerous sketches pinned up on the studio walls, some had been torn off and crumpled into the waste paper basket. She wanted to use the imagery of a parting and yet retain a link between mother and child. She was not satisfied, she couldn't see her way past the absence of her own son. At twelve o'clock she surfaced and decided to break for lunch. She was grateful for an excuse to leave the studio.

Cassie was wearing a sundress with wide straps and a full skirt. She had left Charles' blue-striped shirt that she had appropriated for her painting over an easel. She always wore his old shirts, it had started in the war; she had said then that it made her feel close to him. She noticed on her way up the path that led from the studio to the kitchen door that Edwin was slumped right down. She hesitated for a moment, should she see if Edwin was all right? But then she decided to prepare lunch – she would wake him when it was ready. In the kitchen she arranged fresh bread and deep-yellow butter on a tray, she fetched glasses from the cupboard and poured some of the thick strawberry milkshake that she had prepared in her mixing machine that morning. The scent of the fresh crushed strawberries was quite delicious. It made Cassie ridiculously happy, she loved doing things like that for others. With Tom away she had little opportunity to perform such tasks, which was why she so enjoyed having Edwin to lunch. She knew it interrupted her work, but she was having so little success with her current project that she didn't mind. She had made a salad, and purchased some strong crumbly Cheddar cheese. She was just about to carry the tray out when she remembered the chutney. Edwin always had chutney with his cheese. She put the bottle on the tray, she knew he would scoop huge spoonfuls of it onto his plate. Often she would tease him and tell him that he only ate the bread and cheese so that he could have the chutney. She walked across the grass to him and set the tray down on the table that Edwin had thoughtfully left for just such a purpose. Her own chair was positioned next to his.

He was a dear man, she was so sorry he had never met her mother. Somehow she and Charles had to arrange it. But Jane was so stubborn she would still not come to England, and Cassie knew that Edwin was too frail to go to America. Sighing, she sat down and picked up the glass of pale pink milkshake in one hand and with the other gently touched her father-in-law. He moved slightly in the chair, and then sat up, jerking himself out of his sleep.

'Thank you, my dear. I am so sorry. I must have dozed off.'

'You obviously needed to,' Cassie said, handing him the glass. As he took it she noticed how thin his hand was, the blue veins stood out so clearly. Ridiculously she wanted to snatch it up and kiss it, but of course she wouldn't do such a thing. Instead she contented herself with a brief caress. Edwin returned the gesture with an affectionate smile. He ladled the chutney onto his plate, ate a little cheese and a lot of bread, but studiously ignored the salad.

'Evelyn is coming at the weekend,' Cassie told him.

'Yes, I know. She telephoned me to tell me. Will you do luncheon on Sunday?'

'Of course, and it will be lovely. I just wish Tom was with us.'

'She isn't bringing her family, is she?' Edwin asked. His tone of voice was difficult to interpret, but Cassie knew there was more behind the question.

'Why do you Englishmen think it so wrong that I want to have my child around me?'

'Because the time has come for the child not to want to be around the parents,' Edwin said in a surprisingly sharp voice which startled Cassie. 'I have had a nice letter from Tom,' he continued in an easier tone.

'Oh?' said Cassie, hoping he would give it to her to read. Tom's letters to her were short and rather uninformative. He didn't seem to go into detail any more, perhaps he hadn't the time. But Edwin did not give her the letter, and she felt a little upset, but of course said nothing.

147

Edwin did not pass the letter to Cassie because his much-loved grandson had spent a considerable amount of paper bemoaning his mother's passionate epistles.

*'She has to understand that I am not the little boy who went away to the Army. I don't want to hurt her, but she can't live her life through me any more. It is going to be very hard for us both.'*

Edwin knew the boy was right, he knew he should speak to Cassie, he was closer to her than anyone else, but he was tired, he would do it another day.

He died that evening, quite undramatically, in his bed. His housekeeper found him in the morning. A woman who had adhered to a set timetable all her life, she knew instantly there was a difficulty when she arrived at the house and found the curtains were still closed. She had patted her tightly curled blond hair, checked her make-up in her compact mirror, just to make sure that all was in order – she wouldn't want Mr Bray to see her with anything out of place. She had knocked on the bedroom door, and when she didn't hear a response she had gone straight in – she had been a nurse once. She had found him curled on his side, like a baby, the look of death about him. She telephoned Mrs Bray immediately.

Cassie in her turn telephoned Charles. He met her at the house, she was parking the car as his taxi arrived. They said nothing to each other. Cassie tried to take his hand, as much for her own comfort as for his, but he ignored the gesture, merely pressing the doorbell.

'I have a key,' Cassie said.

'Do you?'

'Yes, Edwin gave it to me some months ago, in case. . .'

The housekeeper, with a suitably respectful expression on her face, opened the door and the business of mortality took over. It seemed to Cassie that there was no time for grief. The doctor was already there, Charles had issued instructions that he should be notified immediately. Death was as a result of a heart attack. 'He wouldn't have known anything.'

'I am glad about that,' Cassie said quietly, but no one seemed to be listening.

Evelyn was to arrive in the afternoon. George would drive her, her daughters would not be coming until the funeral. Cassie could not understand that, she wanted Tom, not just for herself and Charles, but because he was part of Edwin too. They were a family and families needed each other even more, so she felt, in times of joy and in times of grief. That was why she asked, 'How do we get hold of Tom? Do I ring the camp, or what?'

Charles ran his hands through his normally neat hair. Cassie felt such tenderness for him, she wished he could cry. 'He'll have to be told. I'll write to him.'

'Write?' she said incredulously. 'But he has to come home.'

'Cassie, he is in the Army.'

'His grandfather has died, he loved his grandfather. His grandfather is your father, you loved him. He was my best friend in this country, and I loved him. We have all lost someone important. That is why Tom has to come home.'

'I don't think it is necessary, but you must do as you see fit then,' Charles said coldly.

He walked out of the room. He was very tired of Cassie's histrionics. Of course Tom would mourn his grandfather just as he himself would mourn his father. It didn't stop and start with funerals. Cassie required outward show, she never seemed to understand that it was how one *felt* that mattered. He could not help but compare Cassie's behaviour with the restrained dignity in his office. There was sympathy, but of a non-intrusive nature, and at the right moment when no one was around his hand had been squeezed and cool, kind lips had touched his.

Charles walked up the stairs to his father's bedroom. The curtains were still shut, the undertakers hadn't arrived yet so the body still lay in its bed, the white sheet pulled up over the face, the hands crossed over the chest. Charles sat down in the wing-chair that had once graced his father's chambers at 12 King's Bench Walk. He remembered how as a small boy he used to be taken to the chambers on the first day of each school holiday. The ritual was always the same, the small boy trying to climb the thick, winding stairs that led up to the big man's huge room. The clerk, a nice man called Mr Trumpet, would always nod respectfully. 'How are you, Master Bray?' he would say. And Master Bray would nod back and say, 'Very well, thank you,' whether he was or not. Those were formal days. He would go and sit in the chair where he now sat, as a child his feet had just reached the edge of the seat, and each year his legs grew longer until finally, in adolescence, they reached the floor. The chair had always been a symbol of the distance between him and his father. The young Charles would find that once he sat in the chair the room was obscured by its wings and he would only have a partial view of his father sitting behind his huge desk dispensing power and a kindly affection to those around him. But the child was in awe of the man, for somehow his father had not been quite so kind to him as he had to those who worked for him. He remembered how he had choked back his tears when the terrors of prep school loomed. He had wanted to run over to the desk and hide in one of its deep drawers so that they wouldn't know where he was; but he knew his father would have found him so there was little point. The chair had been both friend and enemy – a place of sanctuary and a place of exposure – but it was always bigger than he was, even when he grew up. Now that he sat in it after his father's death, it felt small to him. Charles thought about his childhood, he had never really known his parents when he was young. It was only in his later years, after he himself became a father, that he had begun to understand this man who was now gone from him.

Cassie had telephoned the appropriate personnel and received permission for her son to be flown home on compassionate leave. He would arrive the following evening. Naturally she told Kate, who was torn between sympathy for the bereavement and incredible gratitude for the unexpected time with Tom.

Tom was very sad. He came home in a huge-bellied transport plane. It was not a particularly comfortable flight, but Tom didn't notice. He was trying to deal with the fact that Edwin Bray was no longer alive. He remembered his other grandfather's funeral, and his sense of disassociation from those proceedings. He had stood by the grave, aware of his mother's silent misery, but it hadn't meant anything to him then. He wasn't even aware of the significance of a coffin being consigned to the earth. Not so now. He put his head into his hands and wept. Cassie had taught him how to cry.

When the plane landed a Flight Sergeant offered him a lift into London in his Morris Minor: 'Get you to a tube.'

'Thanks.'

The Flight Sergeant offered a pack of cigarettes. Tom took one. 'Bit of bother then?' the man, short and square with a good face, asked.

'My grandfather died.'

'Not easy, old chum, losing people you care about.'

Tom drew deeply on his cigarette; no, it wasn't going to be easy.

The Flight Sergeant took him right into London.

'No bother, mate, no bother at all,' he said when Tom protested. He dropped him at Oxford Circus, close enough to the underground. Tom was grateful but when the squat blue car had pulled away from the kerb he hailed a taxi. He needed some solitude before facing the bereavement.

Cassie opened the door before he had even rung the bell and he knew she must have been watching for him from the sitting room window. She was not made up, but her blond hair was combed and she wore a navy jumper and a grey skirt. She had no shoes on, it made her look very small and very young. Tom and she put their arms around each other, holding each other, allowing their sadness to unite them. Standing in the hall behind them Kate caught her breath for Cassie and her son looked like a couple. Cassie broke from him first and Kate could see the tears on Tom's cheeks. She was uncertain what to do, wondering if she was intruding on the family, and then she saw that Tom was holding his hands out to her and she ran to him. After a moment he released her and turned back to Cassie.

'Where's Dad?' he asked.

'In his study. He didn't want me to call you back here.'

'Of course not.'

'But I had to.'

'I know that too. And I should be here.'

Tom left his kit bag where it was in the hall and went to his father. He found Charles at his desk. There were a number of papers in front of him, but he was not looking at them. He seemed to be staring ahead at nothing and, aware that Tom must have noticed, he said, 'I can't concentrate.'

Tom nodded. He went to the decanter and poured two glasses of whisky for his father and himself and he thought of how, just a little time before he had gone to serve Queen and country, Charles had performed the same task for him and how he had told him the Army would make a man of him. As he set the glasses down on the desk he realised Charles had been right.

Charles took one of the glasses. 'Thank you for coming back, Tom. I must say that I argued with your mother about it, I didn't think it was necessary. I still don't but nevertheless now that you are here I have to admit to being very glad.'

Tom nodded again. 'To Grandfather,' he said, offering his glass in a toast.

'To Father,' and Tom averted his head to allow his father to deal with momentary, but unwelcome, wet eyes.

'How is it, Berlin?' Charles asked as soon as he could.

'Not that easy,' his son replied. 'The Russians may not be firing bullets at the moment but we all know it is a siege town.'

'Changes you, doesn't it, knowing that?'

'Yes.'

The two men drank quietly together, aware that they were equals, sharing experience – it was the first time that they had ever done such a thing.

·In the kitchen Cassie showed Kate how to thicken a casserole by mixing together a paste of flour and butter. 'It makes the sauce smoother and richer,' she said, and as she talked she was aware that Tom was with his father behind a closed door, separated from her.

That night, in bed, Cassie reached for Charles.

'I'm sorry, Cassie, but I am just not in the mood.'

'Charles, I don't mean sex, I just want to hold you and comfort you.'

'I'm fine, thank you,' he said and turned on his side.

Cassie had never felt so lonely in her life.

# Chapter Seven
## 1960

Kate was working as a journalist on the local newspaper. She liked writing, but she didn't particularly enjoy the sycophantic pieces about local benefactors, or even the business of reporting fires and the occasional crime, mostly robbery – there was very little murder, for Hampstead was a law-abiding place.

When she could, she applied for a job on a national newspaper. She sent some cuttings and was asked up for an interview. She did not know what to expect but she was determined to give of her best.

'What I try to do is to get under the skin of ordinary people in extraordinary situations. Because it is the situation that determines how the person develops, and I think one can say more about robbery by interviewing a thief than by quoting any number of dry statistics and so-called experts. That's why the profile pieces interest me most.'

Kate cleared her throat. She was nervous, but she crossed her legs neatly, conscious that she was displaying just a little of her nylon-clad thighs. She would have liked to have pulled her skirt down, but that would have looked silly. She just hoped she wasn't making too much of a fool of herself.

She was sitting in an Editor's office, overlooking Fleet Street. She had told herself not to be scared as she had walked up from the Temple tube station through Bouverie Street. There was almost a smell of ink in the air. Fat rolls of paper were stacked on the pavements ready for the presses, vans were parked in neat rows waiting for the finished editions. Knots of printers and drivers and security men stood around smoking or watching as they swapped stories. She kept her eyes down as she hurried past them. It was all very different from a local newspaper.

She got a job – on the diary.

Cassie thought it was very funny. She teased Kate gently, she who dreamt of fame and strong, good writing was to work on the social diary. Her own parents, on the other hand, were somewhat impressed.

'You'll meet some interesting people there,' her mother said. She was dishing up the dinner – a shepherd's pie – in the kitchen. It was a simple room – cream cabinets and a lino floor – but there was always a bunch of flowers, whatever was in the garden, on the table. Kate loved her mother's shepherd's pie, there was nothing leftover-ish about Mrs Sullivan's version, just fresh meat and onions and carrots topped with thick mashed potato. The kitchen was warm and smelt of cakes. Mrs Sullivan cooked for the Friends of the local hospital.

'Just get your head down and do your job as well as you can,' Kate's father said. 'That's how you'll get noticed.'

'Cassie thinks it's funny that I am working on a social diary,' Kate told him.

'Mrs Bray is an American lady. I haven't met her, but it seems to me that she has different views to your mother and I.'

'She did ask you both to dinner when Tom came home from Germany on his last leave.'

'Tom is a very nice boy, my dear, but there is nothing formal about your relationship so it would be wrong for us to meet the Brays,' Mrs Sullivan interjected as she carried a tray of three steaming hot cups of cocoa over to the kitchen table where Kate and her father were seated. As she took a cup she realised that all family discussions, for good or bad, took place over the kitchen table, and there was usually a cup of something to help the words down. She wondered where the Brays sat for their discussions.

'Mr Bray was in the Air Force, wasn't he?' Kate's father asked. Kate was surprised as he had never expressed any interest in Tom's family before.

'Yes, I think he was,' Kate replied, glancing up at the photograph of her father and mother on their wedding day. Mrs Sullivan was wearing a borrowed wedding dress and Mr Sullivan was proudly displaying his newly acquired sergeant's stripes.

Kate's first job was to cover the Queen Charlotte's Ball, the debutantes' event of the year. Kate worried about what she should wear, but a seasoned hack of 24 told her that she need not worry, as a representative of the 'penny press' she would not be allowed into the actual ballroom but would be relegated to the balcony from where she would merely watch the events of the evening. Nevertheless she wore a royal-blue taffeta cocktail dress with a sweetheart neckline – her mother had made it. As she zipped it up in the ladies' lavatory at work she pondered on how far she had come since Aldermaston in 1958. She hadn't been on the last march, neither had Cassie. They were paid-up members of CND so they hadn't betrayed their principles, but Cassie had reasoned for both of them that lots of protesters went now. They had gone when it was important, when there had been very few of them.

The ball was an extraordinary experience for Kate. She observed the upper classes presenting their daughters to society in the hope that within the whirl of the 'season' they would find a suitable partner for life – it wasn't a question of having a good time, it was about the serious business of marriage.

The ball heralded the start of it all. Originally, Queen Charlotte, the wife of George III, had invited the daughters of the aristocracy to celebrate her birthday and they had all had a piece of her cake. Now the event was staged for charity and there were no Queens present, but there was an aristocrat. The girls trooped down the wide staircase that led from the balcony to the floor of the great ballroom at the Grosvenor House Hotel, their long white dresses skimming the stairs, and formed rows behind a white birthday cake that was supposed to symbolise Queen Charlotte's. When they had all filed in, they moved forward and curtseyed to the aristocrat.

'They are curtseying to the bloody cake!' one of the older hacks muttered.

After they had both filed their pieces, he invited Kate for a drink. She accepted, feeling extremely silly in her cocktail dress. She pulled her coat over it, trying to hide the voluminous skirt.

'This isn't what I wanted to do at all,' she moaned into her lager.

'You mean you'd like to be at that ball?'

'You must be joking. I want to do serious pieces. All I do is write flippant rubbish.'

She was very upset at the way everyone around her laughed.

While Kate agonised over her professionalism, Tom broke the news to Helga that he would soon be finished with the Army.

'You will go back to England?'

'Yes, I'm going to Cambridge University,' he said, 'and I am going back to Kate.' Helga heard the love in his voice.

'And me?' she couldn't help but ask.

'You've been a really good friend and I care for you very much,' Tom said quietly. He wanted her to understand that he meant what he was

155

saying but as he looked into her face he realised that it was not enough, she was in love with him. It hadn't occurred to Tom that such a thing might happen and he felt deep remorse for the hurt he was causing her. The worst part was that there was nothing he could do about it.

Tom arrived back in a London fog. The thick grey vapour stifled him even as he descended from the train. He walked quickly down the platform looking for Kate. They had not seen each other for nine months and in his impatience for a sight of her he pushed through the other travellers without even noticing them. He saw her standing by the ticket barrier, the schoolgirl raincoat had been replaced by a red winter coat, her hair, damp from the London drizzle, clung to her shoulders. Tom thought she was more beautiful than ever. He held her very tight for a very long time. Neither of them could speak, nor even look at each other, they touched, that was enough.

When they could bear to step back from each other, Tom realised that Cassie had come to meet him too. As he turned to greet her he wondered why she had come to the station, it was Kate he wanted. Then he remembered that whenever he had gone somewhere when he was a child, even if it were only on a school outing, Cassie had always been the one to welcome him home. He had always said, when he was a child, that she was the homecoming. Aware that he didn't want her now, he put his arm around her shoulder in what he knew was a conciliatory gesture.

'How are you, Mum?' he asked.

'Fine, Tom,' she answered, removing herself from his encircling arm. He felt sad that she sensed he was making an effort.

Cassie found it impossible to deal with the surge of pain she had felt at Tom's greeting. She had kept quiet as she walked beside the lovers but she felt so alone. She had suggested, perhaps a shade too brightly, that they sit in the back of the car together whilst she drove. But Tom had asked if he could drive and so she found herself sitting in the back seat whilst Kate took the front.

She excused herself very quickly when they returned to the house. She had prepared dinner, and of course Charles would be there, but it was still only five o'clock and she was going to her studio.

She was working on a series of flower paintings, having abandoned the series on motherhood because she still could not evolve the picture that would symbolise the separation between mother and child. She grabbed some geranium-red paint and splashed a thick but uneven red cross all over the soft flowery hues. She threw the canvas off the easel and pinned up a piece of white cartridge paper, she took black charcoal and started to sketch without a plan or an idea, just wanting to see what would come out. She drew Tom and Kate, kissing – they were deliberately blurred, almost as if the watcher didn't really want to see them. She drew herself at the side watching.

After it was dark Tom came to fetch her.

'Dad's home,' he said. 'He's brought champagne.'

He walked around her so he could see what she was working on, using his old privilege. He stood quietly for a moment and Cassie wondered, momentarily ashamed of her excesses, what he would say.

'Paris again,' were the words he used.

She was shocked. She looked at the work again, it was about being on the outside of love. Once there had been Joshua, was it now going to be Tom?

She got a little drunk over dinner. She looked at Kate sitting opposite Tom, next to Charles, and she told herself that she felt good about the lovers now. Tom was being very kind to her. He kept her glass filled, complimented her on her appearance, told little anecdotes about her. It was very nice.

Kate was bemused by Cassie's behaviour. Despite the American woman's excesses she liked her very much, but Cassie was behaving like a giggling girl on her first date and Tom was pandering to her. He was plying her with wine and to Kate it was almost as if they were flirting with each other. She glanced over at Charles. He looked bored and she knew he had seen it all before.

The familiar black despair hit Cassie as soon as she sobered up. She knew she was mercurial. On a good day the colour of life would be bright and clear, there would be opportunity, work would nourish and excite her, people would be loved, obligations would be met; but on the bad days, when the rats gnawed at her stomach, when there was no light, just an anguish that swamped and swallowed her, she would sink into that terrible apathy. Tasks would be completed, but not willingly, it would be all slapdash shortcuts. In the past she could have turned to her son to break the thick greyness. But now he was no longer there for her, he was in his room behind a closed door and she had to deal with it on her own.

After four days she telephoned Yvonne. The little Frenchwoman came, driving her car precariously through Hampstead; Cassie always worried about her driving. Yvonne, she knew, was frightened of the roads, but as a single woman she would never give in to her fear.

'You are so brave,' Cassie said as she opened the door. She knew she looked awful: no make-up, her clothes slightly too tight. She was eating constantly, little treks to the refrigerator or to the biscuit tin, she just couldn't stop. Usually she managed to control herself, but now she didn't care any more – no one was interested in how she looked.

'Brave?' said Yvonne. She carried flowers – roses, Cassie's favourite. 'Brave at negotiating these horrible little roads, or brave at confronting you?'

Cassie smiled weakly. 'Both,' she said.

'Are you working?' Yvonne asked Cassie as she made coffee. She was at home in Cassie's house. She knew where things were.

'I can't. I have no ideas. No new thoughts.'

'What about the flowers?'

'Trite.'

'No . . . not if you develop the idea.'

'Let's be honest, Yvonne, I'm not really good enough to be great.'

'No, you're not.' Cassie stared at her, shocked. 'But you are good enough to be good. You are stale, Cassie. As an artist you feed on yourself – you should go out and look at others' work. Rauschenberg is interesting, he is an inventive artist doing work that provokes a response.'

'I am far too romantic to have anything in common with Rauschenberg. I'm searching for a way out of this. I'm beginning to read a lot, Conrad interests me. Do you know his work, Yvonne?'

The Frenchwoman shook her head.

'He shapes his plots around the inner personality of the character. That's what I want to do in my art. But I can't get it out, it's stuck somewhere here.' She pointed to the space between her breasts and her stomach. 'I feel as if I am halfway up a mountain and it's covered in clouds. I know that once I get through those clouds the top will be beautiful but there isn't much air and I can't get my breath, and I am suffering.'

'Then get off the mountain,' Yvonne said.

'I can't.'

'Then give yourself a different kind of break. Go into an art college and teach for a while.'

'I'm no teacher.'

'Then go away, get some new air. It will help you.'

Cassie was looking directly at Yvonne. The Frenchwoman realised that the American was still young, and rather beautiful with her straight neck, fine angled chin and those huge wide eyes. If Cassie had heard herself described as beautiful she would have gazed in a mirror and then she would have turned from her own reflection, shrugging off any praise, for she did not believe in her own attractiveness.

Unlike Yvonne, who had long ago acknowledged, and indeed happily accepted, her lesbian status. She had an arrangement that suited her well enough. It was private, she didn't discuss it with Cassie – she was sure that Cassie could never accept her preference for women. Her lover was a married woman, the wife of an eminent art critic. With her Yvonne knew great joy. She was godmother to her lover's second child, a girl, who was now ten; there were four children in all, the other three were boys. Such an arrangement allowed for family intimacies and a sense of belonging. If asked, Yvonne would have said she was a happy woman. Not so her poor Cassie.

'Why not go to America for a while?' Yvonne said, draining her coffee cup. 'You haven't seen your mother for at least a year. Suggest to Charles that you all go. A family vacation before Tom goes to Cambridge.'

'Oh, he won't want to go, he won't want to leave Kate.'

'Then take her with you. What a pleasure to have such a lovely young girl around.'

After Yvonne's visit, Cassie felt stronger and able to contemplate an outing. She decided to pay a call on John Bravington. Bravington loved Cassie but he knew she was far too lacking in awareness of her own sexuality to ever contemplate an affair and he accepted that. On every other level he tried to force Cassie to face herself. They argued a lot, of course, for Cassie was no wimp, and the subject was usually Tom.

'You've always loved that boy too much,' Bravington told her. 'You've used him to block all your discomforts. If you faced the dirtier side of life you might be a better painter.'

'I don't bury myself in a fantasy world. I know what's out there.'

'You don't, Cassie. You don't see beyond your nose.'

Bravington knew he was shouting but he couldn't help himself. Cassie made him so cross. They were in his study at school. She had just popped in on an off-chance, she said. Cassie never normally 'popped in'. She looked sad and wan. A bit of make-up washed over white cheeks, strained eyes and a pinched mouth in a half-hearted attempt at camouflage did nothing to help her. She had mentioned brightly that she wasn't painting.

159

'Yvonne suggested that we should all go to America for a holiday – Kate too. I'll be able to go to some exhibitions. It'll be good for me.'

She was stretched out in a wing-chair, her feet crossed at the ankles, her coat still on, but open so he could see the neat red dress she wore. He hated her in red, but it wasn't his place to say so. He liked her in black but she never wore it during the time of her depression. He always knew when Cassie was gripped by the monster for he recognised it, he suffered himself.

Cassie revealed herself to no one except Yvonne and John. Other acquaintances were part of her social life, giving form to that part of her life which was governed by Charles' requirements. There were business evenings to attend, or perhaps outings with other couples, except that they were not Cassie's intimates. She didn't dislike any of them but they did not touch her inner self. The Sampsons were a particular example, although of course Charles was close to David and as such Marilyn had become his friend too. Cassie knew a number of fellow artists, but surprisingly few had any place in her life for she existed within herself.

On the evening of the day that Yvonne had visited, Cassie and Charles were to accompany Roger and Loretta Mallory to the cinema. There was a new film, *Never On Sunday*, directed by Jules Dassin and starring a voluptuous Greek beauty called Melina Mercouri. The film's irreverent attitude towards sex interested Cassie because it was the first time she had observed that passion might be fun. After the performance was over, Cassie and Charles sat with the Mallorys over dinner at a smart restaurant where the waiters bobbed attention and offered fish covered in different flavoured glutinous sauces with overcooked vegetables. Cassie talked tentatively of the heady atmosphere of the Greek summer.

'We've never been to Greece,' she told Loretta, a heavily made-up woman whose style indicated that she favoured Chanel No. 5 and her husband's millions.

'It's delightful. You must go, all those little tavernas, and the Greeks are incredibly hospitable. And of course you must see the Parthenon, it's quite incredible.'

'What moved you so much about it?' Cassie's tone was rather belligerent. She didn't mean to be, but Loretta's enthusiasm had irritated her as indeed the lady herself irritated her. Loretta was on a committee for children's mental health and she was constantly pestering Cassie for paintings or donations and even expecting her to

160

attend functions. Cassie gave her money while ensuring that she always had a ready excuse for the rest of the demands.

'Well, its lines, its, er. . .' Loretta was obviously flustered and Roger Mallory smoothly interrupted her temporary loss of words.

'It was all knocked down in a naval battle. Stood all those years and then the Venetians aim bloody cannon at it. Disgraceful.'

In the car on the way home Cassie observed to Charles that it was not likely to have been the ecstacy of her response to classical Greek architecture that had prevented Loretta's flow of speech but more likely that she didn't know what to say.

'You are cruel, Cassie. It doesn't matter a toss whether she is articulate or not. She's a good kind woman who couldn't have a child. They adopted a girl when she was two days old and then found out she was a mongol. Loretta insisted on keeping the baby. She said at the time that if she had borne her and she had been a mongol she would have kept her, and now that she had chosen one who was a mongol she would still keep her.'

'I didn't know that,' Cassie said quietly, feeling ashamed.

'There's a lot you don't know,' Charles snapped.

Cassie didn't like Charles' tone, but she was in no mood for confrontation. Her attack on Loretta and her subsequent discovery of Loretta's situation in life was a matter of great concern to Cassie. She had to question her behaviour and her judgements, but she was not prepared to do that even with Charles until she had time for solitary contemplation.

However, such personal thoughts were shelved the following morning when she telephoned Loretta and offered her a painting for her next raffle and Loretta was gushingly nice.

'Oh Cassie, that is lovely of you. Will you come and present it yourself to the lucky winner?'

Cassie drew the line at personal participation and graciously declined, unaware of Roger Mallory's comment as the telephone went down. 'My God, what an arrogant woman she is.'

'I've got a picture out of her and a raffle will raise a lot of money. That's the only thing that is important.'

Roger looked at his wife as she sat at her cream and gold dressing table and noticed that without her make-up she looked desperately tired. He loved her so very much. 'Come back to bed, darling,' he said, patting the sheets.

'To sleep?' Loretta said laughingly.

'Sleep afterwards,' he said, holding out his arms.

Loretta slipped off her pink satin nightdress. As she nestled in her husband's arms she murmured, 'But I can't sleep afterwards. Our little girl will need some help with her breakfast and although Nanny is patient I like to be there.'

'I know you do,' said Roger and kissed his wife so tenderly.

As Loretta and Roger made love, Cassie mooted Yvonne's suggestion of a family holiday in America.

'Why not?' said Charles to Cassie's surprise.

He had actually been dreading the thought of a summer holiday alone with Cassie. Having managed to avoid it the previous year by offering work as his excuse, he had realised that any repetition of that excuse would inevitably bring about some form of confrontation, as had almost happened the previous evening. He had been surprised at himself, but he had been incredibly angry at Cassie's sense of superiority. The whole matter had made him behave totally out of character. Such outbursts were not to his liking, he had always preferred to avoid difficulty. It would have come as no surprise to those who knew him well to have discovered that he had chosen his secretary as his 'friend', as he liked to call her. She was there, in the next office, typing his letters, sharing his thoughts and worries. There was no need to pick up a telephone, or to have the affair intrude on his life at home; but since Tom had become involved with Kate, Charles had increasingly felt Cassie to be the interloper. She had so many requirements. It wasn't that she voiced them but Charles knew she had turned to him as a replacement for Tom. At first he had been glad for he hoped they could at least have a friendship, but Cassie's emotional outpourings and expectations were not what he needed. His secretary and her reserved demeanour (which belied her extraordinary passions in bed) were far more attractive; too attractive, he had begun to realise.

And Cassie, tuned like an instrument to be fragile and susceptible, only heard her own song. She wanted Charles and Yvonne to be her chorus, but she was deaf to the music of a secretary and an art critic's wife.

Kate was anxious about the holiday. She hadn't wanted to accept the Brays' generosity. It wasn't a churlish refusal. It was merely embarrassment at such largesse. She told Tom. They were sitting in a coffee bar just off Fleet Street. It was lunchtime.

'I understand exactly how you feel,' he told her, after the waitress

162

had delivered their cheese sandwiches and lukewarm cappuccinos, 'but without you, I won't go, and without me. . .' He paused, stirring a lot of sugar into his coffee. 'Let's just say my mother will have a bad time and my father will have a worse time.' He sighed and then leaned across and squeezed Kate's hand. 'And anyway, I want you to meet my grandmother. And the wondrous Cleo. She brought my mother up. Unless you meet them you can never fully understand either of us.'

'You certainly have a complex relationship with Cassie. Sometimes I admit it bothers me a little.' The words were out before Kate could stop them.

'What do you mean?' Tom asked, his voice was suddenly quiet.

'Well, I mean when you came back from Germany you didn't greet her like she was your mother. You were angry she was there. But later, at dinner, when she got drunk, you were soft, I know it sounds ridiculous, but it was almost a loving relationship. And then almost in the same breath you can suddenly be very unkind to her.'

Kate was aware she had said too much, but she wasn't sorry. She was so confused by this warm, overpowering woman who treated her as both a friend and a rival. She hoped Tom would help her, but she could see that he wasn't going to, his face had become set, his normally soft, full mouth hard. She pulled her coat on, gathered up her handbag and her gloves.

'I must get back,' she said, too quickly. 'I'll have to think about a way of paying for my own ticket.'

She swallowed her coffee, pecked him on the cheek and walked rapidly out of the coffee bar hearing her own heels clicking across the floor.

Tom made no attempt to follow Kate. He wasn't angry with her for talking about his mother, indeed he understood her distress for he was aware of the unfathomable depths between Cassie and himself. As a child he had relished that closeness. He remembered the hours in her arms, in her bed, after his father had gone to work. They would wait until Charles had gone through the front door and shut it behind him and then they would grab a tray. Cassie would put her coffee on it, and milk for him, and chocolate cookies for both of them. She made wonderful cookies, soft and gooey inside with huge chocolate drops that Grandma Jane used to send from America. Those times were happy and funny. They seemed to laugh so much, whether it was from the tickling, or the silly jokes, or the crumbs in the bed. After he had gone with her to Grandfather Clinton's funeral he had stopped getting into her bed. He was never quite sure why but he had a sense that sleeping with one's mother was not quite right. It was strange but when he was growing up he had never thought of Cassie as an interfering mother. Other mothers interfered, they nagged their children, but she never nagged and yet now it was different, her presence intruded on every private moment and he despaired of ever being free of her. He was about to go to Cambridge University and he wanted to get on with the living of his life and the loving of Kate. He wanted Cassie to let him go. He deeply resented her for not doing so. And yet he knew he loved her nonetheless.

It was Kate's father who solved Kate's dilemma.

'Do you *want* to go with them, or is all this faffing just an excuse?' he asked his daughter. He was a blunt man, not given to artifice.

'Of course I want to go. I want to be with Tom. And I want to see America.'

'Well why don't you use some of that money your mother and I have been saving for you? There's a fair bit there. It's yours to do with what you like.'

Kate knew, of course, that her parents had opened a savings account for her when she was born, but she had no idea how much was there, or when indeed she might use it. Birthday and Christmas money was never put in that account, those presents had always gone into the post office – accessible whenever she wanted. After all that was hers to be talked about and discussed. She remembered an argument about roller skates, she had wanted a pair so badly, her best friend at school had a pair. Her parents had been implacable in their refusal.

'My post office account is mine,' she remembered she had shouted, red-faced with rage.

'You haven't got enough,' her father had told her. 'You insisted on buying that doll at Christmas.'

Kate had been heartbroken at her childish indulgence of just six months previously. She had gone up into her bedroom, slammed the door and thrown the doll into the back of her cupboard. That night as she lay in her bed, she thought she heard her doll crying so she climbed out of the blankets, opened the cupboard door, rummaged at the back and rescued the poor crumpled thing. When her mother came to kiss her goodnight she found her ten-year-old asleep, with the doll in her arms. But the next day it was back in the cupboard, on the shelf with the other toys she no longer used. She never did get her roller skates.

164

And now, all these years later, her father was opening his desk and taking out a bank book. He knew exactly where it was, there were three books with an elastic band around them. The one he wanted was in the middle; he removed it quickly and handed it to Kate.

She wanted to hug him, but she knew better. He would have been very embarrassed. Instead she just said thank you. On her way up to her bedroom she had gone into the kitchen, her mother was washing up. She kissed her on the cheek. She didn't need to say anything.

There was £1090 in her account. She transferred £500 into her current account, went into a travel agent and found out the cost of her air fare to New York. That night she wrote a letter to Charles, enclosing her cheque and sent it to his office. Two days later she received a letter back thanking her for her cheque. She felt very dignified, now she could look forward to her holiday.

'Why did you take it? The girl hasn't much money!' Cassie exploded to Charles.

'Because she wanted me to,' Charles answered firmly.

Cassie decided that because Kate had spent so much money on the ticket she would have little left for frippery. It would be Cassie's responsibility to augment the young girl's wardrobe. With that end in view, she went to Debenham and Freebody. She loved that store with its grand staircase and elegant ladies' cloakroom. If she found the sales ladies a little daunting she kept the information to herself. Cassie shopped carefully, treading the opulent grey carpet backwards and forwards in her attempts to find the most appealing garments. She relied on her artist's sense of what would be right for Kate. Eventually she chose a pretty shirt-waister dress in white broderie anglaise with a pink sash, and a turquoise swimming costume trimmed with a small frill, top and bottom. When the sales lady queried the size, Cassie explained they were for her son's girlfriend.

Kate thanked her profusely enough. It was Tom who told Cassie she had been presumptuous.

If, later, Kate were to try and describe the ecstasy she experienced on that American holiday, she would have found it hard. Passion, joy and happiness are trite words to describe a time of such intense pleasure.

They flew into New York at dusk. The sky was a fondant pink streaked with tongues of grey and the lights on the huge skyscrapers flickered like thousands of candles. In the twilight the Hudson River looked like a shining silver road.

165

'Broadway is just down there,' Tom whispered, pointing through the aircraft window. 'I saw my first play there when I was seven. It was a musical called *Brigadoon*. Cassie took me. That was when I decided that I wanted to work on the stage.' Kate felt as if she had come to fairyland.

When they landed Kate knew she had come out of the world of yesterday into the world of tomorrow. The lights were brighter, the roads were wider, the cars were bigger. The sense of haste confused her. The policemen carried guns and chewed gum. Kate had no idea how she would have coped if she'd been alone.

They were to spend the night at Cassie's mother's apartment. Mrs Fleming was already installed in the house at East Hampton.

'No one spends the summer in the city,' Cassie told Kate by way of explanation.

A cab took them to the corner of Madison Avenue and 81st Street.

'The Upper East Side. Smart!' Charles reported.

A black attendant in a green uniform quietly embellished with gold buttons took their cases. He called Tom 'Master Tom', and Charles and Cassie acquired a Mr and Miss in front of their first names. This, Kate was told, was Henry. He had only been superintendent of the building for ten years, quite a newcomer. As the lift reached the fifth floor the door was flung open and Cassie was embraced by plump black arms and an ample body.

'Child, child,' their owner crooned in what Kate assumed to be a Southern drawl.

After some moments the two women parted, but Cassie still held a black hand. Kate was amazed to see tears on her cheek. Charles received a short and respectful greeting, 'How are you, Mr Bray?'

But then it was Tom's turn. There was no 'child, child', but the greeting was powerful and proprietorial and Kate could see that these people loved each other.

'So you are Tom's girl,' the black woman said.

Kate flushed. No one had called her 'Tom's girl' before.

'I'm Cleo. And I've looked after this boy's mother since she was a small girl.'

It was only then that Kate realised that the woman had grey hair and heavily lined skin.

Cleo informed Kate that she had worked for the Fleming family for thirty years. 'But I never go to East Hampton. Mrs Fleming has Bertha there.' The voice was clipped so Kate didn't ask about Bertha.

The apartment amazed Kate. It consisted of three bedrooms, each with its own bathroom. The walls were hung with Impressionist paintings of the kind she had only looked at in museums. There was a cream carpet and deep luxurious sofas of the same colour. The occasional furniture was antique. She would have liked to have remarked to Tom that only the rich could afford carpets and furniture of such a colour, but then she realised she would have been talking about Tom's grandmother. Kate was disappointed when she saw that all the windows were covered by thick white net curtains so that there was no view. The inner hall was a surprise for it was the only personal area of Jane Fleming's home, lined with books and photographs. A separate dining room was already laid for what Kate considered to be a formal dinner. She realised she was exhausted, her arms felt heavy and she was lightheaded. She glanced at her watch, surprised to see it was only seven o'clock in the evening.

'You've actually been awake for eighteen hours, Kate. And you're probably feeling awful. It's the jet lag. It'll take you a few days to adjust because New York's six hours behind England so to you it's one o'clock in the morning now. You just have to ease yourself in.' Kate wanted to laugh, Cassie suddenly sounded so American.

'Draw yourself a tub,' Cleo said to her; for a moment Kate didn't understand.

'A bath,' Cassie interjected. 'We'll have one of Cleo's delicious dinners in about an hour and then bed by nine o'clock.'

Kate fervently wished she could go to bed straight after her bath, the thought of dinner, however delicious, was not welcome. However she was almost euphoric at the luxury of what had once been Cassie's bedroom. 'Done over' as a guest room since that time, it was still old rose and white, and quite lovely.

Whilst Kate relaxed in hot water enjoying a loving Tom who came to her with coffee and himself, Cassie sat again in the wicker chair in Cleo's kitchen and listened to the sound of her past, allowing it to seduce and comfort her.

'I've missed you,' she said.

'And I miss you, child. Tom's growin' up. Got himself a nice girl.'

'Oh Cleo,' Cassie whispered, 'I have been so lonely.' She held out her hands to Cleo and the black woman took them and pulled Cassie close to her and cradled her and Cassie did not see the anxiety in her eyes.

*

167

In the privacy of his bedroom Charles telephoned his office.

'Just to tell you we've arrived. It's going to be harder to be away from you than I anticipated.'

Kate was unprepared for the heat of the streets in the New York summer, it was quite a shock after the chill of the air-conditioned interiors. She had dressed as Cassie had, in a cotton skirt and blouse, but she had put on a jumper – it was really cold in the Fleming apartment. As soon as she stepped out of the building, the doors held open by the ubiquitous Henry, the hot air stifled her.

'You have to be careful here,' Charles said. 'One can end up with the most dreadful cold from the extraordinary habit of living in a fridge while the outside temperature is at boiling point.'

'I have to say I don't like the air conditioning either,' Cassie said as she hailed a cab, pushing in front of three people trying to do the same thing.

'We're going to the Guggenheim,' Tom said.

'The museum?' asked Kate.

'Yup, that way my father can worship at the feet of Frank Lloyd Wright and my mother can stare at the Cubists like Braque and Surrealists like Magritte and Pop artists like Warhol.'

'Art is more available in this country, Kate,' Charles told her.

'That's because we aren't an elitist society,' Cassie added.

'How can you say that, Mum?'

'We may have our snobbery, but we don't close doors on anyone,' Cassie replied hotly.

'Do you think of yourself as an American?' Kate asked as the cab drew up outside the spiral building that was the Guggenheim.

'I do when I first come home, but after a while I realise I have lived in Europe longer than I lived in America.'

The marvels of modern architecture awaited them. In the cream expanse of a museum unlike anything that even Cassie had ever seen before, Calder's mobiles moved in the air, Segal's statues stood in judgement, Warhol's cans, Rothko's dancing whorls and lines and Pollock's action paintings pursued her and she was an artist again. Over lunch she vibrated with excitement and was perhaps a little argumentative.

'You see, what America is about, Charles, is that there is a freshness here. Even in the architecture individuality is more important than function.'

168

'That's rubbish, Cassie. You know very well that the international style of high-rise housing and offices came out of this.' He pointed to the towering buildings that Kate privately thought turned the streets into cages.

The food was a delicious lobster salad made with crisp green lettuce, unlike anything Kate had eaten at home, with huge chunks of succulent sweet white meat. 'If heaven is to do with food I have arrived,' she said unselfconsciously.

'That's all very well, but how do you feel about the architecture?' Tom said laughingly and Kate was happy to see that Charles and Cassie laughed too.

Cassie seemed to calm down then. 'I am sorry, darling,' she said to Charles, laying her hand over his. 'I just get a bit hyped, it's all those colours and styles and ideas, they've got to me.'

Charles smiled back at her, but he didn't take her hand, he just slipped his away after a moment or two.

East Hampton had white clapboard houses with porches and gardens, and land around each plot. Some of them fronted the beach. There was a little church and just one main shopping street – commercial vulgarity had no place there.

Jane Fleming was a strong crusty lady who wore white trousers and her late husband's old sailing sweaters. She favoured a yachting cap during the day. At night she would change into a cotton skirt and a shirt, presiding over family dinner with authority and humour. Tom obviously loved her. And she made it her business to get to know Kate, but there was no question of her engineering an uncomfortable rendezvous, that wasn't her way.

Jane was still a political woman. Although a Democrat, she had no love of the Kennedys – she still remembered Joe Kennedy's addiction to the Nazi cause. She was a devotee of Adlai Stevenson who'd been defeated in 1956.

'They're conning the people,' she said as she sat in her favourite high-backed chair watching on television as Kennedy thrilled and touched the flesh. 'All the razzamatazz, but none of the stuff of real reform. Mark my words, he'll never bring in civil rights. He hasn't got the savvy to get it through Congress.'

Kate was fascinated by the circus, it was all so different from an English election where the issues were debated in such a glitterless process. If only she could have covered it for the *Mercury*, but her features editor hadn't taken her seriously. When she had broached the subject he had told her just to relax and to have a wonderful holiday. At the time she had been absolutely furious.

So now that she was actually in America, instead of hitting the campaign trail she sat and watched the bandwagon on the television with Tom's grandmother whilst Cassie painted, or sunned herself, or visited with old friends, and Tom fished with his father. Kate had established that demarcation herself. On the first evening Charles had invited them both to sail with him, but Kate had declined. Tom had rushed back early, feeling bad for being away from her.

'You must spend some time with your dad. I don't need you with me the whole time, and anyway little boats make me very seasick. I once went in one with my dad when I was about eight. He lived to regret it, I can tell you.'

Tom laughed. 'But just what will you get up to when I am out?' he said. 'Cassie is off painting and all Grandma does is watch television.'

'I am very happy watching the brouhaha on television with your grandmother, and when I am not doing that I shall lie in the sun and feel the heat eating into me, here between my legs.' She ran her hand over the warm V of her bikini bottom and invited Tom to do the same. As she felt his hand closing over her she whispered, 'And I shall think of you and wait for you to come back.'

So Tom went sailing and enjoyed being with his father. They concentrated on the physical business of sailing, of using the elements to cut through the water in the cleanest, fastest way.

Charles, of course, was captain and Tom crewed. But Charles would step back and allow him the rudder. They both admitted that they would have liked to have faced the danger of a rough sea instead of this gentle warm-weather sailing.

'I'd like to taste the edge,' Charles said. Tom bit his lip and nodded in agreement. He could see how handsome his father was. His skin was lined of course beneath the tan, but the blond hair had aged kindly to a silver grey, the eyes were still clear. 'We could sail harder,' Charles added.

'Let's at least try that,' said Tom, and the catamaran that Jane had purchased for her family was turned into the wind. However, the weather was too kind; there was no edge to be found on those waves.

Cassie invited Kate to visit her old friend Beth with her.

'We were in Paris together,' she told her by way of an introduction to

Beth's role in her life. Kate was delighted for she would have the opportunity to learn more about Cassie. However, the enticement was even greater when she discovered that Beth was a political wife. Her husband was a Kennedy intimate.

Kate confided in Jane. 'Do you think, if I play my cards right, I might get an interview?'

'You'll get nothing interesting 'cause those ladies aren't interesting, but you can try.'

Cassie drove Kate to Beth's house on the other side of town. Kate noticed that she had dressed carefully with just a little pink lipstick. She wore a turquoise silk dress with matching shoes. Kate felt she should put on the broderie anglaise outfit that Cassie had bought her, even though it made her look like a pudding.

'Were you close, you and Beth?' she asked Cassie.

'We were but then we grew apart. I was in love with my glamorous European and Beth went out with Marvin who worked at the American Embassy. And she married him,' Cassie said laughingly.

'What was he like, Cassie?' Kate found herself asking.

'I assume you don't mean Marvin,' Cassie said carefully, not looking at Kate. 'He was very beautiful, at least he was to me,' Cassie replied as she turned into the drive of a stately property that lay back from the beach within its own grounds. She was glad they had reached their destination because she had no wish to discuss Joshua Gottlieb even with Kate. He was private, he belonged to her even if she chose not to think of him.

A butler opened the door. Beth was waiting for them in the garden room. It was an elegant room with iron tables and chairs and a chaise longue. Tea was laid out formally on white cloths; there were scones and jam and sandwiches; not quite the food that Kate had grown to enjoy on her holiday. Jane Fleming offered clams, fresh crab, barbecued ribs, and jacket potatoes with lashings of butter and bowls of creamy coleslaw. There were even homemade corn muffins and waffles and maple syrup; Kate loved it all. In Beth's house now, dressed in her shirt-waister, she declined the offer of a sandwich and allied herself totally with Cassie. Beth, in a yellow dress, was sitting on her chaise longue – and obviously in judgement.

'Your hair, Cassie. You know, you haven't altered the style since you were in Paris. Each time you come I hope you are going to wear something a little more becoming for your age, but look at you.'

'Beth, my dear, you live a more formal life than I do,' Cassie came back easily, 'I just paint.'

'Do you do well?' Beth asked.

'Fortunately I don't have to "do well", as you call it,' Cassie answered tartly, and Kate wondered about their relationship. But then the women shifted in their chairs and tried to be intimate with each other. They asked about the welfare of their respective children and husbands. Beth offered little insight into the life of a woman who dallied in the corridors of power. Kate found it extraordinary that she had so little to say of importance. She discussed how she had redecorated her home in Washington: Jackie had liked it. Kate sat up at that and asked – she hoped innocently – 'What is she like?'

'Like?' Beth asked curiously. 'What do you mean by that, Kate?'

'I mean, what's her substance? She seems so flippant, I am sure she isn't; I am curious about such a woman.'

'She's very pretty, and her clothes, Cassie, they are just gorgeous.'

Kate squirmed, she didn't want to know about Mrs Kennedy's looks, or her clothes. Kate wondered how Cassie had ever been close to Beth.

'Are you all right, Cassie?' Beth suddenly asked, sweeping Kate out of the conversation, 'you really do look very tired.' Beth was pouring tea at that moment, the sun caught her bony wrist as she lifted the silver teapot and played games with the heavy gold bracelets that she wore.

'Why, I'm fine,' Cassie replied, but it was obvious that she had been caught unawares by the question.

'I thought it was your hair when you came in, but it's not, it's your eyes. I can see that now.'

'I've told you. . .' Cassie tried to answer. But the bony wrist shot out and clasped Cassie's slender hand.

'I am your friend, Cassandra Fleming, and I know that it's difficult to catch up on the years when we haven't seen each other and our lives are so different, but I loved you when you were a girl and I still do, and if you are hurt or upset I want to know about it.'

'Oh Beth,' Cassie said and Kate was embarrassed to see the women clasp each other and giggle and touch. 'But I am all right, I promise you. Just a little weary, that's all.' Kate could see that Beth did not believe her friend, but she let it pass and moved on to reminiscences of their childhood because that was easy to talk over. However, before they left, Beth did ask if she might see Cassie's paintings when she came to visit.

'No, you can't.'

'Why not? I can organise an exhibition for you in New York. It's ludicrous that your French gallery owner hasn't done it for you before.'

'Well she hasn't because I don't particularly want it yet. Anyway I'm stultified, I can't work properly, Beth. It's coming back, but it isn't with me yet. Maybe that's what's wrong with me.'

'Oh Cassie, maybe I can help you.'

'I've told you, Beth, I'm fine. I have an artist's block, that's all. Everything,' she pointed to her chest, slapping the bare skin above the neckline of her sundress, 'is stuck here and it won't come out. I have to keep pushing and then it will emerge and I'll feel better.'

'OK,' Beth said and Kate knew that none of them thought it was OK at all.

Cassie was surprised that her feelings were so obvious to others – she really thought she had been successful in camouflaging her distress. Not only was she having difficulty with her work but Charles, except when he was with the others, was withdrawn and quiet. She had even endeavoured to make herself appealing to him, but he had ignored her overtures. She was surprised. Their love-making was spasmodic in England, but usually on holiday Charles wanted her. She liked him holding her, it didn't matter that she didn't have an orgasm, at least she was close to him at those moments.

Cassie noticed that Kate got on with Jane, she was glad, she wanted them to like each other. Sometimes the three of them would watch television together. Cassie enjoyed it even though these days the political connivings held no interest for her. John, of course, always told her that she should care about what was going on in the world, it was irresponsible not to be involved – she was missing his company, but she knew it was only because Charles was distancing himself from her.

She didn't know what made her go through his briefcase that second Monday morning. He had gone sailing as usual and she had gone up to their room to get her sunglasses. She had just shut the door behind her, turned the key in the lock and opened the briefcase. She saw the letter immediately. It was in an envelope marked Confidential. It was quite creased, obviously written some time ago. It was from Margaret.

'My darling Charles,'

Cassie wanted to stop reading, but she couldn't.

'When you left me this evening I could still feel you inside me, it was as if you had not gone. I turned over in the sheets that still smelt of you and we were still fucking.'

173

The explicit sexual need, the graphic descriptions of what her husband had done to another woman, gripped her. She wanted to cry out, but she couldn't. She wanted to be embarrassed and ashamed but she wasn't. At first she sat there, but then she put the letter back into its envelope, back into the briefcase. She said nothing. She went outside, and sat at the end of the garden, hidden under her sunhat behind her glasses. She had no idea what to do. She held onto her body, trying to stop the thumping in her veins. They called her for dinner, she said she had a headache and was going to bed.

Charles found her there.

'You've found out.'

'Yes,' she said.

'How?'

'I read a letter.'

'You shouldn't have done that.'

'You shouldn't have done what you did.'

She lay on her side with her back to him. It was still and quiet in the white room that they always used at the summer house. The net curtains moved in the breeze, the white wooden tallboy with its mirror reflected Cassie's body, curled up under the white counterpane. Charles sat in the white wicker chair. His grey hair was neat, his white face was not.

'What do you want to do?' he asked.

'Nothing,' said Cassie, 'I just want her to go away and leave you to me.'

'Even if she went away, Cassie, she would still leave her mark – on both of us now.'

'I know, I know. And that is why I hate her.'

And Cassie began to cry. The worst part was that the crying didn't help.

The household shifted, rocked by Cassie's pain. Charles admitted his indiscretion to Tom. Tom told his grandmother, but she did not go to her daughter, she would wait until her daughter was ready to come to her. Tom whispered it to Kate and Kate, quite shocked by what she saw as Jane's almost audacious disregard of Cassie's situation, immediately went to the grieving woman.

Cassie let the younger woman stroke and comfort her, but she was embarrassed that it was Kate who was privy to her tears. It wasn't that she didn't care for Kate, she did, but there was no intimacy between them. Cassie needed Tom. She had always been sure, if she was sure of nothing else, that Tom would never desert her. But Tom did not come to her, Tom was with his father.

Tom decided to take Kate to a drive-in movie that night; she'd never experienced anything like it. A movie in the open air, Coke to drink, popcorn to eat and the feel of Tom's fingers roaming at will under her clothes. How she loved the feel of his fingers – everywhere. However, their reason for going was not the need of their own pleasures, they had to get out of the house. Cassie had not come down for dinner. Charles had been polite but quiet, unwilling to pander to Jane's need for a performance. The old lady had behaved throughout dinner almost as if nothing had happened, but the slight turn of the chin, the tautness around the mouth revealed her displeasure. Her mood was tight, starched. It seemed to say, keep your affairs to yourselves, I don't need them to invade my safe-house.

In fact that was not how Jane was feeling at all. She was simply biding her time, waiting for Tom and Kate to leave the house, for then she would have her say. As the porch door shut behind them she turned to her son-in-law.

'Now be so good as to tell me what is happening.'

'I've been having an affair, Jane. Cassie read the lady's letter and now she knows. That's all there is to it, really.'

'That is all there is to it, Charles?'

Charles liked his mother-in-law but he had no wish to talk over his relationships with her. She was a direct woman without Cassie's emotionality so it was easy to say, 'Really I don't think I should be talking to you about it.'

'Perhaps not, but if I may offer one word of advice, why don't you try and talk to your wife?'

Charles smiled politely and excused himself from the room. He had no wish to talk to Cassie – he couldn't face her tears. Instead he walked down to the beach and for the first time seriously thought about the business of ending his marriage.

Jane stayed in the house and kicked the fireplace at least ten times with her right foot. When she had finished she went up to her daughter's room. 'I am sorry, Cassie,' she whispered to the tear-stained woman, who was after all her child, for there was nothing else to say. Now was not the time for might-have-beens.

'It's all quite shocking, really,' Tom had told Kate as they drove to the movie, 'to discover quite how fragile all those links that I take for granted really are. Oh, I've always known about Cassie's obsession

175

with me. And it came as no surprise really to discover that Dad has been playing away for so many years. It's the fact that no one talks. Form has to be maintained, that is all that is required. So when that goes we have no resources.' He sighed.

'You all give the illusion of closeness, but in fact you're all quite unfeeling,' Kate said.

'Kate, I'm not unfeeling. I just couldn't deal with my mother's emotions, there's nothing complicated about that. I could understand my father. He is having a physical affair that's become, well, rather important.'

'What is he going to do?' Kate asked almost fearfully. 'Because if he leaves your mother. . .'

'I know,' Tom came in, 'that's why I couldn't go to her.'

He pulled Kate towards him. He buried his head between her breasts, breathing in the smell of her. He pulled her scooped neckline down – she was wearing a shimmering black blouse with a white skirt – and ran his lips over her skin. He undid her bra so that he could graze his teeth over her nipples – she loved that. He heard her moan and move closer to him and suddenly even the drive-in was too public. He pushed her away and reversed his grandmother's Ford out of the parking lot, onto the highway. He felt her fingers touching him, undoing his zip, reaching in to touch his penis, and then her head went down and her teeth nipped him, her lips caressed him. He felt as if he were flying. He drove past his grandmother's house onto an empty piece of land that opened onto the beach. The wheels of the car screeched as he spun them in his haste to be rid of the responsibility of driving. He managed to turn off the engine before the coming drowned out the world.

'I still don't want you to leave,' Cassie told Charles, 'I want you to leave her.'

'I know you do,' he replied. They were walking on the beach outside the Fleming house. It was a still night, the only sound was the lapping of the waves as they slapped off the wet sand and the crunching of Charles' and Cassie's feet. 'But we have to be honest, Cassie, and face the fact that Margaret is not responsible for the problems in our marriage. If you like, she is the result of them.'

'Charles, please.' Cassie knew she was begging.

'No, don't do that, Cassie. It won't help either of us.'

Cassie turned to face Charles. Her sadness was easy to see in the white moonlight.

'Do you love her?' she asked, knowing the answer.

'Yes,' he said, turning away from her, unable to look at her any more.

On the day of their departure for England Jane Fleming had warned her daughter, 'Charles'll go. He has to. He may come back, of course, because of the guilt – but that, naturally, is up to you. What you mustn't do is tighten the screws on Tom. Let him go too, Cassie. He's a man now. God knows how he'll deal with the knot of love you've got yourselves in, but the least you can do now is to let him out.'

Cassie heard her mother. The trouble was she didn't know what she was talking about. As far as Cassie could see, Tom and Kate had each other; what had she got?

Charles left Cassie just two weeks after they returned from America. It was the beginning of September, the heat was still in the air, but the freshness had gone out of the summer. Nature was making its preparations for the business of yearly death. Kate, ripe with her love, watched caringly and not without some anxiety, as Cassie contemplated her empty life.

In a small flat in West London Margaret welcomed her lover. She had telephoned her parents and her married sister earlier in the day. 'He's coming to me. I told you he would eventually. I didn't believe it possible to be this happy.'

Before he went up to Cambridge Tom did his best for both his parents. He talked to Charles at the office – he didn't like to ring him at Margaret's flat. Margaret had invited him for dinner. He'd declined, explaining that there was not enough time. She had realised, as soon as she had put Tom through to his father, that she had been hasty. She apologised to Charles.

'Don't worry,' he said, 'I'm sure Tom will come in his next vacation.'

As for Cassie, Tom felt helpless. He was going away from home, what could he do? She cried a lot. On the first weekend he and Kate had taken her to the theatre, to see *Fings Aint What They Used To Be*. He tried to talk to her about the play. She answered but it was just words, she wasn't interested. She looked nice, if you didn't examine the pale face and shadowed eyes too closely. She wore a dark-green cocktail dress with a row of pearls. It was not her usual style, far too formal for Cassie. Tom held Kate's hand tight and tried to ignore the bad feeling inside that he knew to be not only guilt at leaving Cassie alone, but guilt too for not being part of her pain when she, who had always been part of his life, needed him so much.

It didn't take Tom long to understand that Cambridge was a very different establishment from the British Army. There was a parallel in matters of etiquette, but whereas the British Army laid down its rules as principles of survival, the University camouflaged theirs in older traditions.

On his second evening as an undergraduate Tom forgot to put on his gown. He was walking along the Backs indulging himself in that atmosphere of heady history which characterises the English institutions, and thinking of Kate. She had described the architecture of Trinity and King's and St John's Colleges as giant wedding cakes embellished with lashings of intricate icing and had wondered what was inside them: were they full of juicy currants, or crawling with maggots? He was smiling at her analogy when he was intercepted by two guardians of university morality, known as Bulldogs. They always wore bowler hats.

'Excuse me, Sir,' one of them said, 'I notice you are without your gown. I shall need your name and your college.'

'Why?' asked Tom.

'You are without your gown, Sir,' the Bulldog repeated.

Tom wanted to laugh but he could see by the expression on the men's faces that this was not a humorous matter. The Proctor was informed of his crime and he was fined the sum of six and eightpence.

When Tom first arrived his landmarks were the shops and street names, but in time he noticed only the colleges. He himself was at King's – a college for winners. However, it did not take him long to realise that there were two worlds at Cambridge: the academics and the rest. The tutors themselves selected who did and did not fit the 'academic' label. Those dedicated to study were noted down by their tutors. There was the in-joke, a definite degree of intimacy and the stilted cocktail parties where the only drink was sherry. Others outside the inner circle were free to pursue their favoured activity, be it sport, politics or the theatre. Having acquainted himself with the best places to eat, where his lecture halls were and the location of his tutorials, Tom turned his mind to his main ambition – to direct as many plays as he could whilst he was at University. He had elected to read English, for such a degree would be compatible with his ambitions. His introduction to the world of the 'dramas' took place just a few short days after his arrival. At the Societies Fair the Freshers were invited to acquaint themselves with the various societies eager to welcome new blood. However, Tom found no such cordiality when he approached the famed Footlights Society and enquired how a freshman might 'get a chance'. He was told curtly it was by invitation only.

Edward O'Conner, who was to become a close friend, but who at the time was simply a bystander, shed light on the darkness. 'When they think you have something to offer, you get invited to a "smoker".'

Tom's bemused expression demanded more explanation.

'It's an unrehearsed performance. They drink and smoke and you offer your talent. If you can make them laugh they'll invite you to join, if not, forget it. They have what they call a "rehearsal room" in Falcon's Yard, above a fish shop. It's actually their club. I understand they do a very good lunch.' Tom saw that Edward O'Conner had what would be described as a real 'twinkle' in his eyes.

'A man who knows his priorities, I see,' he said

'Oh yes,' O'Conner replied. 'Perhaps you'd like to join me in finding a way to join their charmed circle.'

'Why not? But I am going to do a play first.'

'The famed Amateur Dramatic Club, known as the ADC?'

'Is that where we are supposed to go?'

Tom was not as naive as he seemed, for Bravington had prepared him well. His former English master had also taken the precaution of contacting an old friend who knew an old friend whose son was the President of the ADC.

So whilst most undergraduates acquainted themselves with the ways of the Proctors and the Bulldogs, and the pleasures of 'sporting the oak' when one wanted privacy (shutting the oak outer door as well as the plain painted door of one's rooms ensured that callers were kept out) and of discovering the King Street Run (if one was a pub man), Tom was pushing to direct a nursery production for the ADC – not an easy task for a first-year student.

Tom had decided his first play should be Sartre's *Huis Clos*. He considered it a masterpiece of psychological terror – the concept of three people trapped in a room for eternity left only with their thoughts was perfect. He made his proposal to the Committee of the ADC. The President suggested that Tom Bray should not be considered presumptuous despite his audacity at wanting to direct during his first term, and a three-act play at that. Mr Bray had put forward an interesting idea, and he, the President, had heard good things about him.

Thus the freshman got his nursery production.

Kate came off the diary. To her great relief she could put the frocks away and start writing features. Euphoric at the change in her fortunes, she eagerly accepted her first assignment.

At 12.30 the call came from Michael Stillet, the features editor.

'Sylvester is opening at Covent Garden tomorrow. They've mucked us around for days, but he's finally agreed to squeeze an interview in at three-thirty today, which means we'll have to have the piece by six at the latest if it's going to get in. See what you can do.'

Kate quaked. She was in awe of Stillet, a fast-tongued man who knew how to drink, a Fleet Street 'star' guaranteed a role as one of the great and the good.

She arrived at Sylvester's dressing-room door on the dot of 3.30. And that was the day Kate became a real professional. The celebrated tenor sat opposite her, on a plush pink velvet settee, totally naked. She told herself not to look at him, just to get on with the interview. There was nothing else she could do. She had to get the piece in.

Kate made it her business to telephone Cassie every day. She would recount her little activities and Cassie would listen and recount her little activities in turn. It was hard.

There were others who tried to help Cassie. Evelyn contacted her as often as she could, Yvonne was there for her, and, most surprisingly, Loretta Mallory. Cassie was ashamed that she had been so dismissive of Loretta, for although she could not deal with Loretta's social invitations she certainly found her easy to talk to. She even went to visit her one afternoon when Loretta was looking after her daughter. Cassie observed the motherly care that Loretta showered on her child and she was ashamed of the jealousy she felt.

It was around that time that Cassie wished she drank, but, not liking the taste of alcohol very much, there was nothing to deaden her pain. At times she was consumed with such hatred for Margaret that she planned humiliations in her mind – taking pleasure in the most minute detail. Charles telephoned her often, finding excuses for his calls. At first she was quite rude, but after discussing it with Kate she decided to be nice; after all perhaps domestic bliss with Margaret wasn't quite what he had expected.

180

For Charles the biggest change was the peace. Margaret made no demands on him, she was just there, not intrusive, not demanding and most of all not needful. However, he found it difficult in her flat. The remnants of her single life littered her new-found domesticity. She didn't have a washing machine, nor a lady that came to 'do'. At first, during the week they would have dinner out, it was easier after work. But seeing his tiredness, Margaret insisted that they go home. He would have a bath, having prepared their drinks, whilst she would cook. After their meal he would wash up whilst she lazed in hot water. Her single girlfriends still telephoned for the first few weeks, but they had little to say to Charles nor indeed he to them. Margaret's parents lived in Bournemouth, her sister was married to a transport manager and had three children. They were invited to Sunday lunch but that was a failure. An architect of Charles' stature had little in common with a couple who had no interest in his personal battle between form and function. It removed Margaret from them too, for she had aligned herself with Charles and his needs, submerging herself in him. She had worshipped Charles from the first moment she had met him. She knew he was not happy and she consciously wooed him, staying late whenever he needed her, and when he didn't, monitoring his calls, opening his letters. He would say affectionately, 'Margaret runs my life now.'

And Margaret did. If she lost him there would be nowhere else for her to go, for Margaret was a woman who had assumed that there was to be no love in her life; the advent of Charles had brought a passion that she had never even imagined. There had been a few boyfriends, but no one who was important. She was a woman who had established a life for herself as a competent secretary. She went to cordon bleu cookery courses and to the opera as often as she could, but however comfortable she had made her life, it seemed as disposable as blotting paper, ready to be ripped off the block whenever a new sheet was required.

After several weeks Charles insisted that they find a house.

'You can keep this flat if you like. It'll give you some security.'

'Are you going back to her?' she asked him, suddenly fearful.

Margaret was not a young woman any more although she wore her 38 years well. With her small body, shoulder-length hair and partic-ularly nice light-brown eyes shaped like almonds, she could pass for a much younger girl, except from an angle which exposed her chin – then her jowls gave her age away. Charles asked her if she would like to stop working. She said she couldn't, that working for him was as much a part of her life as the loving. His partners complained, of course, because it was difficult for the rest of the staff. But Charles was the senior partner so there wasn't much they could do about it. They had very little social life and Margaret preferred it that way for she was having to learn how to live with a man for the very first time and there were moments when she found it difficult. However, Margaret did acquire a new friend in Marilyn Sampson.

David Sampson had not endorsed Charles' decision to leave Cassie. They had met in one of those smart restaurants that pretend they are clubs where the discreet can meet and talk and be looked at.

'I know she is not an easy person, Charles, but you have a lot of mileage behind you; is it worth throwing that away?'

'I have never been happy and neither has Cassie. At least she'll have a chance of finding someone who she can live with – she deserves that. She's a good woman.'

'She *is* a good woman, Charles, but neither of you realises that you are a couple; perhaps this madness of yours will help you to understand.'

'What an extraordinary thing to say.'

Marilyn, on the other hand, threw her lot in with Margaret.

'For the first time Charles has a woman around him who will nurture him,' she told David.

'Cassie nurtured him.'

'She is so very demanding.'

'No, you're quite wrong. You don't know Charles as Cassie knows him, or indeed as I know him. He has a need for warmth that that girl won't be able to give him, you'll see.'

'Well I think she will make him very happy. At least I can talk to her.'

'That's no basis for *their* relationship,' her husband told her.

David did wonder whether he ought to contact Cassie, but in the end Marilyn persuaded him that his place was with Charles.

And so the divide started. Charles had his remnants of their life together and Cassie had hers.

John Bravington telephoned her one Monday morning after a horrific weekend when the reality of her changed condition had tortured Cassie. His tone with her was clipped. He was angry that she had not contacted him after her return from America. Then she told him that Charles had left her.

John came to the house that night at six o'clock, a wet, un-distinguished evening. Cassie had used no make-up, she had brushed her hair and she wore a clean black sweater and a black skirt, but she still looked as if she no longer cared about herself. John Bravington wanted to put his arms around her. Instead he allowed her to pour him a drink. They sat in Charles' study, an unusual choice, Bravington felt, but she explained quite simply, 'The other room feels so big.'

She made no attempt at small talk. It was left to him.

'Have you heard from Tom?' he asked her.

She nodded.

'How is he?'

'Very well. Organising his first play.' She drank from her glass, wrinkling her nose. He noticed she had given herself only a tiny amount of brandy – she obviously didn't like it. Why, he wondered, did she bother? He could see she was trying to make an effort. 'He's doing *Huis Clos*,' she said.

They drank, both of them. Cassie was rubbing her arm, her wedding ring flashed as it moved up and down in the electric light. He felt awkward but still he stood up and moved over to her chair. He put his hands on her shoulders and pulled her towards him. He wondered if she would push him away, but she didn't – she curled into him like an animal. She didn't cry, she didn't make a sound, simply laid her head against his chest, her shoulders huddled over, her spine bent. Bravington ran his hand over the curvature. She sighed and pulled her head up.

'Thank you for your kindness, but I'd like you to go now.'

'I'd like to see your studio,' he said.

She shrugged and led him into the garden, down the little crazy-paving path into her world. She took the key from underneath a flower pot, unlocked the door and turned on the light. It was a large room, stacked with canvases. The roof was glass, as was one wall. Obviously architect-designed, he thought wryly. She let him look through her work which lay on the floor. And then he walked towards the easel.

'No,' she said.

'Pardon?'

'I said no. There is only one person who is allowed to see my work before it's finished.' Her voice was sharp.

'I'm not trying to take Charles' place. But I am your friend,' Bravington said softly.

'Oh, Charles never saw my work on the easel. Only Tom did that.'

Tom's auditions were crowded. A first-year directing a nursery production at the ADC, when normal practice was to act first, had attracted a great deal of interest. Edward O'Conner was working as his assistant director. They sat together on wooden chairs in the middle of the bare room they were using as their venue. One by one the hopeful filed in. There were 32 of them. Expectant stars, however good, were not welcome in Tom's production. Carefully and considerately he would explain his premise, evolve the play for each individual, listen to them read and always thank them.

Six were called back. Knowing there were only three principal parts, plus one – the valet – nerves were short, stomachs hurt. Four females and two males awaited the director and his assistant. Tom hadn't meant to be late, at least he said he hadn't; Edward wondered though, for Tom found every excuse to delay their departure: first he couldn't find his text, then he had forgotten his wallet, and then he checked his watch. They would arrive just five minutes after the call.

'You've done this deliberately,' O'Conner insisted as they approached the audition room.

'Of course I haven't, Edward. It's important to be courteous, it's hard enough auditioning,' and he checked his watch again – this time he walked faster. 'But,' he added, almost as an afterthought, 'it'll sort out those who've got bottle.'

By the time they reached the hall, the six, having done some voice exercises, were trying to be nice to each other. Tracey Roberts, her mass of blond curls hiding her face, sat with her head over her book reading her lines. Belinda Pollard a slender, black-haired nymphet who interested Tom, was on the floor in a yoga position, her arms stretched out at her sides, her breathing deep and even. Rachel Marcus, another blonde, but with disciplined hair, was talking to David Jones, a thickset, wiry Welshman. Juliet Harrison, a lush, dark, deepset girl, almost a woman, was just quietly waiting. Jonathan Brown, a handsome boy, picked at his nails.

Tom was apologetic, just enough. He watched them all, and Juliet Harrison watched him watching them. It amused him.

First he asked them to improvise. They were all of them locked in a room, and each one represented one deadly sin – he was going to offer Belinda lust, but he changed his mind and asked Juliet to perform that role. He gave Tracey Roberts sloth, to Belinda he gave envy, to Jonathan pride, to David gluttony, to Rachel hate. Tracey Roberts remarked that there were seven deadly sins. He'd left out avarice. For the sake of structure, Tom invited Edward to complete the cast list. His performers played their roles, exposing themselves in just the way Tom wanted. He had cast them well: Belinda was so envious of Jonathan's pride; David didn't care about anyone else, gluttony was his sin; Rachel hated; Tracey, like David's gluttony, allowed her sin to swamp her. The surprise was Edward's avarice – or was it?

Later that evening he made his choices: Tracey was to play Estelle, Rachel would be Ines, but his coup was Garcin – it had to be Edward.

Edward O'Conner was a handsome man with thick, jet-black hair and strong blue eyes. His nose was straight, not long, and his mouth was full, but quite hard. He knew what Tom wanted and he played his ruse because he didn't mind being an actor. Edward O'Conner was a performer and he was hungry for experience of any kind of stage for he had resolved to come to Cambridge to get an English education: he needed it for his work. He was a political man, but not the kind that would have appealed to his hosts at Cambridge University, for Edward O'Conner, born in Northern Ireland, raised as a Catholic, was of Republican stock, and he intended to serve his blood. The great-grandson on his mother's side of a hero of 1916, he resented the partition of his land and the natural presumption of the Protestants. He had seen his mother kicked out of the way of an Orange Day March, he had seen his father grovel for work in the docks at Belfast, he had grown up with 'Papist' as his badge. At seventeen he had sought out a history teacher at school who he knew had the right contacts south of the border. Despite his tender age, he was made to go through the recruitment classes like all volunteers and there he met a man who was to become Director of Operations in the Republican Army. This man told Edward O'Conner that he was to get himself an education, the best he could, and then he could go to work for the Cause. So Edward went back to school and studied very hard. He passed all the necessary examinations and was accepted at Cambridge University. His friends in the South organised the necessary monies.

Tom, of course, knew nothing of that Edward O'Conner. He knew the man who, like himself, did not have the pedigree of the true-born Englishman. Tom found it easy to talk to Edward – it was as if they came from the same place. However, it did not take Tom long to discover that there was a fundamental difference between the two of them: Tom wanted to make his mark at Cambridge, Edward had no intention of becoming known.

'I am not a remarkable person,' he told Tom. Tom wanted to laugh out loud, Edward could never pass as an unremarkable person. On one

185

occasion, two young girls, possibly language students – he could tell they were not undergraduates because they wore huge skirts and a lot of make-up – had both stumbled over the edge of the pavement in their eagerness to look at Edward as he passed by them.

Kate had taken to going to the pub, the Quill, just opposite the *Enquirer*. Each newspaper in Fleet Street had its own place to drink, its 'club', so to speak, and the *Enquirer* had the Quill. Of course there were neutral places, like El Vino's where everyone went, but a woman wouldn't be served at the bar there. Kate had confided the secret of Sylvester's naked state during her interview with him to the women's page editor, Estelle Winters. Unable to keep such a titbit to herself, Estelle Winters had told Sally Stone, the fashion editor, who was rumoured to be sleeping with Michael Stillet, Kate's features editor.

When she arrived at the Quill on the day that Stillet had been told the story she was surprised to find him offering her a drink.

'Well done, you've handled yourself rather well,' he told her.

As she drank deeply from her glass she realised that she could actually feel the heat from his body as he stood next to her. He was a thin man, with soft brown hair. It embarrassed her to realise that he made her feel awkward.

Cassie sat on one of Yvonne's comfortable chairs in her gallery, her legs crossed, her hair pushed back behind her ears, whilst Yvonne got very angry with her. The little Frenchwoman strode around, punching the air, talking loudly.

'You mean this nice man came all the way across London. . .'

'Don't exaggerate. He didn't come across London, just a few stops on the tube.'

'Irrelevant. He came to you and you poured him a drink, told him he couldn't look at your current work because only your son is allowed to do that and then you let him go home! My God, Cassie, your problem is not that Charles left you, but that Tom has.'

'Oh but Tom hasn't left me, he's just gone to university, that's all.'

'Cassie, Cassie.'

'What's the matter, Yvonne? Tom's got a girlfriend. I know that – and you know that I think she's smashing.' She pulled her hair out from behind her ears and fluffed it with her fingers. 'Now, I want to talk about doing a series of faces, almost like photographs – using the seven deadly sins as the theme.'

186

Yvonne stopped pacing. 'That's actually a wonderful idea.'

'I know. I thought of it last night. I've already started some sketches. Do you want to see them?'

'Why not?' Yvonne said. 'How are you going to do envy, Cassie?'

'How do you think I should handle it?'

'Perhaps envy is to do with believing that one is on the outside of love,' Yvonne said as gently as she could.

'What do you mean?'

'You think you are unloved, Cassie. We do love you, all of us, but somehow our love is never enough for you and only you know why that is.'

'If I knew why, Yvonne, I wouldn't feel as desperate as I do,' Cassie said. She got out of the chair and hugged her friend. Then she turned on her heel and walked out to the street as quickly as she could.

# Chapter Eight
## 1961

When Cassie Bray had completed some of the paintings in her series, to which she had given the title 'Seven Portraits', she showed them to just two people, Yvonne and John. Tom, of course, had seen them during the course of their development when he had come home during the University vacations, for the house in Hampstead was still home. He had been stunned when he had discovered her theme. 'But I use that,' he said, 'in auditions, to get the actors to reveal themselves.'

'I suppose it's not that extraordinary. We are mother and son,' she said, without looking at him. And then she told herself to stop being coy, there was no way that Tom could know that she had seen his notes to himself before he had gone up to University: 'seven deadly sins – perfect audition material'.

There were to be 21 paintings in all, three in each group, and devastating, for each one was to be a self-portrait, and each sin would be shown in all its ugliness. She had not spared herself. Greed was a woman, gross and greasy, grabbing at the tree of life, stuffing herself with its apples, her mouth and hands bulging with rich red fruit. Lust was legs akimbo, skirt high, waiting without tenderness for a faceless man. Jealousy was a green canvas, pale figures in a glow of pink, oblivious to a huge female face. Yvonne had been shocked, she did not know what to say, for she was uncertain whether she could sell the works. She could not reveal that to Cassie so she talked instead of her courage.

That was not enough for Cassie, she wanted a date for the exhibition. After some vacillation on Yvonne's part, it was agreed that the exhibition would take place in October 1962, just before Tom went back to University for his second year. That would give Cassie enough time to complete all the works.

She was painting with tremendous energy. Rising late, she would prepare coffee with the rich cream she favoured, orange juice, and toast which she would eat in the kitchen standing by her blue work surface. She would then stack her cup and saucer and plate and glass neatly by the sink for her daily, then she would go to the studio. Some days she would begin work immediately. At other times she would sit and read the newspapers, or fiddle with her paints or prepare some canvases – an onlooker might think she was procrastinating but that was not the case, the thought processes were functioning all the time. Cassie was proud of what she was doing, seeing the paintings as mirrors of an unacceptable reality.

John Bravington, however, did not share that view. He told Cassie she was self-indulgent.

'We are all slothful at times, we are all envious, and lustful, and hateful, and full of gluttony. What gives you the right to take all that for yourself?'

'I am not taking it for myself, I have simply chosen to use my own face as a symbol.'

'Do you have such a distorted view of the human race?'

'I just see life for what it is.' Cassie spoke flippantly, tossing her hair, and moving her shoulders slightly so that she was facing away from him.

They were sitting in the garden of their favourite pub in Hampstead. If it hadn't been for the people crowding around them, or the traffic jammed in the narrow High Street that wound up to the Heath, they might have imagined they were in a country garden.

John had really been an extraordinary friend to Cassie. When she had started this new project she had told him that she couldn't see him. She would be too busy. He had ignored her, and arrived just when she didn't need to see him. He would mess around in the kitchen and produce appalling curries which she had to eat until she finally admitted her aversion to them. Then he changed to egg and chips, which she did quite like. At weekends he would insist she went to the movies, either on Saturday or Sunday. She wondered how he got away from his wife. Once she asked.

His reply was, 'I only go out when I am not needed.'

John didn't change his routine when Tom came down for vacations. At first Tom had been surprised but then he seemed rather relieved. He assumed, of course, that John and his mother were sleeping together.

189

'Don't alter your behaviour just because Kate and I are around,' he had said.

Cassie had been quite shocked. 'There's nothing like that going on.'

'Why not?'

'Because I am not that kind of. . .'

'Mum, you're a grown woman, you aren't a girl.'

And Cassie knew he was right, but there was nothing like that between her and John. She still missed Charles. Not for the physical act but for the touch of him. Charles had such a beautiful body, and Cassie had so appreciated that beauty. They saw each other occasionally for dinner and sometimes he would come to the house 'to check up on things'. Cassie hated it when he left.

Christmas had been bad. Her mother had suggested that she come to America, but a dinner with just the two of them was not something Cassie even wanted to consider. Tom had gone to Kate's family. So Yvonne had insisted that Cassie go to the Winstons. 'You know I am godmother to the little girl.'

Cassie had always prepared her own Christmas dinner; ever since Tom had been a little boy, they had always eaten at about four o'clock. The mornings were for opening presents, and drinking champagne, and preparing the feast.

The Winstons ate at 1.30. Otherwise Selwyn Winston's elderly mother would get acute pains in her stomach. Cassie arrived at 12.30. She was offered sherry. Whilst Selwyn went to deal with the glasses Cassie found herself momentarily alone with Mrs Winston senior. Cassie smiled, Mrs Winston smiled.

'Christmas is nice, isn't it?' said Mrs Winston.

'It's a family time, really, isn't it?' Cassie replied quietly and the full impact of her loneliness overwhelmed her. She looked around her; the room was large, and cold. The only heating came from a wood-burning fire, but the grate was small. A grand piano filled a bay window, otherwise the room contained three settees and several wing-chairs. Cassie wondered where the Christmas tree was. She noticed one of her paintings on the wall nearest the door. She knew she should be glad, Selwyn was known to be highly discriminating. Why could she derive no pleasure from her successes? All she wanted was to excuse herself and run from the house, go to her bed, pull the covers over her head and pretend that Christmas didn't exist. But her host had returned, genial and pink-faced.

The tree was in the dining room, the fairy lights blinked on and off throughout lunch. The turkey was dry, the children noisy, Yvonne and Miranda Winston intimate. Selwyn occupied himself with his food. And Mrs Winston was deaf. Cassie, during the pudding, envied her. She managed to excuse herself after the Queen's Speech.

When she returned, her house was unoccupied, too neat. The Christmas tree, festooned in white and gold with real candles and ribbons, mocked her. She couldn't even look at it. She went into the kitchen, took a bottle of champagne out of the refrigerator, set it on a tray with one glass and took it into her sitting room. She turned the television on, drew her curtains – she would lock the world out, it could all go away.

She heard the key in the lock. For one wild moment she wondered if it was Charles.

'Mum?'

'I've just opened champagne.'

'I don't suppose you got me a glass.'

'I didn't expect you.'

'No?'

She heard him rustling around in the kitchen; he seemed to be doing something more than just getting a glass. She was surprised. They had exchanged presents in the morning, before they had both left. Briefly she wondered why he had come home. Maybe it had been awful for him too. At least they had each other. Cassie sat up and put her fingers through her hair, rearranging it so that it was more becoming. She was so much better off than Yvonne, she was not alone, she had a child.

Tom came into the sitting room. He was carrying his glass and a huge bunch of golden chrysanthemums. As her son's arms went around her, Cassie bit back her tears, this was not a time to cry. They sat together on the floor and watched television eating dates and nuts. Tom complained that she had not made the usual treat of dates actually stuffed with almonds.

'You are eating almonds and you are eating dates, so what's the difference?'

'You haven't slit open the date, taken out the stone and put the nut in its place, nor have you rolled it in sugar.'

'I used to do that, didn't I?' Cassie said, ruffling his hair.

'You did it last year and I shall look forward to it next year,' her son told her.

'You want Christmas at home next year?' Cassie asked him.

'I want my stuffed dates, and I want my cake, and I want cranberries,' Tom replied by way of an answer.

They watched television and laughed at the dreadful jokes, they even played a bit of Scrabble, but Cassie wasn't really concentrating properly. At eight o'clock she said, 'Don't worry about me, I'm fine now. You go back to Kate, she'll be wondering where you are.'

'She knows I'm with you. She understood that you and I needed some time together today.' Cassie put her arms around Tom and hugged him. He hugged her back, and didn't move away from her. They stayed on the floor holding each other until Cassie was able to push him away from her.

After he had gone she felt, if not happy, at least calm.

Tom's career as a director had blossomed, not so as a student – he was in trouble for neglecting his studies, being late for supervisions and for sometimes avoiding his lectures completely.

His tutor, a kindly man with a mass of wild hair and a penchant for good claret, told him, 'I foresee difficulties. Your devotion to the theatre precludes all else. Cambridge is here to extend you. Your courses are structured to do that, the way of life of your college is structured for that too. The whole purpose is to complete one level of your education, enabling you, hopefully, to go on to the next. If you only wished to direct you should have gone straight to the theatre.'

Tom took the rebuke. His tutor was right. He should have gone directly to the theatre. However, much as he was obsessed by his work as a director, he reasoned that there were things to be learned, so he took more interest in his scholastic life too.

*Huis Clos* had been a wonderful success, reviewed by the local press, and, at Kate's instigation, by the drama critic on the *Enquirer*. He and Tom had liked each other.

'What's next?' he had asked.

'It must be Shakespeare,' Tom had replied. 'In my last term at school I tried a modern-dress *Hamlet*. It didn't go down well in the corridors of tradition, but the boys loved it.'

'Ambitious,' said the critic, an untidy man who smoked too many cigarettes, the ash settling in the creases of his trousers and on the front of his jacket.

Tom was not quite ready to expose his *Hamlet* to the public. He had work to do first. Together with Edward and Jonathan Brown he had formed a small experimental group utilising the Method school of acting; eventually they would give readings and performances, but first there were the classes. Tracey Roberts and Juliet Harrison were the first to join them. Others came too, but the original five formed the nucleus. They nourished each other, they pushed each other, they learned to know each other.

Tom wanted them to understand the Chinese philosophy that the reed cannot change its place in the field, but can only survive if it learns to bend with the changing elements. He told them they were trees, anchored into the earth by their roots, but slowly swaying in the breeze, enjoying the gentle air as it stroked their leaves. He changed the climate, the wind became harsher, it whipped those leaves, slashed at those branches and then it got worse. The wind turned into a storm, it was cold but the trees had to stay in their place and deal with the conditions as best they could. They rocked backwards and forwards. Tracey cried out, 'I am breaking, but I cannot move. I am breaking into two.' She shook violently, screaming out 'help me!'

'Bend, bend at the waist!' Jonathan shouted back. 'You must move with the wind. If you don't you'll die.'

'I can't,' she wailed, there was a terrible cracking noise from her throat and she keeled over onto the floor. Tom left the others still rooted to the ground, mourning the dead tree. After some moments he released them and together they all cuddled Tracey.

He watched them all, they were his friends now, his intimates. It was Edward who was in control. He sat Tracey up and rubbed her back and asked Juliet to get a glass of water. Tom could see that Juliet watched Edward, Juliet liked Edward. Tom smiled softly to himself for Edward did not look back at Juliet. He had told Tom that he had a friend in Ireland, a special friend. Tom remembered how in Berlin he had turned to Helga out of loneliness. He wondered if Edward would succumb, for Juliet was a sensual woman.

Jonathan sat at Tracey's feet. He was courting Tracey, he obviously considered her to be the brightest and the best, and she was certainly the most passionate. But Tom could not share Jonathan's passion for her, he could see it in his eyes, but he had no sense of it himself. He liked the slender handsome young man, he was a wonderful actor, but he would never be as close to him as he was to Edward. Edward O'Conner was his friend.

Jonathan had no knowledge of Tom's reservations. He worshipped Tom. Whilst Jonathan did indeed care for Tracey, the true object of his desire was Tom. But it was a private fantasy that he knew could never

193

be realised. In moments of dreams he wondered how it would be if Tom were to respond to his longings, but then he would push the thought away, guilty at its implications. A virgin, fearful of what lay beyond that barrier, Jonathan had constructed a careful façade. As a child of the rich he lived behind their barricades, cushioned by their power from the business of living. His family name was actually Lytton-Brown, but he had dropped the Lytton when he went up to University. No actor in the egalitarian Sixties would survive the boards with the double-barrelled calling card of the rich, Jonathan knew that. And he intended to be an actor.

His father, his father's father, and his father's father's father had spent their growing years in Lytton Hall, a stone structure built at the end of the eighteenth century. The means to construct such a fortress against the more unpleasant aspects of life came from cotton. An unfortunate involvement with slave-trading was never discussed in company.

Jonathan had a lonely childhood. A stately home and substantial acreage were no substitute for playmates. Jonathan's one great friend during his childhood was Des Watson, his father's estate manager. An unhappy relationship with a father who required a more resourceful son was mollified in the shadow of Des Watson. Watson was a big man, with big hands and a ruddy face and hair that had once been the colour of sand. He had a wife, Maureen, who cooked comforting breakfasts and huge teas. They had no children. 'Maureen isn't much good that way,' Watson had once confided.

When Jonathan was six years of age his father had introduced him to the rigours of deer-stalking. When the boy had cried that the toiling up hills and down the other side, through rough undergrowth, along river beds, over rocks, was too much for small legs, his father had said, 'Nonsense, boy – the tracking is what it's all about, us against him. It's the scent of the stalk, don't you see?'

Watson had said nothing, but after the boy had fallen, and was crying a little in pain, he said respectfully, 'May I, sir?' and before Jonathan's father could say no, he had picked Jonathan up and put him across his back as if he were of no more inconvenience than a coat. Jonathan, aware of the strength of the man beneath him, cuddled his neck, and loved him.

Boarding school had been hell – except for an English teacher who had opened the curtains to the world of make-believe where Jonathan had shone. University was the first pleasurable experience of Jonathan's life.

After several weeks of intense exercises, Tom decided he was ready to start work on his *Hamlet*. He discussed it with Edward as they walked together from a lecture. The Cambridge stones glowed gold in the late afternoon sun. The students thronged the streets, their black gowns flapping around them like bats' wings.

'We're ready to begin rehearsals,' Tom said, slipping his arm through Edward's.

'Jonathan for Hamlet,' said Edward.

'I want you to play Laertes,' Tom said.

'I am going to play Claudius.'

'I think you would be a powerful Laertes.'

'I know I'm right for Claudius. You play Laertes.'

'I'm not an actor. I work with actors.'

By now they had reached the Round Church which concealed the little path that led to the Cambridge Union. Tom noticed that Edward glanced at the building, just as he did every time they walked past it.

'Why don't you join the Union?' Tom asked him.

'I have no wish to.'

'You would be a great orator, my friend.'

'But not at the Cambridge Union.'

'It's as good a place as any.'

'Not for me.'

It was hard for Edward to lie to Tom. He wanted very much to speak at the Union. But his orders were to be inconspicuous.

'All right, I'll play Laertes,' he said.

Tom invited Cassie to the first performance. Unfortunately Kate could not be there, she was covering a story in Leeds. Cassie brought John Bravington with her for although he was no longer Tom's mentor he was still curious about Tom. Cassie wore a dress of midnight blue, she had washed her blond hair and brushed it until it shone. Her skin glowed, her eyes were deep bronze. She looked wonderful and Tom was thrilled with her.

'You are magnificent,' he whispered to his mother and she blushed like a girl. John would have liked to have told Cassie how lovely she looked but his tongue felt like cotton wool in his mouth and he couldn't get the words out properly.

The *Hamlet* was a sensation. Tom had taken the play and stripped it bare. He had examined the speeches and pared them down to their essential meanings. He had then taken those meanings and created pictures, for as Cassie's son he understood the physical power of images. And from those images he had created a modern play about a passionate man obsessed by the need to discover himself. Unwittingly Tom had created a play of his time; like his idol Osborne, he had attempted to give youth a voice and to take the theatre back to its people. So in his version Hamlet wore blue jeans and carried a guitar. This time *The Times* and the *Manchester Guardian* reviewed him as well as the *Enquirer*. The *Daily Telegraph* decided that an interview was in order. Tom's bandwagon was beginning to roll.

He decided that he had to take a play to the Edinburgh Fringe. Kate agreed with him. The big question was which play. He talked to his tutor, to the drama critic on the *Enquirer*, to Edward, to Jonathan, to Tracey and Juliet. Kate read for him, tirelessly.

One night, in April, Edward came to Tom's rooms. He was carrying a script in his hand. Tom held out a hand for it.

'You may not like it. I wrote it.'

Tom raised an eyebrow.

'It's a prophetic piece, I'm afraid. I've projected forward. Ireland in 1985. It's a love story between a British soldier and an Irish Catholic girl.'

Tom didn't ask any more. He just took the script and read.

Set during a civil war, O'Conner had used the past to give form to the future. The English Army has come into the North to protect the Catholics from the Protestants. But, as in all matters of war, principles become blurred, visions fail under the bullet and victories are won. Ireland again spills her blood. A young English boy, no more than eighteen, offers his heart to a seventeen-year-old Irish girl. Their fear-ridden love is destined for horror and O'Conner had spared his audience nothing.

Tom was deeply moved by what he read. Within a love story Edward had encapsulated the tragedy of the individual's impotence against the manipulations of power.

Tom had found his play.

Jonathan Brown was cast as the young English boy. Edward wanted him.

'He has the right kind of fragility,' he told Tom.

Tom chose the girl, he wanted Juliet for the part. Tom would have liked to have involved the whole group by offering Tracey the part of the mother, but after a stunning performance as Gertrude in their *Hamlet* Tracey had been invited to perform in a professional production at a small theatre in London.

196

'Will you forgive me, Tom?' she had asked him when she had declined his offer of the role.

'Of course I will, but I will miss you. We are family now, the five of us, and it won't be the same without you.'

'I think it's better than family, Tom.'

'I think so too,' Tom replied and he hugged Tracey very hard and wished her luck from his heart.

Kate was missing Tom, but not as much as she had thought she would. Michael Stillet liked her, so it seemed. She got the good jobs, and, after a particularly delicate interview with the wife of a convicted murderer, a byline.

She had been drinking with a group of young journalists when one of them congratulated her on her elevation. She was so excited, she left her drink and ran out of the Quill, and across Fleet Street back to the paper. She knew Stillet was there putting the paper to bed. He was on the back bench, checking a last-minute feature with the Editor. She managed to burble out her thanks, aware that the sub, and the Editor, were watching her with some amusement. Awkwardly she turned to leave again.

She had reached the lift when she heard Michael calling her.

'Kate, wait.' She turned to look at him. He had joined her by the doors. 'You're going to be good,' he said, and he kissed her, using his tongue.

She was shocked at how much she enjoyed it.

John Bravington took Cassie out to dinner to celebrate the completion of her 'tour de force', as he called it. She hadn't really wanted to go. Normally when she finished a project she liked to watch television and potter around her house and sleep a great deal. But he had been a wonderful friend and she didn't want to disappoint him.

John had been planning this evening for many months. He was deeply in love with Cassie and he wanted her so much. He had held himself back because he had known that the time was not right, but on the night of Tom's opening at Cambridge he had seen how glorious Cassie had looked and he could no longer restrain himself. Sick with nerves, despite the longing to feel her naked flesh against his naked flesh, he was terrified lest he damage their beautiful friendship.

He took her to L'Etoile, a French restaurant in Soho. The service was attentive, the decor plush. Other diners wore dark suits and neat little cocktail dresses. Cassie had on the requisite neat little cocktail dress, but John Bravington hadn't changed out of his usual baggy grey teaching suit. She noticed he was sweating and she realised that she much preferred him as a zealot – at least then he had passion; as a supplicant he was unattractive. She concentrated on eating her asparagus and kept wiping her lips, aware that the butter was making them greasy. She just hoped her lipstick hadn't smudged. She tried to be gay and interesting, recounting little titbits of gossip in the art world that Yvonne had passed on to her.

John laughed in the right places, offered encouraging noises, was altogether quite unlike himself. Halfway through the dessert, Cassie put her knife and fork down.

'We haven't argued once this evening,' she said.

'That's good.'

'That's bad.'

They both fell silent and concentrated on eating. Cassie couldn't tolerate the tension.

'Talk to me, John. I thought this was supposed to be a fun evening.'

'I'm not in my natural habitat,' John told her, 'I find this all quite awesome.' Cassie laughed. So that's what it was, it was all right then. 'I'd be happier if we had coffee at your house,' he told her.

'Well if that's all it is, let's go,' Cassie said, laughing. John was thrilled, could it be, dare he hope, that Cassie felt the same as he did?

As soon as they got back to Hampstead, he took off his jacket and undid his tie. Cassie realised he looked rather nice, especially without the jacket. He had good shoulders too – funny, she hadn't noticed that before.

John saw the approbation in her eyes and suddenly he was on top of her, trying to kiss her.

'No,' she said, trying to push him off.

'Cassie, please, I love you. I have been so patient. I ache for you. I want to feel you, to be inside you, I need you.'

'No,' she said again.

His tongue was inside her mouth. It felt wet and big. She hated it. His hands were pulling at her zip, pushing her skirt up. She didn't want him. She tried to push him off but he was too heavy for her. He was pulling at her pants, trying to push his fingers into her. She was being violated. She wouldn't have it. She pulled her knees up and pushed hard at his now erect penis. She hurt him.

'Oow!' He cried out and rolled off her.

'Get out,' she said.

'Cassie?'

'Get out.'

After he had left she ran up to her bathroom and ran a hot bath. As she lay in the water she forced herself to concentrate on her anger rather than the revulsion. If she could stay angry she knew she would be all right.

John got into his little grey Austin – chosen for its economic use of petrol – but he didn't start the engine. He sat in the driver's seat, buried his head in his hands and cried unashamedly. He loved Cassie, why couldn't she love him? She must have known how he had felt during all the years of their friendship. And now it was over, for he could never forget the look of repulsion in her eyes.

The following morning he telephoned her. By then Cassie was in control. She had taken a sleeping pill so she had slept, but now she was heavy-headed and nauseous.

'I am sorry, Cassie.'

She could hear how quiet he was. 'I am not angry that you tried, I am angry that you didn't listen when I said no,' she told him.

Tom's play, *An Irish Love Story*, was to open in Edinburgh on August 2nd. Cassie waited for her invitation to attend the opening night, but none came. Eventually she felt she had to ask Tom if she might attend the first night. She was proud of herself, believing that she was learning not to expect to be a part of Tom's world as her automatic mother's right.

'I absolutely want you to come up,' Tom told her, 'I would be furious if you weren't here,' and then he added, 'Dad's coming too.'

Cassie's heart jumped. She rang Kate at the newspaper. 'Shall I ask him if I can go up with him?' she asked her.

Kate appeared to be considering her reply. 'No. Why don't you come up with me? We can take the sleeper.'

Cassie bought a new dress, a black and white cross-over with a full skirt and three-quarter-length sleeves. She knew it looked wonderful on her. She was meeting Kate at the railway station and, arriving early, she purchased magazines, including the *Arts Review*. She realised it was the first time she had bought the magazine since Charles had left. That morning Cassie had noticed the weather, it was warm, but overcast. God, how she longed for sunshine.

She saw Charles before he saw her. She was about to run over to him, to say something, anything – and then she realised he had Margaret with him. For the first time she really looked at her, wondering what it was that Margaret possessed which she had lost, or perhaps had never had. Despite being a passionate woman, Cassie Bray was blessed with a mind that, whatever its stresses, could still appraise; that was the gift of the artist. She saw a slender woman, a body that was almost male in its line – was that what it was? Margaret offered none of the femininity that Cassie knew she herself possessed. The Englishwoman had a spare quality about her that reminded Cassie of Charles' mother. As she looked at Margaret, Cassie wondered what Edwin would have made of her. Deirdre would have liked her: Margaret did not look the kind of woman to get excited about her son's first erection.

'You knew, didn't you?' Cassie said to Kate as they sat in their compartment.

'I didn't know how to tell you,' the younger woman said.

The two women did not talk much on the journey. Kate would have liked to have comforted Cassie, but she sat in the corner of the carriage keeping her gaze fixed on the vanishing countryside as the train sped north, deliberately discouraging any conversation.

Cassie was in fact quite unaware of the passing scenery or of Kate's wish to console her. She was aware of only one thing, the brainwashing sentence that she made herself repeat over and over again: 'I must be charming, I must be controlled, I must not let myself down.' Even in the night as she lay on the narrow bunk between the coarse white sheets whilst the train jogged and shunted its way north, she continued with her one sentence, 'I must be controlled and charming, I must not let myself down.'

At Edinburgh station Cassie managed well when they finally came face to face in the taxi rank.

'See you tonight,' she said gaily as she walked quickly with Kate towards an empty taxi. Tom had booked her into the George, one of the more distinguished hotels in the city and close to the Assembly Rooms where the play was being performed. Charles and Margaret were staying at the Royal Northern Hotel, a huge tribute to Victorian grandeur in a different part of the city. Kate, of course, would be lodged with Tom.

Kate was so impressed by Cassie. She wished that Cassie would let her show her support, but she understood that Cassie had to deal with her discomfort on her own. All the same, she did manage a 'well done' as they climbed into the taxi. Cassie glanced back at her and managed a smile.

Margaret was relieved, for it had occurred to her that Cassie might be difficult. Charles, however, was worried: this was so unlike Cassie's normal behaviour. He hadn't wanted to bring Margaret, but she had made it clear that she would not be left behind.

As soon as the taxi drew out of the station Cassie was herself again. She liked Edinburgh immediately. Somehow, although it was not the same kind of city, she was reminded of Paris. There were gracious squares, tiny cobbled streets and away, at the edge of the vista, she could see the rolling green of Scotland and beyond that the sea itself.

As soon as Kate arrived, she was pressed into service organising presents for the cast. That was what they did in the proper theatre. She had to buy wine too and food for the first-night party. Cassie offered to help.

'It's all right,' Cassie heard Tom telling her, 'why don't you go to the gallery or something? Kate can manage.'

'But why can't I help? I am your mother.'

'Mother, I need Kate, that's all. OK?'

'I don't have anything particular to do. I'd really like to help.'

'Edinburgh is a wonderful city. There's a festival going on too so there are exhibitions and performances all over the place. I am sure you'll find lots to entertain you.'

'But Tom. . .'

'Look, Mother, I don't mean to be unnecessarily hard, but I have a lot on today and I can't deal with you as well. See you tonight.' And her son was gone, back through the swing doors into a darkened auditorium. Cassie could not follow him there.

As she walked from the theatre, her face hot and red, Cassie noticed an exceptional young man. He was watching her kindly, but there was nothing condescending about him. She registered that he had a young face, but the look he offered her was old with understanding.

Edward had grown to love Tom Bray, but as a wise young man – beyond his years almost – he realised he might not *like* Tom. He knew that Tom used people. Not many people saw that, for he seemed so soft and charming. Edward hadn't minded that aspect of his friend's personality until he had seen Tom being unkind to his mother. He wondered what she was like.

If she had been of a mind to notice such things, Cassie would have enjoyed the little cobbled streets of the old town with its hidey-holes that housed dwellings, restaurants, shops and galleries. But the sharp edge of rejection ran through her and there were no pleasures anywhere.

At around five o'clock in the afternoon she returned to the hotel and prepared herself for the evening. She dressed as well as she could and reminded herself again and again of her determination to be controlled and dignified. She would do her best for Tom's sake. It was his moment. God knows, she told herself, she had had enough of those times herself to know what he was feeling. Cassie knew she wanted to be a part of his excitement, but Tom had been telling her at the theatre that she had no place in it. Cassie wondered where she was supposed to put all her care and all her love now that Tom was too old to need it.

Later, as the four of them, Cassie and Kate and Charles and Margaret, sat watching the play, Cassie let Kate hold her hand – both of them were nervous. But it was to Charles that Cassie turned when the audience stood on their feet and cheered. It was for their son and briefly they were united.

In the thrill of the surge of applause Cassie caught sight of a small, quiet couple sitting just to the side of them. They too had a look of tearful, incredulous pride and Cassie realised they must be Edward O'Conner's parents.

On the stage Edward too took his bows, alongside Jonathan, Juliet and Tom. Juliet had her supporter in the audience, a boyfriend from another university. She was not the kind of girl to lie alone in her bed. Jonathan had no one, his mother was in the South of France, his father in New York. So Tom and Edward gathered around him. For a moment he was their star, their man. He had indeed triumphed, and Jonathan glowed in their praise. He would have liked to have hugged them both, as he had seen Edward hug Tom, briefly, in the wings, kissing him quite shamelessly on both cheeks. The men, for Jonathan could see they were men, had exchanged almost passionate intimacies. He had heard them.

'You're a bastard, Bray, but you'll make it.'

'And you are a great writer. And I love you,' Tom said quickly.

'I love you too,' Edward replied. He didn't need to say the words quickly, he wasn't threatened by them.

For a moment, Jonathan's memory of what he had seen and heard all but extinguished the flush of his success.

Charles and Cassie met the O'Conners, and Margaret watched them. She had known even as she had insisted that she had a right to be present, that she shouldn't have come. But she had expected Cassie would be there and she hadn't felt she could afford to let Charles be alone with his wife. She felt awkward, but she had waited long enough for Charles and she intended to keep him.

'You look beautiful, Cassie,' Charles told her quietly, as they left the O'Conners. Before she could thank him he had moved back to Margaret.

Tom, triumphant, emerged from the hidden world backstage to embrace his parents, to share his success with them briefly. Like a hero he appeared to be sprinkling the magic of stardom, touching those closest to him with its glory, and they drank it in eagerly allowing it to transform them for just a moment.

'Cassie, Cassie – I did it,' her son whispered to her, laying his head on her shoulder, and she held him tight. But then he was gone, clutching Kate, back to the intimate, incestuous world of the victors.

'They're having a party,' Cassie said to no one, for no one was there. They had all gone. The O'Conners had returned to their hotel – they were tired, they said – and Charles was walking ahead with Margaret.

'I'm going to ask Cassie to join us for dinner,' Charles told her.

'That'll be awkward, won't it?' Margaret found herself saying.

'It won't be awkward for Cassie and me. We are celebrating our son's success,' Charles found himself snapping.

He found Cassie in the auditorium. She had gone back to look at the set. 'The real world is a dark place,' she commented to Charles as they both stood looking at the stage, at the bleak room that Tom had constructed for his lovers. There was peeling wallpaper, an iron bedstead, cups and saucers on a brown table, two straight-backed chairs.

'You always said that colour was clearer and sharper in the clean, fresh air of America.'

Cassie smiled, but ironically. 'Maybe I thought it was, who knows? But I stayed here, embraced it, loved it, because my men were here.' She ran her hand over the back of a chair. 'And now I am having to find out whether I really like it for myself. I'm not sure, Charles. It's a lonely place.'

Charles grimaced. 'Don't you see our glorious friends?'

'Our "glorious friends", as you call them, have called from time to time, but it's embarrassing, isn't it? To be forced to take sides. But I have to say to my shame that Loretta always calls.'

'I told you she was a good woman. I see the Sampsons of course, but

203

as for the others, well . . . I suppose it would be fairer to say that they haven't taken sides. I don't see them either.'

'That's the British for you. Scrupulous fair play. We're both drowning, but at least no one can accuse any of them of rescuing one without the other.'

Charles laughed wryly. 'Cassie?' He took her hand, she wanted to cling to his fingers, but she made herself hold back. 'Will you have dinner with me? We should be together.'

'With us,' Cassie corrected him. 'You are here with Margaret. No, I won't, thank you. I would find it too difficult, frankly.'

Charles watched her leaving the theatre. He was struck by her dignity. It jolted him, 'dignity' was not a word he would have used when describing Cassie.

It was over her difficult dinner with Charles that Margaret realised her mistake in coming to Edinburgh. Her sister had warned her, but she hadn't listened. She resolved never to interfere again when Charles was on family business. She kept herself quiet, not even attempting to lighten the atmosphere. She would wait until they got back to London.

Cassie resolved to walk to her hotel, she kept thinking of Charles and Margaret together – it hurt.

'Mrs Bray?' A voice interrupted her – Edward O'Conner. 'I'm not much of a party man myself. May I escort you to your hotel?'

Cassie, as ever, still loved beauty, and she found Edward O'Conner quite beautiful. She let him take her arm, she let him lead her to her hotel. He invited her to have tea with him in the lounge.

'Wouldn't you prefer to be at your party?' she asked him.

'No, I wouldn't.' He was looking at her levelly over the edge of the white china cup that he was lifting to his lips. 'I want to make love to you.'

Cassie looked down sharply at her own cup. She was incredibly embarrassed. 'Whatever for?' she heard herself ask. And then she felt Edward O'Conner's fingers slip into her own fingers and she didn't want to be alone any more. She let him wait for her whilst she asked for her key, and then she let him come up to her room.

She stood silently in the dark as he took off the black and white dress, she pulled in her stomach muscles as he eased off her black pants, she gasped as he undid her black bra, she shivered as he caressed her erect nipples with his tongue. She trembled as he pushed her onto the bed, she lay still as he touched her thighs. She shook as he parted them and ran his fingers between them. And then she stopped gasping and trembling and shivering and shaking for he was using his lips on her and she began to feel, she was feeling again, it was pounding over her, the waves of a sweet wondrous ache that had been absent from her for so long. She threw her arms back over her head, she couldn't lie still, she wanted his tongue higher into her, and she told him so, crudely. Her fingers grasped the pillows, it was coming, it was coming, it was from somewhere deeper inside, it was pouring over her, out of her, and then it was there, and she screamed with it.

Tom shimmered and shone through his first-night party. It was intimate, nobody was there but the players and the managers; except for Kate, of course, and she was there because she was Tom's girl. She wore a slim turquoise shift dress. She still wore no make up, she didn't need it for Kate was a gorgeous woman. She trapped her own admirers, particularly, it seemed, Jonathan, who simpered around her in a quite charming manner.

'My father has a house not too far from here. After the play finishes I am going to invite Tom to come deer-stalking there. I'd be very pleased if you came too.'

'Deer-stalking?' Kate queried.

'Yes. It's very interesting. A contest of strength between deer and men.'

'I don't think so,' Kate said sharply.

'Oh, you must see it. It's a triumph for the deer.'

'In that case I'll come.'

She turned around to look for Tom. She noticed the leading lady, an extraordinarily pretty leading lady, kissing Tom. He was kissing her back. She had a sharp feeling somewhere between her breasts, but quickly she told herself, this is the theatre, they all behave intimately, it's an intimate business.

Tom was suddenly by her side, whispering in her ear, 'Bid them all farewell. I must fuck you.'

Kate laughed low in her throat.

Even when they got back to the little room, he was charged, high, exultant.

'I've got to get noticed now,' he told her.

'Now?' she whispered, pulling open his shirt, licking his chest.

'I'd make the front pages,' he whispered back, undoing her zip.

'We'd make the front pages,' she said, pulling her dress off for him.

And she was there in front of him, naked except for her small white pants. He sank onto her, gripping her hair, sucking at her nipples. He could feel her under him, her legs curling up behind him around his back, opening herself wide for him. Quickly he pulled off the rest of his clothes, but without ceasing his sucking. He heard her moan and arch under him. He could feel her fingers pulling at her little white pants, trying to guide him into her, but he pulled her hands away. He wanted her wild for him, he wanted her to scream for him. Her body was moving – she was beginning, yes, he could hear her begging, 'Tom, please. Tom.'

He ripped the pants down, drove into her, feeling her wet and throbbing cunt pulling him in, and in, and in. He knew nothing but sheer pleasure.

He held her close afterwards, staying inside her, kissing her, touching her. She felt warm and soft to his touch. He reached up and turned the bedside light on.

'I want to look at you,' he said quietly, realising how much he loved her. He could feel the want again, but slowly this time, deliberately he thrust into her, and he felt her thrust back, on and on, looking into each other, feeling the need build, letting it build, until he saw her eyes change, and her breathing change, and he felt her body convulse under his. He took a pillow from under her head and put it under her buttocks so he could ride her harder. She jerked herself away from him, and lay on top of him so he could feel her breasts pressing into him. She pulled his penis out from her and moved further down his body, so it lay in between her breasts – he could feel her sharp nipples. He turned quickly so he could reach her, feeling the wetness of her on his tongue. Her mouth was on him and her tongue worked on him, and he drove his high up into her, tasting himself, working on the folds of flesh, biting and nibbling as she was doing to him. Who was she? She was woman, any woman, all woman – he felt himself shudder and groan as his climax came and he cried out his love for women.

Cassie lay beside the young man on her bed who had made her feel so wonderful. She admired his gorgeous body, it was so long since she had touched young smooth flesh. She flexed her muscles, feeling her own skin as if for the first time.

'You have made me feel wonderful, Edward.'

'Keep touching me, Mrs Bray,' he said, with a heavy emphasis on the 'Mrs Bray', 'you are a wondrous lover.'

'Cassie,' she said, pulling him on top of her.

# Chapter Nine
## 1961

It was very hot in Berlin in August 1961 and Rebecca Gottlieb did not like the heat. The room she shared with Elizabeth, so cold and inhospitable in winter, was airless. She felt stifled and uncomfortable. It wasn't just the summer. People were leaving the East in droves. Some were attracted by the lure of higher wages and a softer life, others were tired of the constant intrusion of the State in their personal lives; of being continually lectured and cajoled to do better and to sacrifice more for the greater good. Others were simply fearful, widespread arrests did nothing to limit the loathing directed towards the authorities. Rebecca knew that the State would not continue to tolerate the mass exodus through the various crossing points. The labour drain was too acute to be ignored. Something would be done, cheap housing and cheap food were simply not enough to keep Berliners in the East.

There was an atmosphere about the Eastern Sector of the city that worried her. A rumour had been put around that West Germany was suffering from a polio epidemic. Police scoured all trains from East Berlin into West Berlin. People carrying luggage were immediately searched. Those thought to be trying to get to West Germany were immediately arrested. Patrols combed the forests and fields around East Berlin to winkle out anyone who might be trying to make their way westward on foot.

Former friends of Rebecca's from the days when she had known Dietrich had joined harassment groups, haranguing those Berliners who still worked in the Western Sectors (mostly chambermaids and hotel workers culling Western currency for its greater purchasing power). It was not an ideologically acceptable thing to do, but these people were not ideologists – they just wanted the better wages.

Rebecca, too, was anxious to be on her way. She had prepared two small cases for Elizabeth and herself and she was ready. But try as she might, she could not persuade Elizabeth. Her daughter was dancing at the Komische Oper and dancing was Elizabeth's life. She had no other needs.

Except that she was in love.

Mikhail Novotny had been a dancer at the Kirov, and a good one, until a back injury had ended his dreams of stardom. He had taken a position with the Berlin Company. Despite a wife and a child in Moscow, he had quite deliberately seduced Elizabeth, not because he found her particularly beautiful, or indeed appealing, but because he recognised that she had the potential to be a very fine dancer. He saw himself as her mentor fulfilling his dreams of stardom through Elizabeth – perhaps she might even dance at the Kirov one day.

He supervised her classes personally, working her slowly, methodically, always inspiring her to do better. He was never a bully, but he was an unceasing taskmaster. His control over Elizabeth was insidious, quiet and totally effective. Through his gentle manipulation, Elizabeth's body and mind listened to him. So when Rebecca talked of the West, Elizabeth told Mikhail and Mikhail told her that Rebecca was a tired lady who had loved and lost. And Elizabeth, soothed by Mikhail's words, went home to her mother and soothed her in turn, saying, 'Soon, soon we'll go. Mikhail has suggested Giselle. He thinks I have the maturity to dance her now. He has some ideas, of course.'

And Rebecca remembered how Elizabeth had once danced Giselle for her.

Rebecca did not like Mikhail Novotny. She feared the influence he had over her daughter. Nor would she have derived any comfort from knowing how Novotny exercised his real power over her daughter.

'Come, little one,' he would say, and he would take her hand and lead her to the small rehearsal room. He would lock the door and with his gentle, tender voice he would entice her to bend over a bench. He liked to pull up her skirt, pull down her pants, and push himself into her, always from behind. She balked at the hardness of him, he always hurt her, but he would tell her, 'When you are a woman you will enjoy sex, and then it won't be uncomfortable.'

But Novotny had no intention of helping Elizabeth to discover the essence of her womanhood through the pleasures of love-making. His excitement came from her dry, tight fear.

Elizabeth had no idea what Novotny meant by her not being a woman. She felt so ashamed, she was obviously lacking some element within herself. But she had no way of knowing what it was. She would surreptitiously look at her mother and wonder if she was different from Rebecca, was her mother a woman? She wished she could talk to her, but there was no question of that. Novotny was right, Rebecca was a tired old lady. Her hair was quite grey now, her fingers horribly deformed by the swellings of her arthritis, her skin was sallow, her eyes were those of a dead person. She talked simply of going to the West. What difference would that make, Elizabeth wanted to know. At least here in East Berlin Elizabeth had a future, and, as her mother had always told her, if she was good enough no harm would come to her. Then she would be able to improve Rebecca's situation.

They had little in common any more, she and her mother. She was tired of Rebecca's constant misery. She knew her mother had had a hard life but, as Novotny pointed out, Rebecca never made things better for herself. She locked herself away from people, she did nothing to elevate her status at work.

'Elizabeth, she need not just wash clothes all the time. She could find some other work. Perhaps she wants to be a martyr.'

'She did a great deal for me, Mikhail. She was always there when I needed her. It wasn't easy, she must have been very lonely sometimes.'

'Of course she must have been lonely. And I love her for being good to you. I wish I could help her, but unless someone helps themselves what can we on the sidelines hope to do?'

The discipline Novotny imposed on Elizabeth's life left little time for her to persuade her mother to help herself. Besides when she was with Rebecca they argued, mostly over food, for Novotny had decreed that Elizabeth was too fat whereas Rebecca was appalled by her daughter's lack of nourishment. She would go to great lengths to provide Elizabeth's favourite foods, to tempt her, even to please her. But her efforts never met with success. On one particular evening she had managed to procure some pork. She had gone to West Berlin and smuggled it back in her bag. She had been quite frightened for while she was on the train the woman next to her was searched. The guards had found some watches that she was bringing back to the East. Despite the woman's tearful protestations that they were for her children, they had manhandled her out of the carriage; Rebecca had scarcely been able to control her own trembling. She had managed to get back to the little room where she had carefully braised the pork with potatoes and cabbage. She had set the table and waited for her daughter.

Elizabeth had come in later than her usual nine or ten o'clock. It was closer to midnight, and Rebecca had had to keep turning the oven on and off so the food would not dry out. She was tired, her legs ached, particularly her ankles.

Elizabeth smelt the food as she came up the stairs, the stench of it made her feel sick.

'Oh no,' she said as she walked into the little room, 'I can't possibly eat, I feel quite sick.'

'You feel sick because you don't eat. I got this meat specially for you. Just eat a little.'

'Mutti, leave me alone. I don't want to eat any more. I have already eaten tonight.'

'But I prepared this especially for you.'

'I can't help that.' Elizabeth avoided the table, she went and sat on the brocade settee and took her ballet shoes out of her bag. She had to wash her ballet shoes for the morning, the ribbons were grubby, she could not possibly wear them as they were. On her way to the shared bathroom she pointedly opened a window. When her daughter shut the door behind her, Rebecca Gottlieb cried.

Elizabeth was grateful for the cool air of the bathroom. She really couldn't bear the smell of cooked food. She knew her mother was upset but she couldn't help that. Even if she was hungry, which she wasn't, she couldn't have eaten it because Novotny required a slender almost fleshless line if she was to perform the movements he required of her. Sometimes he wouldn't show her a position, he would simply pull her leg or her arm into shape.

'It is not just the step, it is the movement too that is important. Ease into it, don't force anything.' His voice was never hard or strict, it was always soft, always persuasive. And Elizabeth wanted so much to please that voice. Nothing else mattered at all.

On the night of August 12th, Rebecca could not sleep. At first she thought it was her nerves, but then she became aware of a drone of motor vehicles rumbling down the normally silent, night-time streets. She got up, hastily pulled on some clothes and ran down into the square. She was not surprised to see others there.

'Something is happening,' Dr Kindt, a neighbour, said.

Rebecca sensed it – she knew: they were going to fence them in. She ran towards the Brandenburg Gate. There were police and tanks, the drills were digging deep into the Berlin soil, making the holes for the posts that would hold the wire. Rebecca didn't wait. She ran back to the apartment house and roused Elizabeth from her sleep. The girl protested, at first she was merely confused, then angry.

'I'm not going, Mutti, I've told you.'

'No.' Rebecca said. 'No. I won't listen any more. We are going.'

She hustled the startled girl into her clothes and down the stairs. She was glad that she had packed their cases. Dragging Elizabeth by the hand, she headed off towards an apartment building that bordered the British and Soviet zones. Elizabeth trailed behind her, trying to hinder her, shouting at her, 'Leave me here, this is my home.'

'They are going to fence us in, we'll never get out if we don't go now.'

Rebecca was surprised at her own strength, in the last few years she had felt like an old woman, but not on this night. She was holding the two cases and pulling her reluctant daughter. People heard Elizabeth shouting. Rebecca had to get her inside the building before they attracted the wrong attention. She got to the main door, opened it and virtually pushed Elizabeth up to the first floor. There was a large window that looked out onto the street, onto West Berlin. Rebecca pulled the shutters open, pushed the window open and shoved her still-protesting daughter onto the window ledge. Elizabeth clung to the shutter. She wouldn't jump, she was terrified. She didn't want to go.

'Jump! Come on, jump!' a voice shouted in English.

Elizabeth didn't understand, she was too terrified to think.

'Come on – they're sealing the borders, building a barbed-wire fence all around the Eastern Sector. *Come on!*' the voice said again.

Rebecca turned to her daughter, she translated the sentence and added, 'You can stay if you want. But I won't be locked in by anyone.'

And she threw down her suitcase, leaving Elizabeth's on the ledge. Hands reached up to her. She lowered her legs carefully, someone grasped them and eased her down.

'Mutti. . .?' Elizabeth cried, 'Mutti. . .?'

'Jump!' someone shouted in German. Behind her there was confusion. She heard voices. A man pushed past her, he was in his nightclothes. He was going. She watched as hands reached up and helped him. She thought of Novotny and she turned to go back, but someone else was on the ledge beside her. 'Go on, others are waiting. You are stopping us.' His hands scrabbled at Elizabeth, they felt like claws, his nails were scratching her. She shut her eyes, pushed her suitcase off the ledge and eased herself down from it. Someone grabbed her and she was down – on the other side.

She was tired and confused. People were talking everywhere. A car appeared as if by magic. The man who spoke in English helped them in: Elizabeth, Rebecca and the man in the pyjamas. He drove them to

211

Marienfeld, the refugee centre. She heard Rebecca talking to him in English. If she had wanted, she could have concentrated and she would have understood, but she was too tired, too confused and far too frightened. Where were they going? What would happen to them? Where would she dance? And Novotny, oh Mikhail, when would she see him again?

The car stopped, they seemed to have arrived at some sort of building. She didn't like the fact that the man who had driven them there was sorting out a camera and then taking a photograph of them, particularly concentrating on her.

'What was that about?' she asked.

'He's a newspaper man. I told him you were a ballerina. He'll make sure you are on the front pages of every newspaper.'

Elizabeth gazed at her mother uncomprehendingly. 'What have photographs on a front page to do with me being a ballerina?'

At that moment a hand took Elizabeth's arm. 'Welcome to the West,' said its owner, a kindly looking woman with a full face and silky white hair.

And that was how, on the morning of Monday August 15th as the sun was beginning to make its presence felt through the open window of her blue and yellow kitchen, and the scent of her rich dark coffee mingled in with the fresh roses which she had picked the day before, Cassie Bray saw a photograph of Rebecca and Elizabeth Gottlieb on the front page of her daily newspaper – heroines of a night of horror when half a city had been walled up. She wasn't surprised at the searing pain that burnt through her. It seemed that the slightest reminder of Joshua shook her physically, as if her nerve ends went into spasm even at the very thought of his name. She could best describe the effect as like an electric shock. Cassie supposed it was because all her loving and all her longing had, in the end, done her terrible damage.

Cassie put the newspaper down, then picked it up again. She carried it over to the window and carefully laid it out on the counter. She forced herself to pour her coffee. What could it have been like, to know that an army was bent on encasing its city in an iron perimeter to stop its people from getting out? How had Rebecca escaped? She had to read the story properly, but she couldn't – not immediately – so she simply scanned the page. It was enough to know that the Gottliebs, a mother and her ballerina daughter, had taken just two small suitcases and left their life in the East behind.

She sat for many hours in her kitchen, thinking of Joshua. Despite her son, her successes, even her new found sexuality, the photograph of Joshua Gottlieb's daughter had still reminded her that she had not been good enough for the man she had really wanted. On impulse she decided to telephone Edward, perhaps with him she would find some sort of release from the dreadful hurt. He had given her a number where she could reach him whilst he was in London. She was rather nervous, but he said he was pleased to hear from her and when she asked him to visit her, he said, 'Of course I will. I would enjoy that so much.'

As soon as he put the receiver down in his room in a small hotel in a part of King's Cross that discouraged visits by his fellow Cambridge undergraduates, Edward bade farewell to a group of three men, Irishmen like himself. He told them he would meet them a week later. He wanted to see Cassie. He found her unique, he enjoyed her excesses. He reconciled his need for her with his other life in Ireland by telling himself that Cassie was a woman who wouldn't have any expectations of him. They could pleasure each other – even love each other a little – without fear of consequences.

When he arrived he found that Cassie was disturbed. She would not tell him what was wrong. He wondered whether Tom had upset her.

'No, it's nothing to do with Tom. Listen, Edward,' she was unbuttoning her blouse in her bedroom, a yellow room, 'I don't want to discuss Tom with you. It's an intrusion on your friendship with me and with him, and on my relationship with my son.'

'What a wise woman you are,' Edward told her. He held out his hands to her, he was already without his clothes. 'I'll do that,' he said and took over the business of the unbuttoning. Cassie lost herself in the physical pleasures that Edward offered her. She was amazed at herself, her body felt soft and weak with wanting.

'I don't understand it,' she told him.

'Why don't you understand? You are a woman and you want a man, what's so wrong about that?'

'I am old enough to be your mother.'

'Ah, but the important thing is that you are not my mother,' he said, laughing at her and kissing her neck, just below her ear.

Charles telephoned her the next morning.

'Are you all right?' he asked.

'Of course,' she said brightly.

'Have you seen the news from Berlin?'

'Yes. Is that why you telephoned?'

'It is. I thought you might feel strange.'

'It's kind of you to think about me, Charles. I admit that when I saw Rebecca's photograph it shook me a little, but I feel better now.'

She put the telephone down and turned back to Edward.

When Edward had left her Cassie wrote a letter (having obtained the address from the Foreign Office) to Mrs Rebecca Gottlieb, c/o Marienfeld Absorption Centre, Berlin, West Germany. After all, Rebecca was Joshua's widow and she ought to offer to help her. She rewrote the letter four times before she felt she had got the wording right.

*Dear Rebecca,*
> *I saw your heroic escape and want to help you. Perhaps you and your daughter will come to England and stay with me. I am married and have a son. I am sure I can help you.*
> *Affectionately, Cassie Fleming (now Bray)*

Tom was rather surprised by Jonathan's invitation to go deer-hunting. He was fond of Jonathan but he didn't really expect an invitation to his home. It implied an intimacy which Tom found a little uncomfortable, for he was not totally at ease with Jonathan. As performer and director, he and Jonathan had a perfect understanding. It was in their private life that there was unease. Tom discussed it with Kate. 'It isn't that I can actually locate anything wrong within our relationship. . .'

'What a dreadful American word.'

'What?'

'Locate.'

'Kate, it means to find.'

'Tom, I know. Actually, I don't want to go, even if he did say that it's a triumph for the deer.'

And they wouldn't have gone, except that neither of them had the courage to tell Jonathan.

So Tom and Kate were driven even further north by a euphoric Jonathan. He had a pale-blue Morris Minor; Kate thought the car looked like an unfortunate slug, despite its pastel colour. At first she and Tom were bemused by Jonathan's excessive excitement, but after a short time first Tom, and then Kate, was infected.

It took three hours on small roads through spectacular countryside to reach Jonathan's home. Lytton Hall stood large and bleak against the deep blue of an early autumn sky. Kate got out of the car first.

'What an extraordinary place to build a home,' she said quietly.

'Oh, they didn't build it to be a home. It's more of a statement really – "we own the land, we will dominate it".'

'Do your parents live here?' Tom interjected.

He was standing slightly behind Jonathan and Kate, but nearer to Kate.

'Not all the time,' Jonathan replied, turning his head slightly so he could look at Tom. 'There is a house in London. My mother and father are divorced. She lives in Wiltshire. But the agreement was that I should stay with my father, so I grew up here, till I was old enough to go to boarding school.'

'How old were you, when you went away from home?' Kate asked gently.

'Oh, seven when I went to prep school.'

'The upper classes amaze me. They have children, have them brought up by someone else and then despatch them off to a boarding school. They learn to be adults before their time.'

'Everyone in England does that, Kate,' remarked Tom. 'The only reason I didn't go away was because my mother was an American and she wouldn't have it.'

'I've always known your mother was a highly intelligent woman,' said Kate.

Tom laughed at her. She turned to hit him and missed, he grabbed her arms and on the lawn in front of a house that had never seen such frolicking, Tom wrestled Kate to the ground.

'Give in?' he shouted.

'No!' she shouted back. So he tickled her until she begged for mercy and he kissed her and she kissed him back, holding him so tightly that Jonathan thought she was actually taking him into her body.

Later after a heavy dinner they played records in the drawing room and Helen Shapiro shattered the customary calm. Maureen Watson, the wife of Desmond Watson – the estate manager whom Jonathan loved so much – jigged a little in the hall outside.

Desmond called her sharply. 'What do you think you are doing?'

'Oh it's lovely to hear that music and to think of young Mr Jonathan having friends.'

'Stop making a show of your body like that, it's not proper.'

'No, Desmond,' Maureen said quickly, moving away from the door, but still hearing the music and still wanting to dance.

The deer-stalk started very early in the morning. Kate was surprised at the amount of equipment that was packed into the van. She didn't look at the guns. A rather fine black and tan dachshund accompanied them. Kate fondled and touched him, she liked dogs.

At first it seemed like a rather pleasant ramble, the countryside was phenomenal: wild bushes had rooted themselves spontaneously in the soil; coarse grass and dense foliage would suddenly give way to flat open spaces; gentle hills would grow into sharp inclines. There was little sound, just the swish, swish of the feet of the walkers, or perhaps a crack as a dry twig snapped underfoot. They moved slowly, leisurely almost. Watson would stop a lot, looking, he told them, for signs of deer activity – slot marks, fresh droppings, scrapes, fraying. They would stop so he could spy from behind a tree, or a bush, or even the occasional fence. He ensured that the party crept stealthily around the curve of a hill, moving along a line separating peat from heather. Kate could have laughed at the elaborate precautions. Then the game grew tighter, Watson had found droppings that indicated that deer were nearby. He made them make a detour to take up a higher position so they could keep watch. Kate giggled, but just then a family of deer came into view. They stopped and began to graze peacefully around the stag. Kate held her breath.

'Too young,' Watson intoned.

Kate breathed again. Perhaps they wouldn't find an appropriate victim, she hoped, and proceeded to enjoy the countryside and the trekking. And so they continued, for long enough to allow Kate to think there would be no killing that day. But no, something was happening, Watson was holding up his hand. The party, as one, dropped to the ground, hiding in the foliage. A stag proudly displaying its superb antlers was watching over its young, or so it seemed to Kate. Unaware of the impending disaster, they quietly grazed. The stag, as if bidden, raised its nose, sniffed the air. Kate stopped breathing again as Jonathan reached for a gun.

'No, you'll catch a young'un,' Watson hissed.

Jonathan moved around on his belly, aiming his gun.

'Careful now,' she heard Watson say.

The crack of the bullet frightened her, she shut her eyes briefly, but then she saw the deer rear up. It was wounded in the leg. It managed to get up, swaying its head, and charged off on three legs.

'God!' Kate whispered.

'Come on,' spat Watson. 'That was stupid, Jonathan. Bad shot.' Jonathan looked suitably rebuked. Kate wanted to be sick.

The stalking continued, the dachshund was off his lead, racing after the wounded deer. The animal had to be found, finished off, killed. Kate wanted it to get away, to be free. She would have liked to have run off herself, but there was nowhere to go. After two hours of stalking, the dog sniffing out the way, they found the injured deer. Tom was offered the shot, Kate willed him to say no, but to her horror he took the gun, aimed it and shot. Again the bullet cracked out, the deer sank to the ground.

'Good,' said Watson.

He stood up and as Kate looked on, sickened, he and Jonathan walked to the still-writhing animal. Jonathan put his feet over the antlers as Watson plunged a knife in under the skull, cutting the spinal cord.

That was still not enough. The knife was stuck into the deer's chest and worked around and around, until the blood gushed out. Jonathan raised the poor creature's body and pumped it behind the shoulder area, increasing the flow of blood.

Kate wasn't actually sick until they turned the deer on its back with its head pointing up the hill and disembowelled it. She was trembling and still heaving as they thrust bracken into the deer's rib cage. An insertion was made through the deer's nose and a rope was threaded through and knotted. Another rope was tied around the deer's hind feet. Watson carried the rope in the front, Jonathan the one at the rear.

Kate stumbled behind. Tom wanted to help her, but she wouldn't even let him touch her hand.

'The buck's end was not a pretty sight,' he said later, when they got back to the house.

'You shot it.'

'I had to. The gun was offered to me.'

'You didn't have to take it,' Kate screamed.

Jonathan could hear her, downstairs in the hall. He half-smiled and poured two whiskies, one for him and one for Tom. He was not anticipating Kate's company that evening.

Tom came down shortly afterwards. He took the drink Jonathan held out to him.

'Women!' Jonathan said disparagingly. 'They eat the meat, but they don't like the sight of the blood.'

'Kate's not like that,' Tom said sharply.

'I wasn't attacking her,' said Jonathan lightly as he led the way into the dining room.

Tom and Kate left the following morning. Jonathan drove them to Edinburgh from where they were to take a train to London. Kate was not rude, but the conversation was dominated by Tom and Jonathan. They talked of the theatre.

In the train, travelling down to London, Kate said, 'I just can't imagine loving a man who can be a party to that slaughter.'

'Oh grow up, it's not my kind of sport, but that's the way it is. Real life is about killing or being killed.'

'Is that your thesis, Tom?'

'Yes, that's my thesis, Kate.'

'You'll read mine in the paper.' She took out her pad and studiously ignored Tom whilst she wrote her notes for a piece that she would offer Mike Stillet.

Kate and Tom went their separate ways at the railway station: Tom to his home and Kate straight to the newspaper. It was 4.30. She made her way through clacking typewriters and noisy phones to her desk in the features department. She waved hello to anyone who happened to raise their head in her direction. She sat down, threw her coat over the back of her chair, put some paper in her typewriter and wrote her story on deer-stalking. Her fingers sped over the keys, she didn't need to stop to think, the words just came out. She was unaware that Michael Stillet was watching her. After about half an hour, he stood up and went to a cupboard behind his desk. He brought out a bottle of whisky and two glasses, poured two measures, and then trudged to the gentlemen's lavatory where he added water. He walked back to Kate's desk and put the glass by her side. 'Drink up,' he said.

She looked at him, surprised.

'Do you want to tell me what you're writing?' he asked.

'Deer-stalking.'

'Let me see it when it's finished.'

He went back to his desk, talked on the phone and sat and waited. Kate swallowed her drink, grimacing as the liquid went down; she didn't like whisky. When she had finished her copy she took it out of the typewriter, checked the number of pages and took it over to Stillet. He indicated a chair next to his desk, poured her another drink, and himself a third.

'This time you get the water from your lavatory,' he said.

Kate smiled and picked up the two glasses. Stillet had already started to read. She went to the ladies, carefully poured half her whisky away, added the same amount of water to both and then took the two glasses

218

back to Michael's desk. He didn't look at her – he was still reading her piece. Her stomach turned to water and she fled back to the sanctuary of the ladies. She carefully washed her hands, ran her fingers through her hair, rubbed her lips and smoothed her eyebrows, and then returned to her desk.

Stillet was watching her again now.

'Well?' she said, she knew her voice was too high. 'What do you think?'

'Good, very good.' He looked at his watch, she automatically looked at hers. She was surprised to see it was 6.30 – the editorial floor was beginning to thin out, the nightly trek to the pub by the feature writers had begun although the news writers would be around till 7.30 or 8 o'clock.

'If I could have had it by five I would have run it today, but it will go in tomorrow.'

He held out a hand to her, but before she could respond a shout went up from the night news editor.

'Michael, come here. The Russians have shot an eighteen-year-old boy who tried to escape to the West. We'd better have a feature.'

Mike turned to her. 'Kate, get the cuttings out on that girl ballerina who escaped the other day. Ring Tom Westcott in Berlin – see what he can tell you about her. Also the stringer, tell him to find out where she is and see if he can get some quotes. Highlight it against the tragedy of the boy's death, you know what I want. Lots of human interest, OK, Kate?'

Kate was confused for a second, but only a second. She got the cuttings out on Rebecca and Elizabeth and rang Berlin; she got a little, but not very much. The stringer told her that the girl dancer had signed an exclusive with an American photographer.

Kate checked the teleprinters and Reuters.

'Try AFP too,' the night foreign editor told her, but no one had anything new on Elizabeth Gottlieb so Kate sat down and wrote about the promise of life, love and success for the young dancer. Whilst she typed Mike had already drawn up a new rough, given it to the art department, sorted out some pictures and worked on a new headline. As she finished each sheet it was passed to the back bench and subbed.

'You'd better come down to the stone with me and we'll check it there,' Mike told her when she'd finished the last sheet.

Kate barely had time to be excited. Journalists were never allowed into the domain ruled by printers, editors were just about tolerated, but a rush was on now. Kate watched as her piece was set in metal type by the compositor who stood on one side of the stone whilst she and Mike stood on the other and tried to read it upside down.

'It's going to be three inches too long, darlin'. You'll have to cut it in,' the compositor told her as he set the extra pieces of type at the side of the page. He took a huge inky roller and whipped it quickly over the type. Then he put a large piece of wet paper on top and another hand-held roller was pressed down and rubbed over the page. The sheet was lifted off and handed to her, and another copy was then prepared in the same way and passed to readers in another room who checked it for 'literals' – typographical mistakes.

'Try and make straight paragraph cuts,' Mike told her as they both read it through. 'Look, here, you can take that description out.'

The compositor listened, took the appropriate metal letters out and reset the lines. He ran off another sheet which this time was set to dry on a huge hot plate.

'That's for the editor. A messenger will take it up to him,' Mike said.

'His will be dry when he reads it. I suppose that's the perks of the job, clean fingers,' said Kate.

Mike laughed.

As they left Kate saw that the whole page of type was now locked together, it was loaded onto a trolley and wheeled past her.

'They'll make the cast from that,' said Mike.

'And then the paper will be printed from that.'

'After a bit more fiddling. You've got the idea, Kate,' he said and blew her a kiss.

She was pleased. Very pleased.

Tom found Cassie in the studio. She was quiet, but contained. He asked her how she had spent the last few days.

'With a friend.'

'How is Bravington?'

'Bravington?' she asked, surprised. She had quite forgotten about him. 'Oh, fine,' she said quickly, hoping Tom hadn't picked up her lapse.

Tom *had* noticed his mother's slight hesitation at the mention of John Bravington's name. There was obviously a new man in her life and he wondered briefly who it might be. But Cassie's permutations were not his concern.

He had started to climb the stairs to his bedroom when he heard

Cassie call him, 'Tom, I want to show you something.' She was holding a newspaper in her hand.

'Do you know who this woman is?'

'What woman?'

'Don't tell me you haven't heard what is happening in Berlin. They've built a wall around the Eastern Sector.'

'Oh God. But I can't say I am surprised. I wonder how Helga is?'

'Helga?'

'A friend of mine.'

'If she's in the West she'll be all right. How come you didn't know about it?'

'There were no newspapers at Jonathan's house and I didn't bother to buy one at the station.'

'A woman escaped over the wall, with her daughter.'

He walked back down the stairs. His mother, standing by the kitchen door, suddenly looked very small.

'Who was the woman, Cassie?'

'Rebecca. She married Joshua Gottlieb. This is a photograph of her daughter.'

Tom didn't look at the newspaper. He put it down on the hall table by the telephone, took his mother in his arms and stroked her hair and tried to comfort her.

'I wrote her a letter,' Cassie told him.

'Why did you do that?'

'She will need help.'

'But you hate her.'

'I know.'

'So why help her?'

'It makes me feel better, Tom.'

'Then I hope she accepts your help.'

Cassandra Bray hugged her son very tightly, she loved him so much.

Tom read Kate's piece on the ballet dancer, he thought it very good but he tore it up before Cassie saw it. When, later, she asked for the newspaper, Tom said, 'They didn't deliver it. When I rang they said there was some foul-up over deliveries. They asked if we would like a *Telegraph* or maybe a *Times*.'

'Oh darling, would you pick something up for me? I can't go through the day without a newspaper.'

Tom collected a copy of *The Times*, having first checked that there were no photographs of any defecting Germans in it.

221

At eleven o'clock he telephoned Kate at her office.

'Hello,' he said.

Kate was so happy to hear his voice. The euphoria of the night before had already disappeared by the time morning had come. She had woken with the dawn. At first she had lain in her bed in her small pink and white bedroom dwarfed by a huge cream dressing table with its curved mirror – a thirteenth birthday present – and wondered what was bothering her. Then she had experienced the sharp gut-ache of love gone wrong.

Kate had got out of bed with difficulty. She had selected a lime-green skirt and a navy sweater from the wardrobe and tossed them on her unmade bed. She had tried the outfit on and then taken it off again. Then she had put on a blue dress but that looked too formal. Several other items of clothing were pulled out and rejected. She had returned to the original sweater and skirt. Unable to face her parents, she had left the house, shouting a hurried farewell. Kate felt bad, she knew they would have wanted to share her success with her.

She had sat at her desk staring at the phone, trying to find a proper excuse to call Tom, praying that he would ring her. All the accolades would mean nothing without his approbation.

'It's a good article, Kate,' he said softly.

'Thank you. Can we see each other later?'

Over a celebratory bottle of wine at lunch Tom told Kate about the identity of the ballerina.

'Don't say anything to Cassie. It's stirring up a lot of wounds. Let it be.'

Kate nodded.

Back at the office, of course, she took out the photographs. So this thin, grey-haired woman was Cassie's rival. She tried to concentrate on her but it was the daughter who interested her more. She was obviously beautiful, with straight black hair, a small nose, wide eyes, and a full mouth – her face disturbed Kate. It must have been the girl's obvious distress that communicated itself even across the grainy surface of a newspaper photograph.

# Chapter Ten
## 1961–1962

It was six weeks later that Kate realised she might be pregnant. At first it was just a nagging worry at the back of her mind, but as two weeks passed with no sign of the once-inconvenient monthly blood-letting, the threat of a personal crisis loomed larger with each until, after the date of the second period had come and gone, it overwhelmed her. She kept telling herself it was ludicrous, she had always used the cap, but she knew she never bothered to insert more cream when they made love twice, or maybe three times in one evening.

Nor could Kate overlook the changes that were taking place in her own body – the transformation from a single person to a life-support system could not be ignored. Her breasts had altered shape, they were sore and the nipples were browner – they seemed to have spread – and there was sickness in the morning too. After the fourth morning of flight to the lavatory she wondered how much longer she could conceal her situation from her parents. She made an attempt to swallow a breakfast of bacon and egg. Even tea had assumed an unappealing tang. She poured herself a glass of milk.

'Milk?' her mother exclaimed. 'You hate milk!'

'I'm acquiring a taste for it.'

'Pregnant women drink milk,' her father said, laughing.

'It isn't Kate's turn yet,' her mother retorted. 'Why, she and Tom haven't even set a date.'

If Kate hadn't already been so preoccupied she would perhaps have noticed that her mother's voice was falsely gay, that her face was worried, and that her hand trembled a little. Kate's mother had gone off cooked breakfasts and tea when she had been carrying Kate. But Kate noticed nothing. Her mother's hand strayed over her hair as she sat, head bent, at the kitchen table. But she could do no more than that, for Kate's father sat there too.

Later that day, Mrs Sullivan rang Kate at the office; not something that she normally did. 'Are you all right?' she asked her daughter.

'Why?' Kate was defensive.

'Nothing,' her mother said. 'Nothing at all. I just thought you looked a bit peaky. That's all.'

Oh my God, Kate thought, she knows, she knows, what am I going to do? The shame of it will destroy our relationship. Who can I turn to? Who can help me?

Kate's mother thought, speak to me, I'll help you. I am your mother. Let me into your life.

But neither of them spoke.

Kate telephoned Cassie and Cassie was delighted to hear from her. However, when Kate asked rather speedily for a lunch date – and away from Fleet Street – Cassie did wonder why.

As soon as she saw Kate, who was already seated in the restaurant, she knew. Kate's face was different. She was pale and wan, of course the worry must have been making her ill. Cassie wasted no time. She was not a woman to do that.

Once the ritual pleasantries had been exchanged she said, 'My poor darling, how late are you?'

Kate wanted to cry. Was it so obvious? 'Two months, I think.'

'Does Tom know?'

'No. I haven't told him yet.'

'What do you want to do?'

Kate did cry then. She felt ridiculous.

'Do you want me to help you organise it?'

Kate paused a little. 'It' was an abortion. Of course she had to have an abortion. There was no alternative . . . really. She made a great effort to stop the tears and looked Cassie in the eyes.

'Would you?'

'Of course I will. It'll be all right. You'll feel nothing. You'll just go to sleep and when you wake up it'll all be over.' She put her arm around the girl's shoulders, she wanted to comfort her. 'I promise you.'

'I'll have to tell Tom.'

'Of course,' Cassie replied, 'but leave all the practical stuff to me. Now what would you like to eat? And don't tell me nothing. How about a salad? That won't be too squeamish.'

Throughout lunch Cassie covered her own feelings with bright chatter. She felt so sorry for Kate, but of course there was no question of them having the child, they were far too young. The thought of Tom

224

marrying was ridiculous. He had hardly started his life yet. She knew that she must not allow anyone to think of what was happening to Kate as anything but an unwanted pregnancy. 'It' must never be referred to as a baby. She knew that they would be unable to bring themselves to terminate a life if it assumed an identity. Things had to be progressed quickly, before the foetus grew much more. But try as she might Cassie still felt a great sadness.

Kate telephoned Tom that same evening.

'I need to see you,' she said, 'it's urgent.'

They arranged to meet in Harrods.

'Upstairs in the Georgian Restaurant at eleven o'clock, if you can make it,' Kate told him.

Tom was confused by her choice of venue.

'It's anonymous,' she told him, 'I like that.'

Tom was not an insensitive man. An anonymous venue was not a flippant choice – there must be reasons. It did not take long for him to come to the conclusion that his girlfriend, whom he did love, was pregnant. At first the thought of the impending child terrified him, but he told himself that Kate had to have the choice of what they would do. She was the one who was carrying the child. 'Their child.' As young as he was, the very words excited him – it made him realise that their passion had made a living being. The enormity of the conception swamped him. A baby, a tiny baby. He found himself looking at prams. A ridiculous thing to do, but he was going to have one of those. Momentarily he was tearful. He discussed the situation with no one, it was a private time, but he couldn't help but wonder about his father and whether he had felt as Tom himself was feeling now when Cassie had presented him with the reality of his own birth. He resolved to ask him, when he could. Fatherhood, he thought, created its own club.

He arrived at Harrods at 10.45. It seemed ridiculous to be meeting someone he knew so intimately in so remote a place. He felt oddly awkward so he spent his time wandering around the men's department and then he took the lift, manned by a Harrods commissionaire in olive green, to the fifth floor. The restaurant was a feminine affair with a patterned carpet and heavy chandeliers. He was shown to a table with a perfect view of the entrance. Women came in with other women, mothers with children, and a few fathers for Saturday morning coffee. Kate arrived late, at 11.10. He stood up, wanting to kiss her, but she was distant with him. He didn't mind, it confirmed his explanation for the meeting.

225

Just as his mother had, Tom said simply, 'You're late.'

'Yes.'

He tried to take her hand, but she wouldn't allow it. That worried him.

'We have to talk,' he said cautiously.

'That's why I asked you to meet me.'

'Look,' he said, suddenly making a decision, 'I don't particularly want to stay here. I can't touch you, or talk to you properly. Let's go. We'll drive somewhere, or. . .' He had already stood up.

'I don't want to go anywhere. Here is fine. Sit down, Tom. You see I've talked to Cassie and she'll arrange the abortion for me.'

'Cassie!'

If Kate hadn't been so distraught she would have noticed how dangerously quiet Tom's voice had become.

'She's been wonderful, Tom.'

'I couldn't care less what Cassie has been. It is nothing to do with my mother and I don't understand why it was discussed with her before you told me. I am the father.'

'I had to talk to someone.'

'You didn't need "someone". You had me.'

'But how can you understand what I am feeling? You can't have a baby, you're a man.'

She knew as she said it that it was a stupid thing to say. She hadn't meant it to come out as it had sounded. She would have apologised, but he had such a hurt expression on his face she wanted to laugh. Why was he upset, how could he understand how she was feeling? He wasn't carrying the baby. His body wasn't changing.

Tom was not sure at whom his anger was directed, Kate or Cassie. He burned with intolerance and indignation. How dare these two women presume to discount his feelings! The baby was half his and he had the right to be part of the jury that judged its future. He spoke with sharp, harsh words.

'I don't know what you have decided with my mother, but those decisions are actually irrelevant. It is you and I who have to make those choices, not Cassie.'

'Cassie didn't involve herself in any way other than to offer to make the arrangements.'

'It isn't for her to do anything. It is for me to do it, if that is what we decide is best.'

'There are no other choices, Tom. Be practical.'

'Practical? We're talking about. . .' He had stopped, the waitress was standing by the table, her small pad at the ready, her pen poised, her ears keenly trained on their conversation.

'Tea,' he said.

'Milk,' said Kate.

Tom looked at her inquisitively.

'I can't stand the taste of tea or coffee,' she told him.

He smiled wistfully. Kate put her hand over his. 'I know you feel somehow overruled. But can't you see, we need Cassie to help us.'

'I should have been told first.'

'Oh Tom, if you are practising power-play with your mother, go and do it somewhere else. Not over me. I'm not available.'

'We're talking about our child,' Tom said. His anger was visible now, it was a hot anger, his face was red, his eyes blazed.

'How dare you?' Kate said.

'How dare I what?'

'Talk about "our child". Don't you understand, if you give it an identity, I can't go through with the abortion.'

'But you don't have to. We'll get married, we'll. . .'

'No. I don't want it, I'm not ready for motherhood, and as long as I don't think of it as our child, it will be all right. Try to understand that. Cassie does, talk to her.'

She got up and left just as the waitress was bringing her milk.

Tom made no attempt to stop her. He left too, after he had paid the bill. He would certainly not talk to his mother, his rage against her was terrible. She had no right to intrude in his affairs, no right to decide his child's fate.

Cassie did not inform Charles of what was happening. If she had, she would have found him unmoved. He would have said it was a matter that had nothing to do with either of them. Cassie knew that so she decided if Tom wished his father to know he should should tell him himself.

She took Kate to a small flat off Seymour Street. There was a very nice man there, a doctor. He examined her, washed his hands and then told her to go and have a bath. Cassie was confused, but he explained that he wanted to minimise the risk of infection. Of course Cassie could stay.

After she had dried herself Kate was given an injection and Cassie held her hand until she fell asleep.

Whilst she waited in the rather neat sitting room, over-furnished with red velvet and mahogany, Cassie remembered Tom's birth and tried not to think of the foetus as Tom's child. She told herself that this was the right thing to do, the only thing to do. Tom could not contemplate marriage at his age, it just wasn't possible with Tom studying, and in any event Kate was just beginning her career. But try as she might Cassie could not block out the memory of her fight to bring Tom into the world. She remembered how she had called him 'little thing'.

Kate felt nothing when she first woke after the operation. She was in a bed in a nice room, white and anonymous, almost like a hospital. It seemed as if she were in a day-dreaming state, semi-conscious, but nothing more. She let Cassie dress her and take her back to her house – she had told her parents she was away on a job. She had told Michael Stillet that she needed a day's holiday that Friday.

'For a special weekend?' he had asked.

'Sort of.'

She dreamt of babies that night. They were in their prams, they all had bright little faces shining with happiness. Kind hands tickled and played with them. There was a pram at the end of the room. It was the only one without a mother standing by it. Kate knew it was her baby, she ran over to it, wanting to pick up the little one and hold it. But the pram was empty, there was nothing there except neatly folded blankets and sheets.

'Oh, that baby died,' another mother said.

'What was it like?' Kate heard herself asking.

'Oh, no one knows, no one saw it,' the same mother told her.

The anguish of her dream woke Kate up. The feeling of loss overcame her and she cried bitterly. She wanted Tom with her.

He came the next day, courteous, with flowers and chocolates.

She told him of her dream.

'Well. . .' he said awkwardly.

'You mean, what do I expect?'

Just as his mother had done the day before, Tom sat with Kate, and even held her hand, until she fell asleep.

He came down the stairs quietly; it was his intention to leave without seeing Cassie, but she was waiting for him in the hall. She greeted him with her usual warmth and a degree of passion.

'Darling, how are you? I've made some coffee, it's in the kitchen.'

'I don't want coffee with you, Cassie. I am leaving. You have involved yourself in my life, in my affairs, without asking me whether I wished you to do so. You abetted my girlfriend and not once did you consider whether it was what *I* wanted.'

He could see she was shocked. He knew it was not so much what he had said that mattered, but the way he had said it. He had never been so cold with anyone, he had never wished to be so cold with anyone.

It was Jonathan who had suggested that Tom might go to America.

'To get away from it. You could get a job in summer stock. It'll give you a breathing space and time to get over it. I am sure you must be going through some sort of bereavement.'

Tom was astounded at Jonathan's sensitivity. He had no idea that the pretty young man had so much understanding.

'I can understand, Tom, that you feel very bad,' commented Edward, 'but you weren't carrying the child. Kate was and I think she'll need your support for quite a while. If it doesn't work after that, well, so be it, but for now she needs you.'

'I won't go yet, Edward. But Jonathan's right, I need to get away.'

They were in Tom's rooms. They had taken to spending their evenings there since Tom had told them about Kate's pregnancy. Edward was frustrated for it was impossible for him to offer Tom the proper privileges of friendship at a time when Tom most needed him. How could he talk openly to Tom about his mother, when he, Edward, was sleeping with her and enjoying every minute of it? However, he could not condone her interference in Kate's pregnancy. He told her quite forcefully. She resented him for saying it.

'We agreed that we would not discuss Tom,' she said.

They were speaking on the telephone. Cassie had telephoned him, needing him.

'Cassie, we have a relationship. We sleep together. That gives us both the right to express our opinions to each other.'

'I told you the terms of the relationship. Tom is forbidden territory.'

'Tom is my friend.'

'And he is my son.'

'So we have to talk about him. We share him, as well as each other.'

'We don't share him, Edward. I've told you, he is my son.'

'Don't be ridiculous, Cassie, it sounds as if you think you own him.'

'I don't "own him", as you put it. But as his mother. . .'

'Cassie, stop interfering in Tom's life. You have to let go of him. He's a grown man.'

'He isn't a man yet.'

'He's the same age as I am.'

'Yes, but it's different, you aren't. . .' Cassie stopped, she was going

229

to say 'my son'. Suddenly she equated Edward with Tom and she didn't want to do that. If she thought of Edward as Tom's friend she would not be able to continue her relationship with him.

'Go on, Cassie.' She could hear Edward's insistent voice on the telephone.

'There is nothing to say. I don't know what I wanted to add. Tom is my son, you are my friend. I don't want to mix you up. What's wrong with that?'

'Why don't you want to "mix us up", as you put it?'

'Because if I think of you as Tom's friend it will seem wrong for me to sleep with you.'

'Really?'

'Don't get clever with me, Edward.'

'Why is it wrong, Cassie?'

'You're pushing me.'

'Yes, I am. Why is it wrong?'

'Because it's dirty!!'

'If that's how you feel, Cassie, then I wish you well.'

Cassie heard the phone click. She gasped. What had gone wrong, what had Edward made her say? She wanted him, she wanted to be with him. But he'd twisted the conversation, he had brought Tom into it. And now she would not be able to see Edward again. She could feel her body going numb. What was happening? Why was her life so awful? Oh she felt so bad, and there was no one she could turn to for help.

Edward was not surprised at himself. He had pushed Cassie quite deliberately. He knew what Cassie felt about Tom and he wanted no part of her complex needs. He was sad though, she was a wonderful lover and quite a woman. He could have fallen in love with her very easily, if it weren't for Tom. So it was lucky really – loving an older, married woman living in England was not part of the master plan. He wondered if he had made her face herself. But even as he thought about it he knew that Cassie would gloss over their conversation. She would never be able to face the truth about her Tom. How could she? So it was over, the story of Edward and Cassie. He wanted to shed tears but he told himself that at least now he could return to Tom.

He and Jonathan chose to support Tom during those weeks. He was not very communicative but they didn't force anything, just made themselves available. Jonathan was euphoric, he felt he was one of them at last.

However there was one night when Edward was not there. He had received a telephone call summoning him to a pub not far out of Cambridge. There was bad news from home. A key man had been lost in an ambush. Edward had sent a message that he felt the informer who had revealed the man's whereabouts should be shot. The Army Council had decided that his plan should be discussed and one of their Commanders was despatched to London to meet him. There was no question of Edward returning to Dublin. His cover had to be maintained.

'I suppose it's that mysterious girl – the one you're having in London,' said Tom, managing a little of his old humour. He didn't want Edward to go. He knew he was being morose and difficult, but at least he managed a cheery farewell as Edward walked through the door. He set a bottle of whisky on the brown wooden table that served as both a dining table and desk and poured out two glasses. He offered one to Jonathan.

They drank companionably. In a short while they were both drunk. So it was understandable that Tom did not over-react when Jonathan's hand brushed his penis. And when the fingers lingered and he felt himself becoming erect, it felt all right. But when Jonathan took Tom's fingers and placed them gingerly on his own erect penis Tom did react. He pushed Jonathan away. 'Jesus,' he said, rubbing his hand over his befuddled head, as if to clear his brain. 'Get out, Jonathan, this isn't for me. You've got a wrong number.'

Jonathan left, his cheeks flaming with embarrassment. He wasn't too drunk to realise that his relationship with Tom could never be the same.

Tom said nothing to Edward, but his Irish friend perceived that something rather serious had happened to alter the situation between Jonathan and Tom when Jonathan no longer joined them for coffee at The Whim – even more so when Tom discouraged his enquiries. His suspicions were confirmed when he saw Jonathan in the company of some of Cambridge's exclusively male set. He didn't mention it to Tom.

Rebecca received Cassie's letter on the third day after her arrival in the West. She remembered her, the blonde American who had adored Joshua. She had written to her, herself, when Joshua had died. But all that was a long time ago. They had never been friends. Rebecca had always found her rather patronising. She wrote what she hoped was a polite letter, thanking Cassie for her interest but declining her offer of help.

Rebecca was anxious about Elizabeth, the girl was so withdrawn and difficult. When Rebecca asked her what was wrong she told her, 'Why did you make me come? I won't be able to dance here.'

'You will, you will. Adam says that you will shortly receive an invitation from the ballet company at the Hannover Opera House.'

'Who is Adam?' Elizabeth asked.

'The man who rescued us at the wall. He is a journalist, he is going to help us.'

Elizabeth shrugged. Mikhail was right, her mother was a stupid naive woman. Elizabeth hated what had happened. Why did her mother have to change their lives? It was a stupid situation. She cared nothing for politics, she only cared about dancing – and without Mikhail she was not sure she could dance. He was her motor, he propelled her, motivated her, taught her. What could she do without him? Her life was ruined. She went to her bed and lay on it, wishing it would swallow her up.

Rebecca waited anxiously for Adam Brodin to visit them. He had promised he would do something for Elizabeth. He had said something about exclusivity for five years, but Rebecca didn't know what that meant. The camp was not an easy place. They slept in dormitories and ate in a canteen. There were interviews and forms to fill in and bureaucrats to talk to. Otherwise they were left very much to their own devices, prey to boredom and insecurity.

Adam arrived to see Rebecca the following day.

'You have news for me, I hope,' she said to him.

'Absolutely, good news.' Adam Brodin was a young man, with a soft face, and short American-style hair.

'Shall we go?' he said, offering her his arm. 'I'd like to tell your daughter where she is going; we can take a few photographs.'

'More photographs?'

'Yes, of course. It's part of the exclusivity deal. We're going to chart her progress from a broken young girl to a star.'

'She's not broken,' said Rebecca, suddenly worried.

'No, of course she's not, it's just a manner of speaking. She's lost her home. . .'

'And she thinks her future as a dancer has gone too.'

'Yup, and we're going to change that right now.'

They found Elizabeth sitting on her bed, her face to the wall, avoiding the other refugees who sat in groups and talked quietly. Some of the men played chess, some of the women knitted, some did nothing, they were all waiting.

'You are to join a ballet company in Hannover. It's all set. This is the beginning of your life, Miss Gottlieb,' Adam told a bemused Elizabeth as he took his pictures. Rebecca signed the exclusive contract with the journalist: it seemed a small price to pay for her daughter's place in the Hannover Ballet Company.

Elizabeth tried to feel happiness, but what she really felt was fear. Without Mikhail she could not dance; it was ludicrous to think otherwise. She would be exposed and ridiculed. She had to run away, somehow she had to get away. She was desperate, but suddenly the answer to her problem became clear. She would get back to the East, back to Mikhail, she would go that night, no one would know. It would be done quietly. She would leave Rebecca a message on her pillow and when she had sorted everything out she would bring her back too. Mikhail would help her. There would be no problem, and all this would be nothing more than a passing nightmare.

Elizabeth waited until everyone was asleep, and then in the dark she slipped her shoes on, pulled off her nightdress, and silently put on her clothes. She left her letter on Rebecca's pillow and padded out of the room. She was halfway down the road when a jeep with four soldiers in it drew alongside her. The men were all talking in loud voices, she supposed it was English, she didn't know; men in uniform frightened her. She kept walking, with her eyes fixed on the road.

'Fräulein?' one of them said.

Still she didn't answer – she had to run, there was nothing else she could do. She turned into the field that ran by the road. She could feel her heart banging against her chest, her breath came in short bursts. The men had stopped the jeep, one of them was running behind her, he was gaining on her, she was desperate. She tripped and fell, and he was on top of her. What was he going to do with her? She was crying, shouting. But he did nothing, he held her hands by her side to stop her scratching him. She could feel his uniform, it was rough against her skin.

'Shush, shush,' he kept saying.

And then she realised he was not going to hurt her. She let him pull her up and take her back to the jeep.

One of the soldiers, he was black, offered her a cigarette. She shook her head. The one who had chased her had a nice face, she could see that, he was blond; Mikhail had been blond.

'Marienfeld?' the black one asked her.

She nodded and they drove her back. She got back into the room and

233

went over to Rebecca; her mother was still asleep. She took the note from the pillow and tore it up, took off her clothes, and climbed into bed. She dreaded tomorrow.

# Chapter Eleven
## 1963

After the abortion Kate had become less independent, somehow more clinging. It was as if the unborn child tied her more to Tom than if it had been given a chance to live. She had become melancholy, taken to seeking out babies, caressing the handles of prams as if she wanted to whisk the occupant away into her own world.

Tom continued to blame his mother, and Cassie seemed to accept that. She had told him, in an outburst, that whilst she had been waiting for Kate in the doctor's surgery she had relived his birth.

'I wanted more children,' she had said, 'so I didn't offer abortion as an easy option. It was to save you.'

'Save me!' he had exploded. 'Save me from what?'

'The responsibilities of parenthood at this stage of your life.'

'And Kate, your great friend Kate, what did you want to save her from?'

'I am fond of Kate, but she is not my child,' Cassie answered very honestly. 'I worried for her, of course, but my main concern at the time was for you, I admit it.'

'Whatever you say, you can never justify your behaviour in my eyes,' Tom told her.

Tom still loved the theatre, but he had tired of the posturing of undergraduate and fringe productions. He wanted the discipline of the commercial world. He had no wish to align himself with the 'let's-take-culture-to-the-masses' faction. Tom Bray had a simple ethos: if the work is good enough, the masses will come to you. He saw the theatre both as a circus for talent and as a statement that could challenge both eye and ear in a more direct way than cinema or television. Given that, where else could he go, he had reasoned with a distraught Kate, other than America?

'I don't want you to leave me,' Kate told him.

'I am going to go, Kate, and you must accept it.'

He gave her what he could but even he knew that it wasn't enough. He noticed after a while that she brought a journalist, Michael Stillet, into their conversation whenever she could. Tom hoped that her relationship would flourish with him. He, of course, had spent a last weekend with Kate before leaving. They had gone to Kent; England at its best with its soft green fields and the remnants of the strawberry harvest seemed appropriate for a farewell. Kate had been emotional, loving. He'd tried, because she was his friend and that would never change. But the passion was gone for him.

Of them all, Tom had regretted leaving his father the most. Tom knew he was happy now. He had dined with him and Margaret in their elegant flat with its clean lines and floor-to-ceiling windows that looked out onto a neat terrace that housed a square box for plants. Despite himself, Tom suddenly thought of Cassie's squashy settees and huge fireplaces and recognised that Charles' home wasn't really the kind of place where one could put one's feet up.

Over a quiet drink before dinner he had told Charles of Cassie's role in Kate's abortion.

'She would have done it because she felt it was for the best,' Charles told him.

'It wasn't her business,' Tom answered. 'Dad?' He swallowed, he was not used to being familiar with his father, but for a short time he had been a father too. 'How did you feel, when you knew I was going to be born?'

'Awed, because pregnancy is a female affair. It carries a mystique that excludes us men. But the reality of the child belongs as much to us as to them. I am not sure they totally realise that.'

Tom had reached over and taken his father's hand. He was pleased to feel Charles grip him back.

Charles was grateful to Cassie – she had brought up their son well. He was aware that he himself had abdicated his responsibilities towards Tom. He had missed Tom's growing years and he regretted it. However, Charles was sure that he was a lucky man. At last he had found a peace and a companionship that he treasured. Margaret was unobtrusive, she made no demands on him, but she did organise him and she did care for him. 'As long as I have you, I need nothing else,' she told him.

She never failed to excite him in bed. She was aggressive with him, using him as if she were the male, and he the female. He liked that. It had come about quite suddenly when they came home from Edinburgh. They had been making love, Margaret had been on top of him, her small breasts flattened as she moved on him, head back, gripping his ankles. She ran her hands up his calves, under his thighs, under his buttocks, and further. He'd cried out when he'd felt her fingers inside him.

Margaret had rubbed her tiny breasts up and down his chest. She knew he would never leave her now. And nor would it be long before he would divorce Cassie and make her his wife.

They began to create their rituals. As each habit was formed Margaret felt she was untying the bonds that bound Charles to Cassie. Every week they had dinner with David and Marilyn Sampson. They played bridge together. She liked seeing four people seated around her table.

Margaret was quite glad that Tom had gone to America; somehow he was the last tie with Cassie. With him gone she felt Charles was really hers.


With his grandmother's help Tom obtained the position of assistant director at the Boston Playhouse in the United States. It was a good theatre in a theatrical wasteland for it seemed that politics and music found more favour with the neighbours of Harvard University. But for Tom it was the promised land.

He had been working as assistant director at the Playhouse for just one month when they murdered President Kennedy. The impact on the state that had spawned the hero was devastating. Tom, despite his intellectual contempt for the Kennedy bandwagon (given life by his grandmother and nurtured at the breast of the theatrical left in England), was engulfed in the national mourning.

It was Tom's habit to take his breakfast in the drugstore opposite the theatre. He had ordered his eggs sunny side up and his bacon crisp every day since he had arrived at the beginning of September. He sometimes went back at lunchtime for a sandwich, but he was seldom alone then. As befitted the role that nature and luck had handed him – for one without the other would not have done the trick – Tom attracted attention, and not just from women. He was careful, however, to remain aloof from the men, save for the artistic director, Sidney Fleistein, a tyrant of a man only saved from universal hatred by his sheer commitment.

Fleistein had reformed the Boston Playhouse himself when it was threatened with closure. He had bullied, wheedled and performed, and gone to extravagant lengths to get the money he needed to create his idea of a theatre. He wanted a season of plays, four perhaps, to run through the winter. In a smaller auditorium, he would pander to musical taste – concerts and ballet would be on offer. He insisted on excellence. And he got it.

Tom was lucky that not only was Fleistein an ex-Communist who truly worshipped at the feet of Jane Fleming because she was one of the ones who had never turned her back during those mad McCarthy years, but he had also been at Edinburgh when Tom had directed *An Irish Love Story*. He had been curious about a young man arrogant enough to direct a new play when he himself was an untried director. Fleistein had found fault with the production, of course, but it was brave, and good – in parts. So when Jane Fleming had offered $25,000 for her grandson's participation in his 1963/64 season he had felt obliged to tell her that the money wasn't necessary: Tom had talent. Jane Fleming informed him that she knew that, otherwise she wouldn't have even telephoned him, and he was a fool not to take the contribution. By the time Sidney Fleistein, a name for which he would never forgive his mother, had managed to get the sentence out to say that he would be happy to take the contribution, Jane Fleming had put the receiver down.

When Sidney met Tom for the first time he bellowed, 'Your talent cost me $25,000 – you had better be worth it.'

And as if to make him earn every penny of the loss he worked Tom as he worked no one else in the company. He abused him, he cajoled him, he pushed him – but he never praised him.

Fleistein had invited a prominent German ballet company from Hannover to perform for two weeks in his smaller theatre. They were good, that was his reason, but they were also German, and it was less than twenty years since the war. There were times when Fleistein regretted his decision: born a Jew, despite his now atheist beliefs, he had little reason to honour anything German.

The Hannover Company were due to arrive on the day the President's funeral took place; instead they arrived a day late. So it was that on the Tuesday Tom noticed a small slight girl sitting at the counter in the drugstore. She was so thin he thought he would be able to count the bones in her back. She was drinking black coffee.

'She should eat, that girl,' his waitress Cecile told him. 'She's German though.'

Tom would have liked to have told her that being thin was certainly no national trait among the German people, but Cecile had no wish to talk of foreigners. She had devoured the preceding days' events and it was that which chiefly occupied her now.

Tom picked up his coffee, full of cream as he liked it, and walked over to the counter and the girl. When she heard him speak in German she looked up. He was about to smile his way into an introduction, but he found himself quite unable to go through the pleasantries for when he looked into her face he saw in the wide green almond-shaped eyes and the snub nose and the small mouth an animal-like quality of such sensuality that he reacted physically to her: his stomach contracted, his heart started beating – was this called falling in love, he wondered. The girl, who knew nothing of Tom's startling response, was merely surprised to find herself conversing with someone in her own language. Tom pulled himself together and explained that he had served in Berlin in 1958.

'I lived in Berlin then,' she said, 'but in the East.'

He raised an eyebrow.

'A sensational escape on the night the wall went up, all stage-managed by my mother.'

'The wall too?' Tom asked.

'No,' she replied, smiling suddenly, transforming the little face, but even so Tom could see that there was nothing young about her. 'Not even she could do that.'

'My mother knew someone who escaped that night – she had a daughter too.'

'There were so many of us.'

Tom made no comment but he knew who the girl was even before she gave her name. It was extraordinary. Here he was confronted by the daughter of a woman who had haunted his mother for all these years. It didn't occur to him to mention the coincidence to Elizabeth, it was nothing to do with her – that was Cassie's business and he would never discuss it.

'My name is Tom Bray. I am an assistant director at the Boston Playhouse, for the moment.'

'And I am Elizabeth Gottlieb. A dancer.' She looked down at her coffee as if to study the deep, dark liquid.

Tom was totally aware of her. He could almost smell her and he felt the sex roll off her. He could scarcely look at her, but he managed an invitation.

239

'Are you free this evening? Would you like to have dinner with me?'

'I don't like to go to restaurants.'

'I'll cook you something. Will sausages and sauerkraut be OK?'

She nodded her head. He could see she was awkward too.

Tom thought of her all day. He even sneaked into the theatre to look at her as she danced. It was an extraordinary thing for him to watch a dancer use her whole body to tell a story. It was mime of course, but in its most beautiful form. The production was *Sleeping Beauty* and Elizabeth was the Princess Aurora. She flitted across the stage, clutching the dreadful spindle behind her back, ignoring the pleas of her distraught parents. Tom was excited by the beauty of her dance. It was as if she brought together every possible means of expression into one form, creating a moving picture on the stage. But more than that she *was* Aurora, she *was* the capricious girl. As Tom watched her body move to the music she aroused something primeval in him, perhaps it was her legs, or maybe the line from her head to her hip bone, but he had an overwhelming desire to hold her, to subdue her, even to protect her.

Tom's own work was less romantic. The play was Tennessee Williams' *A Streetcar Named Desire* – Blanche Dubois was no Princess Aurora, and for a moment Tom dallied with the idea of having Blanche dance – a grotesque parody of a princess. But the realities of his position in the company precluded any such fantasies. Tom was an assistant director and an assistant director is not supposed to be creative, he merely echoes his director. Tom wondered how long he would be able to provide such a service. It seemed that his main task was to follow Fleistein around, note instructions together with any little asides, and ensure that the great man's words were followed through into action. Such a task was broad-based, from a briefing to a designer to ensuring that the coffee machine was working. But Tom was interested in the way Fleistein worked, for this was his first experience of the professional theatre. Fleistein seemed to be formal. On the first day that the assembled company had come under his scrutiny, he had laid down his guidelines, the underlying credo of which was: 'I am the boss.' He had organised a structured read-through, followed by a précis of his interpretation of the play and the way it was going to be performed. Tom had wondered if any of the actors would demur, or suggest their own interpretation, but the cast, even the Hollywood Star specifically cast to give added sparkle, had been docile enough. Tom was disappointed, rehearsals weren't going to be very interesting.

Tom collected Elizabeth at the stage door that evening. He heard her coming for she was arguing loudly with a young man who had obviously taken her company that evening for granted. Tom had to laugh, the young man was so indignant and so pompous. As they rounded the corner Tom was treated to a view of the forsaken man who at first sight seemed rather small with enormous shoulders. The effect was frog-like. He wore his coat slung round his shoulders like a cape, and his hat was large. Anglo-Saxons would have branded him as gay, but Tom knew better. He immediately christened him the Frog Prince. Elizabeth thought that very funny, she threw back her head and laughed loudly. Tom had never seen a woman do that before.

He bought the food on the way back to the apartment. Boston encapsulated American history and American opportunity although, with its cobbled streets and village greens, it would have been easy to have dismissed it as merely an extension of little old England. The old families here clung to their privileges and their exclusivity with much more determination than their cousins across the sea. There were enough immigrants to flavour the city: there were the Irish, and the Jews, and the Italians, the Greeks, the Chinese. But despite having had a Catholic son of Boston in the White House, the old families still had their way.

Tom was lucky to live on Beacon Hill. He liked the steep incline that led up to his house, the black street-lamps that cast a romantic glow over the red brick of the houses. There was no sporting the oak here, but there was a front door that locked, two rooms – one for sleeping, and one for sitting – a small kitchen and a bathroom. It was furnished simply, with lots of wooden furniture but a very comfortable bed and a sofa that encouraged lounging.

Tom was aware of being nervous – it was stupid, he was never nervous with women. He made a lot of gestures, showing her the bathroom, the view, even the kitchen, and then he offered her a drink which she refused.

'Well, coffee then?'

'Yes, black.'

'You drink a lot of black coffee.'

She shrugged. She was wearing a sweater and black trousers, he could see she wasn't wearing a bra and he wondered what she would look like, lying on her back with her hands stretched behind her neck.

Realising he was staring at her, he turned and walked into his little kitchen. He made fresh coffee and invited her in to talk to him whilst he cooked. He noticed her little face was pointed upwards and away from the stove, almost as if she were avoiding the smell of food. She didn't offer to help.

He decided to ask her to lay the table. She did that nicely, even asking him for candles. She re-arranged the flowers that his landlady always put in his rooms every Friday, together with a plate of cookies.

Tom cooked the sausages carefully, opened the tin of sauerkraut and heated it, adding a little more sugar and vinegar, and served it, he hoped in a German way. She ate little, and rather tidily, cutting her sausages up into small pieces, chewing them very carefully. Halfway through the meal she excused herself and hurried to the bathroom. She ran the taps, she didn't want him to hear her being sick.

Elizabeth did hate the smell of food, and particularly of cabbage. It always made her recall the meal Rebecca had prepared when they still lived in East Berlin. But she was very attracted to the young man who was courting her so well. He had an extraordinary face with a beautiful mouth, and wonderful tapering fingers, but it was his eyes with their dark lashes and their hint of coldness that aroused her. Mikhail had that quality too. She had missed him badly in the beginning. She had written to him. He had sent a polite note back wishing her well and extolling the virtues of a new ingénue. It had hurt at first, but dance helped. And then a brief lighthearted tryst with a fellow dancer had enabled Elizabeth to discover that it was not that she was not a woman, but that Mikhail was incapable of loving someone who asked for pleasure too. Quite deliberately, in someone else's bed, Elizabeth had banished Mikhail and promised herself she would never be fucked from behind again.

Tom was worried, he knocked on the door, trying to be polite.

'Are you all right?'

Elizabeth opened the bathroom door, he could smell perfume on her.

'Yes, excuse me. I am fine,' she replied in English.

It surprised him, he had no idea that she spoke any English at all.

'You've let me disgrace myself with my terrible German whilst all the time you could have spoken English.'

'I thought you wanted to speak German,' she said.

She moved past him to go into the sitting room. He touched her arm and saw the black fabric of her sweater as it moved over the swell of her

242

breasts. She turned to him, shifting her shoulders. He reached for her, pulling the sweater up and running his hands over her small breasts to feel the sharp nipples against his fingers. He could feel her grind herself into him, pulling his mouth onto hers, pushing her tongue against his teeth. She was taking off her own trousers and his. Her legs were around his back, he was inside her and she felt wonderful.

Elizabeth stared into the face of the man above her, the man who held her. She could feel him move in her, she wanted to watch his face. She liked that best when she was with a man. The shudder started, and the sweet wet ache filled her.

He slept afterwards, that amused her, he was like all men, they got so tired after so little exertion. They should try the ballet. She got out of the bed and stretched a little, bent her legs; when she got cramp it helped.

She went into his other room and sat on the couch. They hadn't pulled the curtains so the street lights lifted the dark. She was glad she was alone, she needed time to think. The extraordinary young Englishman had lit a fire in her, she had never felt that way about any man before. Since Mikhail she had used them, but Thomas Bray was different. She ran her fingers over her mouth, all that had happened between them had been so special, so exciting, it had been pure pleasure. Up to that time only dancing had given her that special ecstasy, now a man, this man, had shown her that it wasn't just the union of music and movement that could create such beauty – she loved it, she would never let him go.

Elizabeth's life had changed so dramatically since that jump out of the building – from one country to another. The discovery that she could actually dance without Mikhail to support her was phenomenal in itself. The American journalist, Adam Brodin, had taken her and Rebecca to Hannover. She had felt as if she were going to die, her throat was closed, her muscles ached, her stomach contracted.

She had auditioned in front of three men and a woman. She hadn't looked at them, she didn't want to watch their disgust at her humiliation. Instead she had warmed up at the bar, working her limbs, trying to ignore the fluttering that she knew to be her heart.

It was time to dance, and she did.

They applauded when she had finished. It was then that she looked at them and saw the admiration in their faces.

'Elizabeth Gottlieb.' She heard Tom pronounce her name softly, in the English manner, she liked that, and she turned towards him and saw him naked – he enthralled her, and she held out her slim hand to him.

She told him about Adam Brodin in the morning.

'My mother signed a contract with him. For five years he has the right to record every moment of my life with his camera. The transformation of the Eastern European victim into the West's passport to the good life.'

'Is he a friend now?' Tom was spreading butter liberally on a thin slice of toast which he offered to her. She would eat the bread, but without all that grease.

'You eat that one,' she said, picking up another slice and spreading it with as little of the butter as she could. 'No, he is like a spider, creeping all over the floor. I can't ignore him because I can see him and he disturbs me, but I know I could squash him with my foot if I wanted.'

Tom raised an eyebrow.

'He has the right to always be there. I resent it.'

'Do you really dislike it here that much?'

'No, no I don't. It's just that I am realistic, the prisons are here too, and so are the victims.'

Tom smiled. 'And after Kennedy's Camelot, we will have to see what Lyndon Johnson's Texas can offer.'

'I saw him, you know, in Berlin.'

'Ich bin ein Berliner.'

Elizabeth nodded, smiled into him.

'It was electrifying. He was a young god, kissed by the sun. He stood in front of us all, Arthur himself, he should have had Excalibur in his hands.' She spoke an accomplished English now.

'You know the legend too.'

'Dancers can read.'

'Bitch,' said Tom gently, reaching for her, pulling her towards him by her long black hair.

She moved in with him that day, collecting her cases from the hotel herself. He was at rehearsal.

That night, as she prepared herself for bed, Tom watched her.

'It's ridiculous. I've only just met you and all I can think of is that you are only here for two weeks and how will I cope when you're gone?'

'We're touring in America for three months. I shall come back all the time.'

244

Content then, Tom went back to the business of loving her.

In London Kate lay in her bed and longed for Tom. During the days she could cope with his absence, but in the darkness his image came back to her and she wanted him. She knew it was over, she'd known before their weekend in Kent. It was the way he held her – that spoke more clearly than words. Oh, he wasn't selfish, he hadn't used her, he'd been careful of her needs, too careful, as if he were a guest at a dinner party, mindful of his manners, respectful of the meal in front of him, remembering to finish every morsel, and of course to praise the manner in which it had been prepared. She'd hated him for it.

She tried to concentrate on her work, she covered her stories, created some of her own, but she knew she was removed, so to speak, from the activity around her. She wasn't even aware of Michael Stillet until he asked her for lunch.

They took a taxi from Fleet Street to the West End. 'We'll go to one of those anonymous hotels where they serve good food in clean surroundings,' he said.

She had to laugh. They had gone to the restaurant at the top of the Hilton. She could see the gardens of Buckingham Palace from its windows, it would have looked nicer if it hadn't been for the hideous grey walls with their spikes at the top, all the sharper to put a head on.

For a brief moment she relished the thought of Tom's head on one of those spikes, dripping red blood, the lips still moving, mouthing her name, 'Kate, Kate, I love you.'

'So he's gone then,' Michael said.

She looked at him questioningly.

'Don't be coy with me, Kate. I am thirty-eight years of age, and I've been around a lot. I like you, you like me – I know you do, I felt it when I kissed you. I am a married man. I am not going to give you the bullshit of the misunderstood husband because it wouldn't be true. My wife is a nice woman, and I have three smashing kids, but there's something about you, you're under my skin, girl.'

Kate slowly shook her head. She shook her head in the hotel bedroom, she shook her head as he took off her clothes, but she stopped shaking her head when she felt his mouth on her skin. She wanted it to be good, she wanted to feel that earth move, she wanted just to forget herself.

'It'll get better,' he said afterwards, 'I promise you that.'

And she was grateful that she wasn't expected to lie.

245

They had lunch again, a week later. He'd been circumspect in the office, careful not to reveal their intimacies to the outside world. Kate took his lead, but if they met alone in a corridor he would touch her breast, or run his hand over the curve of her stomach. Those light touches excited her more than the coupling. She didn't know why.

He'd changed their lunchtime venue, this time it was a smart club off Conduit Street. He caressed her under the cover of the table cloth, and she squirmed for him. She wondered if she were going to fall in love with him. She wanted to, she wanted to stamp out the memory of Tom, deflect his image with Michael's. So what if he was married? She could cope.

The loving got better.

'I told you,' he said softly. She turned to look into deep blue eyes and told herself she was in love.

It wasn't difficult to love Michael Stillet. He was such an attractive man, not tall, but not small either. Thick, greying hair and sensual lips, and an almost animal ambition served up with a lot of charm was a good cocktail to offer Kate. She decided, after the fourth hotel visit, that the time had come for her to get a flat. Her parents were very supportive, they knew it was right. She found a three-roomed place in an anonymous block in St John's Wood. It had ugly grey carpet and floral chipboard wallpaper with several generations of emulsion over it. The bedroom curtains were grey-patterned velvet to match the carpet. There was a tree outside the bedroom window which belonged to the Catholic Church next door. Kate formed an immediate allegiance with that tree, it was the only reminder around that somewhere there was growth.

She told Michael that she would change it all, when she was rich enough.

'Is that a hint?' he asked, pouring champagne into two tumblers.

'No, I don't work like that.'

'Neither do I.'

The exchange was sharp enough – there was no need for further amplification.

Whilst Tom and Kate re-arranged their lives in keeping with their new circumstances, Cassie agonised over her son. She told no one of her despair. She took to looking at old photographs of him, ones taken when he was a boy. She remembered how close they had been. It seemed ridiculous that she couldn't talk to him. She tried telephoning, of course, but he was distant and difficult, using the phone to mask his feelings. He was polite, but he didn't give anything of himself. And that was worse than the harsh words.

She wrote to him, as honest a letter as she could, telling him that she apologised unconditionally. She had not meant to tamper with his life. He wrote back – accepting her apology. But it was a formality, she knew that, he hadn't forgiven her.

Cassie missed Edward too. He had awoken her body, and she was finding it hard to put away her physical needs. At night she would lie under her sheets and long for the feel of a man. She would use her fingers on herself, that helped, but afterwards she would lie there knowing she was alone.

She turned to her art, using it as surrogate lover and son, but she knew the work she was producing was pallid, she had lost her confidence. Yvonne had never shown 'The Seven Deadly Sins', first she had delayed the exhibition, and then she had told Cassie bluntly that the work had been too self-indulgent, it wouldn't sell.

She had preserved her privacy so jealously that there was no one there for her. She contemplated ringing John Bravington, but balked at the idea in the end. She allowed less intimate friends whom she found through Loretta to fill her hours. She even went to their charity events. Men flirted with her, but stopped the moment their wives appeared. It wasn't an easy time for Cassie.

She confided to Loretta that one of the husbands had even taken to dropping in for coffee. 'The awful part is I actually stop work and talk to him.'

'Why is it awful? Do you like him?'

'He is very married and he doesn't understand anything about painting.'

Cassie Bray was not a happy woman, but she knew she had to find a place for herself in the world of 1963. All around her she saw an explosion of talent – and it was young talent – demanding its place and its voice. Cassie suddenly felt old. Her art no longer nourished her. Doubt had become her bedfellow. She understood that art was essentially performance and required an audience. She knew she had to be not only conscious of her own role as a creator, but also in a sense aware of herself as a performer. In previous epochs the point of contact between the performer and their audience was religious or even social. In Cassie's era the artist had to turn to other forms of art to provide the stimulus. And Cassie did not know how to do that.

Nor could she talk to Yvonne: Yvonne was enmeshed in that new era.

'I love the egalitarianism of it all, Cassie,' she would say. 'Art is no longer the right of the rich.'

'But the paintings are getting even more expensive.'

'Yes, the originals. But more people come to see them now. And there are other techniques, silk screen for one, that enable you to provide maybe a hundred and twenty copies of the same work.'

'How you've changed, Yvonne,' Cassie told her. They were having dinner together in one of the smart new Italian restaurants off the King's Road in Chelsea where the new elite ate their pasta and drank their Frascati and courted the object of their desires.

'And you have not, my dear Cassie,' Yvonne told her before she turned to wave to a newly arrived diner who just happened to be a new dear friend as well as one of those clever new film directors.

'Darling,' he said, 'what a wonderful party last night. Who was that little friend of yours? Such a pretty girl.'

'She is, isn't she?' said Yvonne. 'And what about you? Left very early, didn't you?'

'Don't like being around vengeful husbands,' he said sharply.

Cassie was embarrassed, not only by the fact that she had no idea what they were talking about, but also because they totally ignored her.

She knew she should find another gallery, but she had no idea where to begin. Yvonne had always exhibited her work. She wondered briefly whether she might not telephone Charles, but she dismissed the thought – he had gone from her life too, although they had not yet divorced. She was waiting for him to make the request, dreading it almost, for she would not have refused, but he didn't, so they remained married and he still paid all the household bills. She often wondered why, but she supposed it was because it assuaged his conscience.

Cassie still had one friend from her past, one who would never forsake her: the black despair which embraced her and cuddled her and said, 'I'll never leave you.' Acquiescent, she locked her studio door and looked for other ways to fill her day.

She took herself off to her dress shops, but they didn't help. It seemed the clothes were for another generation and another shape, they made her feel ugly. She watched the men and the women in the streets as they passed her by, they all looked as if they had somewhere to go and she envied them.

Cassie read of John Bravington's activities on the front page of the *Daily Telegraph*. A reader of that august organ had accused the schoolmaster of exerting prejudicial influence over the boys in his class; his crime was to spell out the evils of nuclear war, and the reader, a parent by the name of Roger Standish, had called for his dismissal. Cassie was righteously indignant. She telephoned Kate at the *Enquirer* to find out if the story was true. She and Kate didn't see much of each other now. The abortion had blighted their relationship and with Tom's departure from Kate's life there was no call for contact.

'Yes, I am afraid it is true. We carried the story too. Mr Bravington is newsworthy now.'

'What does that mean?'

'His story will be carried by everyone, written up in the leader columns, and there will be a lot of readers' letters. The best thing you can do for him, Cassie, is to lobby as much support as you can. Try to make as much fuss, you know, build public sympathy, although word is that he will lose his job. Perhaps,' Kate could be heard clearing her voice, 'it might be a good idea if you contacted Tom. He could write an open letter to one of the newspapers. You know the kind of thing – "I owe my success to John Bravington".'

After the usual platitudes and promises to see each other very soon the conversation ended. Cassie realised she had not seen Bravington for a long time and she was aware that a renewed contact might prove embarrassing.

She decided that a note expressing her outrage and offering her help (and Tom's, of course) would be in order. She wrote it quickly and posted it before she had the chance to change her mind.

She waited for Bravington's reply. It came soon enough.

*My dear Cassie,*
*Thank you so much for your offer of support. I am confused, I confess. Any help would be most appreciated.*
*As ever,*
*John Bravington*

They met at the Dorchester for tea. The cream-painted room with its graceful panels and neat antiques served as ballast for both of them as they sipped their tea from china cups and ate their cucumber sandwiches.

'Just tell me what happened,' said Cassie.

She had taken care with her appearance that day, brushing her hair till it glowed, applying her lipstick neatly and not too overtly. She even put on a little rouge, she didn't want to look pale. She noticed that John looked very tired, his clothes were just the same, dishevelled but not shabby. His hair was neat enough, but his eyes were the eyes of a disappointed man – the zealot was quite gone.

'I don't really know where to start. I behaved as I always have. I have been scrupulous, as you well know from Tom, in my behaviour at school. But if the boys wanted to know what my personal views were outside school hours, I would tell them. There were those who were opposed to my point of view and I always thought it was rather a democratic way to spend an afternoon.'

'What do you mean?' Cassie said carefully.

'Well, since the trial of some of the Committee of 100 – you know, those of us who were a bit more active in our objections to the Bomb – there were summonses under the Official Secrets Act. I felt one should try to redress the balance, so to speak.'

'Oh no,' Cassie couldn't help but say, 'what were you thinking of?'

'Look, Cassie, I didn't organise anything in the school. I invited some of the boys for tea and discussion. I thought it was helpful. Standish was one of my stars, I thought he was a bit like Tom. It has all been quite a shock really.'

'They never turn out the way we think they will,' Cassie said softly.

'I beg your pardon?'

'Our children. We have dreams for them, and we plan their lives so they can achieve those dreams, and when they get there it isn't like we thought it would be.'

'Our own parents probably felt that way about us, Cassie,' Bravington said gently.

'Probably.' She shook her head, her hair shifted over her shoulders. 'Look, John, frankly I don't think you stand a chance in hell in this England of yours. Your country is still split between Empire and protest, and the Empire is still winning. Maybe in ten years it will be different, but by then we'll be too old to care.'

'In ten years you'll be fifty-six, that's hardly old.'

'It's old enough for things not to matter any more.'

'They'll always matter to you, Cassie.'

'I'll write to Tom, he'll help as much as he can, I'm sure of it.'

'How is he? What is he doing?'

Cassie could see that Bravington was hungry for news of his protégé. She realised then how hard it must be to prepare the young and then lose them. She held back a sigh and reported what little she knew of Tom's life in America.

'He went off with his head held high, the arrogance fairly obliterating him from view. But he is just an assistant director, which doesn't mean very much, and I think he'll be chafing at the bit soon.'

Bravington smiled. 'I doubt it, Cassie. He'll stick at it until he has learnt what he needs and then he'll find a way out into the spotlight.'

How well John Bravington knew her son.

As she poured more tea from the same silver, Victorian-style teapot that had always been in use in London hotels – thank heavens some things never changed – Cassie asked how his wife was coping.

'She's appalled, of course. The life of a policeman's daughter does not prepare one for a radical husband!'

'Why do you stay together?'

'Pardon?' Bravington's voice was shocked.

'You never spend any time together. From what I know, you have few interests in common. What binds you?'

Even as she said the words Cassie knew she had erred. It was not acceptable to probe. The manufacture of an unacceptable partner is a perfect analgesic against the reality of one's own failings – the unfailing source of excuses: all the 'if only's', and the 'I can't because's'.

Suddenly she couldn't look at John Bravington because, if nothing else, Cassie was an honest woman. She excused herself as quickly as she could, trying to minimise the embarrassment with promises of help and support.

Cassie wrote to Tom as soon as she got home, sending him copies of all the newspapers, simply outlining what Kate had suggested. As she sealed the letter she realised that perhaps for the very first time she had made no personal requests of Tom, nor volunteered any information about herself.

In the safety of her kitchen Cassie contemplated the wasteland of her life. She thought about Edward – she had so enjoyed him. She wondered where else she might go for solace. It did not take long for her to realise that there was an alternative for her: she had her work. Like a starving creature, she raided her paints and her crayons, looking for an idea to bring a new theme to her work. She haunted the art galleries searching for inspiration. Days became weeks until, in an obscure gallery, she found a sketch by a German artist, Käthe Kollwitz.

Joshua had first introduced Cassie to the work of Käthe Kollwitz in Paris. Born in 1867, Kollwitz had struggled to cope with the duality of being an artist and a woman, trying to balance the needs of both elements within her. She lost her son in the first weeks of World War I;

it aroused within her an implacable hatred of war. The Cassie of another time had found her too political, and perhaps too dour, but now Cassie understood the sensuality and irony in her work. Kollwitz saluted the mothers of the world; that would be Cassie's work too. She wouldn't be a party to the mourning of their losses any more, she would praise their victories.

She was irritated by the physical limitations of painting in the face of such a task. She wondered about using collage. She spent her hours experimenting with papier mâché, building up outlines, experimenting with texture. So immersed in her work was she that she forgot her despair.

Tragedy comes into a family unbidden. Sometimes it lurks quietly, creating small crises and then departing, at other times it strikes, swift and deadly.

Charles Bray had a sore throat. Well, it wasn't so much a sore throat as a feeling as if there was something stuck in his throat. He ignored it, of course. He had other things on his mind: he had been shortlisted to design a major new shopping complex, like those vast American shopping malls, something new and innovative for England. He wanted the job badly, he saw it as his responsibility to make utilities more comfortable and usable in a society that had great need of them. He had prepared a proposal which would incorporate moving staircases, shopping collection points, comfortable seating areas, facilities to care for a baby, clean lavatories, playrooms, accessible telephones, banks, restaurants, car parks – a utopia for the consumer. It was his statement on how to live.

'This is a much better way to improve living conditions,' he told Margaret. He cleared his throat and sipped some water. 'Better than all the marches and campaigns.' He felt so damn sick.

He started throwing up that night. At lunchtime the following day Margaret called the doctor.

Charles' doctor, Alec Rose, was a nice man. Once he had been a rather good horseman, now he played golf. Margaret liked him. As a doctor he was a cautious man, not prone to exaggeration. When he told Margaret, quietly, that Charles should go into hospital, she did not demur – experience had told her that Alec would only take such an action if he deemed it essential.

Charles protested, 'For God's sake, man, I have a stomach bug, that's all.'

'I think we should run some tests.' Alec was firm, it was a voice Charles recognised – his housemaster all those years ago had had such a voice.

They operated two days later. When they opened Charles up they found that there was nothing they could do: he was riddled with a cancer that would kill him. It was Alec who told Margaret that she should telephone Cassie.

'She has a right to know, Margaret.'

It was hard for Margaret. She was, after all, the other woman, Cassie was the wife.

Cassie came immediately. She asked if she might see Charles alone.

'He doesn't know,' said Margaret, 'I feel it's right that way.'

'He isn't a child, Margaret,' Cassie said quietly.

Her composure and control worried Margaret, but then Cassie had always worried Margaret. She stood in the corridor whilst Cassie went in to her husband.

Charles lay quite still on his bed, his hair lank against his head, his skin whiter than usual. His face, though, was unlined, as if he had somehow regained his youth. Suddenly Cassie saw him as he had looked that evening at Sacré Coeur when he had asked her to marry him; he had been so handsome, he still was so handsome. What a dreadful, dreadful thing this illness was. She loved him, she knew that. Gently she smoothed his hair away from his forehead. She bent her head and gently pressed her lips against the damp skin.

'Cassie?' The voice was weak.

'Yes.'

'I smelt you.'

She smiled at him.

'You still wear your Guerlain perfume.' He took her hand. 'I am sorry.'

'I am too.'

'Are we friends?'

'We were friends first.'

He smiled into her and for a moment she thought she would break down.

'I'd quite like to see Tom,' he said.

'I'll call him.'

'Thank you.' He turned his face away. 'I'm tired, Cassie, could you tell Margaret.'

'Tell Margaret?'

253

'Tell Margaret that I'm tired.'

'Of course, I'm sure she'll understand.'

'No, you don't see. I want her here with me, so I can sleep.'

'Of course,' she said.

She left the door open and walked over to where Margaret stood, her head against the wall.

'He wants you,' she said. There was no attempt to hide the pain in her voice.

Tom had managed to organise a season in summer stock – as a director. Such an achievement was not to be overlooked. Assistant directors, he had discovered, did not have much clout. Fleistein allowed him to hold rehearsals when he himself was preoccupied with administration, but as for a creative thought, or an original idea – that was not to be tolerated on the curriculum. It was Fleistein's idea that Tom should try for one of the American repertory companies who performed throughout the summer season. After an agonising wait Tom heard that he had been appointed artistic director of the Little Theatre near Pittsfield in the Berkshire Mountain region – just two and a half hours from New York or Boston, and a lush, rolling area, rich in American history. It was also heavily populated with the kind of people who would go to summer stock.

Elizabeth and Tom had celebrated with a weekend away. They had borrowed a house belonging to Tom's landlady, it wasn't far, just up the coast. Situated right on a pebble beach, the white clapboard house with its huge verandah was the perfect place for lovers.

'Oh Tom, this is paradise,' a euphoric Elizabeth told him.

They had brought food and wine with them, and flowers, and candles. Elizabeth had shopped.

'I want to. A whole two days alone, it will be so special, and I want to make it so with extra things.'

Whilst Tom set a fire Elizabeth laid the table with the candles and flowers. She laid out all the food on the side: steaks, chicken and potatoes – and a lot of salad. She could eat salad easily. Tom was to prepare the food, for that was something she still could not do.

When he had lit the fire and prepared the steaks Tom looked for Elizabeth. She had gone outside and was sitting on the verandah, huddled in a woollen jacket, looking out to sea. Tom watched her and marvelled at how quickly they had become a couple. There was never a shortage of things to say, they shared a passion for the performing arts.

Tom was fascinated by ballet, he wanted to learn more about the art of movement. Elizabeth needed to learn about acting.

'You cannot dance without conveying the essence of the story in your movement. You have to learn how to communicate that.'

'I see. You have to teach me, Tom. Show me now.'

And he would take her through different exercises in order to teach her how to express her feelings, to talk about them. He told her she was a car going down a hill at speed, overtaking the other slower vehicles, tasting the wind, testing her nerves.

'I am the best!' Elizabeth had shouted.

'Aren't you frightened?'

'What of?'

'Losing control – perhaps your brakes don't work?'

'Who cares. I can hold the road, I can do anything. I am in love.' She stopped being a car, and turned to look at Tom, the yearning in her eyes was wonderful for him.

But he said, 'Cars don't fall in love,' because they were in the middle of working.

Now he moved over to her and the boards of the verandah creaked under him. The moon cast little silver lights over the inky black sea. The waves made little splashing sounds as they lapped the shore. The wind was soft and the trees rustled at its touch. Elizabeth heard him behind her. She stood up and took off her sweater and then her trousers and then her shirt and stood naked for him in the night air by a cold Atlantic Ocean and held out her arms. Tom felt the blood rush up to his face, he had never seen a more wondrous sight than Elizabeth, her skin touched by silver, open for him.

'I cannot think of a time when I shall not love you,' Tom whispered.

Elizabeth was not going to return to Germany. She had auditioned for the New York City Ballet, an awesome experience. Tom had driven her to New York and stayed with her at the Algonquin, a splendidly romantic relic of another era, the writers' hotel.

Jane had wanted them to stay with her, but Tom had declined.

'She'll be very nervous,' he told his grandmother and he arranged instead to meet her for lunch at the Writer's Club the next day.

His suggestion for the evening was Broadway. He wanted to see George C. Scott appearing as Ephraim in *Desire Under the Elms*. He'd heard that Scott was an acerbic actor who saw acting as an antidote to self-hatred. That interested Tom, and he had spent many hours contemplating the idea that he himself had retreated into the world of make-believe as a means of avoiding personal confrontation. Perhaps, in spite of Cassie's careful rearing, he was just like his father.

Elizabeth didn't care where she went – her nerves were torn like fine fibres which at the moment of her own meeting with fate would knit together into a taut web connecting limb with brain, allowing a perfectly disciplined body to dance. None of the rest mattered. She managed to sit through the performance, she managed to retain a sense of occasion whilst Tom fawned his way into Scott's presence after the performance; but in the restaurant all pretence went. She shook so violently that they had to leave an excellent lobster and its companion jug of iced water (she had refused wine, it would dull her responses and she couldn't have that) and return to the hotel. Tom cradled her shaking body all night. She had neither held him, nor acknowledged his caresses, it was as if she were in a stupor, consumed with fear in a place he could not reach.

In the morning she would not allow him to attend to her. She wanted nothing from him, he was banished from her world. She thought of Rebecca, she worried that she was not with her mother.

As Elizabeth thought of her mother, Tom was walking down Fifth Avenue and remembering the first time he had done that, with Cassie. How English he had been in his neat clothes – how beautiful and flamboyant his mother had seemed to him. He remembered how he used to love to touch her, to kiss her, to hug her. When she hugged him he had felt as if she were taking him back into her own body. He felt safe with her surrounded by her soft perfumed flesh, her thick long hair. What had happened to that Cassie, he wondered, as he crossed obediently at the flickering instruction on the road sign.

'WALK' and everyone walked. 'DON'T WALK' and nobody walked. For such an undisciplined place, New Yorkers were surprisingly obedient when it came to street behaviour. Tom loved the smell of New York, from uptown to downtown there was a speed and excitement in the air that smelt of purpose, it intoxicated him. New Yorkers had things to do, they were smart, they had places to go.

He was more aware of art in New York than he was at home. He often wondered why Cassie had never used any of Jane's contacts to further herself. That irritated Tom, he couldn't understand why his mother didn't make the most of all her opportunities. It made him think she wasn't quite professional enough.

His grandmother, he discovered, was now an old lady. It wasn't a sudden transformation to grey hair and wrinkled skin, she had always

256

had grey hair and wrinkles, it was her manner, her behaviour. She was sitting in a chair as if she had shrivelled into it, merging with its cream textures as if she were an old doll someone had left there. The shock was quite horrifying, it had happened suddenly, since he had last seen her. He was going to suggest that they stayed in, that she didn't tire herself, but she wouldn't hear of it. She was looking forward to an outing.

The Writer's Club in New York was 'a piece of England' but somehow, like all American pieces of England, it was much more 'English' than the original, but at the same time, it was too new, too smart, too well done, to be wholly convincing.

Throughout lunch Tom had a terrible feeling that all was not well, he wondered if this would be the last time he had such a lunch with his grandmother. He became maudlin and emotional.

They talked of this and that, and then, as if reading his mind, Jane had her say: 'My time is coming, Tom. I have cancer, a bad one.' She put her hand over his. 'Now don't say anything because there isn't anything to say. You know I have always loved you best. I sometimes think that Cassie and I were always rivals, first for your grandfather's affections, and then for yours. Oh, it was never an overt thing, it was always unspoken, but there nevertheless. Perhaps that is why Cassie is so obsessive about her loves, she never gets quite enough. The tragedy is, of course, that she could have had enough from Charles, but she never wanted him.'

'What do you mean, she has never had quite enough?'

'When you were a little boy, she had you. She held onto your love as if it were a fire in a cold, cold room. I warned her, of course, that you were not hers. She had you on loan, so to speak, until you were grown and then you would have to leave her. If you hadn't you would have been lost, floating somewhere without any identity. She could never see that, she always thought you and she would stay as one for ever.'

'No mother and child stay as one.'

'No, of course not. It isn't healthy, one generation holding onto the other, there has to be freedom on both sides. I think you and I have that. Perhaps you and Cassie will achieve it, after I am dead.'

'If you died, I would fall apart for a bit.'

'For a bit,' Jane repeated, 'when I die,' and she toasted him with her champagne. 'Go for it,' she whispered, 'all of it, for me.'

*

257

On that day in New York God smiled on those who went for it. Elizabeth was accepted for the New York City Ballet and Tom discovered that Edward O'Conner was in New York.

The two men, quite by chance, passed each other on the crowded windy sidewalk opposite St Patrick's on Fifth Avenue. It was Tom who stopped first. He saw Edward, muffled in his winter clothes, talking to two men. He went straight to him, butting in on the conversation – after all, Edward was his friend. They shouted in a thoroughly un-English manner, clasped each other, kissed each other, held each other as New Yorkers jostled past in their impatience to get somewhere.

The other two men excused themselves quite quickly. Edward didn't even introduce them to Tom. He just told them he would meet them, as arranged, that evening. Tom would have questioned the speed of their departure if he hadn't been so overjoyed to see Edward.

'Why are you here? What are you doing?' Tom asked him.

'Just visiting,' said Edward. He couldn't tell Tom that he was now a Commander in the Irish Republican Army and that he had come to America to talk to people about arms. Although officially the campaign of resistance to the British occupation of Ireland had terminated in February 1962, Edward O'Conner's job was to make sure that when the war started again the Army had its supplies. To Edward O'Conner and his friends it was a war. They believed that the partition of Ireland was illegal and they were determined to end it by armed conflict – there was no other way that the British would listen. Support had fallen away in America; Clan na Gael, the Brotherhood of Ireland, formed as a part of the struggle to unify the country and once an active participator, had disintegrated. People in the New World no longer cared about the old country. It was Edward O'Conner's business to make sure that they cared again, and enough. There was little or no activity in Ireland itself now, but Edward knew the time would come when it would begin again and he needed to prepare. However, none of this was any concern of Tom Bray.

They retired to a bar off 52nd Street. It was a long, low affair with dark-green walls embellished with hunting prints, polished tables and comfortable chairs. 'Not the place for undergraduates,' Edward remarked.

'We're not undergraduates any more. Come on, what are you up to?' he repeated.

Edward cuffed him playfully in the stomach. 'I've told you, Tom,' he said.

Tom smiled and shrugged his shoulders. He didn't really care what Edward was doing there, he was just very glad to see him.

They ordered whisky sours and caught up with one another's news.

'Jonathan is a star in Aberystwyth.'

'What?'

'He worked in a festival there, got a good notice in *The Stage*.'

'And now. . .?'

'Who knows, my dear?'

'And you?' Tom asked.

'I am writing.'

'Anything for me to see?'

'When it's ready, Tom, when it's ready.'

'I'm doing summer stock. How about letting me do *An Irish Love Story*?'

'Yes.'

'Good, then that's settled.'

'That's settled.'

The men drank, companionable and familiar with each other.

'Tell me about Cassie,' Edward said lightly.

'She is in England. I am here.'

'Have you made your peace?'

'She's my mother.'

Edward smiled. He would have liked to have told Tom how Cassie was always saying that Tom was her son. Instead he asked, 'How's Kate?'

'I don't know. It's Elizabeth now.'

'How's Elizabeth?'

'Elizabeth's. . .' Tom smiled, 'not like any woman you've ever met.'

Cassie had been trying to telephone Tom during the two days he had been in New York, his landlady told him on his return to Boston.

He didn't call her back immediately. He and Elizabeth had other things on their minds.

'So I have got you back again,' he said as he slid into her. The telephone rang again. Anticipating Cassie, he did not remove his penis but shifted his position so that he could reach the receiver. It was a shock to hear Kate.

'Tom, I am sorry to call you. Cassie has been trying to reach you. When she couldn't she telephoned me and asked me to keep trying.'

'What is it?' Tom asked, horribly aware of his nakedness.

He turned away from Elizabeth, his back was to her, his mouth tight against the receiver, wanting to protect one woman from the other.

'Your father is ill.'

'My father?'

'It was quite sudden.'

'My father?' He knew he was repeating himself. Jane was ill, not Charles, it was ridiculous to assume otherwise.

'When will you come? You must, you see. . .'

Tom stood up and moved away from the bed.

'What's he got, Kate?'

'Cancer . . . and it's bad.'

'Oh my God!'

God? Was there a God? Who knows? But at those moments there has to be one – we need Him.

Tom was crying. Elizabeth was with him, trying to take the phone away from him, trying to talk into the receiver. No, no, Kate mustn't know about Elizabeth, it would hurt her. He kept the telephone close.

'I'll get a flight as soon as I can.' He cleared his throat. 'How's Cassie?'

'Bad. She wants to be with your father, but he wants Margaret. She feels very alone, Tom.'

'Take care of her for me, till I get back.'

'Tom, Tom,' he could hear her tears too, 'we love you.'

'I know.'

Elizabeth had moved away, sitting in the chair across from him, crosslegged yoga-fashion, showing the deep rich redness that just a few minutes before he had kissed and sucked.

'And I love you both. My father? My father, does he know?'

'No. They operated two days ago, they thought he had an obstruction in his stomach. He's heavily doped, he thinks they cleared it. Cassie wants you home before he is told that they didn't.'

'Yes.'

'Let me know your flight number, I'll meet you.'

'Yes,' he said, wanting Cassie, wanting Kate, wanting his father.

Elizabeth helped him pack, she was quiet after he told her. Whilst he booked his ticket she made coffee.

'Do you love your father?'

'Yes, very much.'

'And your mother too?'

'Yes.'

'And the one who rang you?'

'I beg your pardon?'

'The one you wouldn't let me speak to on the telephone.' Then she threw the coffee at him. It missed, which was lucky because it was very hot.

'You bitch! All you can think about is yourself.'

'Yes, all I can think about is myself and you. Don't cut me out, Tom, I am with you now, and you are with me.'

'I'll be back,' he said.

'You are not doing anything to tell me that you will be back. We are making love and then you get a phone call and you are gone from me. What am I to think?'

'I have just heard that my father is dying, it's hardly the time for a fuck.'

'Perhaps it is just the time for love and for comfort.' Elizabeth felt as if she were the one who was dying, not the faceless man from over the water. She had grown to love Tom, they were two of a kind, they needed each other. When she had been in New York and she had been so frightened he had held her and asked for nothing. Now that he was in pain he would not let her hold him. It was wrong, so wrong. Where was their love?

'Just a week ago, Tom, you said you could not think of a time when you would not love me.'

'Elizabeth, please. I can't deal with your selfishness now. If you love me, as you say you do, then leave me be. Don't hassle me, not now.'

Neither of them spoke further, there was nothing to say.

Tom telephoned Jane in New York, but she already knew. Cassie had spoken to her.

'I am sad, Tom. Charles should not be going before me. It's my turn. He has to have another twenty years.'

'From what I hear he doesn't have that.'

'Oh my dear,' his grandmother said and Tom wished he were with her.

When the taxi arrived Elizabeth didn't go to the airport with him.

'I won't bid you farewell for the other one to pick you up at the other end.'

'Kate is my best friend, I won't apologise for that,' Tom said as he left the house.

Elizabeth cried that night, and the following morning. But she got up and went to class, working her body, punishing her body, trying to expunge Tom Bray in her sweat.

Kate met Tom at the airport. It was strange how quickly she had become part of the Bray family again. She had gone to see Cassie as soon as she had telephoned her. She felt useless but at least she could be there, making a drink when Cassie wanted it, answering the phone when it rang, holding Cassie when she needed it.

Cassie had been nervous about facing Tom, even at a time of such sadness, so she had waited at home while Kate went to the airport. Tom had hugged Kate at the airport, she was ashamed that she had wept a little. He hadn't minded, but he didn't shed tears then. Those came when he saw his mother standing by the front door. She looked so tired and so vulnerable, how could he tell her that her mother was dying too? Then there would be just the two of them. But then he supposed there had been just the two of them in the beginning.

Tom held Cassie that night. They didn't go to bed, they lay together on the couch in the sitting room. They both cried.

'I am sorry for what I did.'

'Don't,' Tom whispered, 'don't.'

'I know you don't believe me, but I love him, Tom.'

'Have you ever told him that?'

'No.' She shook her head.

'You could try now.'

'How can I? There is Margaret now.'

But somehow, with Tom's return, there was less of Margaret. When Tom arrived at the hospital, he came with Cassie. He was nice to his father's lover, but quite clear. 'I need some time with my parents. I am sure you understand. Would you excuse us this afternoon?'

And Margaret did.

She walked into Regent's Park. It wasn't far from the hospital. She sat by the large pond, there were children there feeding the ducks. Margaret had never wanted a child. Loving Charles had been enough, but she knew now that he was gone from her. She'd known that when he'd asked her what was wrong with him, and she had said it was just a blockage in his stomach and they had taken it away. He had just looked at her and said 'Never mind. I'll find out from Tom, he'll tell me the truth.' Tom mattered too much, and with Tom came Cassie. There would not be enough room for her as well. She began her grieving then.

She didn't weep, she kept it inside. On the way back from the park she stopped at an employment agency and offered her services. She didn't want a big job, just something that would earn her enough money and utilise her shorthand and typing. She couldn't face decisions at such a time.

Cassie, Charles and Tom sat in Charles' hospital room having tea, the weak winter sun was trying to penetrate the peculiar hospital well, where the smells of cooking and the clanking of hospital life were centred. The nurse had brought three cups with three scones and three little sandwiches. Cassie thanked her.

'What happened to Bravington?' Tom was asking. 'I wrote to *The Times*, you know.'

'Oh, he got the bullet of course.'

Tom smiled at his mother. 'You are still very American.'

Charles, now very weak in striped pyjamas, propped up on hospital pillows that made his frail body even more uncomfortable, listened to his son and watched his wife. And then, when they had finished their scones, he said, 'When are you going to have the guts to tell me?'

'Tell you what?' Cassie's voice was too high, too pained, she was gripping the first finger of her left hand with the whole of her right hand.

Tom could see his father's distress, the muscles in his thin face were working very hard, a little saliva dribbled from his mouth. The man had become a child, but he still had a man's rights.

'Do you want it straight, Dad?'

Charles nodded, overriding Cassie's quiet plea, 'No, no, Tom.'

Tom took both their hands in his, putting them together, covering them with his own, so there were six hands on the bed, two frail and trembling, two fearful and shaking, two strong and hard.

'You have cancer of the stomach, the prognosis is a fast one.'

The pain for these three people was unbearable, but they bore it. They talked of the past, of each other, but not of the future.

In front of Tom, Cassie told her husband how much she loved him.

'I've always loved you, Cassie,' Charles told her.

Tom left them. Kate was waiting at the end of the corridor, and he let his best friend put her arms around him and take him home.

'We have to make our peace,' Charles told an already grieving Cassie. 'I think I would like to come home. I've looked at you and Tom today and I realise that is where I should be. It's not that I don't care about Margaret. I would be glad if she could come and see me. Would that be too difficult?' Cassie shook her head. 'She's been very good to me, you see. I do care about her. But now that I know I am dying I need to be with you and Tom. I asked her to tell me about the cancer, but she wouldn't.'

'It wasn't "wouldn't", Charles, it was "couldn't". I'm not sure I could have done either. It was Tom who knew what to do.'

Margaret said she would cope with Charles' decision, but Cassie could see how hard it was for her. She put her hand on Margaret's shoulder, wanting to comfort her. 'You must come when you want to,' she told her. 'It isn't easy for any of us.' And then she and Tom took Charles home.

Cassie wondered whether he would want to sleep in the bedroom alone, but he made it clear that, if she didn't mind, he wanted to be with her.

'It will give us more time together, to talk,' he said.

'I'd like that,' said Cassie, 'I do love you, Charles.'

'And I love you, Cassie. The sadness is that we are such different kinds of people, you and I.'

'I am not so sure we are, Charles. I just think we had different ways of saying the same thing.' Cassie stroked his cheek and smiled into his eyes; she was very glad when he smiled back and even touched her hair.

During the day they made him a bed in his study so he could hear them, like he used to when they were all young. In the morning Tom would carry his wasting father down the stairs, trying not to cry at the ease with which he carried the man who had once carried him, swinging him around his head, throwing him up into the air, the golden-haired man who was his boyhood hero. How little he knew him. They tried to make up for it, of course, trying to cram a lifetime into the ebbing hours.

Cassie would sit quietly on the floor, leaving only to make food or answer the phone. She hated going out of the house – even to do the shopping. She let others do that. But sometimes she would leave the little room – just so that Tom and Charles could have some time alone. Kate came every day, after her work. They wanted her there, she was a friend. Sometimes she would read to Charles, so that Cassie could sleep and Tom could breathe.

Other friends, close ones, offered their time too. Yvonne, of course, was one of the most regular visitors, and David Sampson. Before Charles became too frail, David would walk him around the garden, very slowly, and with an arm not too far away. They would drink whisky (David's heavily loaded, Charles' with just a tip of amber liquid in water, which he despised) and play the 'Do you remember when?' game.

Yvonne forgot the need to be seen and to see. She would spend hours cooking little French delicacies in the hope that Charles would eat just a little of something. Cassie too had to be tempted for she had no interest in food.

'You must eat,' her friend told her.

'I know,' Cassie would say and she would set about laying the table. When the meal was ready they would walk Charles to his place at the head and Cassie would bring in Yvonne's goodies, or her own food, or Kate's. She would serve a little for Tom, a little for Kate, next to nothing for Charles – although she would spread it over the plate so it looked more – and a little for herself. No one ate very much, but everyone tried.

'This is jolly good, Kate,' Charles would say.

'Then try to eat it,' Yvonne would answer on the days she was there, 'because I cooked it, not Kate.'

'You and your ego,' Cassie would riposte, because they were all trying to be normal. Evelyn telephoned a lot, she was distressed she could not visit Charles but her own husband was a sick man too. Mostly they were alone. Margaret came once, but it was difficult for all of them. She stayed with Charles for just twenty minutes. When she left she was in tears, and was unable to talk.

'I told her I loved her,' Charles told Tom, 'and I do. But she has no place here now. We've said goodbye. Be nice to her, afterwards.'

Tom just nodded. He could not bear to think of afterwards.

Charles was the calmest of them all. He knew he just had to wait and he was happy that he had made his peace with them all.

Jane announced that she wanted to come over, but Cassie told her she had not come during the good times and she certainly didn't want her to come during the bad. And in any event Tom had told her that Jane was frail too, although he hadn't told her about Jane's cancer – his mother had enough anguish.

When Charles' pain started to get very bad, Alec told Tom he was going to have to use morphine.

'Discuss it with my father,' said Tom.

'Well, I don't think. . .'

'He means he is too ill,' Sally, Alec's wife, interjected, 'he can't know what is right for himself.'

265

'He must know. He is in charge of his own destiny. Once he starts on that morphine he won't be able to make those judgements any more,' Cassie said firmly and Tom loved her for her strength.

Charles was very upset that night. 'I've had enough,' he told his son, as Tom carried his useless body to his bedroom.

When Cassie woke the next morning she gently called Charles' name, a habit she had acquired since his illness. He would normally reach out and squeeze her hand. It was funny now, at last, when the body no longer needed it, they had become lovers. But Charles did not reach out. Cassie lay quietly for a moment and then touched him. She felt the cold of death. She didn't cry then, she kissed his eyes and his nose and his lips and went to get her son.

'How will I cope?' she said to Tom later, before the outsiders came, 'when you go back to America, and Kate goes back to her newspaper?'

Jane died two weeks after Charles' death. Cassie and Tom flew to New York for the funeral. Beth met them at the airport. Cassie, utterly swamped by her grief, held onto her son. And he, swamped too, held onto his mother.

He contemplated ringing Elizabeth, but it was too complicated. He had time only for Cassie. Cassie needed him, so his place had to be in England now. He would find work there. If he was honest, he needed Cassie too. Kate understood that, but Elizabeth would never have coped with having to share him.

Edward came to the funeral too. He noticed that Cassie clung to him. Tom hoped Edward didn't mind.

# Chapter Twelve
## 1965

It had been a bad period for Cassie after the deaths of Charles and Jane. She had found it particularly difficult to deal with her mother's passing – she had used up all her emotional resources in the final weeks of Charles' life. Although Jane lived in America, she was nevertheless as central to Cassie's life as if she had been just around the corner. It wasn't that they were constantly in touch, it was simply a matter of her being there. And now she wasn't. Cassie couldn't paint, she felt dried up, the rich, solid essence that had kept her living and fertile wasn't there any more. Without it she was a dead leaf, ready to crumble at the slightest touch. She turned to Tom, needing his support, and he gave it unstintingly.

They went for a lot of walks on Hampstead Heath. Cassie, wrapped in a huge shawl and wearing dark glasses, attracted more attention than she would have without them.

Tom had to laugh. 'You still manage to look dramatic.'

'I feel such a failure. You know, I was reading this book about bereavement. It said you go through various stages, anger at "why me?", before you get to acceptance. I am going through the "why me?" '

'At least you did get Dad back, Cassie, at the end.'

'Yes, I did, and I am very lucky because we made our peace, even if we didn't talk very much about things. It must have been very difficult for Margaret. I have thought about her a lot. I wanted to ring her to see if she was OK but I thought she might think I was being patronising.'

'I don't know, she might be glad to talk to you. After all, you are a part of Dad.'

'I don't know either, Tom. Perhaps I'll ask David, he knew her quite well.'

As she walked off to throw a ball back to a child Tom pondered his mother's thoughtfulness.

Cassie seemed content enough to spend her hours quietly with Tom by her side. She took pleasure in her new domesticity. Kate came to visit them both, it was an easy relationship – she deferred to Cassie's need for Tom. After three weeks Yvonne telephoned and invited Cassie to go out for dinner with her, but Cassie declined.

'I'm not ready yet,' she told Yvonne just as Tom happened to walk into the kitchen. He went to the refrigerator and took out a bottle of milk, removed its silver cap and drank straight from the bottle. As Cassie remonstrated with him, he realised that she probably didn't want to go out to dinner with Yvonne because she liked things just the way they were – it was time for both of them to get back to the living.

'You must start to work again,' he said, 'there are no other choices for you. I am going to go out tonight.' He didn't wait to see the expression on Cassie's face.

Tom took her car and drove north, through the neat suburbs, out of London to green countryside. He parked in a layby. It was time to think about Elizabeth – and Kate. He had been shocked by his feelings when Kate had telephoned him in Boston. Despite his immediate grief at the news of his father's illness, he had felt compelled to protect her from knowing about his relationship with Elizabeth. Elizabeth had sensed that, at once, that was the reason for her terrible anger at him. She was justified. They had been making love. He groaned, the sex was powerful with Elizabeth: he only had to think about her and he wanted her. It seemed to him that no matter where she was or how she was dressed, she always looked as if she were just about to slip out of her clothes. He remembered that most of the time she did precisely that for him, whenever, wherever and however she could. She had devoured him. His need for her overwhelmed him. And he wasn't sure he wanted that kind of relationship any more. There were other needs – and to allow them a chance to develop he had to distance himself from Elizabeth's passion. Kate was so different from Elizabeth, she gave so generously, she demanded so little. He felt comfortable with her, safe with her. He suddenly realised he wanted her back.

After some preliminary skirmishes Tom was invited to join a prestigious theatre near Watford which was near enough to London to attract attention. He was delighted, for it would give him the opportunity to work with a repertory company and produce the kind of plays that he wanted to do. He was even more delighted to discover that one of the actresses there was Tracey Roberts. There was a lot of hugging when they rediscovered each other and then they went off and got drunk.

Tom poured his heart out to her, retelling all the events of his life from the abortion onwards.

'Anything else to add to the pie?' asked Tracey.

'Oh yeah, Jonathan. . .' He stopped. That wasn't right. He wouldn't discuss Jonathan.

'Jonathan made a pass at you.' Tom turned away from Tracey. They were sitting in a local pub, unappealing brown tables with huge ashtrays gave the measure of the place. 'He was in love with you. Anyone could see that.'

'Except me.'

'Which one of them do you love?'

'Not Jonathan.'

Tracey laughed and lit a cigarette. 'I didn't think it was Jonathan, but seriously, you have talked about both of these women in great detail but you haven't told me how you really feel about them.'

'I love Kate.'

'Are you sure?'

'Yes, yes, I'm sure.'

'Then do something about it.'

Tom smiled and drank more from a glass of not very good red wine.

'And you, Tracey, what about you?'

'I am in love with my best friend so I am really lucky. He's going to be a barrister and when the time is right we'll have the big wedding and everyone will cry. It'll be wonderful. You'll have to come with . . . with Kate!' Tom grinned. He had forgotten how much he liked Tracey.

He was actually rather nervous about ringing Kate, but he managed it and arranged to see her at her flat that evening. He borrowed Cassie's car again – he would have to get one of his own, hers was a bulky Rover.

He parked in the U-shaped drive in front of the block of flats, close to a wall. He had to ring an outside door bell to get in and it was a few minutes before Kate answered.

'Come up, Tom,' she said.

Inside the flat Kate surveyed herself in the mirror that dominated the hall. When she had moved in it had had pink embellishments on either side. She had taken those off and left herself with a simple mirror. She pinched her cheeks, she didn't want to look pale. She was wearing a yellow dress that she had worn all day. She contemplated changing, but decided not to, she didn't want to look as if she had made any special effort. She had spent most of her time since the phone call wondering what Tom had to say; she supposed he was going to re-emphasise that their relationship was over, or, worse, he was going back to America.

He had brought flowers and a bottle of wine for them to drink. She went into her bright orange and white kitchen and searched around for a corkscrew. What had she done with it? She'd used it just two days previously when Michael had last been with her. She pursed her lips and pulled in her cheeks and tried not to think of the usual inhabitant of her sitting room.

Tom was sitting in one of her dark-green chairs. She hated her furniture but her mother had persuaded her it was a sensible buy – wouldn't show the dirt. She remembered Jane's apartment in New York, the cream carpet and the cream furniture.

'Kate, we need to talk.'

'Yes.'

'I still love you.' The words were so easy once they had been said.

'I still love you,' she whispered back and after that it was easy.

When Kate and Tom came down the next morning Tom discovered that his car was very firmly blocked in by a small Triumph Herald at the back and a larger Cortina in front. Kate laughed and laughed as Tom tried to manoeuvre the ungainly Rover with its impossible lock out of a tiny space. In the end he gave up and Kate went to work by bus whilst Tom fumed and waited for the owners of the other two cars.

They decided to get married when they were in a fish and chip shop on the evening of the first-night party to celebrate Tom's production of *King Lear* in modern dress. The food at the party had been awful and they were very hungry so they drove around Bromley until they found a chippie which was just closing. Tom said if Kate could persuade a tired man to put two fresh pieces of cod and a double portion of chips into oil that needed heating, he had better make her his wife. Kate was about to decline his proposal when Tom refused to put vinegar on the chips, but the owner of the chippie forced a compromise. 'Vinegar on one,' he said. He was a romantic and he'd remembered what his Clara had been like when she was young.

When they told Cassie she cried – from happiness, she said. She invited Kate's parents to dinner. The evening had been an extraordinary success. It was as if it marked the end of the mourning. Tom had poured and spilt champagne, Cassie had burnt the potatoes. Frank Sullivan took over the champagne and Kate's mother the potatoes.

They'd laughed a lot. When the three parents had enquired as to the nature of the wedding they were told that Tom and Kate were planning it themselves and that the ceremony would be at a small church in Hampstead with the reception in the garden of a local hotel. Kate particularly liked that garden, there were great big grey paving stones and roses everywhere.

She wore a white silk sleeveless mini-dress with a mandarin collar, white tights and shoes and there were small white roses entwined in her long thick hair. And on her wedding night she stopped taking her contraceptive pill.

Tom had never contacted Elizabeth again. Sidney, as he now called Fleistein, had arranged to have his things sent back to England.

Fleistein had not been particularly kind to Elizabeth, but he had assumed that Tom did not mind about that. He was wrong, Tom would have minded, but Tom could not face Elizabeth's tears and recriminations. The artistic director of the Boston Playhouse had gone to the little apartment on the top of Beacon Hill one evening at seven o'clock.

Elizabeth had been in New York earlier that day, arranging her new accommodation. Through another German friend, Otto Munch, who was already dancing with the New York City Ballet, she had visited a clairvoyant.

Elizabeth's faith in the supernatural had been fuelled while she was still in the DDR. One of the dressers, Sofia Steiner, had a pack of tarot cards and some of the girls (and some of the boys too) would go to her in the privacy of the costume store where she would lay out the cards amidst the net and glitter of make-believe. The little wiry woman with grey hair and a hook nose and eyes like small pieces of jet would study the images on her cards and offer her promises for the future. Those in love would hold their breath, for Sofia Steiner shattered so many dreams. For Elizabeth it was nothing more than a game until Sofia Steiner told her, 'You will go away from here, you will find much fame, you will find much love, but he will break your heart. You will cut across his life, as he will cut across yours. You are two parts of a whole: like a peach when the fruit has been cut in half, the stone is red and bleeding, but when you put it together you cannot even see the join, so it will be with you and this man. You will suffer, both of you, but you will never be parted even when you are separated.'

She had thought at the time that Sofia was speaking of Mikhail. But now she knew the clairvoyant had foreseen Tom. And Elizabeth needed to know how to cope with the pain of the separation. In Tom's absence she had taken to eating – nothing sensible, just biscuits and cake and bread and potatoes with lashings of salad cream. At night she would make herself sick; a few days before she had coughed up blood. It nauseated her so she stopped the binges, but the hunger spasms racked her together with her anguish at his loss.

Now the clairvoyant in New York had promised happy ever after.

'Are you sure?'

'You will have your tears, I see him offering you a handkerchief for them, but a little further along life's path he will come back to you.'

'When?'

'Time, my dear, if only we knew time.'

Despite the prediction, it was a horrible thing to see Fleistein organising Tom's things, taking them away from her.

'What are you doing?' she shouted.

He didn't even bother to answer her.

'Where is Tom?' she screamed. 'How do I contact him?'

'I would imagine you don't. And if I were you I wouldn't even try to speak to him. I understand that he is reconciled with his English girlfriend.'

If Fleistein had admitted the pleasure he felt in inflicting the deadly cut he would have justified himself by saying, 'If my grandparents had stayed in your country they would have been made into soap.'

Perhaps he would have been more charitable if he had known that Elizabeth's grandparents had actually been candidates for such a terrible end.

Elizabeth was desperate for it seemed impossible for her to escape the terrible anguish she was suffering. Little Peter Clark, a young choreographer with a girlish giggle, offered her a cigarette one evening. She had gone to his place, one room in a peeling house. Nothing was put away, tins and soap powder and lavatory paper were strewn over table and work surfaces. There were some fresh vegetables, and a loaf of bread, already cut, its crumbs soaking in some juice that had leaked from an orange-juice carton. She wondered how he could live like that. He had already lit the cigarette and was holding it out to her.

'I don't smoke,' she said, 'I am a dancer!'

'This isn't just any cigarette. It's medicine, baby.'

Unbelievingly she took the proffered gift. It was badly rolled, and the wet paper clung to her lips. She breathed deeply, feeling the smoke burning all the way down to her stomach. She coughed and coughed till the tears came to her eyes. Peter had taken the cigarette back from her and was drawing deeply and contentedly. She thought he looked funny, and she told him so as she reached out for another pull on the rapidly burning butt.

One evening a few weeks later, when the bad feeling had been banished by little red pills, new goodies that Peter had brought her, Elizabeth telephoned Rebecca.

That day Rebecca had bought herself a birthday present, a pearl necklace. She knew no one else would do such a thing, and she did so love pearls. She had had pearls when she was a little girl, she had always worn them – until Joshua had sold them. He had said they needed the money, she'd cried a lot that day. Rebecca didn't need money now. The West German Government paid her money because her parents had died – they called it reparation.

Elizabeth had been bright on the phone – at least she had thought she was, chatting on about everything and nothing. On the other end of the telephone Rebecca fidgeted with her pearls. 'Are you well, my daughter?' she asked, knowing that Elizabeth was not well; she recognised the high-pitched voice which at times was near hysteria.

'I am absolutely fine. What an extraordinary thing to say.'

'You are not fine. I am coming to New York. Something is wrong.'

'Stay away from me, you are not to come. When you interfere in my life you change things. This time stay away. I know what I'm doing.'

Elizabeth had slammed the phone down on her and Rebecca had been very shocked.

Of course she heard from Elizabeth a few days later, but Rebecca could not reconcile the screeching, irrational girl with the slender young dancer who was her daughter. She wondered what Elizabeth was doing with her life.

Elizabeth had felt quite dreadful after Peter's little pills. She resolved never to take them again. She liked the cigarettes, though, for they helped her to forget.

Just as Elizabeth was discovering the pleasures of marijuana as an antidote to loneliness, over in England, Tom also discovered the drug, but only as a simple way to have a good time. It didn't take him long to become a connoisseur of the weed, offering it at dinner parties much as one might offer a glass of brandy. He took to growing a plant himself and spent a considerable amount of time tending it and checking that it had sufficient water.

Tom's first production at Watford was Ionesco's *Rhinoceros*.

Although it was the second time the play had been performed – the first had starred Olivier – it was still a triumph. His next production, Chekhov's *The Cherry Orchard*, ran a brilliant course, and transferred to Her Majesty's Theatre in London. The stage was easily filled with Tom's gentle yet irreverent evocation of Chekhov's play. He managed to find the comedy in the piece which Chekhov himself had maintained was the essence of the play, without alienating the established view that it was a serious drama of Russian life. The critics loved him.

Kate conceived some three months after their wedding. She told him over a dinner in a fashionable Italian restaurant that specialised in stuffed vegetables and bowls of huge prawns that had had the taste frozen out of them. The heavily built Italian with the regulation humour had just finished his performance with the wine when Kate reached over and took Tom's hand. One by one, she kissed each finger. He'd reached over and touched her hair, lingering over it.

'We're going to have our baby now,' she said.

He couldn't answer.

'It would have been three now,' she said very quietly.

'I didn't want you to have the abortion,' he said, trying not to remember his fury at Cassie.

'I love you, Tom,' said Kate. 'I want our baby to grow up to be just like his father.'

Kate carried her child with joy. It was as if she had been someone quite different before the conception who looked as she looked, but not quite, and who certainly didn't feel as she now felt. Michael Stillet called it 'womanliness'.

She had ended her affair with Michael when Tom came back.

They were good friends nonetheless. If the passion was still there neither of them spoke of it. Michael had given her the opportunity to write a column.

'We need one, and it'll give you a profile. There'll be less need for you to be in the office – you can write it at home, if you like.'

Prior to the birth Kate hadn't liked to write at home at all, but after little Charlie Bray, as his grandmother Cassie called him, was born she loved it.

Although they had a nanny, Kate would sneak into the nursery and sit on the floor and gaze at her son. Sometimes if he was awake she would sweep him out of his cot and nuzzle him and cuddle him. She loved feeding him, the quiet moments when they sat together and he guzzled her milk.

Charlie was christened just two months after his birth. Swathed in lace and a hand-crocheted shawl he bawled his way through a celebration that his father deemed unnecessary, but which his mother wanted.

'So you can see just what goes in our marriage,' an elegant Tom told his friend Edward O'Conner as he filled his glass with yet more champagne during the reception after the event at Tom and Kate's smart house in Holland Park.

Edward, who had stood up as the child's godfather despite being a Catholic, was flushed with his own – and Tom's – success. *An Irish Love Story* had opened in the autumn of '64 to rapturous reviews, and just the week before they had heard that the play's Broadway transfer had been confirmed.

Tom lifted his glass to Edward. 'Tomorrow Broadway, the day after the world.'

'Ah, the two stars,' said Yvonne, looking chic in a Jackie-Kennedy-style black and white suit. Her greatest success was Cassie Bray. Cassie's collage 'Motherhood – a Homage to Käthe Kollwitz' had taken the art world by storm. Once a cautious artist, she had become a real force and Yvonne knew that Cassie loved it. Yvonne admitted quite openly that she had rejected Cassie, not to inspire her to greater things, but because she felt she could no longer sell her work. When her friend had produced such staggering pieces she admitted equally openly that she had grovelled to take her back.

Kate had invited Michael to the christening.

'And the family,' she had said in a loud voice in the office. 'It's time I met those kids of yours, and your wife.'

He had brought them all, three nice children of ten, nine and seven, and a pretty, blonde, anxious wife.

'I met Michael at school,' she told Kate, as she chucked Charlie under his chin, 'fell in love with him and stayed in love with him.' She took a deep breath and looked at Kate. Kate found it hard to return her gaze.

'Do you think she knew?' Kate's old friend, Lucy, whispered in a rare moment of privacy.

'I really hope not. She loves him.'

'So did you.'

Kate nodded. 'I did, but there was always Tom too.' She bent her head and concentrated on the task of cleaning Charlie's neat little bottom as her baby gurgled his contentment with the world.

When Kate came back downstairs most of the guests had gone. Cassie had stayed behind of course. She had kicked off her shoes and curled up with a glass of champagne on the burnt-brown sofa above which hung one of her latest works. Kate had modelled for it, cradling her baby in her arms. It was a tender piece, Cassie had called it simply 'Love'.

'All right?' Kate asked her.

'Fine. I think this is happiness,' Cassie said softly, and Kate nodded, the warm feeling had smothered her too.

Edward would have left, but Kate and Tom persuaded him to stay. Lucy was staying on.

Edward didn't appear to have a girlfriend. There had been some romantic interludes, actresses mainly, but despite Tom's probing he kept his private life to himself. Once, irritated, Tom had exploded, 'I don't care if you are gay, just tell me!'

Edward had merely laughed.

Cassie had tried to re-establish her relationship with Edward. Shortly after he returned to England they had lunched at a smart fish restaurant off Leicester Square. Cassie had invited him to 'catch up – as friends'. She had been subtle but had made it clear that she was available to him. He had declined, but kindly. 'I am not what you need, Cassie.'

'Oh, I don't know, Edward. I think you are just what I "need", as you put it.'

'No, Cassie. We're friends now. It would be too complicated.'

'Of course, you're right,' Cassie said quickly. She smiled and patted his hand and tried to make it a maternal gesture.

Neither of them had told the truth. Cassie was aching with disappointment. She needed Edward. He made her feel so good, most of all he made her feel as if Tom were still hers.

Edward knew there could be no question of his going to bed with Cassie again but, still, he could not help but regret it.

They managed to preserve their friendship and Edward would often just telephone Cassie to find out how she was. She looked forward to his phone calls. They were catching up with each other's news at the end of the christening party when Tom started to collect the dirty glasses.

'Leave them, darling, they can be dealt with tomorrow,' Cassie called over to him.

'With respect, Cassie, this isn't your house. I deal with things in my own home in the way *I* want to,' Tom answered sharply. He didn't know quite why he had spoken in such a tone – he supposed Cassie's proprietorial manner had got to him. He could see she was shocked. Well, so what? He wanted her to go. Kate's parents had left with Kate's aunt and uncle at the proper time with all the other guests. Why was Cassie hanging around? His anger was building, he could feel it. Kate was standing with him, her arm around his waist. He hadn't even seen her come over to him. She put her head on his shoulder and discreetly licked his ear. He squirmed and was reminded that they hadn't made love since the baby was born. It wasn't that Kate didn't want him to, it was just that he hadn't felt like it.

'Shall we clear up whilst this indolent lot just lie around?' she said. 'Edward and Lucy can help us.'

'What about me, Tom?' said Cassie, her voice had a hard edge to it.

'Oh, I'm sure you've got things to do, haven't you? I'll get your coat.'

As she left, Cassie heard Lucy say with astonishment in her voice, 'You threw your mother out.'

As Cassie drove home she was consumed with rage. So this was nemesis for mother love. She went straight to her studio and started to work; her lines were violent slashes on the paper. She drew the Goddess of Night with thick angry strokes. So engrossed in her rage was she that she didn't hear the telephone ring.

At the other end a quietened Tom told his wife, 'She's not there,' as he replaced the receiver.

'The trouble is,' Edward said complacently from behind the sweet-scented smoke ring of an excellent joint, 'you're too passionate about your mother. Stop caring about her so much and it'll all be all right. I don't have problems with my mother.'

'It's not me that cares too much about her, she cares too much about me.'

'Really?' said Edward quietly.

Tom went to see Cassie the next morning. He still had a key to the house. He parked his new car in the drive behind hers, let himself in and went into the kitchen where he made some fresh coffee. He loaded up the tray with two cups, the jug, and a carton of cream – he shared his mother's taste for cream with coffee – and walked out of the kitchen door and down to her studio. He didn't knock, he hadn't done that when he was a child. She was at her easel, her hair pulled back with two grips. She wore glasses now when she worked, thick-black-rimmed ones – they suited her. When Cassie heard Tom she poked her head out

277

from behind the easel. She looked defiant, like a small child. He strode round to view her work and then stopped, staggered. He and Kate, ugly little gnome creatures yet with completely recognisable faces, were depicted worshipping at the feet of the Goddess of Night. He knew that was who it was: Cassie had scrawled the title of the work all over the top of the paper. He looked at his mother, she was looking at him as she poured cream into her own coffee cup, obviously ignoring his, and he threw back his head and roared his approval of her. She smiled back at him, but still didn't put any cream in his coffee.

# Chapter Thirteen
## 1968

During the three years since he had left her, Elizabeth Gottlieb had known exactly how Tom Bray was living his life. At least she thought she did. Through a prodigious use of tarot cards, press cuttings, acquaintances, and the occasional private detective she managed to ensure that she kept pace. In the meantime her career as a dancer flourished, despite what some might have judged an inordinate indulgence in marijuana.

She ate a little more now – she had fainted once during class and a doctor's examination had ensued. Mild malnutrition was diagnosed and she was warned that if she did not eat she would not dance. That was enough for Elizabeth, she only lived in order to dance, so she became more disciplined about her food. She had her lovers too but they never lasted long. She used them to satisfy her physical needs but when they encroached on her life she discarded them. She told Peter, her confidant in all matters, 'When I get tired of my own hand, I use a man, and when I get tired of the man I go back to my hand.'

'Lonely, isn't it?'

'Yes.'

Elizabeth was merely a good dancer until she appeared in a work choreographed by Stephen Grieg, a brilliant young man nurtured in the tradition of Hollywood extravaganza and matured in the classical world of ballet. For Elizabeth he created a piece of such devastating beauty and poignancy that, like a fairy tale, it enabled her to become a star overnight. The applause was a greater high even than marijuana.

Elizabeth had asked Rebecca to come to New York for the opening. It was the first time she had asked her mother to attend a performance, but the sense that she was a winner was in the air and she wanted Rebecca, who was the real architect of her triumph, to be with her. But

Rebecca would not leave her little home. Age had made her fearful of leaving what was familiar. She had no wish to participate in the glitter. It was enough that her child should. So she had simply said 'no' when Elizabeth had sent her a ticket. Elizabeth had been very angry.

Rebecca did not deem it necessary to explain herself. It was a private matter. Rebecca believed that she was ugly and because she was unable to come to terms with her physical deterioration she lived indoors, venturing out only to get her food, or her books – she read all the time – or perhaps to walk a little, if the weather was good. Once, on one of her rare outings, she thought she had seen Dietrich, he was with a young woman. At first she had assumed it was his daughter but then she had noticed his hand slip up underneath the girl's blue sweater and she knew she was no daughter. She had turned quickly and cut down a small side-street and told herself that it could not have been him, but it could have been. She went home as quickly as possible. She had not been surprised that she was shaking. She made herself a glass of tea, picked up her volume of Proust; she was reading Proust's *Remembrance of Things Past, The Captive*. The very words calmed her:

> *When we have passed a certain age, the soul of the child that we were and the souls of the dead from whom we spring come and bestow upon us in handfuls their treasures and their calamities, asking to be allowed to cooperate in the new sentiments which we are feeling and which, obliterating their former image, we recast in an original creation.*

She shut the book for a moment and lay back in her chair, closing her eyes. Who was she, she wondered? Did she even exist? Had she ever existed? Rebecca contemplated her own reality. Was she merely the link between her dead parents and her living child? Her father, her charismatic father, her sweet mother, how they would have loved Elizabeth. And her, what would they have made of her? She didn't care. Elizabeth was their inheritance.

On the morning after her triumph Elizabeth dressed early, she put on a soft flowered skirt, a T-shirt and sunglasses. She pulled a big hat onto her head, not as a disguise, she knew she didn't need that, but out of vanity, her hair needed washing. She grabbed a raincoat and slammed out of her apartment. She lived in one of those anonymous blocks on the Upper West Side. She would have liked to have lived in the Village but she had never got it together to move. Instead she lived in white space, cared for by the building superintendents and Clara who came twice a week. She waited impatiently by the elevator, drumming her fingers on the nicely painted beige walls. When the lift arrived she pushed in with the business community.

'Well done, Miss Gottlieb,' said Mrs Macnamara.

Mrs Macnamara lived two floors up and paid her subscription to the *Metropolitan*. She told anyone who would listen at the doctor's clinic where she worked as a receptionist (just a little something to do, the kids really needed her – despite the fact that they were nineteen and twenty-three and spent most of their time out of the apartment, and her husband who worked downtown as a financial analyst didn't want her to do too much) that there was a dancer in her block. Now she could say Elizabeth Gottlieb lived in her block.

Elizabeth glanced at her over her dark glasses.

'Thank you.'

'It must have been wonderful.'

Elizabeth nodded, more out of gratitude that the elevator had finally reached the ground floor. She sped out of the building, waving, of course, to the superintendent, she never ignored him.

'Want a taxi, Miss Gottlieb?' he shouted after her.

'Yes. I have to go somewhere before class,' she shouted back.

She turned to look at him, her skirt blew up and he thought she looked for all the world like Marilyn Monroe – except she had black hair.

'She's got everything now,' Mrs Macnamara remarked to Mr Kingsley who lived opposite.

It took a few minutes to get a cab. New York in early May had a particular clarity about it, and the heat was coming, people knew that, their winter coats were off. Elizabeth felt stifled in her raincoat, she wished she had taken a sweater. A cab was coming, she stepped out and hailed it.

'Uptown, please. East 90th and Second. I'll walk from there.'

The cab swung into the stream of traffic.

'You German?' the driver asked Elizabeth.

'It's all right,' Elizabeth answered, 'I'm Jewish too,' and she looked out of the window, discouraging conversation.

It hadn't taken her long to discover her Jewishness in New York. It had nothing to do with faith for in a city of immigrants, two million of whom were from the same stock, she didn't have much choice but to acknowledge her heritage, however little it mattered to her.

She paid the cab driver off and walked the half block to her destination. In a part of the city that showed its warts Elizabeth made her way to the back of a crowded drugstore, she went through a doorway marked Private and walked up a small flight of stairs. A door was half open. She didn't knock, just pushed it open. An old man with white hair and a bushy moustache sat at a table covered with a black cloth. On it were packs of tarot cards, and a crystal.

'Herman, how are you?'

'To see you I am better. See,' he waved his finger at her, 'I told you, you were a triumph, and this is just the beginning.'

'Yes, but does *he* know?'

'Elizabeth, stop it. You know, you want only to hear about him. You hear about your career, I try to tell you of your mother, but nothing moves you. . .'

'I know, no lectures today, Herman, just tell me.'

She put fifty dollars down on the black table.

The old man shrugged. He handed her a pack of cards, she could see that his mouth had twisted into a tight line.

'Don't be angry, Herman. Don't you remember what it's like to be in love?'

'Love yes, obsession no.'

'Just tell me,' she said, handing him back the shuffled cards.

He laid them out carefully. After several minutes, he nodded. 'Yes, he will see it in the English newspapers. He will feel bad, but he will push you out of his mind.' It was Elizabeth's turn to tighten her mouth into a line. 'But the time is coming. You will have an offer to dance in Europe. Take it, you will see him again, there.'

'Will it be fate?'

'Fate steered by you,' Herman answered, sweeping the fifty dollars up and pocketing it.

Tom did read of Elizabeth's triumph and it jolted him to see her picture in the newspaper. A twinge of remorse tugged at him, but he deliberately turned his thoughts away. Life was to do with now. Elizabeth was a success and he was glad for her but she was part of his past.

Cassie also read of Elizabeth's triumph. She remembered, with a sharp twist in her stomach, that she was Joshua and Rebecca's girl. She had hoped she would hear no more of the Gottlieb women after Rebecca's rejection of her offer of help. Now she was confronted with the girl's smiling face in the newspaper. Why did Rebecca Gottlieb still blight her life? She wanted nothing to do with her, she wanted to forget that the German woman had ever existed. Why did she have to have a daughter who was a ballerina? Cassie wished the girl had been a secretary or a dentist – anything, as long as she didn't have to read about her.

Tom had just finished a production of a new play, *The Uninvited*, which Edward had written, again about Ireland. Set in the Twenties, it was the story of a household with three children, two boys and a girl, whose lives are permanently altered by the arrival of a lodger.

Tom remarked that Edward's blossoming Irish consciousness seemed to be going hand-in-hand with the Irish civil rights movement.

'Possibly,' said Edward, in a way that made Tom curious but which precluded further enquiry.

Charlie Bray was now three and Kate's beloved. She still wrote her column and occasionally she appeared on television; she had an agent now. And she was going to bed with Michael again. Tom just didn't seem to want her as much since Charlie was born.

'I can't explain it,' she told Lucy at one of their lunches which they tried to do at least once every two weeks. 'It's as if he thinks it isn't quite nice to fuck. I told him he isn't committing incest, I'm Charlie's mother, not his.'

They met at El Surpriso in Kensington – on Saturday. That was the time that Tom spent with Charlie if he wasn't working. They'd both agreed he needed some time to be with his son alone.

'As long as you can control your feelings about Michael you may have found the perfect solution,' Lucy commented. 'But the problem is that I'm not sure we can control our feelings. I think we find it hard not to confuse sex with love. Maybe it's the guilt of the pre-pill generation.'

'Well, we're not really pre-pill, are we?' Kate replied.

'Our training was. When we grew up, nice girls didn't.'

'Well we soon learnt that that was a lie,' Kate rejoined.

The cackles of locker-room laughter could be heard around the restaurant.

Cassie had carved a life for herself. She had her work, and she had her family and her friends. She spent a lot of time with Loretta, whose child had become too difficult to manage at home. Roger had insisted she go and live in a home.

'I'll never forgive him for doing that,' Loretta told Cassie.

'He had no choice. Now what about this Ball for Great Ormond Street Hospital? Do you want a painting for the raffle?'

'Oh, I'm not involved, Cassie, I'm just too tired these days.'

'Loretta, you are not allowed to be too tired. Those children need money and you are the person to get it for them.'

'Oh Cassie, all those years ago, when we first met, you won't believe it, but I thought you were a real cow.'

Cassie had the grace to blush.

She found Kate difficult sometimes, which surprised her. They had always been such good friends, but when she dropped in to see Charlie, if she happened to be passing, Kate could be almost unwelcoming. She couldn't understand it. All she did was go up to the nursery and take over Charlie for a while. Well why shouldn't she? She was his grandmother after all. He was Tom's little boy. She loved to play with him, the feel of his chubby fingers and the smell of his skin – he was just like Tom. Sometimes she would take him to her studio. She prepared the same little table that Tom had used when he was little. She would put out some watercolours and crayons and a huge white pad clearly marked 'CHARLIE'S' and she would watch him as he splashed paints onto the clean surface. Those were the best times, but Kate didn't allow them to happen too often. She said that Charlie was too young. Cassie worried about Kate, she confided to Yvonne that she felt she was rather possessive about Charlie.

'It's natural, you were the same.'

'I never resented Charles' mother.'

'Charles' mother never came to see Tom uninvited, nor did she sweep him off to her house.'

'Times were much more formal then,' Cassie told her.

Cassie kept track of Beth too; with age they had become better friends. Cassie needed Beth, she was the link to her childhood, and Beth needed Cassie – she was very lonely. Marvin was a senator now, his life was his politics and Beth was right behind him, usually at home in New York – whilst he was in Washington. Her daughter, as was expected, had married well, and she worked too – in television. 'She's working her way up the ladder,' Beth would say. 'She has her father's tenacity. After she has finished for the day she and her husband like to see their friends – he's in broadcasting too – it just doesn't leave a lot of time for the parent bit.'

Cassie would have liked to have pointed out that Beth had never had much time for her parents, but it would have been too cruel. She did wonder about Beth's friends. 'Well, a woman on her own – without her husband, that is – is difficult to entertain.' Cassie understood that only too well.

Unexpectedly, for there had been a silence since their tea at the Dorchester in 1963, Cassie received a letter from John Bravington. He was coming to London and he would like to come and see her. She wrote back immediately saying she would be delighted; she suggested lunch at home, and then perhaps a walk on the Heath. When he arrived, the following Tuesday, she greeted him warmly. Old friends, she reasoned, were precious.

They ate in the dining room – a roast, and then one of her apple pies.

During lunch John entertained her with anecdotes about his life in Devon. After the scandal he had taken a job there as a schoolmaster in a local grammar school.

'We've all flourished there. My wife is happy, of course.' Funny, Cassie thought as she swallowed some wine, he had never used his wife's name, only a proprietorial 'my wife'. Briefly she remembered the skirmish on the settee; it didn't matter now.

'And the girls have found husbands, both of them. And I'm not an oddball there. Perhaps I should never have worked in a Public School – wrong atmosphere.'

'But I'm glad you did, for Tom's sake,' Cassie said, squeezing his hand.

They walked on the Heath, companions at last, two people amongst others walking down the slopes past Kenwood House, enjoying the swollen azaleas bursting with the end of their flowering.

Elizabeth received her invitation to dance in Paris just three weeks later. The director wrote to her saying what an honour it would be. Mindful of Herman's prediction, she wrote back suggesting they might do something different. Perhaps they ought to try to combine ballet with opera. It was a revolutionary idea but it would interest her a great deal. She understood that Thomas Bray was a director who was not scared of innovation. Perhaps Monsieur le Directeur might like to contact him.

It wasn't long after Elizabeth's letter must have arrived in Paris that Tom's agent, Andrew Masters, a distinguished man who only represented the best, telephoned him saying that he had received a very interesting proposition. How would Tom like to direct an opera which would incorporate ballet? Would he give it some thought?

At first Tom thought it was a ludicrous idea but then a thread slowly spun in his mind, fragile, perhaps, but worthwhile – Puccini's *Butterfly* juxtaposed with dance – almost as if there were two performances: one real, one unreal, one sung, one danced. He would need a prima ballerina, of course, perhaps even Elizabeth Gottlieb.

He and Andrew flew to Paris. Tom liked that city with its wide boulevards, and graceful gardens, but he didn't know it well – he had only ever visited it with his school. He was intrigued, of course, and he admitted to himself that the curiosity had something to do with Cassie.

They were collected at the airport and told they were to be driven directly to the Opera House. As they drove across Place de l'Opéra Tom stared at the ornate façade of one of the most extraordinary buildings in the world and wondered how he would feel if indeed he was to mount a production within its prestigious walls.

'It was in fact Elizabeth Gottlieb who suggested we contact you,' the artistic director told Tom.

Tom wanted to smile: so it had come at last. The confrontation with Elizabeth. He wasn't sure how he felt for the moment, he certainly wanted to work with her. He remembered watching her dance, her wonderful fluidity. And then he remembered her body, silver in the moonlight of a cold Atlantic Ocean. His mind played tricks, he saw Elizabeth on a stage, taking the bows, the flowers raining down on her.

The negotiations were difficult. The Opera House was nervous, Tom wanted a free hand. Elizabeth wanted her own choreographer; Tom wanted – no, insisted on having the choice of choreographer. Elizabeth, through her business manager, retorted that he wouldn't even know what a choreographer was supposed to do. The battle lines were drawn. The production looked as if it were lost, but then Elizabeth – in a written note from Berlin, where she was now visiting her mother – enquired which choreographer Tom intended to use. The reply was Stephen Grieg. Elizabeth wrote back that it was an excellent choice. The contracts were drawn up and signed.

Then Tom told Cassie that he was going to work in Paris.

'Now you will have to go back there.'

'Only for you, Tom. But not till the opening.'

'Why do you feel that way about such a beautiful place?'

'I was very unhappy there, I don't want to relive those feelings again.'

286

'You won't. You'll see your son achieve a great triumph.'

Cassie ruffled his hair. 'Your ego, young man.'

'You should see the egos I'm having to deal with.'

'Who are you using? Kate said it was rather exciting. Something to do with ballet.'

'Oh a prima ballerina will dance as the prima donna sings. Can you think of anything worse?' Tom said quickly. He had not forgotten Elizabeth's connection with Cassie's past. He had no intention of telling Cassie that Elizabeth Gottlieb was the dancer. She would find out on the first night, but hopefully the excitement would mitigate her unhappiness. Anyway, he had his own problems about seeing Elizabeth.

Kate remarked that Miss Gottlieb had the ability to make Tom quite angry.

'No, not really,' he replied, 'I just can't bear people with monstrous egos.'

He asked Kate if she would like to live in Paris with him whilst he rehearsed. She said no, he could get home at weekends, she had her own job.

The Opera House rented a magnificent apartment for Tom in the 8th arrondissement, off the Champs Elysées. Its hall was lined with books, its salon was an elegant navy, its bedroom swathed as only the French can swathe, but he hated it. 'When you go out at night,' he complained, 'you might as well be living in Surbiton. There isn't even the sound of a cat in the streets.'

They found him another place underneath Sacré Coeur, just down from Montmartre, in Boulevard des Batignolles.

Elizabeth did not want to be in an apartment. She requested, and got, a suite at the George V Hotel.

She had planned, and replanned, her first meeting with Tom. She intended to sweep onto the stage, not even to look at him, but to dance with such exoticism that he would squirm with the need to touch her. And she would leave, with the most attractive young man she could find. But then she decided that plan was too direct. She would be ladylike and cool, she would be perfectly dressed and enquire after his wife and child.

As it was, it didn't happen like that at all. She had arrived at the Opera House to investigate her dressing room facilities and he'd been there, standing by the stage door, talking to Paolo Enzerotti, the Italian tenor who was to sing Pinkerton.

When she saw him she felt sick, her heart fluttered in her chest, her stomach hurt, she wanted to run to him, to throw her arms around his neck – no, she wanted him to run to her. He didn't actually run, but he came straight over to her.

He must have simply left the singer standing at the stage door. But that wasn't enough to mollify her. She remembered her humiliation at the way he had left, she remembered her loss. And she wanted to kill him. She turned on her heel and walked rapidly towards her dressing room. He was running after her, she could hear him, she would not stop. She would get to her dressing room, shut the door in his face, and then she could consider how she felt.

'Elizabeth, wait, please.' His hand was on her arm. Despite herself she whirled around and faced him.

He saw the fury in her eyes. She lashed out at him silently, hitting him, kicking him. He tried to hold her arms, but he did nothing else – he accepted her rage as her right. That was the easy part.

'I am sorry,' he said.

'You bastard,' she said impotently, her rage was finished, and she felt no better.

He wanted to kneel at her feet, to do something, to do anything. How could he have left her? 'We are working together, let's try to talk.'

Elizabeth knew then that she wanted him at any price. Having him was better than not having him.

They walked across Place de l'Opéra to the Café de la Paix. They both ordered coffee and to his surprise Elizabeth chose a tart. He wanted to touch her, she wasn't quite so thin. He noticed she ate carefully, chewing her food as if it were a chore, but she did eat. Her hair was longer, she was well dressed, chic, he supposed – she had the look of New York about her.

She wanted to touch him, he was thin. She noticed he didn't eat, just drank his coffee and smoked his cigarettes, his hair was longer, he was wearing jeans and a jacket – he had the look of London about him.

It took no time for hands to touch, for flesh to meet. They left the table silently. Tom called a taxi to drive them back to her hotel. It smelt of Gauloises and old leather. She wanted a window open, she said the smell made her feel sick. Tom leant over and unwound the one next to her, it was easy to kiss her then.

'You bastard,' she told him as he removed her clothes and nuzzled her skin, cradled her breasts.

'You hurt me,' she screamed at him as his penis pushed into her.

'What about me?' she shouted as he rode her, rammed her, used his hands on her, sucked her until she whimpered, 'I love you.'

She wouldn't move in with him. 'You'll leave me again,' she said.

He did leave her at weekends, in the beginning. 'I have to see Charlie,' he said. Elizabeth thought she hated Charlie.

Kate knew immediately. It wasn't that he didn't make love to her, it was the fact that he did. In the dark she sensed that she was someone else and it hurt her terribly.

She told Michael, they were together at one of those anonymous hotels during a lunch hour.

'I'm sorry, I can't see you any more. I know you'll think it's peculiar, after what I've been doing, but I can't explain it very rationally. It's just that I want Tom back, you see, and therefore I have to stop this.'

'I love you, Kate, and I am ready to end my marriage.'

She was shocked. 'You told me that no one breaks off a marriage for another person, it doesn't happen that way. The marriage has to be wrong in the first place, and I know yours isn't.'

'Maybe it is now.'

'Pardon?'

'Annie is a lovely lady, but we can't talk. I suppose if I'm honest I've grown out of her. They've offered me the *Sunday Enquirer*.'

'Oh, Mike.' Kate hugged him, squashing him against her big white breasts, curling over him in her pleasure at his advancement. 'Mr Editor.'

'Yes,' he said. 'But Annie doesn't want me to take it. She says she can't be an editor's wife.'

'She doesn't have to work on the bloody newspaper. What's the matter with her? You're the one in the firing line, all she has to do is provide tea and sympathy and turn up when she has to.'

'That's it, and she says she can't.'

Kate turned away from him and poured out two glasses of wine from a bottle that was sitting on the bedside table. She suddenly realised what an ugly room it was with its stained furniture and grubby walls and brown geometric curtains over unwashed windows. She handed him one of the glasses.

'Michael, whatever problems you have with Annie you cannot involve me, I hope you understand.' She was very sad.

Tom bought Elizabeth flowers at the airport. After they'd loved each other he showed her a picture of Charlie.

'I don't know anything about children. I know about ballet, and I know about you.'

She ran her hand over his skin, softly, delicately. She loved his smooth sensual body; he had no hair on his chest, she liked that so much.

'As you learned about ballet, as you learned about me, so you'll learn about Charlie,' he said softly.

They stopped talking, both of them. He looked at her, a question in his eyes.

Elizabeth's heart was beating – two halves of a whole, the peach had come together and you couldn't see the join. 'I'll learn about Charlie,' she said softly.

The production took over, the tempers, the anguish, the highs, and the despairs. Tom worked to turn the company into a family, what happened in the outside world was over there, nothing to do with them. Tragedy, comedy and romance was exclusive to them. They would rediscover the rest after opening night.

Tom knew he should talk to Kate, but he kept putting it off until after the opening. He had no time even for Charlie.

He hadn't been home for three weekends when his little boy telephoned him and begged, 'Daddy, Daddy,' and Tom almost wept with the wanting of that little body close to him.

'Daddy will be home very soon,' he said, shocked at his own emotions, even though he knew they were merely expressions of his fatigue. Or were they?

Tom loved Elizabeth, he knew that. But he dreaded the ensuing confrontation with Kate. He was a weak man in matters of love, not through lack of principle, but because of the need to avoid the infliction of pain at all costs. He told himself that during the production he could not allow himself to think about any of it. He brought a wall down, imprisoned his family on one side, and Elizabeth on the other. That way he was safe, there could be no mixing of the two. He would deal with it all later. Still the coming apocalypse wrought havoc on his mind. Fear was his greatest tormentor, playing games with him, trapping him in a black hole of indecisiveness.

For a number of weeks Tom successfully contained his family within their allotted space and lived his life with Elizabeth, but on the day before the opening night Kate and Cassie arrived in Paris. They broke out of his safe-house and walked down the aisle of the auditorium straight back into his life.

He had been watching the wedding. Maria Donato, the prima donna, was centre stage, Elizabeth was behind her, on a raised platform, dancing as Maria sang, both of them Butterfly. The small light over Tom's desk, which had been attached to one of the seats, was the only illumination in the dark place, so everyone in the auditorium was in silhouette, but Tom didn't need light to recognise his mother and his wife. He drew breath sharply, waited till the sequence was over and then stood up. Elizabeth came centre stage to see Tom, she shaded her eyes.

'Well?' she said.

'Wonderful.'

He stood up, blew her a light kiss and then walked deliberately slowly over to the two women. He just hoped that Elizabeth would see and understand.

Kate got up too and walked over to Tom and kissed him on his mouth, as a wife would.

Elizabeth couldn't understand what was happening. Who was that woman? She was looking at Tom the way women look at the men they love, it was horrible, that woman was kissing him on the mouth. It was then that Elizabeth screamed.

Kate froze. She looked at Tom. Not getting the response she wanted, she turned on her heel and left the auditorium. As Kate walked away from him Tom felt the tears grab his throat, but there was no place for that here.

'Tom, I want an explanation,' howled a voice but it wasn't Elizabeth, who had stopped screaming now; it was Cassie.

'There's nothing to say, Mother,' he said. 'Now please get out of here, I have a rehearsal to take.'

'I repeat, I want an explanation.'

'Kate has left – would you please do me the favour of following her?'

He turned his back on her, his face was set and cold, he tried to block out the terrible hammering of his heart. He ignored Elizabeth, who still stood centre stage. He moved over to Maria, giving her notes, concentrating on her. And Maria, a woman in her forties who understood passion, helped him swallow his embarrassment in work.

Elizabeth tried to speak to him, but Tom kept his back to her. She went to her dressing room and waited for him. He came three hours later and found her sitting huddled on the floor.

'I was shocked. I am sorry.'

'Get up,' he said, 'and get to work.'

He went back to the apartment that night and let himself in, wondering what he would say to Kate. He was numb. Kate was not there, she had taken her case and gone back to London. It was Cassie who was waiting for him.

'Well, Tom?'

'Well, what?'

'That's Elizabeth Gottlieb, isn't it?'

'Yes.'

'And you are going to leave your wife and son for her, aren't you?'

'I love her, Cassie.' Tom sank onto a small black chair that stood in the hall of the apartment.

'Really? And what about your wife?' Cassie was leaning against the door to the salon, her arms crossed over her chest. She was white, like a corpse, Tom thought irrelevantly.

'I know, Cassie, I know. Do you want to eat?' he asked his mother.

He got up and walked into the kitchen. Cassie followed him.

'I can't believe you know what you are doing,' she said.

He ran his hands over his head; for one stupid moment he wanted to sink to his knees and put his head in her lap, as he used to do when he was a little boy, to have her stroke his head, to soothe away the pain.

'I need to sleep, I have an early call tomorrow. We open tomorrow, and I have problems with the set, and Maria doesn't marry in totally with Elizabeth.'

He turned on the kitchen light and opened the refrigerator. He was taking out some cheese when he heard Cassie say, 'It was her mother who stole Joshua from me.'

'I know.'

'What?'

He turned around to face his mother, he was beginning to get irritated with her. 'Cassie, come on. Of course I know who she is, but I have never discussed it with her.'

'What has discussion got to do with it? I left this city with your father because that woman's mother stole my lover and now she has stolen my son. She is hurting me.'

'Hurting you? No one is hurting you. Kate is hurt. Charlie will be hurt. I am hurt. Elizabeth is hurt, but you. . .?'

'Elizabeth? What right have you to mention her name? She's broken my family.'

'Cassie, I don't understand you. No one has broken your family. Your husband is dead, but your son is alive, your grandson is alive, your daughter-in-law is your friend. What has Elizabeth done to you?'

'I've told you, she has broken my family. My daughter-in-law is heartbroken, and she has taken my son from me.'

'Oh my God, Cassie, you're sick. How can a woman I love steal me from my mother?'

'Don't do this to me, Tom. I can't bear it again.'

'Again? What do you mean, Cassie?'

'I love you.' Cassie stepped towards him. Tom moved back from her, retreating from her, his back was against the kitchen wall.

'You don't love me like a mother should. You want to possess me. I think you are in love with your own child.'

'No!' Cassie couldn't believe what she was hearing; what was Tom saying?

'Yes.' He was screaming at her, his face was ugly.

Tom was consumed with hatred for Cassie. 'You're not worried for me, or for Kate – or even for Charlie. It's you, you're the only one you care about – and you hate Elizabeth because you think she's taken me from you. It's your marriage that has broken up. You made Kate into you so that you could keep me. How did you cope, Cassie, when I screwed her? Did you feel that too?'

Cassie turned and ran from the kitchen, down the hall, out of the apartment. Tom ran after her, screaming his abuse at her.

'You think Rebecca took Joshua from you, I would have thought he would have run to her, as I am going to run to Elizabeth. Away from you.'

She was running down the stairs, he ran after her. He had more to say. He heard the front door of the apartment building slam. She wasn't going to get away from him that quickly, she was going to listen to it all. He wrenched the huge brown door open. He saw Cassie run across the road in between the traffic. He saw her try to hail a cab, he saw her heel twist on one of the damn cobbles. He saw the taxi swerving, trying to avoid her, he heard the screech of brakes, the sound of horns and the shouting. He saw her turn, she looked at him, he was sure of that, and then the taxi hit her. And in the rain of the Paris night Thomas Bray saw that his mother was dead.

He ran over to her, he tried to pick her up, to hold her, but he couldn't move her, something was holding her down – he realised it was the wheel of the car. He bent his head down to her, he touched her lips with his.

'Cassie, Cassie.' He whispered her name over and over. Someone tried to move him away from her, but he wouldn't let go – not until they took away that dreadful car that had crushed the life out of her.

They lifted the car off her, and he could pick her up then – she was so light. 'I love you,' he whispered, but she said nothing back to him. They took her away from him and he could not stop them. Someone said he ought to get himself cleaned up and he looked down and saw the blood – his mother's blood. Someone else was picking up her shoe, the one that she had caught in the cobbles.

'Please,' he said, 'please give it to me, it's my mother's.' He raised his head and saw that the person who was holding the shoe out to him was a young woman. He wanted to thank her, but the words wouldn't come out, he couldn't speak. Cassie was gone from him and he did not know how he would ever be able to cope with the terrible searing pain.

In the early hours of the following morning Tom telephoned Elizabeth from the police station. He told her that Cassie was dead, and that they had had a horrific argument about him leaving Kate, and that he had said some very terrible things to his mother.

She wanted to go to him, but he said, 'No, I have things to do.'

'I want to hold you.'

The silence on the phone terrified her. Had she lost him? 'It's not the time now,' he said quietly.

'I understand that, but I just wanted to comfort you.'

'Thank you. Well, *merde* for the opening. I won't be with you, but I'll call you, when I can.'

'I'll speak to you on the telephone, before the curtain goes up, won't I?' As she said the words she knew she shouldn't have asked the question.

'Elizabeth?' His voice was very soft. 'Dance well for me.'

She knew of course that the mourning would be a family affair, and she feared for the possible ramifications. After all, she had lost him before when his father died. She missed Peter, she needed him, she had no other friends. Elizabeth was not someone who found it easy to make relationships. When she was not dancing, she spent the day closeted in her dressing room, she only spoke when she had to.

Maria knocked on her door in the afternoon.

'I am sorry,' Elizabeth said, not wanting to be rude to a prima donna, 'but I have a terrible headache.'

'I have some good pills,' came the reply.

'It's kind of you, but I have already taken some.'

'Perhaps they are not the right ones.'

'Sorry?' Now the voice was sharp. 'I just want to be alone.'

Elizabeth stared at the closed door, she felt so empty, there was no one there for her. All she had was her work, could her creativity comfort her? She shivered, of course the work nourished her, but it could not replace the coldness of a life without love. She telephoned Rebecca.

'What is it?' she heard her mother ask her.

She would have liked to have replied differently, but when she heard a voice that loved her she could only say, 'Oh Mutti, Mutti, help me.'

Rebecca was very anxious. She had never heard Elizabeth speak in such a voice.

'I will help you, just tell me, slowly,' she said.

'In America, when I first arrived, I met a man. We became lovers, but he left me and married his English girlfriend. I never got over him, you remember when I was so ill?'

'Yes, it was the only time I wanted to come to you, and you wouldn't allow it.'

'No. . .'

There was a pause, a difficult one, they both remembered that time.

'Go on,' Rebecca said, breaking the silence, but in a very gentle voice.

'We met again here in Paris. Everything began again because it had never finished. His wife and mother came yesterday. His wife kissed him, I screamed, I could not help it. We were going to be together and I could not bear to see them like that. He had a terrible row with his mother, over me, of course. He said he said horrible things to her, she ran out of the apartment building and she was run over.'

'I will come to you,' Rebecca said, 'I will get a plane.'

'Yes,' said Elizabeth.

Rebecca arrived in the early evening. She was wearing a neat little black coat, and a small neat beret. She carried a brown suitcase and a small black handbag. As she removed her coat Elizabeth thought briefly of her impression of Cassie Bray, a willowy blonde woman, still young. But that woman was dead now. Rebecca wore a blouse, a cardigan and a black pleated skirt. Around her neck there was the string of pearls. Her mother sat down by her side, and stroked her hair as she had done when she was a little girl.

'What is his name, the young man?' she asked levelly.

'Tom Bray, the director.'

'Yes, I saw the name when I came in. And the mother was called Cassie, and she was an American.'

'How do you know?'

'I didn't, not until I walked into this place.' Rebecca shifted slightly, curling her feet under her. For a moment she looked almost young. 'Settle into me, little one, I have things to tell you.'

Elizabeth listened as her mother, quietly and without preamble, told her that when she arrived in Paris in 1938, a penniless refugee, a rich young American girl had helped her. 'Unfortunately I fell in love with the American girl's boyfriend, a refugee like me – and a Jew like me. It was your father. She took what she saw as his betrayal very badly. The young woman's name was Cassie Fleming, she married an Englishman called Charles Bray.'

Elizabeth was stunned. No wonder Tom and his mother had fought over her. How could the mother have coped with such a thing? Would she, Elizabeth, lose him? No, she couldn't lose him. His mother had loved her father, it would be right for them to be together. She would tell him that.

The build-up to the opening night passed Elizabeth by. She thought only of Tom and of the performance. All the newspapers, of course, headlined the story that Tom's mother had died. The more popular press reported the rumours that Elizabeth was responsible for the collapse of Tom's marriage. She had to ignore it all, she had to pretend that nothing was amiss. The performance was what mattered. And once again Elizabeth's solace was her work. As she eased herself into the role of Butterfly, first at her dance class, then in quiet contemplation, she began the transformation into the young Japanese girl so in love with her Pinkerton. By the time her make-up was finished and her costume was on she was no longer Elizabeth Gottlieb. She danced as she had never danced before. Through the silent dialogue of ballet she offered the passion and the anguish of Butterfly's love. She entered through a gate into the soul of the music and she became the wronged lover. As she performed her last pirouette before she took the knife and went through the ritual of death she was performing her own destiny.

The audience roared its approval – Tom had created a masterpiece of theatre. It was Maria Donato who spoke at the twelfth curtain call.

'This is for Tom Bray. We love him. We are with him.' And the audience stood and cheered.

Elizabeth chose not to go to the opening night party. Everyone asked her to attend but she had no wish to celebrate even her own performance. She had done her best because that was the way she was.

Tom did not know how to deal with his grief. He could not go to his own home, so he went instead to Hampstead. The personal litter that awaited him, which he would never have touched in Cassie's lifetime, was a dreadful proof of his mother's death. He went first to the studio, there was a sheet of cartridge paper on a board on the easel, she had been working on a new idea around some sort of theatrical theme. He knew there would be notes somewhere – he would find them, but he didn't want to look now. It was all just too horrific. He wondered if he might stay with Edward, he wasn't sure he could face Kate.

He walked back through the garden into the house again, there was someone in the kitchen. He didn't need to wonder who it was, he knew it was Kate. She was brewing some coffee, he could smell it – how many times had he brewed some for Cassie? It was so painful. And now Kate, he had to face Kate. He set his shoulders and opened the door.

'How did you know I would come here?' he asked.

'Where else would you go but home?'

'Home is. . .' He stopped in mid-sentence, she had turned to look at him, she had no tears, but her face was quite simply ravaged with anguish. Those who love, and those who are loved are the hapless ones on whom the gods wreak their vengeance.

They took their coffee into the sitting room, by unspoken mutual consent they avoided the little study that Cassie had taken to using since Charles' death. Of course, there was no cream, Cassie had not expected to be home for several days. 'She was going to stay in Paris and go to some exhibitions,' Kate volunteered.

'I said some terrible things to her.'

Kate kept her head down, didn't look at him.

'I said she wanted me for herself, she didn't care about you or Charlie, or even me, that all she cared about was herself. I asked her if she felt it when we made love. She'd moulded you into her, she'd. . .'

'No, Tom, I am not Cassie. I don't have her dedication.'

She could see him looking at her questioningly, like Charlie.

'You didn't know your mother, did you? You have no idea what she was like. Cassie was a star, Tom. She loved being the centre of attention – just like you. She was disciplined and committed to her work, and to her love object, and nothing could come in the way of those two things. The tragedy for her was that her love object was her son so that she could never have a happy relationship with anyone else. No one could match you. She dreamed of the perfect love and she had him in her son. And you shared her passion in just the same way. I love you, Tom, just love you, want you, care about you, but I am not a star. I would never have screamed if I had seen your wife kiss you, but Cassie would have, and she did.'

They were sitting together on the settee. Tom was in shock, he didn't know what to say. Was it true? Perhaps it was, he felt bad enough inside for it to be so.

Kate was still speaking: 'I don't want you slipping away under the sackcloth and ashes. I have some confessions of my own. I was having an affair with Michael Stillet.'

Tom sat up straight. Kate having an affair, that was ludicrous, his wife wouldn't do anything like that, she couldn't – but Tom knew that Kate never lied. He was deeply shaken, he knew he had no right to feel that way, but the thought of his wife with another man was horrible.

'Did you love him?' he found himself asking, not wanting to hear the answer.

Kate shrugged. 'You stopped wanting me, after I became your son's mother. Fucking mothers is not quite so nice, is it, Tom?' He turned his head, he couldn't bear to look at her. 'I had been involved with Michael when you were in Boston. So it was natural to pick it up again, easy, I suppose.'

'You said "had". . .'

'I ended it when I realised you had someone else in Paris. I, er. . .' She looked down, embarrassed, and curled over her nails to hide them when she saw that the white frosted polish was chipped. She'd meant to have a wonderful bath in Paris, do her nails, wash her hair, wear her beautiful new black dress, and seduce her husband. She felt the tears come, angrily she blinked them away – this wasn't the time for tears. 'I wanted you. And now we have the wreckage of a marriage.'

'Kate, may I stay with you – till the funeral and afterwards for a while?' he asked.

'It's your home, and your child. And I am still your wife,' she said.

It was a big funeral; it was the scandal, of course, that brought the oglers, but Kate stayed near to Tom.

Afterwards he meandered around the house, unable to concentrate, trying to cope with the surge of realities that had hit him.

Kate dealt with John Bravington and Yvonne and Beth, who had come with Marvin. She kept them from him, protecting his inability to face them, shielding him from their loss. He played with Charlie a lot, taking him to the zoo and the playground, trying not to allow himself to dwell on that nightmarish night.

It was on the fourth day after the funeral that Tom realised he had not seen Edward. Where was his friend, where was Edward? He wanted Edward. He was coming back from the park at the time. He raced into the house, into the kitchen. Kate was there with Lucy. He felt suddenly angry. She had her friends, he wanted his friend. 'Where's Edward?'

Kate bit her lip and then went to the kitchen drawer from which she took a newspaper. Tom had thought she was keeping the papers from him because of the scandal, but when he looked at the front page he realised that that had been the last thing on Kate's mind: Edward O'Conner had been arrested in Belfast for trying to kill a respected Protestant clergyman.

Tom did not argue with Kate for hiding it all from him, he just packed a case and asked her to come to Northern Ireland with him. Lucy said she would stay with Charlie.

Tom and Kate went straight to Edward's family home. Mr and Mrs O'Conner were quiet and welcoming.

'You can see him, I think,' said his mother.

'What's it all about? Edward is not a violent man.'

'Little John is a quiet boy, he was walking to the shops when the vicar, a so-called man of God, invited him in for tea. The vicar had other things on his mind, he buggered little John,' Mr O'Conner told them. Kate drew in her breath sharply. 'No one believed the boy at the police station. His mother was hysterical, she wept and cried, and they thought her a stupid woman because the vicar is a man of God, everyone knows that. Edward came home on a week's visit. He brought presents for his mother and me, and for John Donovan. When he found out what had happened he took one of his guns and tried to kill the vicar. He did that.'

'One of his guns?'

'I had better tell you, although you shouldn't know, but you are Edward's best friend. My son is a member of the IRA, Mr Bray. It's ironical that they should have got him for a criminal offence; he handled everything so well, but when it came to the little boy he just couldn't control himself,' said Mrs O'Conner.

'We have to trust you now, Tom,' Mr O'Conner said. He glanced over at his wife. 'By all that's right we should never have told you.'

'Why didn't he tell me himself? I knew him at Cambridge, we were friends.'

'And why would he tell you, Mr Bray? It's not your war.'

'Whether it is our war or not, Edward is our friend,' Kate said quietly.

They took a taxi to Crumlin Road Prison. Edward was on remand so they could see him. The gaol was a huge Victorian edifice and conditions were cramped and appalling. Edward was kept in a cell that was heated by steam pipes, his enamel eating bowl was balanced on top of them, underneath were the chamber pots and the dustpan and brush. Tom and Kate saw nothing of that. They waited in an uncomfortable room whilst a warder collected Edward.

It was a terrible shock for Tom and Kate to see their friend incarcerated. It was difficult, too, trying to come to terms with the knowledge that there was a whole part of a loved human being which was wholly alien, unknown. It was as if he, their friend, had became a stranger.

'I am sorry about Cassie,' Edward said. He was rougher somehow, less amenable.

'Thank you,' said Tom quietly.

'God, man, you are like her. She would have said that.' Tom looked at Edward quizzically. 'I wasn't sorry for you. I was sorry for me.' Edward moved backwards just a fraction, but it was enough. 'We were friends, Cassie and me.'

'I know you were,' Tom answered.

'Close friends, very close friends.'

Tom smiled.

Suddenly Edward lost his temper. 'We were lovers too for a while.'

Tom's head jerked backwards. Cassie sleeping with Edward? It was ridiculous. Edward was his friend, Edward was his age. Kate was covering his fingers with her own. He wanted to hold onto them, but all he could do was think of his mother sleeping with his friend, doing with his friend what he had done with his girls. He felt sick, it was revolting.

Kate was aware that Tom was suffering, but there could be no confrontation in that dreadful place.

'What can we do to help you?' she asked Edward.

'Nothing. I don't want your help.'

'We are your friends.'

300

'In London. The Edward O'Conner who lives in London is your friend.'

'Why, Edward?' Kate asked. 'At least tell us why.'

'Because no one is going to bugger my little boy.'

'The boy is yours?'

'His mother is my wife.'

'And what about my mother?' said Tom.

'What about her? What existed between Cassie and me was to do with the two of us. You were her son, I was her lover. Even if she couldn't learn that there was a difference in the love between a parent and a child, and the love between lovers, *you* are going to have to. It broke us up, her obsession with you. Are you going to let your obsession with her fuck you up too?'

There, it was said, without platitudes or evasions. Kate envied Edward his composure.

Tom rocked back on his chair. She drew in her breath, glancing at Tom. His face was contorted, she knew he was trying to master his emotions. She knew how much he loved Cassie. But Tom was unable to cope with emotional confrontation, and Edward had thrown the maelstrom of mother-and-son passion right into his face. Kate wondered how he would respond, if he would respond. It was a dangerous moment, she knew that. She sensed that Edward was trying to anticipate Tom's reaction too.

The fine-boned Englishman leaned forward. He picked up the Irishman's stubby brown hands. He ran his thumb over the fleshy palms. It was almost a sexual moment. Edward closed his fingers over Tom's hand.

'I told her I loved you,' he said, 'she told me you were her son. I could have killed her for that.'

'I could kill you for screwing her,' said Tom, he was crying.

'It was good between us, Tom,' said Edward.

A harsh voice said, 'Stop that. No touching.'

Tom stood up, scraping his chair on the floor. 'Will we ever see you again?' he asked.

'When I come to London,' Edward replied and turned to the warder who was ready to take him back to his cell.

Kate and Tom went back to their hotel, a huge mausoleum of a place with pillars and a black and white marble floor. They sat together in the hotel lounge, quietly drinking tea. They didn't speak, it would have been far too difficult to find the right words.

301

They were surprised when a man joined them. He was polite enough, and introduced himself as, 'Matthews, Special Branch.' He showed them his identification.

'We know you saw Mr O'Conner today.' He smiled at them both, showing his teeth. He was a nice-looking man with smooth cheeks and neat brown eyebrows above small, bright eyes. His hair was black, slicked back from his forehead, and he wore a brown suit and carried a brown hat – he was very well dressed; a contrast to Tom in his blue jeans, and Kate's white plastic mac.

'Did he tell you anything about himself that we might find interesting?'

The question was so innocuous it was quite shocking.

It was Kate who answered. 'Just that the little boy was his child, and what did he think we would have done about it. And we had to admit that if someone interfered with our little boy, one of us might do something we would regret later. Mightn't you too, Inspector?'

'Quite so,' said Matthews and prepared to leave. He got up and turned away from the table, then turned back. 'Oh, Mr Bray, one other thing.' Tom looked up quickly, he hoped he didn't look worried. 'Could I have your autograph for my wife, she's a great fan of yours.'

'Of course, Inspector,' Tom said, producing a pen.

'Mr Matthews,' the policeman said.

Tom told Kate that he would not be going back to London. He had decided to fly directly to Paris from Belfast.

'I have to see Elizabeth,' he told Kate. 'I won't be staying with her, whatever happens. But I must tell her myself.'

'I see.'

'It's impossible. All that has happened . . . it wouldn't work. I can't explain myself. I need you, Kate. Can you understand that?'

'Yes,' Kate said carefully.

'That's not enough, is it?'

'No.'

'I want you and I want us to try again. Will you consider it? We have a son.'

'What about me, Tom? I have feelings too.'

'I love you, Kate.'

'I don't know, Tom, I don't know.'

# Epilogue
## 1985

In the summer of 1985 Tom Bray decided to mount a retrospective of his mother's work. In the years after Cassie's death he had become a director of major importance whose fame had even allowed him to work in the Soviet Union. Kate was a television presenter, her show went out on Monday nights.

They had had two more children, a daughter, Laura, known as Lu, who was now sixteen, and Ben the youngest child, born just eight years previously. Ben was quite special to them both, Charlie and Lu doted on him and he was a particular favourite of his godfather, the playwright and Sinn Fein activist Edward O'Conner. Home was a huge old house in Barnes, stuffed with antiques and comfortable furniture and Cassie's paintings.

Those who read the colour magazines would have been forgiven for assuming that it was an enviable life. And so it was, except for the shadow of Cassie's death. Tom had come to terms with her loving, the reality of her affair with Edward had helped that, but the manner of her death still afflicted him. Kate often felt that Cassie was the sixth member of the family, never to be exorcised. Ben helped, as indeed did the other children, but they never quite managed to lay her to rest.

Elizabeth was expelled from their lives. Kate had banished her the moment Tom informed her that the affair was over. He had flown to Paris to see Elizabeth as soon as they had returned from Ireland. Kate had not asked him any questions on his return, nor did she mention her disquiet that he had stayed away for two days, instead of the one that had been planned. The extra night had been bad, she had walked around the house, hugging herself, trying to hear his voice saying, 'I am coming back to you, Kate. I just need more time,' and not the little echo in her brain that said it shouldn't take the night hours to say goodbye.

But he had returned the following night and that was enough. If he looked tired and sad Kate chose to ignore it.

After three weeks he had come back to her bed. It had taken time for the sex to be good again, but Kate had been patient. They had gone to Italy on a family holiday and when one night Tom had shouted out her name at the height of his orgasm, she had almost cried with the relief of it. She hadn't faked her own response that night, the heat and the wine had helped. Afterwards he said, 'I thought you were never going to forgive me.'

She was shocked, 'Tom, I. . .'

He interrupted her, tracing the outline of her nipple with his finger. 'I only minded that you pretended.'

Kate turned on her side to look at Tom. 'I thought you didn't want me.'

'I came back to you.'

Tom never told Kate of his anguish at leaving Elizabeth.

He had gone straight to her hotel suite. She had run to him, wrapping her arms around his neck, kissing his cheeks, his mouth, his eyes.

'My darling, my poor darling. I know, I know everything. My mother told me about how your mother loved my father. Here, come and sit down.' She led him to the couch, took off his coat, took off his jacket, ran her hands over his face.

'You see, it is ordained. We have to be together. Your mother loved my father. So at least her son will be happy with the daughter of the man she loved.'

'It isn't like that, Elizabeth.'

'What!'

She was sitting next to him, her feet drawn up under her. She wore a cream satin dressing gown, her skin was the same cream colour. Tom could not help himself but reached forward and touched her – just where the dressing gown skimmed her breasts.

'Forgive me, but it would never work.'

'Why? Because of her?' said Elizabeth.

'Yes.'

'But you love me.'

'Yes, yes, I do. But I love Kate too.'

'You can't love two women.'

'I don't love you in the same way.'

'Tom, don't leave me.' She touched his hand.

304

'Elizabeth, please, I do love you, but I need Kate – she is the only one who can help me.'

He had offered her a final loving. He had thought she would refuse but she had taken it, and the passion of that coupling had imprinted itself on him. He had known that he would never be able to put the memory away, but he resolved to bury it under the business of living. He knew that Elizabeth had become a dancer of great importance. She had never married, but she had a child. He knew it was a girl, but beyond that nothing, and he wanted to know nothing. The child was protected from the public eye. She lived with her grandmother in Berlin.

Yvonne helped Tom with the retrospective. But she only organised the administrative aspects of it. He chose the paintings and arranged them as he believed Cassie would have liked them to be arranged.

The exhibition was opened by a Royal, and was covered by all the major newspapers and television channels. It was regarded as a media event, people fought for invitations. John Bravington came, of course. Tom saw him sitting quietly in front of 'The Seven Deadly Sins', he was sure his old master was crying.

Kate stayed close to Tom as the crowds flocked and cooed and worshipped. Cassie Bray was as much a celebrity in death as she had been in her life.

'Look at Beth,' Kate whispered to Tom as she pointed to a slim dark woman attracting considerable attention. Beth's husband was going to run for President. It was Beth's duty, so she had told Kate, to do her job as well as she could.

'What job?' Kate had asked.

'Why, as his wife, of course.'

Kate smiled, she remembered Beth's devotion to Jacqueline Kennedy, never seeing the woman, just the role. She kissed Beth on the cheek. 'And you will be superb,' she told her, meaning it.

Charlie was so proud of his grandmother. He knew that Lu was bored by it all, but then she had never known Cassie. He couldn't remember her, but it was enough to know that he featured in her work. He wondered where Lu was, and Ben for that matter. He looked around the room, and then he forgot about his sister and brother. For standing in a space, in front of Cassie Bray's 'Homage to Käthe Kollwitz' was a young girl. She was tall and blonde with an open face and huge grey eyes and a wide generous mouth. She had a sketch pad in her hand and a pencil between her fingers. Charlie went over to her, he could see she was drawing. 'What are you doing?' he asked.

'Sketching,' she said. 'I think this is the most extraordinary of all her pieces. Her perception of motherhood was so painful, I wonder she could stand it.'

She looked at Charlie and she smiled, she had a wonderful smile. Charlie wondered if he might be falling in love with her.